Bestselling author Clive Cussler is as active an adventurer as his fictional heroes. Whether searching for lost aircraft or leading expeditions to find famous shipwrecks, he has garnered an amazing record of success and, with his NUMA crew of volunteers, has discovered more than sixty lost ships of historic significance. Clive is also an avid collector of classic cars and has eighty-five examples of hand-built coachwork and 50's convertibles. He divides his time between the mountains of Colorado and the deserts of Arizona.

Also by Clive Cussler

Shock Wave
Flood Tide
Serpent

CLIVE CUSSLER

Blue Gold

POCKET
BOOKS

LONDON • SYDNEY • NEW YORK • TORONTO

First published in Great Britain by Simon & Schuster UK Ltd, 2000
First published by Pocket Books, 2001
This edition first published by Pocket Books, 2010
An imprint of Simon & Schuster UK Ltd
A CBS COMPANY

3 5 7 9 10 8 6 4 2

Simon & Schuster UK Ltd
1st Floor
222 Gray's Inn Road
London WC1X 8HB

www.simonandschuster.co.uk

Simon & Schuster Australia
Sydney

A CIP catalogue record for this book is
available from the British Library

ISBN 978-1-47110-040-6

Printed and bound by CPI Group (UK) Ltd, Croydon, CR0 4YY

ACKNOWLEDGMENTS

THANKS TO PILOTS BILL ALONG, CARL Scrivener, and "Barefoot" Dave Miller, who gave so generously of their time and expertise.

PROLOGUE

São Paulo Airport, Brazil, 1991

WITH A POWERFUL KICK FROM ITS twin turbofan engines, the sleek executive jet lifted off the runway and shot into the vaulted skies above São Paulo. Climbing rapidly over the biggest city in South America, the Learjet soon reached its cruising altitude of thirty-nine thousand feet and raced toward the northwest at five hundred miles an hour. Seated in a comfortable rear-facing chair at the back of the cabin, Professor Francesca Cabral peered wistfully out the window at the cottony cloud cover, already missing the smog-cloaked streets and sizzling energy of her hometown. A muffled snort from across the narrow aisle interrupted her musings. She glanced over at the snoring middle aged man in the rumpled suit and wondered with a shake of her head what her father was thinking when he assigned Phillipo Rodriques as her bodyguard.

Extracting a folder from her briefcase, she jotted notes in the margins of the speech that she planned to deliver at an international conference of environmental scientists in Cairo. She had gone over the draft a dozen times, but her thoroughness was entirely in character. Francesca was a brilliant engineer and a highly respected professor, but in a field and society dominated by males, a female scientist was expected to be *more* than perfect.

The words blurred on the pages. The night before Francesca was up late packing and pulling together scientific papers. She had been too excited to sleep. Now she cast an envious glance at the snoozing bodyguard and decided to take a nap. She set the speech aside, pushed the back of her thick-cushioned seat into its reclining position, and closed her eyes. Lulled by the throaty whisper of the turbines, she soon dozed off.

Dreams came. She was floating on the sea, gently rising and falling like a jellyfish buoyed by soft billows. It was a pleasant sensation until one wave lifted her high in the air and dropped like a runaway elevator. Her eyelids fluttered open, and she looked around the cabin. She had an odd feeling, as if someone had grabbed at her heart. Yet all seemed normal. The haunting strains of Antonio Carlos Jobim's "One Note Samba" played softly over the sound system. Phillipo was still out cold. The sense that something was amiss would not go away. She leaned over and gently shook the sleeping man's shoulder. "Phillipo, wake up."

The bodyguard's hand went to the holster under his jacket, and he came instantly awake. When he saw Francesca he relaxed.

"*Senhora,* I'm sorry," he said with a yawn. "I fell asleep."

"I did, too." She paused as if she were listening. "Something isn't quite right."

"What do you mean?"

She laughed nervously. "I don't know."

Phillipo smiled with the knowing expression of a man whose wife has heard burglars in the night. He patted her hand. "I will go see."

He got up and stretched, then went forward and knocked on the cockpit door. The door opened, and he stuck his head through. Francesca heard a murmured conversation and laughter.

Phillipo was beaming broadly when he returned. "The pilots say everything is okay, *Senhora.*"

Francesca thanked the bodyguard, settled back in her seat, and took a deep breath. Her fears were foolish. The prospect of being freed from her mental meat grinder after two years of exhausting work had given her the jitters. The Project had consumed her, drained the hours from her days and nights, and demolished her social life. Her gaze fell on the divan that stretched across the rear of the cabin, and she resisted the impulse to see if her metal suitcase was still safely stored in the space behind the sofa cushions. She liked to think of the valise as a reverse Pandora's box. Instead of evil, good things would pour out when it was opened. Her discovery would bring health and prosperity to millions, and the planet would never be the same again.

Phillipo brought Francesca a cold bottle of orange juice. She thanked him, thinking she had grown to like her bodyguard in the short time she had known him. With his wrinkled brown suit, balding pepper-and-salt hair, thin mustache, and round spectacles, Phillipo could have passed for an absentminded academic. Francesca couldn't know that he had spent years perfecting the shy, bumbling manner. His carefully cultivated ability to merge into the background like faded wallpaper made him one of the top undercover agents in the Brazilian secret service.

Rodriques had been handpicked by her father. Francesca initially balked at her father's insistence that a bodyguard accompany her. She was far too old to have a baby-sitter. When she saw his genuine concern for her welfare, she went along. She suspected her father was more worried about good-looking fortune hunters than for her safety.

Even without her family's wealth, Francesca would have drawn male attention. In a land of dark hair and smoky complexions, she was a standout. Her blue-black almond-shaped eyes, long lashes, and almost perfect mouth were the legacy of her Japanese grandfather. Her German grandmother had passed along her light brown hair, her height genes, and the Teutonic stubbornness of the delicately sculpted jaw. Her shapely figure, she decided long ago, had something to do with living in Brazil. Brazilian women seem to have bodies especially designed for the country's national dance, the samba. Francesca had improved on the natural model by many hours spent in the gym where she went to relieve the tension of her work.

Grandfather had been a minor diplomat when the Empire of

Japan ended under twin mushroom clouds. He stayed on in Brazil, married the daughter of a Third Reich ambassador similarly unemployed, became a Brazilian citizen, and switched to his first love, gardening. He moved the family to São Paulo, where his landscape company served the rich and powerful. He developed close ties with influential government and military figures. His son, Francesca's father, used those connections to move effortlessly to a highly placed position in the commerce department. Her mother was a brilliant engineering student who put her academic career aside to become a wife and mother. She never regretted her decision, at least not openly, but she was delighted that Francesca would choose to follow in her academic footsteps.

Her father had suggested that she fly on his executive jet to New York, where she would meet with United Nations officials before boarding a commercial flight to Cairo. She was glad to get back to the States, if only for a short visit, and wished she could make the plane move faster. The years she had spent studying engineering at Stanford University in California would always be pleasant memories. She glanced out the window and realized she had no idea where they were. The pilots hadn't reported on the flight's progress since the plane left São Paulo. Excusing herself to Phillipo, she went forward and stuck her head in the cockpit.

"Bom dia, senhores. I was wondering where we are and how much longer we'll be in the air."

The pilot was Captain Riordan, a rawboned American with crew-cut straw-colored hair and a Texas accent. Francesca had never seen him before, but that wasn't surprising. Nor was the fact that Riordan was a foreign national. Although the plane was privately owned it was maintained by a local airline that supplied pilots.

"Bowanis deeyass," he said with a lopsided grin, his Chuck Yeager drawl and butchered Portuguese grating on her ears. "Sorry for not keeping you up to date, miss. Saw you were sleeping and didn't want to disturb you." He winked at the copilot, a thickset Brazilian whose overmuscled physique suggested he spent a lot of time pumping iron. The copilot smirked as his eyes roved over Francesca's body. Francesca felt like a mother who had come upon two mischievous boys about to play a prank.

"What's our timetable?" she said in a businesslike manner.

"Waall, we're over Venezuela. We should be in Miami in approximately three hours. We'll stretch our legs while we refuel and should be in New York about three hours after that."

Francesca's scientific eye was drawn to the screens on the instrument panel. The copilot noticed her interest and couldn't resist the chance to impress a beautiful woman.

"This plane is so smart it can fly itself while we watch the soccer games on TV," he said, showing his big teeth.

"Don't let Carlos blow smoke up your flue," the pilot said. "That's the EFIS, the electronic flight instrument system. The screens take the place of the gauges we used to use."

"Thank you," Francesca said politely. She pointed to another gauge. "Is that a compass?" she said.

"Sim, sim," the copilot said, proud of his successful tutelage.

"Then why does it indicate we're going almost due north?" she said with a furrowed brow. "Shouldn't we be heading in a more westerly direction toward Miami?"

The men exchanged glances. "You're quite observant, *senhora,"* the Texan said. "Absolutely right. But in the air a straight line isn't always the fastest way between two points. Has to do with the curvature of the earth. Like when you fly from the U.S. to Europe the shortest way is up and around in a big curve. We've also got to deal with Cuban airspace. Don't want to get ol' Fidel all haired up."

The quick wink and smirk again.

Francesca nodded appreciatively. "Thank you for your time, gentlemen. It's been most instructive. I'll let you get back to your work."

"No bother, ma'am. Any time."

Francesca was fuming as she took her seat. *Fools!* Did they think she was an idiot? The curvature of the earth indeed!

"Everything's okay, like I said?" Phillipo asked, looking up from the magazine he was reading.

She leaned across the aisle and spoke in a low, even tone. "No, everything is *not* okay. I think this plane is off-course." She told him about the compass reading. "I felt something odd in my sleep. I think it was the shifting of the plane as they changed direction."

"Maybe you're mistaken."

"Perhaps. But I don't think so."

"Did you ask the pilots for an explanation?"

"Yes. They gave me some absurd story saying the shortest distance between two points was not a straight line because of the curvature of the earth."

He raised an eyebrow, apparently surprised by the explanation, but he still wasn't convinced. "I don't know . . ."

Francesca pondered some other inconsistencies. "Do you remember what they said when they came on board, about being replacement pilots?"

"Sure. They said the other pilots were called off on another job. They took their place as a favor."

She shook her head. "Peculiar. Why did they even bring it up? It's as if they wanted to head off any questions I might have. But *why?*"

"I have had some experience in navigation," Phillipo said thoughtfully. "I will go see for myself." He sauntered up to the cockpit again. She heard male laughter, and after a few minutes he came back with a smile on his face. The smile faded as he sat down.

"There's an instrument in the cockpit that shows the original flight plan. We are not following the blue line as we should be. You were right about the compass, too," he said. "We are not on the correct course."

"What in God's name is going on, Phillipo?"

A grave expression came onto his face. "There was something your father didn't tell you."

"I don't understand."

Phillipo glanced toward the closed cockpit. "He had heard things. Nothing that would persuade him you were in danger, but enough so that he would like the reassurance of knowing I would be nearby if you needed help."

"Looks like we could *both* use some help."

"*Sim, senhora.* But unfortunately we must do for ourselves."

"Do you have a gun?" she said abruptly.

"Of course," he said, faintly amused at the hard-nosed question from this beautiful and cultured woman. "Would you like me to shoot them?"

"I didn't mean—no, of course not," she said glumly. "Do you have any ideas?"

"A gun is not just for shooting," he said. "You can use it for intimidation, use its threat to make people do things they don't want to do."

"Like pointing us in the right direction?"

"I hope, *senhora.* I will go forward. I will ask them politely to land at the nearest airport, saying it is your wish. If they refuse I will show them my gun and say I would not like to use it."

"You *can't* use it," Francesca said with alarm. "If you put a hole in the plane at this altitude, it would depressurize the cabin, and we'd all be dead within seconds."

"A good point. It will increase their fear." He took her hand and squeezed it. "I told your father I would watch out for you, *senhora.*"

She shook her head as if it would make the situation go away. "What if I'm wrong? That these are innocent pilots doing their job?"

"Simple," he said with a shrug. "We call ahead on the radio, we land at the nearest airport, we bring in the police, we straighten things out, then we resume our trip."

They cut their conversation short. The door to the cockpit had opened, and the captain stepped into the cabin. He ambled forward, having to bend his head because of the low overhead.

"That was some joke you just told us," he said with his crooked grin. "Got any more?"

"Sorry, *senhor,*" Phillipo said.

"Waall, I got one for you," the pilot replied. Riordan's droopy, heavy-lidded eyes gave him a sleepy look. But there was nothing sluggish about the way he reached behind his back and produced the pistol he had tucked in his belt.

"Hand it over," he said to Phillipo. "Real slow."

Phillipo gingerly opened his jacket wide so the shoulder holster was in plain view, then extracted his gun by the tips of his fingers. The pilot stuck the gun in his belt.

"Grazyeass, amigo," he said. "Always nice to deal with a professional." He sat on an armrest and with his free hand lit a cigarette. "Me and my partner have been talking, and we think maybe you're on to us. Figured you were checking us out when you came up a second time, so we decided to lay it all out so there won't be any misunderstandings."

"Captain Riordan, what is going on?" Francesca said. "Where are you taking us?"

"They said you were smart," the pilot said with a chuckle. "My partner never should have started bragging about the plane." He blew twin plumes of smoke from his nostrils. "You're right. We're not going to Miami, we're on our way to Trinidad."

"Trinidad?"

"I hear it's a real nice place."

"I don't understand."

"It's like this, senyoreeta. There's going to be a welcome party waiting for you at the airport. Don't ask me who they are 'cause I don't know. All's I know is we've been hired to deliver you. Things were supposed to go nice and easy. We were going to tell you we had mechanical problems and needed to land."

"What happened to the pilots?" Phillipo asked.

"They had an accident," he said with a slight shrug. He ground the cigarette butt on the floor. "Here's the situation, miss. You just stay put, and everything will be fine. As for you, *cavaleiro,* I'm sorry to get you in trouble with your bosses. Now I can tie you both up, but I don't think you'd try anything foolish unless you can fly this plane yourselves. One more thing. Up, partner, and turn around."

Thinking he was about to be frisked, Phillipo complied without protest. Francesca's warning came too late. The pistol barrel arced down in a silvery blur and struck the bodyguard above the right ear. The sickening crunch was drowned out by the bodyguard's cry of pain as he doubled over and crumpled onto the floor.

Francesca jumped up from her seat. "Why did you *do* that?" she said defiantly. "You have his gun. He couldn't harm you."

"Sorry, miss. I'm a firm believer in insurance." Riordan stepped over the prostrate form in the aisle as if it were a sack of potatoes. "Nothing like a cracked skull to discourage a man from getting into trouble. There's a first aid kit up there on the wall. Taking care of him should keep you busy 'til it's time to set down." He tipped his hand to his cap, strolled back to the cockpit, and shut the door.

Francesca knelt by the stricken bodyguard. She soaked cloth napkins in mineral water and cleaned the wound, then applied pressure until the bleeding was stanched. She daubed an antiseptic on the scalp cut and the bruised skin around it, wrapped ice in another napkin, and pressed it to the side of the man's head to prevent swelling.

As Francesca sat by his side, she tried to piece the puzzle together. She ruled out a kidnapping for money. The only reason someone would go through this much trouble would be for her process. Whoever was behind this mad scheme wanted more than a scale model and the papers explaining her work. They could have broken into the lab or grabbed her luggage at the airport. But they needed Francesca to interpret her findings. Her process was so arcane, so different, that it didn't conform to the norms of science, which is why no one had thought of it before.

The whole thing didn't make sense! Within a day or two she was going to *give* the process to the countries of the world for *nothing.* No patents. No copyright. No royalty fees. Absolutely free of charge. Anger smoldered in her breast. These ruthless people were stopping her from improving the lot of millions.

Phillipo groaned. He was coming around. His eyes blinked open and came into focus.

"Are you all right?" she said.

"It hurts like the devil, so I must be alive. Help me sit up, please."

Francesca put her arm around Phillipo and lifted until he sat with his back against a seat. She unscrewed a bottle of rum from the bar and put it to his lips. He sipped some liquor, managed to keep it down, then took a healthy swallow. He sat there for a moment waiting to see if his guts would come up. When he didn't vomit, he smiled. "I'll be fine. Thank you."

She handed him his glasses. "I'm afraid they were broken when he hit you."

He tossed them aside. "They are only plain glass. I can see fine without them." The level eyes that bored into Francesca were not those of a frightened man. He glanced at the closed cockpit door. "How long have I been out?"

"Twenty minutes, maybe."

"Good, there is still time."

"Time for *what?*"

His hand slid down to his ankle and came up filled with a snub-nosed revolver.

"If our friend hadn't been so anxious to give me a headache, he would have found this," he said with a grim smile.

This was definitely not the same rumpled man who had seemed more like an absentminded professor than a bodyguard. Francesca's elation was tempered by reality. "What can you do? They have at least two guns, and we can't fly the plane."

"Forgive me, *Senhora* Cabral. Another failure to be forthright on my part." Sounding almost guilty, he said, "I forgot to mention that I was in the Brazilian air force before I joined the secret service. Please help me up."

Francesca was speechless. What other rabbits would this man pull out of his hat? She gave him a hand until he was able to stand on shaky legs. After a minute a new strength and determination seemed to flow through his body. "Stay here until I tell you what to do," he said with the air of a man used to people obeying his command.

He went forward and opened the door. The pilot glanced over his shoulder and said, "Hey, look who's back from the land of the living dead. Guess I didn't hit you hard enough."

"You don't get a second chance," Phillipo said. He jammed the revolver barrel under the Texan's ear hard enough to hurt. "If I shoot one of you, the other can still fly. Which one will it be?"

"Christ, you said you took his gun!" Carlos said.

"You've got a short memory, *cavaleiro,*" the pilot replied calmly. "You shoot us and who's going to fly the plane?"

"I will, *cavaleiro.* Sorry I didn't bring my pilot's license with me. You'll have to take my word for it."

Riordan turned his head slightly and saw the cold smile wreathing the bodyguard's face.

"I take back what I said about dealing with a professional," Riordan said. "What now, partner?"

"Give me the two guns. One at a time."

The pilot handed over his pistol and the one he had taken from Phillipo. The bodyguard passed the weapons back to Francesca, who had come up behind him.

"Get out of your seat," he ordered, backing into the cabin. "Slowly."

Riordan caught the copilot's eye and levered himself out of his seat. Using his body to shield the gesture, he made a quick palm-down flip with his hand. The copilot nodded almost imperceptibly to show he understood.

The pilot followed Phillipo as if drawn by an imaginary leash, as the bodyguard backed up into the cabin. "I want you to go lie facedown on the divan," Phillipo said, keeping his gun pointed at Riordan's chest.

"Hell, I was hoping I could take a nap," the pilot said. "That's real kind of you."

Francesca had backed off the aisle to make room for the two men to pass. Phillipo asked her to get some plastic trash bags from under a front seat. Phillipo intended to use the bags to bind the pilot. With Riordan on ice he would only have to deal with the copilot.

The cabin was about twelve feet long. In the tight space Phillipo had to step aside to let the other man pass. He reminded Riordan not to try anything at close quarters, because it would be impossible to miss. Riordan nodded and stepped toward the rear. They were only a few inches apart when the copilot put the plane over on its left side.

Riordan had expected the move, but he didn't know when it would come or that it would be so violent. He lost his balance and was thrown onto a seat, his head slamming into the bulkhead. Phillipo was lifted off his feet. He flew across the cabin and landed on top of Riordan.

The pilot disentangled his right hand and blasted his big fist into the bodyguard's jaw. Phillipo saw galaxies whirling over his head and almost blacked out, but he managed to keep a death grip on the gun. Riordan brought his arm back for another punch. Phillipo blocked it with his elbow.

Both men were street fighters. Phillipo clawed at Riordan's eyes. The pilot bit Phillipo on the fleshy part of the palm. The bodyguard jammed his knee into Riordan's groin, and when the pilot opened his mouth, Phillipo snapped his head forward, smashing the cartilage in Riordan's nose. He might have gained the upper hand, but at that point the copilot made the plane yaw sharply to the right.

The struggling men flew across the aisle into the opposite seat. Now the American was on top. Phillipo tried to club Riordan with the gun's muzzle, but the pilot grabbed his wrist with two hands and twisted it away and down. Phillipo was strong, but he was no match for the double-teamed assault. The barrel swung closer to his midsection.

The pilot had his hands on the gun and was wrestling it away. Phillipo tried to hold on to the pistol, almost had control of it again, but the grip was slippery from the jets of blood flowing from Riordan's nose. In a wrenching twist the pilot took control of the gun, got his fingertip onto the trigger, and squeezed.

There was a muffled *crack!* Phillipo's body jerked and then went limp as the bullet plowed into his chest.

The plane righted itself as the copilot put it back into its normal position. Riordan stood and staggered toward the cockpit. He stopped and turned, apparently sensing something wasn't right.

The gun he had left behind was propped up on the bodyguard's chest. Phillipo was trying to steady it for a shot. Riordan charged like a wounded rhino. The pistol cracked. The first bullet hit the pilot in the shoulder, and he kept coming. Phillipo's brain died, but his finger twitched twice more. The second shot caught the pilot in the heart and killed him instantly. The third went wild and missed him completely. Even as the pilot crashed to the floor, the pistol had dropped from Phillipo's hand.

The struggle from one side of the cabin to the other had taken only a few seconds. Francesca had been thrown between the seats and played possum as the bloodied pilot was making his way back to the cockpit. The shots sent her down again.

She cautiously stuck her head into the aisle and saw the pilot's still body. She crawled over to Phillipo's side, pried the pistol from his bloody hands, and approached the cockpit door, too enraged to feel fear. Her anger quickly turned to shock.

The copilot was slumped forward, his body held in place by his seatbelt. There was a bullet hole in the partition separating the cockpit from the cabin and through the back of the copilot's chair. Phillipo's third shot.

Francesca pulled the copilot upright. His groan told her he was still alive.

"Can you talk?" she said.

Carlos rolled his eyes and whispered a hoarse "Yes."

"Good. You've been shot, but I don't think it hit any vital organs," she lied. "I'm going to stop the bleeding."

She retrieved the first aid kit, thinking that what she really needed was an emergency-room trauma unit. She almost fainted at the sight of the blood flowing from the wound down his back to puddle on the floor. The compress she applied immediately turned scarlet, but it may have helped stanch the loss of blood. It was impossible to tell. The only thing she knew for certain was that the man was going to die.

With fearful apprehension she looked at the glowing instrument panel, numbed by the realization that this dying man was the key to her survival. She had to keep him alive.

Francesca retrieved the bottle of rum and tilted it to the copilot's lips. The rum dribbled down his chin, and the little amount he swallowed made him cough. He asked for more. The strong liquor brought color to his pale cheeks and the gleam of life back into the glazed eyes.

She put her lips close to his ear. "You must fly," she said levelly. "It's our only chance."

The proximity of a beautiful woman seemed to give him energy. His eyes were glassy but alert. He nodded and reached out with shaking hand to flick on the radio that connected him directly with traffic control in Rio. Francesca eased into the pilot's seat and slipped on the headset. The voice of the traffic controller came on. Carlos asked for help with his eyes. Francesca began to talk, explaining their predicament to traffic control.

"What do you advise us to do?" she said.

After an agonizing pause the voice said, "Proceed to Caracas immediately."

"Caracas too far," Carlos croaked, mustering the strength to talk. "Someplace closer."

Several more moments dragged by.

The dispatcher's voice came back. "There's a small provincial airstrip two hundred miles from your position at San Pedro, outside Caracas. No instrument approach, but the weather is perfect. Can you make it?"

"Yes," Francesca said.

The copilot fumbled with the keypad of the flight computer. With all the strength at his command he called up the international identifier for San Pedro and entered it in the computer.

Guided by the computer, the plane began to make a turn.

Carlos smiled slightly. "Didn't I tell you this plane flies by itself, *senhora?"* His wheezy words had a drowsy quality to them. He was obviously becoming weaker from loss of blood. It was only a matter of time before he passed out.

"I don't care *who* flies it," she said sharply. "Just get us on the ground."

Carlos nodded and set up the automatic descent profile on the flight computer to take the plane down to two thousand feet. The plane began to descend through the clouds, and before long patches of green were visible. The sight of land reassured and terrified Francesca at the same time. Her terror rose a few degrees when Carlos shuddered as if an electric current had gone through him. He grabbed Francesca's hand and held it in a death grip.

"Can't make San Pedro," he said, his voice a wet rattle.

"You've *got* to," Francesca said.

"No use."

"Damn it, Carlos, you and your partner got us into this mess, and you're going to get us out of it!"

He smiled vacantly. "What are you going to do, *senhora,* shoot me?"

Her eyes blazed. "You'll *wish* I had if you don't get this thing down."

He shook his head. "Emergency landing. Our only chance. Find a place."

The big cockpit window offered a view of the thick-grown rain forest. Francesca had the feeling she was flying over a vast unbroken field of broccoli. She scanned the endless greenery again. It was hopeless. *Wait.* Sunlight glinted off something shiny.

"What's that?" she said, pointing.

Carlos disconnected the auto pilot and auto throttles, took the wheel in his hands, and steered toward the reflection, which came from the sun glinting off a giant waterfall. A narrow, meandering river came into view. Alongside the river was an irregularly shaped clearing of yellow and brown vegetation.

Flying almost on automatic himself, Carlos passed the open

area and set up a thirty-degree banking turn to the right. He extended the wing flaps and put the plane in a boxlike flight pattern. With a hard right he prepared the plane for its final approach. They were at eighteen hundred feet, descending on a long, shallow glide. Carlos extended the wing flaps to slow them down further.

"Too low!" he growled. The treetops were rushing at them. With superhuman strength born of desperation he reached out and gave the throttles more power. The plane began to rise.

Through blurred vision he scoped the final approach. His heart fell. It was a terrible landing field, small and lumpy, the size of a postage stamp. They were doing a hundred and sixty miles per hour. Too fast.

A soggy gasp escaped from his throat. His head lolled onto his shoulder. Blood gushed from his mouth. The fingers that had clutched the wheel so tightly were curled in a useless death grip. It was a tribute to his skill that in his last moments he had trimmed the plane perfectly. The jet maintained trim, and when it hit the ground, it bounced into the air a few times like a stone skipped across water.

There was an ear-splitting shriek of tortured metal as the bottom of the fuselage made contact with the earth. The friction between the plane and the solid earth slowed it down, but it was still going more than a hundred miles an hour, the fuselage cutting through the ground like the blade of a plow. The wings snapped off, and the fuel tanks exploded, leaving twin black and orange swaths of fire in the plane's wake for another thousand feet as it hurtled toward a bend in the river.

The plane would have disintegrated if the grass-covered ground had not given way to the soft, marshy mud along the river bank. Stripped of its wings, its blue and white skin splattered with mud, the plane looked like a giant wormlike creature trying to burrow into the mire. The plane skidded over the surface of the muck and finally came to a lurching stop. The impact hurled Francesca forward into the instrument panel, and she blacked out.

Except for the crackle of burning grass, the ripple of river water, and the hiss of steam where the hot metal touched the water, all was silent.

Before long, ghostly shadows emerged from the forest. As quiet as smoke, they moved in closer to the shattered wreckage of the plane.

1

San Diego, California, 2001

WEST OF ENCINITAS ON THE PAcific coast, the graceful motor yacht *Nepenthe* swung at anchor, the grandest craft in a flotilla that seemed to include every sailboat and powerboat in San Diego. With her fluid drawn-out lines, the spearlike sprit jutting from the thrusting clipper bow, and her flaring transom, the two-hundred-foot-long *Nepenthe* looked as if she were made of fine white china floating on a Delft sea. Her paint glistened with a mirror finish, and her brightwork sparkled under the California sun. Flags and pennants snapped and fluttered from stem to stern. Bobbing balloons occasionally broke loose to soar into the cloudless sky.

In the yacht's spacious British Empire–style salon a string quartet played a Vivaldi piece for the eclectic gathering of black-clad Hollywood types, corpulent politicians, and sleek TV anchors who milled around a thick-legged mahogany table devouring pâté, beluga caviar, and shrimp with the gusto of famine victims.

Outside, crowding the sun-drenched decks, children sat in wheelchairs or leaned on crutches, munching hot dogs and burgers and enjoying the fresh sea air. Hovering over them like a mother hen was a lovely woman in her fifties. Gloria Ekhart's generous mouth and cornflower-blue eyes were familiar to millions who had seen her movies and watched her popular sitcom on TV. Every fan knew about Ekhart's daughter Elsie, the pretty, freckle-faced young girl who scooted around the deck in a wheelchair. Ekhart had given up acting at the peak of her career to devote her fortune and time to helping children like her own. The influential and well-heeled guests chugging down Dom Perignon in the salon would be asked later to open their checkbooks for the Ekhart Foundation.

Ekhart had a flair for promotion, which was why she leased the *Nepenthe* for her party. In 1930, when the vessel slid off the ways at the G. L. Watson boatyard in Glasgow, she was among the most graceful motor yachts ever to sail the seas. The yacht's first owner, an English earl, lost her in an all-night poker game to a Hollywood mogul with a penchant for cards, marathon parties, and underage starlets. She went through a succession of equally indifferent owners, winding up in a failed attempt as a fishing boat. Smelling of dead fish and bait, the rotting yacht languished in the back corner of a boatyard. She was rescued by a Silicon Valley magnate who tried to recoup the millions he spent restoring the vessel by leasing her out for events such as the Ekhart fund-raiser.

A man wearing a blue blazer with an official race badge pinned to the breast pocket had been peering through binoculars at the flat green expanse of the Pacific. He rubbed his eyes and squinted into the lenses again. In the distance thin white plumes were etched against the blue sky where it met the water. He lowered the binoculars, raised an aerosol canister with a plastic trumpet attached, and pressed the button three times.

Hawnk . . . hawnk . . . hawnk.

The klaxon's blaring squawk echoed across the water like the mating call of a monster gander. The flotilla took up the signal. A cacophony of bells, whistles, and horns filled the air and drowned out the cry of hungry gulls. Hundreds of spectators excitedly reached for their binoculars and cameras. Boats heeled dangerously as passengers shifted to one side. On the *Nepenthe* the guests wolfed down their food and poured from the salon sipping from glasses of bubbly. They shaded their eyes and looked off in the distance, where the feathery plumes were thickening into bantam rooster tails. Carried on the breeze was a sound like an angry swarm of bees.

In a circling helicopter a thousand feet above the *Nepenthe,* a sturdy Italian photographer named Carlo Pozzi tapped the pilot's shoulder and pointed to the northwest. The water was marked by parallel white streaks advancing as if plowed by a huge, invisible harrow. Pozzi checked his safety harness, stepped out onto a runner with one foot, and hefted a fifty-pound television camera onto his shoulder. Leaning with a practiced stance into the wind that buffeted his body, he brought the extraordinary power of his lens to bear on the advancing lines. He swept the camera from left to right, giving viewers around the world an overview of the dozen race boats cutting furrows in the sea. Then he zoomed in on a pair of boats leading the pack by a quarter of a mile.

The speeding craft skimmed the wave tops, their forty-foot hulls planing with elevated bows as if trying to escape the restraints of gravity. The lead boat was painted a bold firehouse red. Trailing by less than a hundred yards, the second boat sparkled like a gold nugget. The boats were more like star fighters than craft designed for travel over water. Their flat decks connected two knife-edged catamaran hulls called sponsons and aerodynamic wings over the engine compartments. Twin F-16–type canopies were set side-by-side two-thirds of the way back from the sharp-pointed double prows.

Squeezed into the red boat's right-hand canopy, his sunbronzed face fixed in a mask of determination, Kurt Austin braced himself as the eight-ton craft slammed against the concrete-hard water again and again. Unlike a land vehicle, the boat had no shock absorbers to cushion the jarring impact. Each jolt traveled through the one-piece Kevlar and carbon composite hull up through Austin's legs and rattled his teeth. Despite his broad shoulders, his muscular biceps, and the five-point harness system that strapped his two-hundred-pound frame in place, he felt like a basketball being dribbled down the court by Michael Jordan.

Every ounce of strength in his muscular six-foot-one body was needed to keep a steady hand on the trim tabs and the throttle levers and a firm left foot on the engine pedal controlling the pressure in the mighty twin turbos that sent the boat thundering over the water.

José "Joe" Zavala sat hunched over the steering wheel in the left canopy. His gloved hands tightly gripped the small black wheel that seemed inadequate for the task of keeping the boat pointed in the right direction. He felt as if he were *aiming* rather than steering the boat. His mouth was set in a grim line. The large dark brown eyes had lost their usual soulful look as they strained intently through the tinted Plexiglas visor to read the sea conditions for changes in wind or wave height. The up-and-down movement of the bow compounded the difficulty. Where Austin gauged the boat's behavior, quite literally, by the seat of his pants, Zavala felt the waves and troughs through his steering wheel.

Austin barked into the intercom mike that connected the canopies. "What's our speed?"

Zavala glanced at the digital speed gauge. "One twenty-two." His eyes went to the GPS position and compass. "Right on course."

Austin checked his watch and looked down at the chart fastened to his right thigh. The one-hundred-sixty-mile race began in San Diego, made two sharp turns around Santa Catalina Island, and came back to the starting point, giving thousands of spectators along the beaches a view of the dramatic finish. The final turn should be coming up any minute. He squinted through the spray-splashed canopy and saw a vertical line off to the right, then another. Sailboat masts! The spectator fleet flanked a wide swath of open water. Once past the spectators, the racers would pick up the Coast Guard cutter near the turn buoy and head into the last lap. He snapped a quick glance over his right shoulder and caught the reflection of the sun off gold.

"Kicking it up to one-thirty," Austin said.

The hard shocks coming through the steering wheel indicated that the wave height was growing. Zavala had observed white flecks in the water and a distinct marbling to the seas that told him the wind was up.

"Don't know if we should," Zavala yelled over the shriek of the engines. "Picking up a slight chop. Where's Ali Baba?"

"Practically in our back pocket!"

"He's *crazy* if he makes his play now. He should just lie back and let us take the lumps like he's been doing, then go for the home stretch. Sea and wind are too unpredictable."

"Ali doesn't like to lose."

Zavala grunted. "Okay. Take it to one twenty-five. Maybe he'll back off."

Austin pushed down with his fingertips on the throttles and felt a surge of speed and power.

A moment later Zavala reported: "Doing one twenty-seven. Seems okay."

The gold boat fell back, then speeded up to keep pace. Austin could read the black lettering on the side: *Flying Carpet.* The boat's driver was hidden behind the tinted glass, but Austin knew the bearded young Omar Sharif look-alike would be grinning from ear to ear. The son of a Dubai hotel magnate, Ali Bin Said was one of the toughest competitors in one of the world's most competitive and dangerous sports, Class 1 offshore powerboat racing.

Ali came within a whisker of beating Austin at the Dubai Duty Free Grand Prix the year before. The loss in his own backyard before his home audience was particularly galling. Ali had beefed up the power in the *Carpet*'s twin Lamborghini engines. With improvements in its power plant the *Red Ink* squeezed out a few extra miles per hour, but Austin estimated Ali's boat was a match for his.

At the prerace briefing Ali had jokingly accused Austin of calling in the National Underwater & Marine Agency to quell the seas in his boat's path. As leader of the Special Assignments Team for NUMA, Austin had the resources of the huge agency at his command. But he knew better than to play King Canute. Ali had been beaten not by engine power but by the way Austin and his NUMA partner clicked together as a team.

Zavala, with his dark complexion and thick, straight black hair always combed straight back, could have passed for the maître d' in a posh Acapulco resort hotel. The slight smile always on his lips masked a steely resolve forged in his college days as a middleweight boxer and honed by the frequent challenges of his NUMA assignments. The gregarious and soft-spoken marine engineer had thousands of hours piloting helicopters, small jets, and turbo-prop aircraft and easily switched to the cockpit of a race boat. Working with Austin as if they were parts in a precision machine, he took command of the race from the second the referee raised the green starting flag.

They were up on plane at a near-ideal angle and blasted across the start line at one hundred and thirty miles per hour. Every boat had hit the finish line with throttle straight out. Two hard-driven competitors blew out their engines on the first lap, one flipped on the first turn, probably the most dangerous part of any race, and the rest were simply outclassed by the two leaders. The *Red Ink* rocketed by the others as if they were stuck on fly paper. Only the *Flying Carpet* kept pace. During the first Catalina Island turn, Zavala had maneuvered the *Red Ink* around the buoy so that Ali went wide. The *Flying Carpet* had been playing catch-up ever since.

Now the *Carpet* had taken wing and was coming abreast of the *Red Ink.* Austin knew of Ali's last-minute switch to a smaller propeller that would be better in rough seas. Austin wished he could trade in his large calm-water propeller. Ali had been smart to listen to his weather sense rather than the forecast.

"I'm cranking her up another notch!" Austin shouted.

"She's at one-forty now," Zavala yelled back. "Wind's up. She'll kite if we don't slow down."

Austin knew a high-speed turn was risky. The twin catamaran sponsons skated across the surface with practically no water resistance. The same design that allowed for high speed over the wave tops also meant wind could get under the hull, lift it in a kiting motion, or, even worse, flip it back onto its deck.

The *Flying Carpet* continued to gain. Austin's fingertips played over the tops of the throttle levers. He hated to lose. His combativeness was a trait he'd inherited from his father along with the football player physique and eyes the color of coral underwater. One day it would get him killed. But not today. He eased back on the throttles. The maneuver may have saved their lives.

A white-crested four-foot rogue sea was racing in off the port bow, practically snarling as it bore down on them. Zavala saw it angling in, prayed they'd clear it, knew instantly that the timing was all wrong. The wave hooked one of the sponsons like a cat's claw. The *Red Ink* was launched spinning into space. With lightning reflexes Zavala steered in the direction of the spin like a driver caught on an ice patch. The boat splashed into the water sideways, rolled so the canopies were buried, then righted after a few more yaws.

Ali slowed down, but once he saw they were all right, he gunned his engines, throwing caution to the winds. He wanted to finish as far ahead of Austin as possible. Ignoring the advice of his veteran throttle man, Hank Smith, Ali pushed his boat to the edge. The giant rooster tail arced high in the air for hundreds of feet, and the twin propellers plowed a wide and double-furrowed wake for hundreds more.

"Sorry about that," Zavala called out. "Caught a wave."

"Great save. Let's go for second place."

Austin pushed the throttles forward, and with a scream of the engines they were off in hot pursuit.

High above the race course the Italian TV cameraman had spotted the dramatic reversal of the lead boats. The chopper swooped out in a wide circle and came back over the flotilla to hover at midchannel. Pozzi wanted a wide shot of the lone boat speeding past the spectators to the turn buoy for the final approach to San Diego. The cameraman glanced at the sea below to get his bearings and saw wavelets outlining a large, shiny, grayish object mounding at the surface. A trick of the light. No, there was *definitely* something there. He caught the attention of the pilot and pointed straight down.

"What the hell is that?" the pilot said.

Pozzi aimed the camera at the object and zoomed in with the touch of a button.

"It's a *balena,*" he said as the object came into focus.

"For God's sake, speak English."

"How you say? A *whale.*"

"Oh, yeah," the pilot replied. "You see them migrating. Don't worry, he'll dive when he hears the boats."

"No," Carlo said with a shake of his head. "I think he's dead. He's not moving."

The pilot put the chopper at a slight angle for a better view. "Hell, you're right. There's another one. I'm counting three—no, four. Damn! They're popping up all over the place."

He switched to the hailing channel. "Come in, San Diego Coast Guard. This is the TV helicopter over the race course. *Emergency!*"

A voice crackled over the radio. "Coast Guard station at Cabrillo Point. Go ahead."

"I'm seeing whales in the race course."

"Whales?"

"Yeah, maybe a dozen. I think they're dead."

"Roger," the radio man said. "We'll alert the cutter on scene to check them out."

"Too late," the pilot said. "You've got to stop the race."

A tense silence followed. Then: "Roger. We'll try."

A moment later in response to a call from the station, the Coast Guard cutter moved from its post at the turn buoy. Orange signal flares blossomed against the blue sky.

Ali saw neither the flares nor the bloated gray carcass floating in his path until it was too late. He yanked the wheel, missed the obstruction by inches, dodged another body, but could not avoid a third. He veered off, yelling at Hank to cut power.

Smith's fingers flew to the throttle, and the planing hull settled down. The *Carpet* was still going fifty miles an hour when it hit the carcass. With an explosion of foul air, the body popped like a huge blubbery balloon. The boat careened off on one sponson, flipped, somersaulted, and miraculously landed right-side up again.

Ali and the throttle man were saved from fractured skulls by their helmets. Working through a black haze, Ali reached for the wheel and tried to turn, but there was no response from the rudder. He called out to the throttle man. Hank was slumped over the throttles.

On the *Nepenthe* the captain had left the bridge and was down on the deck talking to Gloria Ekhart when the actress leaned over the rail and pointed. "Excuse me, Captain. What's that gold boat doing?"

The *Flying Carpet* was wallowing like a punch-drunk boxer trying to find a neutral corner. Then the twin bows came around, and the boat straightened out, gained speed, and assumed a trajectory aimed at the yacht's midships. The captain waited for the boat to veer off. It kept coming. Alarmed, he calmly excused himself, stepped aside, and whipped a walkie-talkie from his belt. His mental computer was calculating how long it would take the gold boat to hit them.

"This is the captain," he barked into the hand radio. "Get this ship under way!"

"Now, sir? During the race?"

"Are you *deaf?* Weigh anchor and move this ship out. *Now.*"

"Move? Where sir?"

They had a snowball's chance in hell of getting under way in time, and his helmsman wanted to play twenty questions.

"Forward," he shouted, close to panic. "Just *move* it!"

Even as he barked the order the captain knew it was too late. The race boat had already cut the distance in half. He started to herd children to the other side of the yacht. Maybe a few lives would be saved, although he doubted it. The wooden hull would shatter into splinters, fuel would be spilled in a fiery conflagration, and the yacht would go to the bottom within minutes. As the captain grabbed onto a wheelchair with a little girl in it and pushed her across the deck, he yelled at others to do the same. Too frozen by fear to react, Ekhart saw the gold torpedo speeding toward them and instinctively did the only thing she could. She put her arm protectively around her daughter's thin shoulders and held her tight.

2

AUSTIN WAS NOT SURPRISED TO see Ali's boat go out of control. Ali was begging for a flip or a hook. It was the *nature* of the accident that puzzled Austin. The *Flying Carpet* veered sharply in a sloshing, foamy skid, then, living up to its name, went airborne with one side higher than the other, like a stunt car doing a two-wheeler off a low ramp. The catamaran flew bow-first for several boat lengths, landed with a monumental splash, vanished for a moment, then bobbed to the surface right-side up.

Austin and Zavala had found that a speed just under a hundred miles per hour kept them ahead of the pack but was slow enough to deal with changing water and wind conditions. The sea was a mix of small and moderate waves, some longer than others but most crested with white foam. Not exactly Force 12 on the Beaufort scale but nothing to ignore. They kept a sharp eye out for the sudden buildup of an errant sea that could trip them up again.

Zavala had brought the *Red Ink* around in a wide, sweeping curve and pointed the bows toward Ali's boat to see if he needed help. As the boat topped a wave and slid down the other side, Zavala swerved sharply to avoid a gray object longer than the race boat. The boat did a seam-stretching giant slalom run around three more large slate-colored mounds.

"Whales!" Zavala shouted with excitement. "They're everywhere."

Austin reduced their speed by half. They passed another lifeless carcass and a smaller one nearby that could have been a calf. "Gray whales," he said with wonder. "A whole pod of them."

"They don't look healthy," Zavala said.

"Not healthy for *us,* either," Austin said, backing off the throttles. "It's like a minefield out here."

Ali's boat had been slithering aimlessly around in the waves, the propeller chewing at air. The bows rose suddenly, the stern sank, the blades bit hungrily into the water, and the *Flying Carpet* was off like a jackrabbit spooked by a hunting dog. It accelerated rapidly, quickly coming up on plane, and headed toward the spectator fleet.

"Macho hombre!" Zavala said with admiration. "Bounces off a whale and goes to shake hands with his fans."

Austin also thought Ali was taking a bow. Ali's boat streaked across the open water like a gold arrow homing in on a bull's-eye. With his eye Austin drew an invisible line on the water, extending the *Flying Carpet*'s course until it intersected with a big white boat that was anchored broadside to the race chute. The graceful lines identified the vessel as an old luxury yacht. Austin noted with appreciation how the designers had blended form and function in the wooden hull. He glanced again at Ali's boat. It was moving faster, continuing toward the yacht in an undeviating line.

Why haven't they stopped or turned away?

Austin knew a race boat's hull was tougher than nails, but the rudders and the connecting tie bar were exposed. If the bar had been bent, the rudders could have been locked in place. Well, so what? Even if the steering were locked, all the crew had to do was shut down the engines. And if the throttle man couldn't do it, the racer could use the kill switch activated by an arm cord. The boat had struck the whale a glancing blow, but the impact still would have been severe, even worse when it slammed down onto the water. It would have been like hitting cement. Even with helmets and restraining harnesses, Ali's team might have been shaken up, at the very least, or, worse, incapacitated. He looked back at the yacht and saw the young faces lining the decks. Good God! *Kids.* The yacht was full of kids.

There was a flurry of activity on deck. They had seen the oncoming race boat. The yacht's anchor was coming out of the water, but the boat would have to sprout wings to avoid a disastrous collision.

"It's going to hit!" Zavala said, more in wonder than in apprehension.

Austin's hand seemed to move by itself, the fingertips pushing down on the throttles. Engines roaring, the *Red Ink* lurched forward as if it were a racehorse stung by a bee. The acceleration caught Zavala by surprise, but he tightened his grip on the steering wheel and pointed the *Red Ink* at the runaway boat. Their ability to intuit what the other was thinking had saved their skin more than once while carrying out a NUMA assignment. Austin slammed the throttles forward. The catamaran came up on plane and streaked across the open water. They were going twice the speed of the *Carpet,* coming in at an angle. Interception was only seconds away.

"Keep us parallel and come up alongside," Austin said. "When I yell, nudge him to starboard."

Austin's brain synapses danced with enough electrical energy to light up a city. The *Red Ink* went up the side of a wave, flew through the air, and came down with a jaw-jarring splash. The yacht was moving slowly forward. This would give them a slight increase in the margin of error, but not much.

The two boats were almost side by side. Zavala displayed his incredible skill as a pilot, bringing the *Red Ink* closer despite the waves from the broadening wake. Austin let them overtake the *Carpet,* move past it, then slowly pulled back on the throttles to match the speed of the other boat. They were only yards apart.

Austin had slipped into the nether land between intellect and action, pure reflex, his every sense at full alert. The ear-splitting thunder of four powerful engines drowned out attempts at rational thought. He had become one with the *Red Ink,* his muscles and sinews joined with the steel and Kevlar, as much a part of the boat as the pistons and driveshaft. The boats were out of sync, one up when the other was down. Austin fine-tuned the *Red Ink*'s speed until they were like two dolphins swimming abreast in perfect formation.

Up.

Down.

Up.

"Now!" he yelled.

The space between the racing boats narrowed to inches. Zavala eased the steering wheel to the right. It was a delicate maneuver. If it were done too sharply, they would hook hulls and possibly flip into the air in a lethal tangle. There was a loud hollow thump and a screech of tortured carbon composite as the hulls came together, then bounced apart. Zavala brought the boat over again and held it firmly in position. The wheel wanted to tear itself out of his hands.

Austin gunned the throttles. The sound of the engines was horrendous. Again the boats crashed. It was like trying to herd a very large and powerful steer. Eventually the *Flying Carpet* began to yield its forward momentum and angle off to the right. They drifted apart once more. Warmed to the game, Zavala slammed the boats together. The angle increased.

"Haul off, Joe!"

Ali's boat surged ahead on a track that would miss the yacht's stern and sped toward the flotilla. Boats scattered like dry leaves in a wind. Austin knew that battering Ali's boat off-course would send the *Red Ink* off like a cue ball in a game of billiards. He hadn't counted on how long it would take to persuade the *Carpet* to take a hike. Now he and Joe were hurtling toward the moving yacht with only seconds to spare before they struck it. They could see the horrified expressions of the people on deck. The boat was going seventy-five miles an hour. Even if he shut down the engines, he and Zavala would have to be scraped off the wooden sides of the old boat.

"What now?" Zavala yelled.

"Stay on course," Austin shouted.

Zavala swore softly under his breath. He had every confidence in Austin's ability to get them out of a tight spot, but sometimes his partner's actions defied all logic. If Zavala thought the order meant certain suicide, he didn't show it. His every instinct told him to whip the wheel over and take his chances, but he grimly held their insane course as steadily as if the two-hundred-foot boat that filled his vision like a big white wall were nothing but a mirage. He gritted his teeth and tensed his body in preparation for the impact.

"Duck," Austin ordered. "Keep your head low. I'm going to *stuff* it."

He bent and gunned the engines at full throttle; at the same time he set the trim tabs and ailerons. A *stuff* was usually something to be avoided. It happens when a boat comes off one wave and burrows into another. The worst type is called a *submarine,* because that's what the boat becomes when it goes into a stuff at high speed. Far from avoiding this result, Austin was *counting* on it happening. He held his breath as the race boat nosed down at a sharp angle, buried its bows in the water, and kept on going, burrowing into the sea like a badger. With the full power of the engines behind it, the *Red Ink* was transformed from a surface boat into a submersible.

The boat passed under the moving yacht, but not quite deep enough to prevent its canopies from being ripped off. There was a sickening watery crunch. The whirling propellers missed their heads by inches. Then the catamaran passed under the yacht and emerged on the other side. Exploding from the water like a very large and very red flying fish, it came to a halt as the burbling engines stalled out in a cloud of purple smoke.

The boat was built with an interior cage that could resist a herd of overweight elephants. The canopies were more vulnerable. Both Plexiglas covers had been completely ripped off. The cockpits were taking in seas as the boat rocked in the waves.

Zavala coughed out a mouthful of seawater. "You okay?" he asked, a stunned look on his dark, handsome face.

Austin pulled his helmet off to reveal the thick head of platinum, almost white hair. He surveyed the propeller scars on the deck and realized how close they had cut it. "Still among the living," Austin replied, "but I don't think the *Red Ink* was designed to be a convertible."

Zavala felt the water around his waist. "Time to abandon ship."

"Consider it an order," Austin said, loosening his harness. They piled out of the boat into the sea. As part of their certification, racers must pass a dunk test. A cabin cruiser came over and hauled them dripping from the water minutes before the *Red Ink* went to the bottom.

"What happened to the gold race boat?" Austin asked the cruiser's owner, a pipe-smoking middle-aged man who had come out of San Diego to watch the race and got more than he bargained for. He pointed off in the distance with the stem of his pipe. "Over there. The guy plowed right through the fleet. Don't know how he missed hitting the other boats."

"Mind if we check them out?"

"No problem," the man said obligingly as he put the wheel over.

Moments later they pulled up alongside the *Flying Carpet.* The canopies had been pushed back. Austin saw to his relief that the men inside were alive, although blood streamed down Ali's head where he'd bashed it, and Hank looked as if he were nursing a bad hangover.

Austin called out, "Are you injured?"

"No," Ali replied, although he didn't look quite convinced of his own well-being. "What *happened?"*

"You hit a *whale."*

"A *what?"* When he saw Austin's serious expression, Ali's face fell. "Guess we didn't win," he said glumly.

"Don't feel bad," Austin said. "At least your boat doesn't lie on the sea floor."

"Sorry," Ali said sadly. Then he brightened as a thought hit him. "Then *you* didn't win, either."

"Au contraire," Austin said. "All four of us won the prize for being the luckiest men alive."

Ali nodded. "Praise Allah," he said a second before he passed out.

3

Venezuelan Rain Forest

THE THICK CANOPY OF OVERHANGing tree branches blotted out the sun's rays, making the black water in the still pool seem deeper than it was. Wishing that she hadn't read that the Venezuelan government was reintroducing man-eating Orinoco crocodiles into the wild, Gamay Morgan-Trout jackknifed her lithe body in a surface dive and with strong kicks of her slender legs descended into the Stygian darkness. This must be how a prehistoric animal felt sinking into the ooze at the La Brea tar pits in California, Gamay thought. She flicked on the twin halogen lights attached to her Stingray video camera and swam down to the bottom. As she passed over the spinachy vegetation that rose and fell in the slight current as if dancing to music, something poked her in the buttocks.

She whirled around, almost more indignant than scared, her hand going for the sheath knife at her waist. Inches from her face mask was a long, narrow snout attached to a lumpish pink head with small black eyes. The snout waggled back and forth like a scolding finger. Gamay unclenched her hand from the knife hilt and pushed the snout aside.

"*Watch* it with that thing!" The sentence streamed out the regulator as a stream of noisy bubbles.

The thin beak opened in a friendly, sharp-toothed circus clown's grin. Then the river dolphin's face rotated so that it was looking at her upside down.

Gamay laughed, the sounds coming out like the gurgles Old Faithful makes before it erupts. Her thumb pressed the valve that allowed air to inflate her buoyancy compensator. Within seconds her head broke the pool's calm surface like a jack-in-the-box. She leaned back into her inflated BC, whipped the plastic mouthpiece from between her teeth, and broke into a wide grin.

Paul Trout was sitting in his ten-foot Bombard semi-inflatable boat a few yards away. Doing his job as a dive tender, he had followed the foamy air bursts marking his wife's underwater trail. He was startled to see her emerge from the black water and nonplussed at her mirth. Lips pursed in puzzlement, he lowered his head in a characteristic pose, as if he were peering up over the tops of invisible spectacles.

"Are you all right?" he said, blinking his large hazel eyes.

"I'm *fine,*" Gamay said, although clearly she wasn't. Her laughter was rekindled by the incredulous expression on Paul's face. She choked on a mouthful of water. The prospect of drowning from laughter made her laugh even more. She popped the mouthpiece back into her mouth. Paul paddled the inflatable closer, leaned over the side, and offered his hand.

"Are you *sure* you're okay?"

"Yes, I'm fine," she said. She regained her composure and spat out the regulator. After a fit of wet-dog coughs she said, "I'd better come aboard."

Clinging to the side of the boat, she handed her dive gear up to Paul, who then reached down and easily lifted her one hundred thirty-five pounds onto the raft. With his tan shorts, matching military-style shirt with epaulets on the shoulders, and floppy brimmed poplin hat, he looked like a Victorian fugitive from the Explorers' Club. The large tropical butterfly perched below his Adam's apple was actually one of the colorful bow ties he was addicted to. Trout saw no reason he couldn't be impeccably dressed anywhere, even in the depths of the Venezuelan rain forest where a loincloth is considered going formal. Paul's foppish attire belied a potent physical strength built up from his days as a fisherman on Cape Cod. The barnacle-hard calluses on his palms were gone, but the muscles from hoisting fish boxes lurked behind the razor-creased clothes, and he knew how to use the leverage of his six-foot-eight body.

"The depth finder says it's only thirty feet deep, so your giddiness is not caused by nitrogen narcosis," he said in his typical analytical way.

Gamay undid the tie holding back the shoulder-length hair whose dark red color had prompted her wine connoisseur father to name his daughter after the grape of Beaujolais.

"Insightful observation, my dear," she said, wringing the water from her tresses. "I was laughing because I thought I was the *sneaker* when I was really the *sneakee*."

Paul blinked. "What a relief. *That* certainly clears things up. I know what a sneaker is. *Sneakee,* on the other hand . . ."

She flashed a dazzling smile. "Cyrano the dolphin sneaked up and goosed me with his nose."

"I don't blame him." He leered at her slim-hipped body with a Groucho Marx hike of his eyebrows.

"Mother warned me about men who wear bow ties and part their hair in the middle."

"Did I ever tell you you look like Lauren Hutton?" he said, puffing on an imaginary cigar. "And that I'm attracted to women with a sexy space between their front teeth?"

"Bet you say that to all the girls," she said, putting a Mae West huskiness into her voice, which was low and cool by nature. "I did learn something scientific from Cyrano's little love poke."

"That you have a nose fetish?"

She gave him a no-nonsense lift of her eyebrow. "No, although I wouldn't rule it out. I learned that river dolphins may be more primitively developed than their saltwater cousins and more mellow in general than their marine relatives. But they are intelligent and playful and have a sense of humor."

"You would need a sense of humor if you were pink and gray, had flippers with discernible fingers on them, a dorsal fin that's a joke in itself, and a head like a deformed cantaloupe."

"Not a bad biological observation for a deep ocean geologist."

"Glad to be of help."

She kissed him again, on the lips this time. "I really appreciate your being here. And for all the work you've done computer profiling the river. It's been a nice change. I'm almost sorry to be going home."

Paul looked around at their tranquil surroundings. "I've actually enjoyed it. This place is like a medieval cathedral. And the critters have certainly been fun, although I don't know if I like them taking liberties with my wife."

"Cyrano and I have a purely platonic relationship," Gamay said with a haughty elevation of her chin. "He was just trying to get my attention so I'd give him a treat."

"A treat?"

"A *fish* treat." She slapped the side of the inflatable several times with a paddle. There was a splash where the lagoon opened into the river. A pinkish-gray hump with a long, low dorsal fin cut a V-shaped ripple in their direction. It circled the boat, emitting a sneezing sound from its blowhole. Gamay scattered fish meal pellets, and the slim beak came out of the water and hungrily snapped them down.

"We've verified those apocryphal stories of dolphins coming on call. I can imagine them helping the locals with their fishing as we've heard."

"You've also proven that Cyrano has done a good job of training you to give him a snack."

"True, but these creatures are supposed to be unfinished versions of the saltwater type, so it's of interest to me that their brains have advanced faster than their physical appearance."

They watched the circling dolphin with amusement for a few minutes, then, aware that the light was waning, decided to head back.

While Gamay arranged her gear, Paul started the outboard motor and headed them out of the lagoon onto the slow-moving river. The inky water changed to a strained-pea green. The dolphin kept pace, but when he saw there would be no more treats, he peeled off like a fighter plane. Before long the thick jungle along the river gave way to a clearing. A handful of thatched huts were grouped around a white stucco house with a red tile roof and arcade façade in the Spanish colonial style.

They tied up at a small pier, hauled their gear from the boat, and walked to the stucco building, trailing a chattering gang of half-naked Indian children. The youngsters were shooed away by the housekeeper, a formidable Spanish-Indian woman who wielded a broom like a battle-ax. Paul and Gamay went inside. A silver-haired man in his sixties, wearing a white shirt with an embroidered front, cotton slacks, and handmade sandals, rose from his desk in the coolness of the study where he had been working on a pile of papers. He strode over to greet them with obvious pleasure.

"*Señor* and *Señora* Trout. Good to see you. Your work went well, I trust."

"Very well, Dr. Ramirez. Thank you," Gamay said. "I had the chance to catalog more dolphin behavior, and Paul wrapped up his computer modeling of the river."

"I had very little to do with it, actually," Paul said. "It was mostly a question of alerting researchers at the Amazon Basin project of Gamay's work here and asking them to point the LandSat satellite in this direction. I can finish the computer modeling when we get home, and Gamay will use it as part of her habitat analysis."

"I'll be very sorry to see you go. It was kind of the National Underwater & Marine Agency to lend its experts for a small research project."

Gamay said, "Without these rivers and the flora and fauna that grow here, there would *be* no ocean life."

"Thank you, *Señora* Gamay. As a way of appreciation I have prepared a special dinner for your last night here."

"That's very nice of you," Paul said. "We'll pack early so we'll be ready for the supply boat."

"I wouldn't be too concerned," he said. "The boat is always late."

"Fine with us," Paul replied. "We'll have time to talk some more about your work."

Ramirez chuckled. "I feel like a troglodyte. I still practice my science of botany the old way, cutting plants, preserving and comparing them, and writing reports nobody reads." He beamed. "Our little river creatures have never had better friends than you."

Gamay said. "Perhaps our work will show where the dolphins' habitat is under environmental threat. Then something can be done about it."

He shook his head sadly. "In Latin America, government tends to move slowly unless there is someone's pocket to be filled. Worthwhile projects sink into the morass."

"Sounds like home. Our bottomless swamp is named Washington, D.C."

They were laughing at their shared joke when the housekeeper herded a native into the study. He was short and muscular, wore a loincloth, and had large copper loops in his ears. His jet-black hair was cut in bangs, and his eyebrows had been shaved off. He spoke in respectful tones to the doctor, but his excited speech and darting eyes made it clear something had set him off. He kept pointing toward the river. Dr. Ramirez grabbed a broad-brimmed Panama hat from a hook.

"There is apparently a dead man in a canoe," he said. "My apologies, but as the only government representative of any kind within a hundred miles, I must investigate."

"May we come?" Gamay said.

"Of *course*. I am hardly a Sherlock Holmes and would welcome other trained scientific eyes. You may find this of interest. This gentleman says the dead man is a ghost-spirit." Noting the puzzled reaction of his guests, he said, "I'll explain later."

They hustled from the house and walked quickly past the huts to the edge of the river. The men of the village were gathered silently near the water. Children were trying to peek through their legs. The women stayed back. The gathering parted as Dr. Ramirez approached. Tied up to the dock was an ornately carved dugout canoe. The dugout was painted white except for the bow, which was blue, and a blue stripe that extended from the front to the back.

The body of a young Indian man lay on his back inside the canoe. Like the village Indians, he had black hair cut in bangs and he wore only a loincloth. The resemblance ended there. The village men tattooed their bodies or dabbed crimson paint on their high cheekbones to protect them from evil spirits who supposedly cannot see the color red. The dead man's nose and chin were painted in a pale blue that extended down his arms. The rest of his body was a stark white. When Dr. Ramirez leaned into the canoe his shadow startled the green-bottle flies clustered on the dead man's chest, and they buzzed off to reveal a gaping circular hole.

Paul sucked his breath in. "That looks like a gunshot wound."

"I think you're right," Dr. Ramirez said, a serious look in his deep-set eyes. "It doesn't resemble any spear or arrow wound I've ever seen."

He turned to the villagers and after a few minutes of conversation translated for the Trouts.

"They say they were out fishing when the canoe came floating on the river. They recognized it from the color as a ghost-spirit boat and were afraid. It appeared to be empty so they came alongside. They saw the dead man in the canoe and thought they would simply let the boat go on its way. Then they thought better of it, because his spirit might come back to haunt them for not giving him a decent burial. So they brought him here and made him *my* problem."

"Why would they be afraid of this . . . ghost-spirit?" Gamay asked.

The doctor tweaked the end of his bushy gray mustache. "The Chulo, which is the local name for the tribe this gentleman belongs to, are said to live beyond the Great Falls. The natives say they are ghosts who were born of the mists. People who have gone into their territory have never come out." He gestured toward the canoe. "As you can see, this gentleman is flesh and blood like the rest of us." He reached into the canoe and pulled out a bag made of flayed animal skin that was lying next to the corpse. The village natives backed away as if he were brandishing a sack full of black plague. He spoke in Spanish to one of the Indians, who became more animated the longer they talked.

Ramirez abruptly ended the conversation and turned to the Trouts. "They are afraid of him," he said, and indeed, the village men were drifting back to their families. "If you would be so kind, we will haul the boat onto shore. I persuaded them to dig a hole, but not in their own cemetery. Over there, on the other side of the river, where nobody goes anyhow. The shaman has assured them that he can place enough totems on the grave to keep the dead man from wandering." He smiled. "Having the body so near will give the shaman more power. When something goes wrong with his spells he can always say the dead man's spirit has returned. We will send the boat off by itself down the river, and the spirit will be allowed to follow it."

Paul eyed the canoe's fine workmanship. "Seems a shame to waste such a beautiful example of boatbuilding. Anything to keep the peace." He grabbed one end of the canoe. With the three people pulling and pushing, they soon had it up on the shore away from the river. Ramirez covered the body with a woven blanket from the canoe. Then he retrieved the sack, which was about the size of a golf bag and tied with thongs at the open end.

"Perhaps this will tell us more about our ghost," he said, leading the way back to the house. They went into the study and placed the bag on a long library table. He untied the thongs, opened the bag gingerly, and peered inside. "We must be careful. Some of the tribes use poisoned arrows or blowgun darts." He lifted the bottom of the sack, and several smaller bags slid out onto the desk. He opened one and extracted a shiny metal disk that he handed to Gamay. "I understand you studied archaeology before you became a biologist. Perhaps you know what this is."

Gamay furrowed her brow as she examined the flat, round

object. "A mirror? It appears that vanity is not confined to women."

Paul took the mirror from her hand and turned it over to examine the markings on the back. A smile crossed his face. "I had one of these when I was a kid. It's a *signal* mirror. Look, these are dots and dashes. This isn't like any Morse code I know, but it's not bad. See these little stick figures? A basic code. Guy running one way means *come,* facing the other direction is *go,* I'd guess. Here's someone lying down."

"*Stay where you are,*" Gamay ventured.

"My guess, too. These two fellows with spears might mean *join me to fight*. Little guy and the animal could stand for *hunt*." He chuckled. "Almost as good as a cell phone."

"Better," Gamay said. "It doesn't use batteries or cost you per minute."

Paul asked Ramirez if he could open another bag, and the Spaniard gladly assented.

"Fishing kit," Trout said. "Metal hooks, fiber line. Hey," he said, examining a crude pair of metal pincers. "Bet this is a pair of pliers for pulling hooks out."

"I've got you beat," Gamay said, emptying another bag and pulling out a connected pair of small wooden circles with dark transparent surfaces filling their openings. She attached the apparatus to her ears with fiber hoops. "Sunglasses."

Not to be outdone, Ramirez also had been poking through bags. He held a gourd about six inches long, unplugged the wooden top, and sniffed. "Medicine perhaps? It smells like alcohol."

Hanging from the bottom was a miniature bowl and a wooden handle with a flat piece of stone and an irregular wheel on a rotating axis. Paul stared thoughtfully at the gourd, then took it from the other man. He filled the dish with the liquid, brought the wooden device near, and flicked the wheel. It scraped across the stone and emitted sparks. The liquid ignited with a *poof*.

"*Voilà,*" he said with obvious satisfaction. "The very first Bic cigarette lighter. Handy for starting a campfire, too."

More interesting discoveries followed. One bag held herbs Ramirez identified as medicinal plants including some he had never seen. In another was a slim, flat piece of metal, pointed at both ends. When they placed it on a glass of water it swung around until one end pointed toward the magnetic north. They found a bamboo cylinder. When held to the eye the glass lenses imbedded inside offered about an eight-power telescopic magnification. There was a knife that folded into a slim wooden case. Their last find was a short bow made from overlapping strips of metal like a car spring and curved to provide maximum pull for an arrow. The bowstring was of thin metal cable. It was hardly the primitive design one would expect to find in the rain forest. Ramirez ran his hand over the polished metal.

"Amazing," he said. "I've never seen anything like this. The bows the villagers use are simple dowels pulled back and tied with a crude bowstring."

"How did he learn how to make these things?" Paul said, scratching his head.

Gamay said, "It's not just the objects themselves but the material they are made of. Where did it come from?"

They stood around the table in silence.

"There is a more important question," Ramirez said somberly. "Who killed him?"

"Of course," Gamay said. "We were so overwhelmed by his technical accomplishments that we forgot that these objects belong to a dead human being."

"Do you have any idea who might have murdered him?" Paul asked.

A dark cloud descended on Ramirez's brow. "Poachers. Wood cutters and burners. The latest are men who collect valuable plants for medicine. They would kill anyone who got in their way."

"How could a lone Indian be a threat?" Gamay asked.

Ramirez shrugged.

Gamay said, "I think that in a murder investigation you are supposed to start with the corpse."

"Where did you hear that?" Paul said.

"I may have read it in a detective novel."

"Good advice. Let's take another look."

They walked back to the river and uncovered the body. Paul rolled it over onto its stomach. The smaller entry wound indicated that the man had been shot in the back. Trout gently removed a carved pendant from around his neck. It showed a winged woman holding her hands in front of her as if she were pouring from them. He passed it to Gamay, who said the figure reminded her of Egyptian engravings of the rebirth of Osiris.

Paul was taking a closer look at the reddish welts on the dead man's shoulders. "Looks like he's been whipped." He rolled the body onto its back again. "Hey, check out this strange scar," he said, indicating a pale thin line on the Indian's lower abdomen. "If I didn't know better, I'd say he had his appendix out."

Two dugouts arrived from across the river. The shaman, whose head was adorned with a brilliant crown of feathers, announced that the grave was ready. Trout covered the dead body with the blanket, and, with Gamay at the tiller, they used the inflatable to tow the blue-and-white canoe to the other side. Trout and Ramirez carried the body a few hundred yards into the forest and buried it in the shallow hole. The shaman surrounded the grave with what looked like various dried chicken parts and solemnly warned the assemblage that the spot would be forever taboo. Then they towed the empty canoe to midstream, where the current would catch it, and set the dugout adrift.

"How far will it go?" Paul asked as they watched the blue-and-white craft wheel slowly on its final journey.

"There are rapids not far from here. If it isn't broken up on the rocks or caught in the weeds, it could continue on to the sea."

"*Ave atque vale,*" Trout said, quoting the old Roman salute to the dead. "Hail and farewell."

They went back across the river. As Ramirez was climbing from the inflatable, he slipped on the wet bank.

"Are you all right?" Gamay said.

Ramirez grimaced with pain. "You see, the evil spirits have

already begun their work. I've apparently twisted something. I'll put a cold compress on it, but I may require your assistance to walk."

He limped back to the house with a hand from the Trouts. Ramirez said he would report the incident to the regional authorities. He didn't expect a response. A dead Indian was still considered a good Indian by many in his country.

"Well," he said, brightening. "What is done is done. I look forward to our dinner tonight."

The Trouts went back to their room to rest and clean up for dinner. Ramirez collected rainwater in a roof cistern and channeled it into a shower. Gamay had evidently been thinking about the Indian. As she toweled off she said, "Do you remember the Ice Man they found in the Alps?"

Paul had slipped into a silk bathrobe and was stretched out on the bed with his hands behind his head. "Sure. Stone Age guy who got freeze-dried in a glacier. What about him?"

"By looking at the tools and possessions he carried it was possible to picture his way of life. The Indians around here are at a Stone Age level. Our blue-faced friend doesn't fit the mold. How did he learn to make those things? If we had found those tools on the Ice Man, it would be in every newspaper headline. I can see it now: 'Ice Man Flicks a Bic.' "

"Maybe he subscribes to *Popular Mechanics*."

"Maybe he gets *Boy's Life,* too, but even if he got instructions every month on how to make neat stuff, where would he get refined metals to make them with?"

"Perhaps Dr. Ramirez can enlighten us at dinner. I hope you're hungry," Paul said. He was staring out the window.

"I'm starved. Why?"

"I just saw a couple of natives carrying a tapir to the barbecue pit."

4

AS AUSTIN STEPPED THROUGH THE big bay door into the cavernous building at the San Diego naval station, his nostrils were assaulted by a hell smell emanating from the three leviathans whose floodlit carcasses were laid out on flatbed trailers. The young sailor standing just inside the door had seen the broad-shouldered man with the strange white hair approach and assumed from his commanding presence that he was an officer in mufti. When Austin went to identify himself, the sailor snapped to attention.

"Seaman Cummings, sir," the seaman said. "You might want to use this." He offered Austin a surgical mask similar to the one he was wearing. "The smell has gotten real strong since they started pulling out the vital organs." Austin thanked the seaman, wondering whom he had offended to pull such foul duty, and slipped the mask over his nose. The gauze had been sprinkled with a perfumed disinfectant that didn't quite cut the strong odor but subdued the gag reflex.

"What have we got?" Austin said.

"A mama, a papa, and a baby," the sailor said. "Boy, what a time we had getting them here."

The seaman wasn't exaggerating, Austin thought. The final count was fourteen whales. Disposing of their bodies would have been a tall order even without the turf battles. As the first government agency to arrive on the scene, the Coast Guard was worried about hazards to navigation and planned to tow the whales out to sea and sink them with gunfire. The highly dramatic TV reports had gone around the world and stirred up animal rights activists who were angrier over the whale deaths than if Los Angeles had fallen into the Pacific Ocean with all its inhabitants. They wanted answers, fast. The Environmental Protection Agency was equally curious to know what had killed mammals that were under EPA protection.

The city of San Diego was horrified at the prospect of huge, smelly carcasses drifting up to its beaches, marinas, seaside hotels, and shorefront houses. The mayor called the district congressman who happened to be on the naval appropriations committee, and a compromise was reached with amazing speed. Three whales would be brought to shore for necropsy. The others would be towed out to sea and used for target practice. Greenpeace protested, but by the time they mobilized their mosquito fleet, the whales had been blasted to blubbery smithereens by navy gunners.

In the meantime an oceangoing tug hauled the remaining whales to the base. Navy cranes lifted the massive bodies from the water in improvised slings, and they were transported to a vacant warehouse. Mammalian forensic specialists from several California universities went to work as soon as the whales were delivered. An improvised laboratory was set up. Dressed in foul-weather gear, gloves, and boots, the technicians swarmed around and on top of the carcasses like large yellow insects.

The head of each animal had been separated from its body, brain tissue removed and taken to the dissecting tables for tests. Wheelbarrows served the function of stainless steel trays in a human autopsy.

"Not exactly brain surgery, is it?" Austin observed as he listened to the buzz of power saws echoing off the metal walls of the warehouse.

"No, sir," the sailor said. "And I'll be glad when it's over."

"Let's hope it's soon, sailor."

Austin pondered why he had left his comfortable hotel room for this ghoulish watch. If the race hadn't been a flop, win or lose he would have been guzzling champagne in celebration with the other racers and the coterie of lovely women who hovered around the race circuit like beautiful butterflies. A respectable number of bottles were popped, but the festivities had been dampened for Kurt and Ali and their crews.

Ali showed up with an Italian model on one arm and a French *mademoiselle* on the other. Even so, he didn't look particularly happy. Austin elicited a smile when he told the Arab he looked forward to competing against him again soon. Zavala upheld his reputation as a ladies' man by carving a chestnut-haired beauty from the field of groupies on hand for the race finale. They were going out for dinner, where Zavala promised to regale his date with the details of his narrow escape.

Austin stayed long enough to be polite, then left the party to phone the owner of the *Red Ink.* Austin's father was expecting his call. He had watched the race finale on TV and knew Austin was safe and the boat lay at the bottom of the ocean.

The elder Austin was the wealthy owner of a marine salvage company based in Seattle. "Don't worry about it," he said. "We'll build another one, even better. Maybe with a periscope next time." Chuckling evilly, he recounted in loving and unnecessary detail the night a teenage Austin had brought his father's Mustang convertible home with a crumpled fender.

Most grand prix races were held in and around Europe, but Austin's father wanted an American-built boat to win in American waters. He paid for the design and construction of a fast new boat he called the *Red Ink* because of the money it cost him and put together a top-notch pit crew and support team. His father put it with his typical bluntness: "Time we kick ass. We're gonna build a boat that shows these guys that we can win with American parts, American know-how, and an American driver. *You.*"

He formed a conglomerate of sponsors and used their economic clout to bring a major race to the States. Race promoters were eager for the opportunity to tap into the vast potential of the American audience, and before long the first SoCal Grand Prix had become a reality.

NUMA director Admiral James Sandecker grumbled when Austin told him he wanted to work around assignments, whenever possible, so he could race in the qualifying runs. Sandecker said he was worried about Austin being injured in a race. Austin had politely pointed out that for all its dangers, racing was a canoe paddle compared with the hazardous jobs Sandecker assigned him to as leader of NUMA's Special Assignments Team. As a trump card he played on the admiral's fierce patriotic pride. Sandecker gave Austin his blessing and said it was about time the United States showed the rest of the world that they could compete with the best of them.

Austin returned to the party after talking to his father. He quickly tired of the false hilarity and was happy to be invited aboard the *Nepenthe* to meet Gloria Ekhart, who wanted to thank him. The actress's mature warmth and beauty enchanted him. When they shook hands she didn't let go right away. They talked awhile and maintained eye contact that sent messages of mutual interest. Austin briefly entertained the fantasy of having a fling with someone he'd idolized on the big and little screens. It was not to be. Apologizing profusely, Ekhart was dragged off by the demands of her children.

Figuring it just wasn't his day Austin went back to the hotel and answered calls from NUMA colleagues and friends. He had dinner sent up and enjoyed filet mignon as he watched TV reruns of the race. The stations were running slow-motion replays again and again. Austin was more interested in the fate of the dead whales. One reporter mentioned that three whales were going to be examined at the naval station. Austin was curious as well as bored. From what he had heard and seen the whales didn't have a mark to indicate what killed them. The incompleteness of the situation went beyond the loss of his father's boat. It rankled his sense of orderliness.

The autopsy seemed to be winding down. Austin asked the seaman to take his NUMA business card to someone in charge.

The seaman returned with a sandy-haired man in his forties who stripped off his blood-soaked foul-weather gear and gloves but kept his surgical mask on.

"Mr. Austin," he said, extending his hand. "Jason Witherell, EPA. Pleasure to meet you. Glad to have NUMA interested. We might need to utilize your resources."

"We're always ready to help the EPA," Austin said. "My interest is more personal than official. I was in the race today when the whales made their appearance."

"I saw the news clips." Witherell laughed. "That was one hell of a maneuver you pulled off. Sorry about your boat."

"Thanks. I was wondering, have you come up with a cause of death?"

"Sure, they died of DORK."

"Pardon?"

Witherell grinned. "DOn't Really Know. DORK."

Austin smiled patiently. He knew pathologists sometimes cultivated a zany sense of humor to help maintain their sanity.

"Any guesses?"

Witherell said, "As far as we can determine for now, there was no evidence of trauma or toxin, and we've tested tissue for virus. Negative so far. One whale had become entangled in a monfilament fishing net, but it doesn't seem to have prevented the animal from eating or harmed it in any fatal way."

"So at least for now you don't have a clue how they died?"

"Oh sure, we know *how.* They suffocated. There was heavy lung damage that caused pneumonia. The lungs seem to have been damaged by intense heat."

"Heat? I'm not sure I follow you."

"I'll put it this way. They were partially cooked internally, and their skin was blistered as well."

"What could have done something like that?"

"DORK," Witherell said with a shrug of his shoulders.

Austin pondered the answer. "If you don't know *what,* how about *when?"*

"That's tough to pinpoint. The initial exposure might not

have been instantly fatal. The mammals could have become ill several days before their deaths but continued to make their way along the coast. The little ones would have been the sickest, and maybe the adults waited for them. You'd have to factor in the time it would take for the body to decompose and for the putrefaction gases to bloat them up where they'd surface in the race course."

"So if you backtracked you might be able to determine where they were when they died. You'd have to consider traveling and feeding time and currents of course." He shook his head. "Too bad the whales can't tell us where they've been."

Witherell chuckled. "Who *says* they can't tell us? C'mon, I'll show you."

The EPA man led the way past the flatbeds around the puddles of bloody water being hosed into drains. The smell was like a sledgehammer this close to the dead whales, but Witherell didn't seem to be bothered.

"This is the male," he said, stopping by the first carcass. "You can see why they're called gray whales. The skin is naturally dark, but it's blotched from barnacle scars and whale lice. He's a bit chopped up now. When we first measured him he was forty-one feet." They walked to the next flatbed which held a miniaturized version of the first whale. "This calf is also a male, born just a few months ago. There were other calves so we don't know if it belonged to the female." They had paused before the last flatbed. "She's bigger than the male. Like the others, she's got no outward signs of any bruise or laceration that might be fatal. This is what might interest you." He borrowed a knife from a colleague, climbed onto the flatbed, and bent over the whale's fin. After a minute he hopped down and handed Austin a flat square packet of metal and plastic.

"A transponder?" Austin said.

Witherell pointed up. "This old girl's every move was being tracked by satellite. Find out who's been keeping an eye on her, and that person should be able to tell you where she has been and when."

"You're a genius, Mr. Witherell."

"Only a humble government servant like you, trying to do my job." He hefted the transponder. "I'll have to hold on to this thing, but there's a number to call on the back."

Austin jotted the number down in a small notebook and thanked the pathologist for his help.

As Witherell escorted him back to the door, Austin said, "By the way, how'd you choose these particular whales?"

"It was done pretty much by chance. I asked the Navy to cut three representative animals out of the batch. I guess there was somebody on board who actually listened to my request."

"Do you think you would have been more likely to find a cause of death if you had a chance to autopsy the other corpses?"

"I doubt it," Witherell said flatly. "What killed these whales killed the others that were towed away. It's a bit late for that anyhow. From what I understand, after the Navy got through with them there wasn't enough left of the other animals for a plate of sushi."

More autopsy humor. Tossing his surgical mask into a barrel, Austin took a last look at the butchered carcasses that were the sad remains of once magnificent sea creatures. He thanked Witherell and Seaman Cummings and stepped out into the fresh night air. He gulped in several deep breaths, as if he could purge his memory as well as his lungs of the rank smell. Across the harbor sparkled the city-like lights of an aircraft carrier. He drove back to the hotel and walked quickly through the lobby, but not fast enough to avoid a few nose wrinkles from the staff and guests who had picked up the stench of death.

Back in his room Austin threw the khakis and dress shirt he'd been wearing into a laundry bag. He took a long, hot shower, shampooed twice, and changed into slacks and a golf shirt. Then he settled into a comfortable chair, picked up the phone, and dialed the number marked on the transponder. As he expected he was connected to voice mail. The government wouldn't pay someone to sit around and wait for news of a meandering whale. It might take days before someone answered his call. He left no message and instead called a twenty-four-hour desk at NUMA headquarters outside Washington and put in a request. The phone rang about a half hour later.

"Mr. Austin? My name is Wanda Perelli. I'm with the Interior Department. Someone called from NUMA and said you were looking for me. They said it was important."

"Yes, thanks for calling. I'm sorry to bother you at home. You heard about the gray whales off California?"

"Yes. I was wondering how you got my number."

"It was on a transponder attached to the fin of a female whale."

"Oh dear, that was Daisy. It was her pod. I've been tracking her for three years. She's almost like a relative."

"I'm sorry to hear that. There were fourteen whales in all. She was one of those picked at random."

She sighed loudly. "This is terrible news. We've tried so hard to protect the grays, and they've really been making a comeback. We're waiting for a forensics report on cause of death."

"I came from the necropsy a little while ago. Apparently there was no sign of a virus or pollutant. The whales died from lung damage caused by intense heat. Have you ever heard of such a thing happening?"

"No. *Never.* Does anyone know the source of this heat?"

"Not yet. I thought it might shed some light on the incident if we knew where the whales had been recently."

"I'm pretty familiar with Daisy's pod. Their migration is really quite remarkable. They make a ten-thousand-mile round trip. They feed all summer in the Arctic seas, then head south along the Pacific Coast to the breeding lagoons in Baja California, Mexico. They start moving around November and December and get there early the following year. The pregnant females lead the way, then the mature adults and the juveniles, in single file or in pairs. They go pretty close to the shoreline. They start back north in March. The whales with calves may wait until April. Again they follow the coastline closely on the way north. They go real slow, about ten miles an hour on the average."

"There was a briefing before the boat race. We were told to keep a watch for whales, but the race had been scheduled after the last pod had passed. As far as anyone knew there were no whales in the vicinity."

"The only thing I can think of is that they were stragglers. Maybe one of the calves became sick and they dallied somewhere until the calves were well."

"The pathologist had the same theory. Would you have kept track of their migration?"

"Yes. Do you have access to a laptop computer?"

"Wouldn't be without it."

"Good. Give me your e-mail address. I'll tap into the database and get the information to you at light speed."

"Thank you. Can't ask for better service than that."

"You might get the chance to pay me back if we call on NUMA for help."

"Call me personally, and we'll do what we can."

"Thanks. Oh, God, I still can't believe it about Daisy."

Austin hung up, opened his IBM laptop computer, and hooked it up to the telephone. After fifteen minutes passed he opened his e-mail file. A map of the western U.S., Canada, and Alaska appeared. A dotted line ran down from the Chukchi Sea, through the Bering Sea, then along the coast of North America to the tip of the fingerlike Baja Peninsula. The map was labeled "General Whale Migration Route."

Attached to the map was specific information on actual pods. Austin scrolled down until he found the file name "Daisy." The file linked to a map showing the exact route of the Daisy pod. The pod had made steady progress, then had stopped off the Baja coast south of Tijuana. After a pause they started north again, moving slower than before. At one point they looped around as if they were disoriented. He followed their tortuous path until it stopped off San Diego.

Austin exited the whale file and called up several other sites.

After a few minutes he sat back in his chair and tapped his fingertips together. The whales were migrating normally until they reached a certain area. Then something changed. He was pondering what he should do when he heard somebody at the door. Zavala.

"Home from your date so soon?"

"Yeah, I told her I had to get back to check on my sick roommate."

Austin looked alarmed. "You didn't bump your head today, did you?"

"I must admit going *under* a boat was a unique experience. I'll never look at the nautical rules of the road in the same light again."

"Well, for your information I feel fine, so you can go back and pick up where you left off."

Zavala flopped down onto the sofa. "You know something, Kurt, there are times when one has to show some restraint."

Austin wondered if a Zavala clone, stripped of its sexual drive, had walked into the room. "I agree wholeheartedly," he said with caution. "Now tell me the real reason."

"She broke Zavala's rule. I don't go out with married women."

"How did you know she was married?"

"Her husband told me so."

"Oh. Was he big?"

"Slightly smaller than a cement truck."

"Well, restraint was an especially wise decision in that case."

Joe nodded, unconvinced. "God, she was beautiful," he said with a sigh. "What have you been up to?"

"I went to a whale necropsy."

"And I thought *I* was having a bad time. There must be more fun things to do in San Diego."

"I'm sure there are, but I was curious about what killed those whales."

"Did they find a cause?"

"Their lungs were damaged by heat, and they died of pneumonia."

"Strange," Zavala said.

"I thought so. Look at this map on my computer. I got it through a NOAA weather satellite. It shows the water temperature of the ocean. See that little red bump in the water off the Baja? Sudden temperature change."

"You're saying our whales became sick shortly after they passed this area of warm temperature?"

"Maybe. But I'm more interested in what *caused* that change."

"I think you're about to suggest a trip south of the border."

"I could use an interpreter. Paul and Gamay won't be back in Arlington for a few days."

"No problemo. It's important for me to stay in touch with my Mexican roots."

He got up and started for the door.

"Where are you going?" Austin said.

Zavala looked at the clock. "The night is young. Two devilishly handsome and eligible bachelors sitting in their room talking about dead whales and hot water. Not healthy, *amigo.* I saw a beautiful woman in the lounge as I passed by. She looks as if she could use company."

"I thought you were giving women up."

"A momentary delusion caused by my injuries. Besides, I think she had a friend," Zavala said. "And there's a good jazz band playing in the lounge."

Austin's appreciation for cool jazz came right after his love of beautiful women and fast boats. A tequila and lime juice nightcap would taste mighty good. To say nothing about female companionship. He grinned and closed the cover on his laptop computer.

5 "HOW DO YOU LIKE YOUR MEAL?"

Dr. Ramirez inquired.

Paul and Gamay exchanged glances. "It's *wonderful,*" Gamay said. Indeed it was, she thought, surprisingly so. She would have to tell St. Julien Perlmutter, naval historian and gourmet, about this exotic dinner. The thin, tender slices of white meat were spiced with local herbs, accompanied by rich, dark gravy and fresh sweet potatoes. Dinner was served with a respectable Chilean white wine. Oh God! She'd been in the jungle so long she had developed a taste for roast tapir. Next she'd be craving howler monkeys.

Paul displayed his Yankee bluntness. "I agree. It's terrific. We'd never guess it would be so good after seeing the men carry that odd-looking beast in from the forest."

Ramirez put his fork down, a puzzled expression on his face. "Beast? The forest—I'm afraid I don't understand."

"The tapir," Gamay volunteered hesitantly as she glanced down at her plate.

Ramirez looked stunned, then his mustache twitched and he broke out into a deep laugh. He brought his napkin to his lips. "You thought . . ." He started to laugh again. "Excuse me. I am a poor host. Amusing myself at the expense of my guests. But I must assure you that this is *not* the animal you saw being trundled in from the hunt. I bought a pig from a neighboring village for this feast." He made a sour face. "Tapir. I can't imagine *what* it is like. Perhaps it's quite tasty."

Ramirez poured more wine and raised his glass in a toast. "I will miss you, my friends. Your company has been most enjoyable, and we have had many delightful conversations around this table."

"Thank you," Gamay said. "It has been a fascinating experience for us. Today may have been our most exciting day, however."

"Ah, yes, the poor Indian."

Paul shook his head. "I can't get over the sophisticated nature of all those gadgets he had with him."

Ramirez spread his palms apart. "The People of the Mists are a mysterious tribe."

"What do you know about them?" Gamay said, her scientific curiosity aroused. Before she attained a doctorate in marine biology from Scripps Institute of Oceanography, she had been a marine archaeologist and had taken many anthropology courses during her studies at the University of North Carolina.

Ramirez took a sip of wine, nodded with appreciation, and stared off into space as he ordered his thoughts. The buzzing and chirping of millions of tropical insects came through the screened windows, and the concert provided a fitting background for tales of the rain forest.

After a moment's reflection, he said, "First you must realize as we sit here in this island of civilization, with our propane gas stove and our electrical generator, that only a few years ago we would have been dead within minutes had we strayed into this part of the forest. Fierce Indians inhabited the area. Headhunting and cannibalism were commonplace. Anyone, whether you were a missionary bringing in the word of God or a hunter searching for animal skins, was regarded as an intruder who must be killed. Only recently have these people been domesticated."

"Except for the Chulo," Gamay ventured.

"Correct. They retreated further into the forest rather than be pacified. I must confess that I learned more about them today than I knew in the three years I have been living here. I have seriously doubted they even *exist*. With this tribe you must separate facts from legend. The other Indians avoid the forest beyond the Great Falls. They say people who go into Chulo territory never come out. Their fear, as you saw today, is real. Those are the scant facts."

"And the legend?" Gamay said.

"They can make themselves invisible," Ramirez said with a smile. "They can fly. They can pass through solid obstacles. They are more like ghosts or spirits than men. They can't be killed by ordinary weapons."

"The bullet hole we saw puts *that* myth to rest," Paul said.

"It would seem so," Ramirez agreed. "There is another story, even more intriguing. The tribe is apparently matriarchal. A woman leads it. A goddess, in fact."

"An amazon?" Gamay suggested.

In answer, Ramirez pulled an object from his pocket. It was the pendant that had been hanging around the dead man's neck. "Perhaps this is our winged goddess. It is said she protects her tribe and that her vengeance is terrible."

"*She* who must be obeyed," Gamay said dramatically.

"Pardon?"

Gamay smiled. "It's a quote from an adventure story I read when I was young. About a jungle goddess who lived for thousands of years without aging."

Paul took the pendant and studied it. "Goddess or not, she didn't do a very good job of guarding the native we saw."

The older man's face darkened. "Yes, but at the same time . . ."

"Is there something wrong?" Gamay said.

"I'm somewhat concerned. One of the village men came to me. He said there were stirrings of trouble in the forest."

"What kind of trouble?" Paul asked.

"He didn't know. Only that it had to do with the murdered Indian."

"In what way?" Gamay asked.

"I'm not sure exactly." He paused. "Creatures are being killed in this forest at this moment. Insects, animals, and birds are constantly involved in a violent struggle for life. Yet out of this bloody chaos there is an equilibrium." His deep-set eyes seemed to grow even darker. "I fear that the killing of the Indian has disturbed this balance."

"Maybe the Amazon goddess is about to wreak her revenge," Paul said, handing the medallion back.

Ramirez swung the pendant back and forth on its thong as if he were Svengali using it as a hypnotic device. "As a man of science, I must deal with the facts. It is a fact that someone out there has a gun and has no hesitation about using it. Either the Indian strayed out of his territory or someone with a gun invaded it."

"Do you have any thoughts on who this person might be?" Gamay asked.

"Perhaps. Do you know anything about the rubber industry?"

Both Trouts shook their heads.

"A hundred years ago rubber trees grew only in the Amazon jungle. Then a British scientist stole some seeds to start vast rubber plantations in the east. The same thing is happening now. The shaman who accompanied us on our burial detail today is a bit of a fraud when it comes to chasing out evil demons, but he knows the medicinal value of hundreds of rain forest plants. People come here and say they are scientists, but they are really pirates looking for herbs that have medicinal properties. They sell the patents to multinational drug companies. Sometimes they work directly for the companies. In either case the companies make fortunes while the natives who have harbored the knowledge get nothing. Even worse, sometimes men come in and *take* the medicinal plants."

"You think one of these 'pirates' tortured and shot the Indian?" Paul asked.

"It's possible. When millions are at stake, the life of a poor

Indian means nothing. Why they shot him, I don't know. It's possible he simply saw something he shouldn't have. These plant secrets have been with the forest inhabitants for generations."

"Is anybody trying to stop these pirates?" Gamay said.

"It is a problem. Sometimes government officials are in collusion with the drug companies. The stakes are very high. The governments care little about the indigenous people. They are interested only in how to sell the natives' genetic knowledge of plants to the highest bidder."

"So the piracy goes unchecked?"

"Not quite. The universities are sending teams of true scientists to track down the pirates. They are doing research on plants themselves, but at the same time they talk to the Indians and ask if there have been strangers asking questions. Our neighbors in Brazil have tried to stop the theft of genetic resources in the court. They sued a scientist for cataloging seeds and tree bark the Indians use for cures and charged him with stealing knowledge from indigenous people."

"A difficult charge to make stick," Paul noted.

"Agreed. Brazil is also pushing legislation to protect biodiversity, so we are making progress, but not much. We are talking about taking on drug companies with billions of dollars in resources. It is not an even match."

A thought occurred to Gamay. "Has your university been involved?"

"Yes," he said. "We have had teams from time to time. But there is little money for full-time police work."

It wasn't the answer Gamay was looking for, but she didn't persist. "I wish there was something we could do."

"There is," Ramirez said with a broad smile. "I would ask a favor. Please feel under no obligation to grant it."

"Try us," Paul said amiably.

"Very well. A few hours' travel from here there is another settlement on the river. The Dutchman who lives there has no radio. They may have heard about a Chulo being killed. In any event, they should be told, in case there are repercussions." He stuck his leg out. The ankle was heavily wrapped in a bandage. "I can barely walk. I don't think there is a break, but it is badly sprained. I was wondering if you could go in my place. You could make a quick trip of it."

"What about the supply boat?" Gamay asked.

"It is due late tomorrow as expected. They will lay over for the night. You would be back before it leaves."

"I don't see why we can't do it," Gamay said, stopping short as she caught the quizzical look in her husband's eye. "If it's okay with Paul."

"Well—"

"Ah, I apologize. My request has created marital discord."

"Oh, no," Paul reassured him. "It's simply my New England caution. Of course we'd like to help you."

"Splendid. I will have my men gather supplies for you and fuel my boat. It will be faster on the river than your inflatable. She should make the round trip in the same day."

"I thought you had only dugout canoes in the village," Gamay said.

Ramirez smiled. "They serve most of my needs, yes, but occasionally more efficient transportation is desirable."

She shrugged. "Tell us more about the man you call the Dutchman."

"Dieter is actually German. He's a trader, married to a native woman. He comes here occasionally, but mostly he sends his men once a month with a list, and we relay it to the supply boat. He is an unsavory character in my opinion, but that is no reason not to warn him of possible danger." Ramirez paused. "You do not have to do this. These things are really none of your affair, and you are scientists, not adventurers. Especially the beautiful *Señora* Trout."

"I think we can handle it," Gamay said, looking at her husband with amusement.

She was not speaking with bravado, but as part of the NUMA Special Assignments Team she and Paul had been on any number of dangerous assignments. And as attractive as she was, Gamay was no delicate flower. Back in Racine, Wisconsin, where she was born, she had been a tomboy who ran with a pack of boys and later moved with ease among men.

"Well, then, we have an agreement. After dessert we will have a glass of brandy and retire so we can be up at the crack of dawn."

A short while later the Trouts were back in their room getting ready for bed when Gamay asked Paul, "Why were you hesitant about helping Dr. Ramirez?"

"Couple of reasons. Let's start with the fact that this little side trip has nothing to do with our NUMA assignment."

Paul ducked the pillow tossed at his head. "Since when have you gone by the NUMA rule book?" Gamay said.

"Like you, whenever it has been convenient. I've stretched the rules but never broken them."

"Then let's just stretch them a little by saying that the river is an integral part of the ocean, therefore any dead person found on it should be investigated by NUMA's Special Assignments Team. Must I remind you that the team was formed precisely to look into matters nobody else would?"

"Not a bad sales pitch, but don't put too much stock in your powers of persuasion. If you hadn't suggested looking into this thing, I would have. On similarly flimsy grounds, I might add. I have an aversion to someone getting away with murder."

"So do I. Do you have any idea where we might start?"

"Already handled that. Don't let my taciturn Cape Cod nature deceive you."

"Not in a hundred years, my dear."

"Back to your original question, the reason I hesitated was my *surprise*. This is the first time Ramirez mentioned his boat. He's given us the impression he used dugouts. Remember the fuss he made about how great our little putt-putt inflatable was? I was sniffing around one day and found a shed holding an airboat."

She leaned up on one elbow. "An *airboat!* Why didn't he say something?"

"I think it's obvious. He didn't want anybody to know. I think our friend Ramirez is more complicated than he appears."

"I have the same impression. I think he was being disingenuous about sending us scientific geeks off on a potentially dangerous mission. We've told him enough about the Special Assignments Team for him to know what we do when we're not counting river dolphins. I think he wants NUMA brought into this thing."

"Looks like we've played right into his hands, but I'm not sure why he'd be so Machiavellian."

"I've got an idea," Gamay said. "He was talking about the scientists from the university acting as bio police. He is a scientist from a university. He sort of side-slipped the implication."

"I noticed." Paul stretched out on the bed and closed his eyes. "So you think he's actually a bio cop disguised as a botanist?"

"It would make sense." Gamay paused in thought. "I must confess that the real reason I want to investigate was in those bags we found with the Chulo. I'm intrigued at how a backward Indian got all those high-tech toys, aren't you?"

There was no sound from the other side of the bed except that of low breathing. Paul was exercising his famous talent for dropping off to sleep on command. Gamay shook her head, pulled the sheets over her shoulders, and did the same. They would be up with the sun, and she expected the next day to be a long one.

6

THE MEXICAN CUSTOMS AGENT leaned from his window and checked out the two men in the white Ford pickup truck. They were wearing beat-up shorts and T-shirts, Foster Grant sunglasses, and baseball caps with bait shop logos on them.

"Purpose of your visit?" the agent asked the husky man behind the wheel. The driver jerked his thumb over his shoulder at the fishing rods and tackle boxes in back. "Going fishing."

"Wish I could join you," the agent said with a smile, and waved them on into Tijuana.

As they pulled away, Zavala, who was sitting in the passenger seat, said, "What's with the *Spies Like Us* routine? All we had to do was flash our NUMA IDs."

Austin grinned. "This is more fun."

"We're lucky our clean-cut appearance doesn't fit the profile for terrorists or drug runners."

"I prefer to think that we're masters of disguise." Austin glanced at Zavala and shook his head. "By the way, I hope you brought along your American passport. I wouldn't want you to get stuck in Mexico."

"No problem. It wouldn't be the first time a Zavala sneaked across the border."

Zavala's parents had waded across the Rio Grande in the 1960s from Morales, Mexico, where they were born and raised.

His mother was seven months pregnant at the time. Her condition didn't stand in the way of her determination to start life with her newborn in *El Norte.* They made their way to Santa Fe, New Mexico, where Zavala was born. His father's skills as a carpenter and woodcarver brought him steady work with the wealthy clients who built their fashionable homes there. The same influential people helped his father when he applied for a green card and later for citizenship.

The truck was on loan from the *Red Ink's* support team because rental cars couldn't be taken into Mexico. From their hotel they headed south from San Diego, passing through Chula Vista, the border town that is neither Mexican nor American but a blend of both countries. Once into Mexico they skirted the sprawling slums of Tijuana, then picked up MEX 1, the *Carretera Transpeninsula* highway that runs the full length of Baja California. Past El Rosarita with its concentration of souvenir shops, motels, and taco stands, the commercial honky-tonk began to thin out. Before long the highway was flanked by agricultural fields and bare hills on the left and by the curving emerald bay known as Todos Los Santos. About an hour after leaving Tijuana they turned off at Ensenada.

Austin knew the resort and fishing city from the days he crewed in the Newport-Ensenada sailboat race. The unofficial finish was at Hussong's Cantina, a seedy old bar with sawdust-covered floors. Before the new highway brought the tourists and their dollars, Baja California Norte was truly the frontier. In its heyday Hussong's was a haunt for the colorful local characters and rugged individuals, and the sailors, fishermen, and auto racers who knew Ensenada when it was the last outpost of civilization on the eight-hundred-mile-long Baja peninsula before La Paz. Hussong's was one of those legendary bars, like Foxy's in the Virgin Islands or Capt'n Tony's in Key West, where everybody in the world had been. As they stepped inside Austin was heartened to see a few scruffy barflies who might remember the good old days when tequila flowed like a river and the police ran a shuttle service back and forth between the cantina and the local hoosegow.

They sat at a table and ordered *huevos rancheros.* "Ah, pure soul food," Zavala said, savoring a bite of scrambled eggs and salsa. Austin had been studying the sad expression on the moose head that had been over the bar for as long as he could recall. Still wondering how a moose got to Mexico, he turned his attention back to the map of the Baja that was spread out on the table in front of him next to the satellite photo showing water temperature.

"This is where we're going," he said, pointing to the map. "The temperature anomaly is in the vicinity of this cove."

Zavala finished his meal with a smile of pleasure and opened a Baedecker's guide to Mexico. "It says here that the *ballena gris* or gray whale arrives off the Baja from December to March to mate and give birth to its young. The whales weigh up to twenty-five tons and run between ten and forty-nine feet long. During mating, one male will keep the female in position while another male—" He winced. "Think I'll skip that part. The gray was almost exterminated by commercial whaling but was made a protected species in 1947." He paused in his reading. "Let me ask you something. I know you've got a lot of respect for anything that swims in the sea, but I've never thought of you as a whale hugger. Why the big interest? Why not leave this up to the EPA or Fish and Wildlife?"

"Fair question. I *could* say I want to find out what started the chain of events that ended up with the sinking of Pop's boat. But there's another reason that I can't put my finger on." A thoughtful expression came into Austin's eyes. "It reminds me of some scary dives I've made. You know the kind. You're swimming along, everything seemingly fine, when the hair rises on the back of your neck, your gut goes ice-cold, and you've got a *bad* feeling you're not alone, that something is watching you. Something *hungry.*"

"Sure," Zavala said contemplatively. "But it usually goes beyond that. I imagine that the biggest, baddest, hungriest shark in the ocean is behind me, and he's thinking how it's been a long time since he's had authentic Mexican food." He took another bite of his *huevos.* "But when I look around there's nothing there, or maybe there's a minnow the size of my finger who's been giving me the evil eye."

"The sea is wrapped in mystery," Austin said with a faraway look in his eyes.

"Is that a riddle?"

"In a way. It's a quote from Joseph Conrad. 'The sea never changes and its works, for all the talk of men, are wrapped in mystery.' " Austin tapped the map with his fingertip. "Whales die every day. We lose some to natural causes. Others get tangled in fishing nets and starve to death, or they get nailed by a ship, or we poison them with pollution because some people think it's okay to use the sea for a toxic waste dump." He paused. "But this doesn't fit any of those categories. Even without interference from humans, nature is always out of kilter, constantly adjusting and readjusting. But it's not a cacophony. It's like the improvisation you see with a good jazz group, Ahmad Jamal doing a piano solo, going off on his own, catching up with his rhythm section later." He let out a deep laugh. "Hell, I'm not making sense."

"Don't forget I've seen your jazz collection, Kurt. You're saying there's a sour note here."

"More a universal dissonance." He thought about it some more. "I like your analogy better. I've got the feeling that there's a big bad-ass shark lurking just out of sight and it's hungry as hell."

Zavala pushed his empty plate away. "As they say back home, the best time to fish is when the fish are hungry."

"I happen to know you grew up in the desert, *amigo,*" Austin said, rising. "But I agree with what you're saying. Let's go fishing."

From Ensenada they got back on the highway and headed south. As in Tijuana, the commercial sprawl thinned out and vanished and the highway went down to two lanes. They turned off the highway past Maneadero and followed back roads past agricultural fields, scattered farm houses, and old missions, eventually coming into rugged, lonely country with fog-shrouded rolling hills that dropped down to the sea. Zavala, who was navigating, checked the map.

"We're almost there. Just around the corner," he said.

Austin didn't know what he was expecting. Even so he was surprised when they rounded the curve and he saw a neatly lettered sign in Spanish and English announcing they were at the home of the Baja Tortilla Company. He pulled over to the side of the road. The sign was at the beginning of a long, clay drive bordered with planted trees. They could see a large building at the end of the driveway.

Austin leaned on the steering wheel and pushed his Foster Grants up onto his forehead. "You're *sure* this is the right spot?"

Zavala handed the map over for Austin's examination. "This is the place," he said.

"Looks like we drove all this way for nothing."

"Maybe not," Zavala said. "The *huevos rancheros* were excellent, and I've got a new Hussong's Cantina T-shirt."

Austin's eyes narrowed. "Coincidence makes me suspicious. The sign says 'Visitors Welcome.' As long as we're here, let's take them at their word."

He turned the truck off the highway and drove a few hundred yards to a neatly tended gravel parking lot marked with spaces for visitors. Several cars with California plates and a couple of tour buses were parked in front of the building, a corrugated aluminum structure with a portaled adobe façade and tiled roof in the Spanish style. The smell of baking corn wafted through the pickup's open windows.

"Diabolically clever disguise," Zavala said.

"I hardly expected to see a neon sign that said, 'Welcome from the guys who killed the whales.' "

"I wish we were toting our guns," Zavala said with mock gravity. "You never know when a wild tortilla will attack you. I once heard about someone being mauled by a burrito in Nogales—"

"Save it for the drive back." Austin got out of the car and led the way to the ornately carved front door of dark wood.

They stepped into a whitewashed reception area. A smiling young Mexican woman greeted them from behind a desk. *"Buenos días,"* she said. "You are in luck. The tour of the tortilla factory is just starting. You're not with a group from a cruise boat?"

Austin suppressed a smile. "We're on our own. We were driving by and saw the sign."

She smiled again and asked them to join a group of senior citizens, mostly Americans and mostly from the Midwest from the sounds of their accents. The receptionist, who also acted as guide, ushered them into the bakery.

"Corn was life in Mexico, and tortillas have been the staple food in Mexico for centuries with both the Indians and the Spanish settlers." She led the way past where sacks of corn were being emptied into grinding machines. "For many years people made their tortillas at home. The corn was ground into meal, mixed with water to produce *masa,* then rolled, cut, pressed, and baked by hand. With the growth of demand in Mexico and especially in the United States, the tortilla industry has become more centralized. This has allowed us to modernize our production facilities providing for more efficient and sanitary operation."

Speaking in low tones as they trailed behind the others, Austin said, "If the market for Mexican flapjacks is in the U.S., why isn't this place closer to the border? Why make them down here and ship them up the highway?"

"Good question," Zavala said. "The tortilla business in Mexico is a tightly held monopoly run by guys with close government connections. It's a billion-dollar industry. Even if you did have a good reason to locate this far south, why build overlooking the ocean? Nice place for a luxury hotel, but an operation like this?"

The tour went past the dough mixers which fed into machines that produced hundreds of tortillas a minute, the thin flat pies coming out on conveyor belts, all tended by workers in laundry-white coats and plastic caps. The guide was ushering the group to the packaging and shipping department when Austin spied a door with words written in Spanish on it.

"Employees only?" he asked Zavala.

Joe nodded.

"I've learned all I want to know about burritos and enchiladas." Austin stepped aside and tried the door. It was unlocked. "I'm going to look around."

Eyeing Austin's imposing physique and blazing white hair, Zavala said, "With due respect for your talents as a snoop, you don't exactly blend in with the people working around here. I might be less conspicuous than a giant gringo stalking the hallways."

Zavala had a good point. "Okay, snoop away. Be careful. I'll meet you at the end of the tour. If the guide asks, I'll say you had to go to the restroom."

Zavala winked and slipped through the door. He was confident he could charm his way out of practically any situation and had already prepared a story saying he'd become lost looking for the *baño.* He found himself in a long hallway with no windows or other openings except for a steel door at the far end. He walked the length of the hallway and put his ear against the door. Not hearing anything, he tried the knob. The door was locked.

He reached into his pocket and pulled out a modified Swiss Army knife that would have got him arrested in places where possession of burglar tools is illegal. The standard attachments such as scissors, nail file, and can opener had been replaced with picks for the most common locks. On the fourth try he heard the latch click open. Behind the door another corridor slanted down. Unlike the first, this passage had several doors. All were locked except one that opened into a locker room.

The lockers were secure, and he could have opened them with his picks if he had time. He glanced at his watch. The tour would wind up soon. On the opposite wall were shelves piled with neatly folded white coats. He found one that fit and slipped it on. In a supply cabinet he discovered a clipboard. He stepped out into the corridor and continued on to yet a third door. This, too, was locked, but he managed to open it after a few tries.

The door opened onto an elevated platform that overlooked a big room. The platform led to a series of walkways that crossed through a web of linking horizontal and vertical pipes. The low hum of machinery seemed to come from everywhere, and he couldn't trace its source. He descended a set of stairs. The pipes came out of the floor, then disappeared at right angles into the wall. Plumbing for the tortilla factory, he surmised. At one end of the room was another door. It was unlocked. When he cautiously opened it, a cool ocean breeze hit him in the face.

He gasped with surprise. He was standing on a small platform perched high on the side of a cliff, facing out onto a lagoon about two hundred feet below him. It was a beautiful vista, and again he wondered why somebody hadn't built a hotel rather than a factory there. He assumed the factory was behind the edge of the cliff, but he couldn't see it from his angle. He looked down again. The water washed up against the jagged rocks along the shore in foamy ripples. The platform had a gate at one end that led to empty space with no steps going down or up. *Odd.* A few feet from the gate a metal rail ran down the side of the cliff and disappeared into the water.

He followed the rail down to the lagoon with his eye. A section of water appeared to be darker than that surrounding it. It might have been kelp and other seaweed washing against the rocks. As he watched, there was an intense bubbling at the base of the cliff, and a large, shiny, egg-shaped object suddenly appeared from the water and began its climb up the side of the cliff. *Of course!* The rail was for an elevator. The egg rose steadily up the track. It would be there within seconds. Zavala ducked back into the big room with the pipes, keeping the door open a crack.

The egg, made of a dark tinted glass or plastic that blended in with the side of the cliff, came to a stop at the platform. A door opened, and two men in white smocks stepped out. Zavala dashed for the stairs. Within seconds he was back at the storeroom. He tore his coat off, folded it as neatly as possible, and quickly walked along the corridors to the bakery. Nobody saw him step back into the area open to the public. He hurried along in the direction Austin and the tour group had taken. The guide saw him approach and gave him a quizzical and not altogether pleased look.

"I was looking for the *baño.*"

She blushed and said, "Oh, yes. I will show you." She clapped her hands for attention. "The tour is about over." She handed everyone a sample package of tortillas and conducted them back to the reception area. As the cars and tour buses left, Austin and Zavala compared notes.

"From the look on your face I'd guess your little exploration was successful."

"I found *something.* I just don't know what it is." Zavala laid out a quick summary of his findings.

"The fact that they hid something underwater indicates that they don't want anyone to know what they are doing," Austin said. "Let's take a walk.."

They strolled around the side of the factory but only got a short distance toward the water before they encountered a high mesh fence topped with razor wire a few hundred feet short of where the cliff dropped off.

"So much for an ocean view," Zavala said.

"Let's see if we can get around to the other side of the cove."

The two men returned to the pickup and drove back onto the road. Several tracks led down to the sea, but the fence blocked each potential access. They were just about to give up when they saw a man with a fishing pole and a basket full of fish coming from a path that led toward the water. Zavala called him over and asked if they could get to the water. The man was wary at first, apparently thinking they had something to do with the tortilla place. When Zavala extracted a twenty-dollar bill from his wallet, the man's face lit up, and he said yes, there was a fence, but there was a place to crawl under it.

He led them on a narrow path through the shoulder-high bushes, pointed to a section of chain-link fence, and left clutching his windfall. A section of fence was bent back from the ground and a hole scooped out underneath. Zavala easily slithered under to the other side, then held the fence for Austin. They followed the overgrown path until they came to the edge of a cliff. They were near the tip of the southernmost promontory enclosing the lagoon.

A trail that must have been worn by the feet of fishermen descended down the less steep side of the point. The NUMA men were more interested in the unimpeded view across the cove. From this angle the dark metal structure looked like a sinister redoubt out of a *Conan* movie. Austin scanned the building through his binoculars, then pointed them at the side of the cliff. Sunlight glinted off metal about where Zavala had described the elevator track. He let his eyes sweep out to the wide entrance of the lagoon where surf broke on the rocks, then back to the factory.

"Ingenious," Austin said with a chuckle. "If you stuck a big facility out here in the boonies, everyone, like our fisherman friend back there, would talk about it. But put it in plain sight, invite the public to come tramping in and out every day, and you've got an unbeatable cover for some kind of clandestine operation."

Zavala borrowed the binoculars and scanned the opposite cliff. "Why a waterproof elevator?"

"I don't have an answer," Austin said with a shake of his head. "I think we've seen all we're going to see."

Hoping to detect signs of activity around the building or cliff, they lingered a few more minutes, but the only movement they saw was the soaring sea birds. They headed away from the sea and minutes later were crawling under the fence. Zavala would have liked to ask the fisherman if he knew about the elevator or whether he had seen anything unusual in the lagoon, but the man had taken his money and run. They got back into the pickup and headed north.

Austin drove without talking. Zavala knew from past experience that his partner was chewing over a plan and when he had it fully formulated he would spill the details. Just beyond Ensenada, Austin said, "Is NUMA still running those field tests off San Diego?"

"As far as I know. I was planning to check in after the race to see how things were going."

Austin nodded. During the drive back they exchanged small talk, trading war stories about past adventures and youthful indiscretions in Mexico. The long line of traffic at the border crossing was moving at a snail's pace. They flashed their NUMA IDs to save time and were whisked through customs. Back in San Diego they headed toward the bay until they came to a sprawling municipal marina. They parked and made their way along a pier past dozens of sail- and powerboats. At the end of a dock reserved for larger craft they found a stubby, wide-beamed vessel about eighty-five feet long. Painted in white on the greenish-blue hull were the letters "NUMA."

They stepped across the catwalk and asked one of the crewmen puttering on the deck if the captain were aboard. He led the way to the bridge, where a slim, olive-skinned man was going over some charts. Jim Contos was considered one of the best skippers in the NUMA fleet. The son of a Tarpon Springs sponge fisherman, he had been on boats since he was able to walk.

"Kurt. Joe," Contos said with a wide grin. "What a nice surprise! I heard you were in the neighborhood, but I never suspected you'd honor the *Sea Robin* with a visit. What are you up to?" He glanced at Zavala. "Well, I always know what *you've* been up to."

Zavala's lips turned up in his typical slight smile. "Kurt and I were in the offshore boat race yesterday."

A dark cloud crossed his brow. "Hey, I heard about that thing with your boat. I'm really sorry about that."

"Thanks," Austin said. "Then you must know about the dead gray whales."

"I do—a very strange story. Any idea what killed them?"

"We might be able to find out with your help."

"Sure, anything I can do."

"We'd like to borrow the *Sea Robin* and the mini and do a little diving south of the border."

Contos laughed. "You weren't *kidding* about a big favor." He paused in thought, then shrugged. "Why not? We're just about through with our field tests here. If you can get an oral authorization to work in Mexican waters, it's fine with me."

Austin nodded and immediately called NUMA. After a few minutes of conversation he passed the cell phone to Contos. He listened, nodded, asked a few questions, then clicked off. "Looks like we're heading south. Gunn gave his okay." Rudi Gunn was NUMA director of operations in Washington. "Two days at the most. He wants you and Joe back so he can put you to work again. One thing, though. He says he won't have time to get clearance from the Mexican government on short notice."

"If anyone asks, we can say we were lost," Austin said with feigned innocence.

Contos gestured at the glittering array of lights and dials on the ship's console. "That might be a tough story to sell with all the electronics this vessel carries. The *Sea Robin* may be ugly, but she sure knows what's going on in the world. We'll let the State Department iron out any problems if we're boarded. When do you want to leave?"

"We'll pick up our gear and get back as soon as possible. The rest is up to you."

"I'll schedule a seven A.M. departure for tomorrow," he said, and turned away to give the crew its new orders.

As Austin was walking back to the car he asked Zavala what Contos meant when he said he knew what Joe had been up to.

"We dated the same woman a few times," Zavala said with a shrug.

"Is there any female in the District of Columbia you *haven't* dated?"

Zavala thought about it. "The first lady. As you know, I draw the line at married women."

"Relieved to hear that," Austin said, getting behind the wheel.

"But if she becomes divorced, well. . . ."

They got into the car, and as Austin started the engine he said, "I think this would be a good time for you to tell me about the guy in Nogales who was mauled by a burrito."

7

UNDER A CLOUDLESS WESTERN SKY, the teal green McDonnell-Douglas helicopter cleared the rugged peaks of Squaw Mountain, dipped low over the alpine waters of Lake Tahoe, and darted like a startled dragonfly to the California shore. It hovered an instant, then dropped into a tall stand of Ponderosa pine, touching down on a concrete landing pad. As the rotors spun to a stop an elephantine Chevy Suburban lumbered alongside. The driver, who was wearing a uniform the same dark green as the helicopter and the SUV, got out to greet the rangy passenger who stepped from the chopper.

Taking an overnight bag from the passenger's hand, he said, "Right this way, Congressman Kinkaid."

They got into the vehicle, which headed along a blacktop drive through thick forest. Minutes later it pulled up in front of a complex of buildings that looked like a redwood version of the fabled Hearst castle of San Simeon. The late-afternoon sun threw the turrets, walls, and towers into fantastic silhouette. A whole forest of giant trees must have been leveled merely to provide the facing. The sprawling edifice was the ultimate log cabin, squared and cubed in size, a series of connecting outbuildings clustered around a three-story main house.

Congressman Kinkaid muttered, "This place is bigger than the Mormon Tabernacle."

"Welcome to Valhalla," the driver said noncommittally.

He parked the vehicle in front, took the congressman's bag, and led him up a wide stairway to a deck as long as a bowling alley, then into a large foyer paneled and beamed in dark, almost black wood. They followed a series of passageways done in the same dark paneling, finally stopping at a set of high metal doors cast in relief and shaped in a Gothic arch.

"I'll take your bag to your quarters, sir. The others are waiting. You'll find a nameplate designating your seat."

The guide pressed a button on the wall, and the doors opened silently. Kinkaid stepped inside and sucked his breath in as the doors clicked shut behind him. He was in a massive, high-ceilinged chamber. The great hall was lit by the fire from a huge hearth and blazing wall torches that vied for space with brightly decorated shields and pennants, spears, battle-axes, swords, and other instruments of death that recalled a time when war was an exercise in personal butchery.

The lethal artifacts paled next to the object occupying the center of the room. It was a Viking ship about seventy feet in length, its oak planking curved into an upswept bow and stern. The single square hide sail was set as if to catch a following breeze. A gangway near the stern allowed access to the deck and to a long table that ran lengthwise with the mast as its center point.

Kinkaid was a Marine veteran who had seen action in Vietnam and was not put off by the intimidating surroundings. Setting his jaw in an unmistakable expression of determination, he crossed the hall to the ship and went up the gangway. Seated around the table were about two dozen men who halted their conversation and looked at him with curiosity. He sat in the last empty chair and glowered at the others. He was about to strike up a conversation with the man on his right when the double doors at the end of the hall were flung open.

A woman entered and strode toward the boat in the flickering light of the torches, her long legs quickly eating up the distance. As she made her way across the hall, her close-fitting green coveralls emphasized the athletic body, but it was her height that was most imposing. She was nearly seven feet tall.

The woman's body and features were unflawed, but she was beautiful in the way an iceberg is beautiful, and equally forbidding. She could have sprung whole from the arctic permafrost. Her flaxen hair was pulled away from her face and tied in a bun, displaying to the fullest the marble skin and large eyes that were a hard glacial blue. She came up the gangway onto the ship and walked around the table. In a voice surprising for its softness she greeted each man by name and thanked him for coming. When she reached the congressman she paused, boring into his craggy face with her remarkable eyes, and shook his hand in a vise grip. Then she took her place in front of the high-backed chair at the bow end of the table. She smiled a smile that was as cold as it was seductive.

"Good afternoon, gentlemen," she said, her voice rising to the rich tones of a natural orator. "My name is Brynhild Sigurd. Undoubtedly, you are wondering what sort of a place this is. Valhalla is my home and corporate headquarters, but it is also a celebration of my Scandinavian roots. The main building is an expanded version of a Viking long house. The wings are for specialized use, such as offices, guest quarters, gymnasium, and a museum for my collection of primitive Norse art."

She arched an eyebrow. "I hope none of you is prone to seasickness." She waited for the laughter to subside, then went on. "This vessel is a reproduction of the Gogstad Viking ship. It is more than a stage prop; it symbolizes my belief that the impossible is attainable. I had it built because I admire the functional beauty of the design, but also as a constant reminder that the Vikings would never have crossed the sea if they had not been adventurous and daring. Perhaps their spirit will influence the decisions made here." She paused for a moment, then went on. "You're probably all wondering why I invited you," she said.

A saw-edged voice cut her off. "I'd say that your offer to give us fifty thousand dollars or donate it to a charity of our choice may have had something to do with it," Congressman Kinkaid said. "I've donated your offer to a scientific foundation that looks into birth defects."

"I would have expected nothing less, given your reputation for integrity."

Kinkaid grunted and sat back in his chair. "Pardon me for interrupting," he said. "Please get on with your, er, fascinating presentation."

"Thank you," Brynhild said. "To continue, you gentlemen come from all parts of the country and represent many different endeavors. Among your number are politicians, bureaucrats, academics, lobbyists, and engineers. But you and I belong to a common fraternity bound together by one thing. *Water.* A commodity we know to be in very short supply these days. Everyone is aware that we are facing what could possibly be the longest drought in the country's history. Is that not so, Professor Dearborn? As a climatologist, would you kindly give us your appraisal of the situation?"

"I'd be glad to," replied a middle-aged man who seemed surprised to be called upon. He ran his fingers through thinning ginger-colored hair and said, "This country is experiencing moderate to severe drought in its midsection and along the southern tier from Arizona to Florida. That's nearly a quarter of the contiguous forty-eight states. The situation will probably get worse. In addition, water in the Great Lakes is at all-time lows. A prolonged drought of Dust Bowl levels is entirely possible. A megadrought lasting decades is not outside the realm of possibility."

There was a murmur from around the table.

Brynhild opened a wooden box in front of her, dug her hand inside, and let the sand run through her long fingers.

"The party's over, gentlemen. This is the bleak, dusty future we face."

"With all due respect, Ms. Brynhild," drawled a Nevadan, "you're not telling us anything new. Vegas is going to be in tough shape. L.A. and Phoenix aren't much better off."

She put her hands together in light applause. "Agreed. But what if I told you there *is* a way to save our cities?"

"I'd like to hear about that," said the Nevadan.

She slammed the cover down symbolically on the box.

"The first step has already been taken. As most of you know, Congress has authorized private control over the distribution of water from the Colorado River."

Kinkaid leaned forward onto the table. "And as you must know, Ms. Sigurd, I led the opposition to that bill."

"Fortunately you did not prevail. Had the legislation gone down, the West would have been doomed. The reservoirs hold only a two-year supply. After that ran out we would have to evacuate most of California and Arizona and a good portion of Colorado, New Mexico, Utah, and Wyoming."

"I'll say the same thing I told those fools in Washington. Putting Hoover Dam in private hands won't increase the water supply."

"That was never at issue. The problem was not water supply but distribution. Much of the water was being misused. Ending government subsidies and putting water in the private sector means that it will not be wasted for the simplest of reasons. Waste is not profitable."

"I stand by my basic argument," Kinkaid said. "Something as important as water should not be controlled by companies that are unaccountable to the public."

"The public had its chance and failed. Now the price of water will be set by supply and demand. The marketplace will rule. Only those who can afford the water will get it."

"That's exactly what I said during the debate. The rich cities would thrive while the poor communities die of thirst."

Brynhild was unyielding. "So what of it? Consider the alternatives if the water continued to be distributed under the old publicly owned system and the rivers dried up. The West as we know it would become a dust bowl. As the man from Nevada said, L.A., Phoenix, and Denver would become ghost towns. Picture tumbleweed blowing through the empty casinos of Las Vegas. There would be economic disaster. Bond markets would dry up. Wall Street would turn its back on us. Loss in financial power means lost influence in Washington. Public works money would flow to other parts of the country."

She let the litany of disasters sink in, then went on. "Westerners would become the new 'Okies,' straight out of *The Grapes of Wrath.* Only instead of moving *west* to the Promised Land, they would pile their families into their Lexus and Mercedes SUVs and head *east.*" With irony in her rich voice, she said, "Ask yourself how the crowded eastern seaboard would react to thousands, *millions* of jobless westerners moving into their neighborhood." She paused for dramatic effect. "Wouldn't it be interesting if the people in Oklahoma refused to take *us* under their wing?"

"I wouldn't *blame* them," said a developer from Southern California. "They'd greet us the same way the Californians did my grandparents, with guns and goon squads and road blocks."

A rancher from Arizona grinned ruefully. "If you Californians weren't so damned greedy, there *would* be enough water for everybody."

Within minutes everyone was talking at once. Brynhild let the argument go on before rapping the table with her knuckle.

"This fruitless discussion is an example of the squabbling over water that has gone on for decades. In the old days ranchers shot each other over water rights. Today your weapons are lawsuits. Privatization will end this squabbling. We must end the fighting among ourselves."

The sound of clapping echoed in the hall. *"Brava,"* said Kinkaid. "I applaud your eloquent performance, but you're wasting your time. I intend to ask Congress to reopen the whole issue."

"That might be a mistake."

Kinkaid was too agitated to detect the veiled threat. "I don't think so. I have it on good authority that the companies that have taken over the Colorado River system spent hundreds of thousands of dollars to influence this awful legislation."

"Your information is inaccurate. We spent millions."

"Millions. You—?"

"Not personally. My corporation, which is the umbrella organization for those companies you mentioned."

"I'm stunned. The Colorado River is under *your* control?"

"Actually, under the control of an entity set up for that express purpose."

"Outrageous! I can't believe you're telling me this."

"Nothing that has been done is illegal."

"That's what they said in Los Angeles when the city water department stole the Owens Valley river."

"You make my point for me. This *is* nothing new. L.A. became the biggest, richest, and most powerful desert city in the world by sending forth an army of water surveyors, lawyers, and land speculators to take control of water from its neighbors."

Professor Dearborn spoke up. "Pardon me, but I'm afraid I agree with the congressman. The Los Angeles case was a classic case of water imperialism. If what you're saying is true, you're laying the groundwork for a water monopoly."

"Let me pose a scenario, Dr. Dearborn. The drought persists. The Colorado River is unable to meet demand. The cities are dying of thirst. You wouldn't have lawyers debating water allocation, you'd have gunfights at the water hole as in the old days. Think about it. Thirst-crazed mobs in the street, attacking all authority. The complete breakdown of order. The Watts riots would be a schoolyard fight by comparison."

Dearborn nodded like a man in a trance. "You're right," he said, clearly troubled. "But, if you'll pardon me . . . it just doesn't seem right."

She cut him short. "This is a fight for survival, professor. We live or we die according to our will."

Defeated, Dearborn leaned back, arms folded, and shook his head.

Kinkaid took up the cudgels. "Don't let her confuse the issue with her phony scenarios, Professor Dearborn."

"Apparently I have not been able to change your mind."

Kinkaid stood and said, "No, but I'll tell you what you *did* do. You've given me some good ammunition for when I bring this matter up again before committee. I wouldn't be surprised if antitrust action is merited. I'll bet my colleagues who voted for the Colorado River bill would change their minds if they knew that the whole system was going to be under the thumb of one corporation."

"I'm sorry to hear that," Brynhild said.

"You're going to be a damned lot more sorry when I get through with you. I want to leave your private amusement park immediately."

She gazed at him with sadness. She admired strength even when it was used against her.

"Very well." She spoke into a radio she had clipped to her belt. "It will take a few minutes to get your luggage and ready the helicopter."

The door to the hall opened, and the man who had escorted Kinkaid earlier guided him from the chamber.

When they were gone, Brynhild said, "While some may consider this drought a disaster, it presents a golden opportunity. The Colorado River is only part of our plan. We are continuing to acquire control over water systems around the country. You are all in a position to influence the success of our goals in operations in your communities. There will be great reward for everyone in this room, beyond your imagination in fact. At the same time you will be doing something for the common good as well." Her eyes swept both sides of the table. "Anyone who wants to leave now can do so. I only request that you give your word to keep your silence about this meeting."

The guests exchanged glances and some uneasily shifted their weight, but nobody accepted her offer of an exit visa. Not even Dearborn.

Waiters materialized magically, placed pitchers of water on the tables and a glass in front of each man.

Brynhild looked around the assemblage. "It was William Mulholland who was most responsible for bringing water to Los Angeles. He pointed to Owens Valley and said, 'There it is. Take it.' "

As if on signal, the waiters poured the glasses full and retreated.

Raising her glass high, she said, "There it is. Take it."

She put the glass to her lips and took a long drink. The others followed suit as if in a strange communion ritual.

"Good," she said. "Now for the next step. You will go home and wait for a call. When a request is made you will comply without question. Nothing that transpired at this meeting can be divulged. Not even the fact that you were here."

She scanned each face. "If there are no more questions," she said, making clear by her tone that debate had ended, "please enjoy yourselves. Dinner will be served in the dining hall in ten minutes. I have brought in a five-star chef, so I don't think you will be displeased. There's entertainment from Las Vegas after dinner, and you will be shown to your rooms. You will leave after breakfast tomorrow morning, in the sequence you arrived. I will see you at the next meeting, exactly a month from now."

With that, she left the table, strode across the room and through the double doors she had entered by, walking down a corridor and into an anteroom. Two men stood in the room, legs wide apart, arms folded behind their backs, their deep-set black eyes glued to the flickering screens that took up one wall. They were identical twins dressed alike in matching black leather jackets. They had the same stocky physiques, high cheekbones, hair the color of wet hay, and dark, beetling brows.

"Well, what do you think of our guests?" she said with derision. "Will these worms serve their purpose and loosen the soil?"

The analogy was lost on the brothers, who had only one thing on their minds.

Speaking in an eastern European accent, the man on the right said, "Whom do you want . . ."

". . . us to eliminate?" said the man on the left, finishing the sentence.

Their monotone voices were exactly alike. Brynhild smiled with satisfaction. The answer reaffirmed her conviction that she had made the right decision rescuing Melo and Radko Kradzik from the NATO forces that wanted to bring the notorious brothers before the World Court at the Hague charged with crimes against humanity. The twins were classic sociopaths and would have made a mark for themselves even without the Bosnian war. Their paramilitary status conferred semi-legitimacy on the murder, rape, and torture they carried out in the name of nationalism. It was difficult to imagine these monsters ever having been in a mother's womb, but somewhere they had forged the ability to intuit what the other was thinking. They were the same men, only in separate bodies. Their bond made them doubly dangerous because they could act without verbal communication. Brynhild had stopped trying to tell them apart. "Whom do you think *should* be eliminated?"

One man reached out with a hand whose clawlike fingers seemed to be made for inflicting pain and reversed the video tape. The other twin pointed to a man in a blue suit.

"Him," they said simultaneously.

"Congressman Kinkaid?"

"Yes, he didn't . . ."

". . . like what you said."

"And the others?"

Again the video reversed and they pointed.

"Professor Dearborn? A pity, but your instincts are probably right. We can't afford to have anybody with even the trace of scruples. Very well, cull him out as well. Do your work as discreetly as possible. I'm scheduling a meeting of the board of directors soon to go over our long-range plans. I want everything in place before then. I won't tolerate mistakes the way those fools bungled their job in Brazil ten years ago."

She whirled from the room and left the twins to themselves. The men remained there unmoving, their glittering eyes looking at the screen with the hungry expression of a cat choosing the fattest goldfish in the tank for his dinner.

8

THE RIVER SCENERY HAD CHANGED little since Dr. Ramirez waved good-bye from his dock and wished the Trouts a safe trip. The airboat followed mile after mile of the twisting and unbroken ribbon of dark green water. An unyielding wall of trees hemmed the river in on both sides and separated it from the eternal night of the forest. At one point they had to stop because the river was blocked by debris. They welcomed the break from the mind-numbing drone of the airplane engine. They tied lines around the entangled logs and branches and unclogged the bottleneck. The job was time-consuming, and it was late afternoon when the leafy ramparts gave way to brief glimpses of open space and cultivated fields along the river's edge. Then the forest opened up to reveal a cluster of grass huts.

Paul reduced speed and aimed the airboat's blunt prow between several dugout canoes drawn up on the muddy banking. With a quick goose on the throttle, he slid the boat onto the shore and cut the engine. He removed the NUMA baseball cap he had been wearing backward on his head and used it to fan his face.

"Where *is* everybody?"

The unearthly quiet was in sharp contrast to Dr. Ramirez's settlement where the natives bustled about their business throughout the day. This place appeared to be deserted. The only signs of recent human habitation were tendrils of gray smoke that rose from fire holes.

"This is very weird," Gamay said. "It's as if the plague struck."

Paul opened a storage box and pulled out a backpack. Dr. Ramirez had insisted that the Trouts borrow a long-barreled Colt revolver. Moving slowly, Paul placed the rucksack between them, reached inside, unclipped the holster, and felt the reassuring hardness of the grip.

"It's not the plague I'm worrying about," Paul said quietly, scanning the silent huts. "I'm thinking about that dead Indian in the canoe."

Gamay had seen Paul reach into the bag and shared his concern.

"Once we leave the boat it might be tough getting back to it," she said. "Let's wait a few more minutes and see what happens."

Paul nodded. "Maybe they're taking a siesta. Let's wake them up." He cupped his hands to his mouth and came out with a loud "Hallooo!" The only reply was the echo of his voice. He tried again. Nothing stirred.

Gamay laughed. "They would have to be sound sleepers not to hear a bellow like that."

"Spooky," Paul said with a shake of his head. "It's too damned hot sitting out here. I'm going to look around. Can you watch my back?"

"I'll keep one hand on the cannon Dr. Ramirez gave us and the other on the ignition. Don't be a hero."

"You know me better than that. Any problem and I'll come running."

Trout eased his lanky form out of the seat in front of the propeller screen and onto the deck. He had every confidence in his wife's ability to cover him. As a girl in Racine, she had been taught to shoot skeet by her father and was an excellent marksman with any kind of firearm. Paul contended she could shoot the eye out of a sand flea in mid-hop. He scanned the village and stepped onto the banking, only to freeze. He had seen movement in the dark doorway of the largest hut. A face had peered around the corner and disappeared. There it was again. Seconds later a man stepped out and waved. He shouted what sounded like a greeting and started down the slope toward them.

He arrived at the river's edge and mopped his damp face with a sweat-stained silk handkerchief. He was a big man, and the high flat crown of a wide-brimmed straw hat added to his height. His baggy white cotton slacks were held in place around his corpulent belly by a length of nylon rope, and his long-sleeved white shirt was buttoned up to his Adam's apple. The sun reflected off a monocle in his left eye.

"Greetings," he said with a slight accent. "Welcome to the Paris of the rain forest."

Paul looked past the man's shoulder at the sorry collection of hovels. "Where's the Eiffel Tower?" he asked casually.

"Hah-hah. Eiffel Tower. *Marvelous*! Look there, it's not far from the Arc de Triomphe."

After the long river journey in the damp heat Paul had little appetite for witty repartee. "We're looking for someone called the Dutchman," he said.

The man removed his hat, revealing a tonsured mop of unruly white hair. "At your service. But I'm not Dutch." He laughed. "When I first came to this blighted place seven years ago I said I was 'Deutsch.' I'm *German*. My name is Dieter von Hoffman."

"I'm Paul Trout, and this is my wife, Gamay."

Hoffman focused his monocle on Gamay. "A beautiful name for a lovely woman," he said gallantly. "We don't get many white women out here, beautiful or otherwise."

Gamay asked why the village was so quiet. Dieter's fleshy red lips drooped. "I suggested that the villagers go into hiding. It never hurts to be cautious with strangers. They will come out when they see that you are friendly." The empty smile again. "So, what brings you to our poor village?"

"Dr. Ramirez asked us to come. We're with NUMA, the National Underwater and Marine Agency," Gamay said. "We were doing some research on river dolphins and staying with Dr. Ramirez. He asked if we couldn't come in his place."

"I heard through the jungle telegraph that a couple of scientists from the United States were in the neighborhood. I never dreamed you would honor us with a visit. How is the esteemed Dr. Ramirez these days?"

"He would have liked to come, but he hurt his ankle and couldn't travel."

"Too bad. It would be nice to see him. Well, it's been a long time since I had company, but that's no excuse for being a poor host. Please come ashore. You must be very hot and thirsty."

Paul and Gamay exchanged glances that said, *Okay, but be careful,* and stepped off the boat. Gamay slung the bag with the gun in it over her shoulder, and they started toward the cluster of huts arranged in a semicircle at the top of a rise. Dieter yelled in another language, and each hut disgorged a load of Indian men, women, and children. They came out timidly and stood at silent attention. Dieter gave another command, and they began to go about their tasks. Paul and Gamay glanced at each other again. Dieter did not *suggest* in this village; he commanded.

An Indian woman in her twenties came out of the largest hut, her head bowed. Unlike the other women, who were dressed only in loincloths, she had a red sarong of machine-loomed fabric wrapped around her shapely body. Dieter growled an order, and she disappeared into the hut.

A thatched roof stood in front of the hut on four poles. The roof shaded a rough-cut wooden table and stools carved from stumps. Dieter gestured toward the stools, sat in one himself, and removed his straw hat. He mopped his sweating head with his handkerchief and snapped an order at the open door of the hut.

The woman came out carrying a tray with three mugs made from sections of hollowed tree limbs. She set the mugs down and stood respectfully a few paces away with her head still lowered.

Dieter raised his mug. "Here's to meeting new friends." There was a distinct clinking as he swished the contents of his mug. "That's right," he said. "You are hearing the beautiful sound of ice cubes. You can thank the wonders of modern science for allowing me to have a portable gas-powered ice maker. There is no need to live like these brown-skinned Adams and Eves." He slurped half his glass down in a single gulp.

Paul and Gamay took tentative sips and found the drinks cool, refreshing, and strong. Gamay looked around the settlement. "Dr. Ramirez said that you're a trader. What sort of goods do you trade?"

"I realize that to an outsider this must look like a poor place, but these simple people are capable of artistic work that is quite sophisticated. I give them my services as a middleman in marketing their crafts to gift shops and the like."

From the impoverished appearance of the village the middleman must take the lion's share of the money, Gamay guessed. She made a show of looking around. "We also understand that you are married. Is your wife away?"

Paul hid his smile behind the mug. Gamay was very much aware that the native woman was Dieter's wife and she didn't like the way the Dutchman treated her.

Dieter flushed, then called the woman over. "This is Tessa," he grunted.

Gamay stood and extended her hand in greeting. The woman looked at her in surprise, and, after a moment's hesitation, she took the proffered hand.

"Nice to meet you, Tessa. My name is Gamay, and this is my husband, Paul."

The fleeting ghost of a smile crossed Tessa's dusky face. Sensing that Dieter would make Tessa pay for it later if she pushed too far, Gamay nodded and sat down. Tessa stepped back to where she had been standing.

Dieter covered his annoyance with a meaty smile. "Now that I have answered your questions . . . the purpose of your arduous trip?"

Paul leaned forward onto the table and looked up over the top of his nonexistent glasses. "The body of an Indian came ashore upriver in a dugout canoe."

Dieter spread his hands. "The rain forest can be dangerous, and its inhabitants are only one generation removed from savagery. A dead Indian is not unusual, I am sorry to say."

"*This* one was," Paul replied. "He was shot."

"*Shot?*"

"There's more. He was a Chulo."

"That *is* serious," Dieter said with a shake of his jowls. "Anything to do with the ghost-spirits means trouble."

"Dr. Ramirez mentioned that the tribe is led by a woman," Gamay said.

"Ah, you've heard the legends. Very colorful, yes? Of course I have heard of this mythical goddess-chief, but I have never had the pleasure of meeting her."

Gamay asked, "Have you ever run into members of the tribe?"

"I have no firsthand knowledge of them, but there are the stories . . ."

"What kind of stories, Mr. von Hoffman?"

"The Chulo are said to live beyond the Hand of God. That's what the natives call the Great Falls some distance from here. They say the five cascading waterfalls resemble giant fingers. Natives who have gone too close to the falls have disappeared."

"You said the forest was dangerous."

"Yes, they could have been mauled by some animal or bitten by a poisonous snake. Or simply become lost."

"How about nonnatives?"

"From time to time men come this way to seek their fortune. I have given them what poor hospitality I could, shared my knowledge of my surroundings, and, most important, warned them to stay away from Chulo territory." He made a washing motion with his hands. "Three expeditions ignored my cautions, and three have vanished without a trace. I notified the authorities, of course, but they know the impossibility of finding someone once the trees have swallowed them up."

"Were any of those groups looking for plants that could be useful as pharmaceuticals?" Paul said.

"They came looking for medicine, for rubber, timber, treasure, and lost cities, for all I know. Few who pass this way share their secrets. I don't ask questions."

While Dieter rambled on, Tessa had silently raised her hand and pointed toward the sky. He finally noticed the strange gesture and the Trouts' quizzical expressions. His face went rock hard, then the unctuous smile reappeared.

"As you can see, Tessa was most impressed by a group that passed this way not long ago in search of specimens. They employed a miniature zeppelin to move above the tree canopy. The natives were very much in awe of the machine, and so was I, I must admit."

"Who were these people?" Gamay asked.

"I know only that they represented a French firm. You know how close-mouthed the French can be."

"What happened to them?"

"I haven't the slightest idea. I heard they moved on. Maybe they were captured and eaten by the Chulo." He laughed heartily at the prospect. "Which brings me back to the purpose of your visit. I thank you very much for warning me, but now that you know the dangers that lurk here, I trust you will go back to Dr. Ramirez with my appreciation."

Gamay looked at the lowering afternoon sun. She and Paul knew that in the tropics the sun drops with the swiftness of a guillotine blade.

"It's a little late to be starting back," she said. "What do you think, Paul?"

"It would be dangerous trying to navigate that river by night."

Dieter frowned, then, seeing he was getting nowhere, smiled and said, "Well then, you will be my guests. Tomorrow you will get an early start after a good night's sleep."

Gamay half heard his words. Tessa's head was no longer downcast. She was looking straight at Gamay, her eyes wide open, almost imperceptibly shaking her head. Paul caught the gesture as well.

They thanked Dieter for the refreshing drink and his offer of a place to stay and said they wanted to retrieve some gear from the boat. As they walked toward the river the natives shied away as if the couple were surrounded by an invisible force field.

Gamay made a pretense of checking the engine for oil.

"Did you see Tessa?" she said. "She was warning us."

"No mistaking the terror in those eyes," Paul said, examining the dip stick.

"What do you think we should do?"

"We don't have much choice. I'm not enthusiastic about spending the night here in Camp Happy, but I wasn't kidding. It would be crazy to run this river in the dark. Do you have any suggestions?"

"Yes, I do," Gamay said, watching a bat the size of an eagle flit across the river in the failing light. "I suggest that we don't close our eyes at the same time."

9

AS AUSTIN SCUDDED THROUGH THE blue-green Baja waters on the back of a mini-submersible, he wondered how a *National Geographic* photographer filming a whale migration would react if a man riding a giant boot suddenly appeared in his camera's viewfinder. Perched outside, like a rumble seat passenger in an old roadster, Austin could see Joe's head and shoulders outlined by the blue light from the control computer screen inside the watertight cockpit.

Zavala's metallic voice crackled in the headphones of Austin's underwater communicator. "How's the weather out there, cap?"

Austin rapped on the Plexiglas dome and curled his finger and thumb in the okay sign.

"It's fine. This beats muscle power any day," he said.

Zavala chuckled. "Contos will be pleased to hear that."

The skipper of the *Sea Robin* had beamed with pride as he showed Austin the new submersible sitting in its deck cradle. The experimental mini-sub was a marvelously compact vehicle. The operator sat in the dry, pressurized cabin like the driver of a car, legs stretched out into the extended eight-foot-long hull. Two pontoons flanked the miniature cabin, and on the back were the air tanks and four thrusters.

Austin had run his fingers over the transparent bubble dome and said, "I'll be damned. This thing *does* look like an old boot."

"I tried to get you the *Red October,*" Contos said, "but Sean Connery was using it."

Austin wisely kept his silence. NUMA people were known to form personal attachments to the high-tech equipment under their command. The uglier the gear, the more intense the relationship. Austin didn't want to embarrass Contos by explaining how he knew the sub was being field-tested off California where the main components had been assembled. He had commissioned the design and building of the mini-submersible for the Special Assignments Team, and Zavala designed it. NUMA had subs that could go faster and deeper, but Austin wanted a tough little vehicle that would be portable, easily transported by a helicopter or boat. It would have to be unobtrusive as well, Austin specified, so as not to attract attention. Although he had approved the blueprints, this was his first glimpse of the final product.

Zavala was a brilliant marine engineer who had directed the construction of many manned and unmanned underwater craft. For inspiration, Zavala used the DeepWorker, a commercial mini-sub designed by Phil Nuytten and Zegrahm DeepSea Voyages, an adventure expedition cruise company. Zavala extended the range and power and added sophisticated testing capacity. He claimed the instruments aboard the submersible could tell what river or glacier a drop of ocean water came from.

The sub was originally named the DeepSee, an homage to its predecessor and to its intended function as an exploration vehicle. When Admiral Sandecker heard the designation he cringed at the pun. Shown the scale model, he grinned. "It reminds me of one of the brogans I used to wear when I was a kid," he said, using the old slang term for high-topped workboots. The new name stuck.

The NUMA ship cruised south from San Diego into Mexican waters, staying well offshore. Near Ensenada the *Sea Robin* began to follow the coast more closely. The ship passed several fishing boats and a couple of cruise ships. Before long the vessel was about a half mile from the open mouth of the cove Austin and

Zavala had scouted out earlier from land. Austin scoured the rugged cliffs through powerful binoculars and studied the back of the tortilla factory. Nothing appeared out of the ordinary. Large signs posted on either side of the lagoon warned of dangerous hidden rocks. Highlighting the warnings were caution buoys strung across the opening.

The *Sea Robin* sailed beyond the cove and headed into a small inlet. As the anchor slid into the sea, Zavala eased into the mini-sub and made his last-minute checks. With the dome secured the cabin was watertight and carried its own air supply. Zavala was dressed comfortably in shorts and his new purple Hussong's T-shirt.

Austin, who would be immersed in water, was suited out in full scuba gear and extra air tank. He climbed onto the back of the Brogan with his fins resting on the pontoons and fastened a quick-release harness attached to the sub. The dome was latched tight. At his signal a crane hoisted the sub in the air, then lowered it into the sea. Austin unhooked the slack holding lines and gave Zavala the go-ahead to dive. Within seconds they were sinking into the sea in an explosion of bubbles.

The battery-operated thrusters kicked into action with a high-pitched hum, and Zavala steered for open water. The sub rounded the point of jagged sea-wet rocks and followed a course directly into the mouth of the lagoon. They stayed at a depth of thirty-five feet, moving well under Mach One at a comfortable five knots. They used a combination of Austin's observations and the mini's instruments to navigate. Austin kept his head low to reduce water resistance. He was enjoying the trip, particularly the schools of brightly colored fish that scattered like windblown confetti at their approach.

Austin was glad to see fish for a less aesthetic reason. Their presence meant the water was still safe for living things. He had not forgotten that unknown forces killed an entire pod of huge creatures that were hardier and more adaptable to their marine environment than a puny human being. Although sensors in the sub's skin automatically sampled and tested the ambient waters,

Austin knew that by the time he learned conditions were unhealthy it might be too late.

"Approaching the mouth of the lagoon. We're going right up the middle," Zavala reported. "Plenty of room on either side. Mooring line from a warning buoy off to starboard."

Austin turned to the right and saw a thin black line running from the surface toward the bottom. "I see it. Notice anything funny?"

"Yeah," Zavala said as they cruised by. "No rocks under the buoy."

"Bet you a bottle of Cuervo that all the other warnings are phony, too."

"I'll take the bottle but not the bet. Someone wants to keep people out of here."

"That's obvious. How's this buggy handling?"

"Getting into a little backwash from the water swishing out of the lagoon, but it's still easier than driving on the Beltway," Zavala said, referring to the highway that separates Washington from the rest of the country geographically and politically. "She handles like an—*uh*-oh."

"What's wrong?"

"Sonar is picking up multiple targets. Lots of them. About fifty yards dead ahead."

Austin had been lulled into complacency by the tranquillity of the trip. In his imagination he pictured a line of underwater guards waiting in ambush.

"Divers?"

"Sonar hits are too small. Little or no movement."

Austin strained his eyes in an attempt to pierce the gauzy blue.

Thinking ahead, he said, "What's the Brogan's top speed if we have to get out of here in a hurry?"

"Seven knots, pedal to the metal. She was made more for vertical travel than horizontal, and we're carrying a couple of hundred extra pounds of beef."

"I'll join Weight Watchers when we get back," Austin said. "Move in real slow, but be prepared to make a dash for it."

They crawled ahead at half speed. Within moments dozens of dark objects materialized, stretching from the surface to the bottom and rolling off both directions in a great wall.

Fish.

"Looks like a net," Austin advised. "Stop before we get snagged."

The Brogan slowed to a complete halt and hovered in place.

Austin ducked his head in reflex as a streamlined silhouette glided in from above and behind him. The shark was only there for an instant, long enough for Austin to see its round white eye and to estimate the hungry predator's length at more than six feet. Its toothy jaws opened then clamped shut to grab half a struggling fish in one bite before disappearing from sight with a flick of its high tail fin.

Zavala had seen the same thing. "Kurt, are you okay?" he shouted.

Austin laughed. "Yeah. Don't worry. That guy doesn't want a tough old human to chew on when he's got a whole seafood buffet."

"Glad to hear you say that, because he invited some of his friends for dinner."

Several more sharks swooped in, grabbed a bite, then, wary of the sub, quickly left. It was less a wild feeding frenzy than a gathering of discriminating gourmands picking from the choicest items on the menu. Hundreds of fish were caught in the fine mesh. They came in all sizes, shapes, and species. Some, still alive, were making fruitless attempts to free themselves, only to attract the attention of the sharks. Others had only their heads left, and bones marked the remains of many more.

"No one has been tending the net," Austin said.

"Maybe someone hung it here to keep nosy guys like us out."

"I don't think so," Austin said after a moment's reflection. "That net is made of monofilament. You could cut your way through it with a nail clipper. No electrical wiring, so it doesn't seem to have an alarm signal attached."

"I don't get it."

"Let's think about it. Whatever's in that lagoon killed a pod of whales. The locals would begin asking questions if they started seeing hundreds of dead fish. The folks who bring you Baja Tortillas don't like attention. So they stick the net here to keep the fish out and any dead ones in."

"Makes sense," Zavala agreed. "What next?"

"Keep on going."

Zavala's fingers danced over the computer screen that controlled the sub's functions. Two mechanical arms on the front of the Brogan unfolded and extended like a telescope to within inches of the net. The claws at the end of each arm grabbed the mesh and tore it open like an actor parting a curtain. Pieces of fish in various states of decomposition drifted off in every direction.

The job accomplished, Zavala brought the metal arms back to their rest position and increased throttle. With Austin still on the sub's back, they plunged through the hole and into the lagoon. The thirty-foot visibility was cut in half by thousands of tiny particles of seaweed that had washed into the cove to be shredded by the razor-sharp rocks. The sub slowed to a walk, Zavala feeling his way like a blind man with a white cane. They didn't see the huge object until they were almost on top of it. Again the sub came to a stop.

"What *is* that thing?" Zavala asked.

The cathedral light filtering down from the surface illuminated an enormous structure. It was about three hundred feet wide, Austin estimated, and about thirty feet thick, tapered at the ends like a huge metal lens and resting on four thick metal legs. The legs were hidden by boxlike structures where they sank into the sea.

"It's either a big metal spider or a sunken UFO," Austin said in wonder. "In any case, let's take a closer look."

At Austin's direction, Zavala steered the sub off at an angle and cruised along the perimeter as far as they could, then retraced their path and went along the other side. The structure was almost perfectly round except where it butted up close to the undersea cliffs.

"Hey, this is amazing! I'm getting high heat readings."

"I can feel the heat through my wet suit. Someone has cranked up the BTUs."

"The instruments indicate that it's coming from the pillars. Must be conduits as well as supports. Nothing dangerous. *Yet.*"

"Park this thing while I go in for a closer look."

The mini dropped lightly to the bottom and rested on its pontoons. Austin unhooked the harness and peeled off with instructions for Zavala to turn on the positioning strobe light in fifteen minutes.

Austin swam toward the disk, then over it. Except for a circular skylight the odd structure was fabricated of metal painted a dull green, which would have been difficult to see from the surface. He dropped down onto the dome itself and peered cautiously through the skylight.

Below was a network of pipes and machines. Men in white frocks walked about the well-lit cavernous space. Austin puzzled over the function of the machines, trying to put what he saw together with the hot water discharges, but came up with nothing. He undid a portable waterproof video camera from his belt and filmed the scene below. Satisfied with his work, he decided to get an overview. He rose off the disk and was panning the camera when he saw movement out of the corner of his eye.

He froze, floating above the structure. The egg-shaped elevator Zavala had described descended from the shimmering surface. It moved along its track and disappeared into a circular hatch that was opening on the roof of the underwater structure closest to the face of the cliff. Austin resumed his camera work only to be interrupted again, this time by Zavala.

"Better get back here pronto! The water temp readings are shooting up."

There was no mistaking the urgency in Zavala's voice. "On my way!"

Austin threshed the water with strong kicks of his powerful legs, maintaining a rhythm that ate up the yards. Zavala wasn't kidding about the heat buildup. Austin was sweating under his wet suit. He vowed never to boil a lobster again.

"Hurry," Zavala said. "The temp is going off the tracks!"

The Brogan's silvery beacon blinked in the gloom. Austin reached down and switched on a small strobe that hung from his buoyancy compensator. The Brogan moved in to meet him. The heat had become more intense. Austin grabbed onto the back of the moving sub and snapped his harness buckle in place. With Austin aboard, the Brogan quickly wheeled about and was headed for the mouth of the lagoon, motors whining at top speed. Zavala barked, "Something's wrong, Kurt! I am detecting alarms inside the facility." Moments later, Austin heard a loud, muffled *whump.* He turned to look over his shoulder just as the facility exploded in a fiery ball. The inferno instantly incinerated every living thing in the enclosed space. Superheated gas shot up pipes into the tortilla factory. Luckily, the factory was empty because it was Sunday. The Brogan wasn't as fortunate. It was caught by the shock wave and tumbled end over end with Austin desperately clinging on.

Austin felt as if he had been kicked by a giant invisible mule. The harness straps let go, and he was flung forward, arms and legs flailing, in a tangle of air hoses. He cartwheeled for an eternity and might have kept going halfway across the Pacific if he hadn't slammed into the net strung across the mouth of the lagoon. He hit the mesh with his feet, which was fortunate, because a headfirst impact would have broken his neck. The netting yielded, then snapped back. Austin shot out like a rock in a boy's slingshot.

Right into the path of the oncoming submersible.

The mini's dome had been ripped off, and Zavala was no longer inside. The sub tumbled at Austin on a collision course. Austin brought his knees up to his chest and wrapped his arms around them. He seemed fated to be smashed like a bug on a car windshield when the sub did a little hop that took it over Austin's head. He felt a painful impact as a pontoon grazed his shoulder. Then he was buffeted by secondary shock waves from multiple explosions that slowed his velocity and tossed him back after the mini-sub. The Brogan had battered its way through the net, and this time there was nothing to stop him.

Instinctively, he swooped his arm out to retrieve his regulator hose, clenched the mouthpiece between his teeth, and took a breathy gulp of air. The regulator was still working. His face mask was a cobweb of fracture lines where one of the hoses had hit the lens. Better the mask than his face! He whipped the useless mask off, assumed a vertical position, and did a complete turn.

He knew he had better get to the surface, but he wasn't going to do it without Zavala. One more try. He spun slowly around. Without the mask his vision was blurred, but he thought he saw a spot of purple and swam toward it. Zavala was floating a few feet off the bottom. Bubbles were coming from his mouth.

Austin pushed the regulator toward Zavala's face, not sure if it ever found its mark, because the willpower he had been using to operate on was eaten away by the black angry surf crashing against his brain. He reached down and let the quick-release buckle go on his weight belt and groped for the inflation valve of his buoyancy compensator. He thought he heard another explosion. Then he blacked out completely.

10

TROUT STOOD AT THE DOOR OF the hut as motionless as a totem pole, watching and listening. He had been at his post for hours, staring into the darkness, his every sense alert to catch any change in the rhythms of the night. He had watched the day wind down and seen the shadows mix with the false dusk created by smoldering cook fires. The last few natives had disappeared into their huts like sullen phantoms, and the village went silent except for the brief muffled cry of a baby. Trout was thinking what an unhealthy place this was. It was as if he and Gamay had stumbled into a plague ward.

The Dutchman had kicked the family out of the hut closest to his and with a sweep of his hand ushered the Trouts through the door like the doorman at the Ritz. Slivers of light filtered through the grass walls into the dim interior. Hardly a breath of fresh air entered the close confines. The floor was dirt, a couple of hammocks were slung from support poles, and the furniture consisted of two crude stools and a cutting board fashioned out of stumps. The stifling heat and primitive accommodations didn't faze Trout. He was more bothered by the feeling he and Gamay were *trapped*.

He wrinkled his nose, a gesture he'd picked up from his father, a Cape Cod fisherman. Trout could picture his father walking to the end of the pier in the predawn darkness and sniffing the air like an old hound dog. Most days he'd say, "Finest kind, cap. Let's go fishing." But some mornings he would wrinkle his nose and head for the coffee shop without another word. Any doubts about the elder Trout's olfactory prowess disappeared one beautiful morning when he stayed in port and six fishermen were lost in an unpredicted offshore storm. Things hadn't smelled right, his father explained later.

Trout had the same feeling although he was far from the sea in the heart of the Venezuelan rain forest. It was simply too quiet. There were no voices, no coughing, nothing to indicate human habitation of any kind. While it was still light Trout had committed every detail of the village to his near-photographic memory. He began to imagine that the population of the village must have silently vanished in the night. He backed away from the doorway and bent over the still form lying in a hammock. Gamay reached up and felt his face with a light touch of her fingers.

"I'm awake," she said. "Just thinking."

"About what?"

She sat up and swung her feet onto the floor. "I don't trust our friend the Flying Dutchman any further than I could throw him. Not that I would touch him. *Yech.*"

"I agree with your sentiments exactly. I think someone is watching us." He glanced toward the doorway. "This hut reminds me of a lobster trap. One way in, no way out, except to the cooking pot. I suggest we spend the night on the boat."

"Much as I hate to leave these five-star accommodations, I'm ready when you are. Question. How do we sneak off with someone watching?"

"Simple, we go out the back door."

"There wasn't a back door last time I looked."

"Guess you've never heard of Yankee ingenuity," Trout said smugly. "If you would stand watch I'll put my cleverness to work." He slipped a hunting knife from its belt sheath and went to the back of the hut. Kneeling, he slipped the eight-inch blade through the thatch and began to saw. The rustle and snap were barely audible, but to be on the safe side he timed his sawing to the cry of an unknown forest creature that made a noise like a rat-tail file on metal. Within minutes he had cut a rectangular opening about two feet square in the rear wall. He went to the front of the hut and guided Gamay by the arm to the newly created exit. She stuck her head through to make sure it was safe, then was out in an instant. Paul's basketball player body slithered out a second later.

They stood side-by-side behind the hut listening to the symphony of insect buzzes and bird calls. Earlier Gamay had noticed a path that went from behind the huts to the river. They could see the faint outline of hard-packed earth. Gamay led the way, and before long the huts were behind them and their nostrils picked up the river odor of damp rot. The path led to the gardens they had seen from the river in daylight. They walked along the boggy edge of the river and after a few minutes saw the skeletal outline of the airboat's propeller housing. They stopped in case Dieter had someone watching the boat. Paul threw a pebble into the water. The plop failed to draw anyone out of hiding.

They went aboard and readied the boat to leave at the first sign of dawn. Trout tucked a life preserver under his head and stretched out on the deck. Gamay climbed onto the seat and took her turn at the watch. Paul soon dozed off. At first he slept fitfully because of the heat and insects. His exhaustion caught up with him, and eventually he slipped into a deep sleep. In his slumber he heard Gamay calling his name as if from far away. Light was coming through his eyelids. He blinked and saw Gamay, still on her perch, her face grotesque in a flickering yellow glow.

Three dugout canoes were pulled up alongside the airboat. The canoes carried fierce-looking Indians armed with razor-sharp spears and machetes. The raw flames from the blazing torches they held in their free hands illuminated the garish red paint on their bronze bodies and faces. Black bangs came down to where their eyebrows would have been if they hadn't been plucked clean. The Indians were clad in loincloths except for one who wore a New York Yankees cap on his head. Trout eyed the shotgun the man cradled in his arms. One more reason to hate the Yankees, he thought.

Trout grinned and said, "Hi." The granite expressions remained unchanged. The man with the shotgun motioned for the Trouts to get off the boat. They climbed onto the shore where the Indians clustered around them. The Yankees fan jerked the shotgun again in the direction of the village. With the Trouts in the middle, the torchlight procession started up the slope.

"Sorry, Paul," Gamay whispered. "They just came out of nowhere."

"Not your fault. I thought any threat would come from land."

"Me, too. What was the deal with the smile?"

"I couldn't think of anything else to do."

"I guess Dieter is smarter than we thought he was," Gamay said begrudgingly.

"I don't think so. *Look.*"

As they approached the clearing in front of the huts, they saw Dieter. He was looking very pale and frightened in the torchlight and for good reason. More Indians surrounded him, their spear points inches from his ample belly. Sweat dripped off his face, but he couldn't get to it because his hands were in the air. As if he didn't have enough to worry about, two white men had their handguns leveled at his heart. They were dressed identically in cotton pants, long-sleeved T-shirts, and high-topped leather boots. Both wore what looked like wide leather linesman's belts with metal clips attached. One was a hulking slovenly type who badly needed a shave. The other was short and slim and had the dark, flat eyes of a cobra. The boss Indian handed him the Colt. The hard eyes studied the Trouts for an instant, then flicked back to the Dutchman.

"Here are your couriers, Dieter," the man said with a French accent. "Do you *still* deny that you tried to double-cross me?"

Dieter began to sweat even more profusely, the perspiration coming off his face like a waterfall. "I swear to God I never saw them before this morning, Victor. They simply showed up here and said Ramirez sent them to tell me about the dead Indian and to warn trouble was brewing." A sly look came into his yellow eyes. "I didn't believe them. I put them in the hut where I could keep an eye on them."

"Yes, I noticed your extraordinary security measures," Victor said with undisguised contempt. He turned to the Trouts. "Who are you?"

"My name is Paul Trout. This is my wife, Gamay. We're researchers working with Dr. Ramirez on a river dolphin project."

"Why are you here? There are no dolphins in this part of the river."

"That's true," Paul said. "We found the body of an Indian in a canoe. Dr. Ramirez thought trouble might be brewing and wanted us to warn this village."

"Why didn't Ramirez himself come with this warning?"

"He hurt his ankle and couldn't walk. Besides, we wanted to see more of the rain forest."

"Convenient." The Frenchman hefted the Colt. "Is this part of your scientific equipment?"

"No. It belongs to Dr. Ramirez. He insisted that we take it in case we ran into trouble. From the looks of things, I'd say he was right."

Victor laughed. "Your story sounds so stupid it might actually be plausible." He appraised Gamay as only a Frenchman could look at a woman. "*Gamay,* an unusual name with French roots."

Gamay recognized lechery where Victor saw charm, but she was not above using her feminine attributes for leverage. "The Frenchmen I have met in the past would have introduced themselves by now."

"Ah, pardon my bad manners. It must be my association with people like this *cochón* here." Dieter flinched as Victor waved his pistol barrel under the Dutchman's nose. "My name is Victor Arnaud. This is my assistant, Carlo," he said, indicating his silent companion. "We are employed by a European cartel that is seeking the acquisition of rare biological substances from the rain forest."

"You're botanists, then, like Dr. Ramirez?"

"No," he said with a shake of his head. "The work is too rigorous at this point for botanists. We have a working knowledge of biology, but we are the advance collection team who will bring back interesting specimens for the scientists to analyze. They will come later when we have paved the way."

"So you're looking for pharmaceuticals?" Paul ventured.

"Perhaps, as a by-product," Arnaud said. "It is no secret the next cure for cancer may be growing in the wondrous biological treasure house above our heads." He tapped his long nose, then his lips. "We are here primarily seeking fragrances for perfumes and essences, tastes for the food industry. If we come across medicinal extracts, so much the better. We have the permission of the Venezuelan government, and our operation is entirely legitimate."

Paul let his gaze drift over the ferocious-looking painted savages, the leveled guns, and the patently terrified Dieter. He didn't believe for an instant that these jungle thugs were doing *anything* legitimate. He didn't want to set Arnaud off by being too inquisitive, but he knew it would seem peculiar if he didn't show curiosity.

"You'll hardly be surprised if I observe that you're quite heavily armed for a scientific party," Paul said.

"Of course," Arnaud said, taking the comment in stride. "Ramirez's fears were not without foundation. You can see how dangerous the forest is. You yourself have seen a dead man." His mouth curved in an ironic smile. "You must wonder what our relationship is with this wretched creature," he said, speaking of Dieter. "He has given us the men of this village to help in our search for biological specimens. They know the forest better than anyone. He is paid handsomely, I might add."

Paul grinned. "Looks as if you're about to fire Mr. von Hoffman from his job."

"And for good reason. Even if what you have to say about yourselves is true, that you are not couriers, this does not change the fact that Dieter here tried to steal from us. We had been looking for an extremely valuable plant that could be worth millions, billions possibly, to the pharmaceutical, food, and perfume industry. It's quite a wonder. We were going to take samples to Europe for analysis. The natives have been using it for decades, although not for perfume, unfortunately."

"You seem to have solved your problem," Gamay said. "You have both Dieter and the specimens."

"I wish it were as simple as that," Arnaud said with an edge in his voice. "True, we have this pig, but our valuable plant samples seem to have disappeared."

"I'm afraid I don't understand."

"We had heard of this amazing plant from the natives, but none of them was able to locate it. We had gone far beyond our original area of operations into uncharted parts of the forest which is where we came across the Indian you were later to find dead. He had samples of the plant in his possession. We offered to pay him to show us where he got the specimens, but he refused. We made him our guest in the hopes we could persuade him to change his mind."

Paul remembered the welts on the Indian's body. "So when he wouldn't talk, you shot him."

"Oh, no, nothing so simple as that. In fact we were doing our best to keep him *alive.* Dieter was in charge of providing hospitality and safeguarding the specimens. He got drunk one night and let him escape. The poor devil was shot stealing a canoe. We assumed he got away with the specimens. In which case he would have had them when you found him."

"What did these specimens look like?" Paul asked.

"Quite unimpressive, really. Small tapered leaves with red veins which give the plant its local name, blood leaf."

"We examined the contents of the Indian's bag," Paul said.

"There was a medicinal pouch full of folk medicine herbs. Nothing like you described."

"So," Arnaud said. He turned a scornful eye back to Dieter. "You said the Indian left with the plant in his possession. Who is telling the truth?"

"I don't know what they're talking about," Dieter countered. "The Indian took his bag and everything in it."

"I don't think so," Arnaud said quietly. "If they had the plant specimens, they would not have come back and acted so stupidly. I think you have what we want." He cocked his revolver. "And if you don't tell me where it is, I shall kill you."

"Then you'd *never* find it, Arnaud," the Dutchman said, dredging up a shred of defiance. It was bad timing. Arnaud was clearly in no mood to dally.

"True, but before I killed you I'd turn you over to my painted friends here. They would have no compunction against skinning you like a monkey."

Color drained from Dieter's florid face. "I did not mean I would *not* tell you. I only meant there must be room to negotiate."

"All opportunity for negotiation has passed, regretfully. I'm tired of this affair. I'm tired of you." He raised the pistol to Dieter's lips. "I'm tired of your lying mouth."

There was a tremendous boom, and the lower half of the Dutchman's face disappeared in an explosion of crimson from the point-blank shot. The monocle popped from his unbelieving eye, and his body toppled over backward like a tree felled by a chainsaw.

The Frenchman turned the smoking gun on Paul. "As for you, I don't know if you are telling the truth or not. My instinct tells me that you are. It's very unfortunate that you happened to visit this pig. Nothing personal, but I can't let you carry away news of what has been going on." He shook his head sadly. "I assure you, I will make it quick for your beautiful wife."

Paul was light-years ahead of the Frenchman. He'd been

shocked by Dieter's summary execution, but he knew immediately what Arnaud's move meant for Gamay and him. No witnesses. Trout's lanky body and normally languorous movements were deceptive. He could move quickly when he had to. He tensed his arms, ready to grab Arnaud's wrist and twist him to the ground. He knew that at the best he would take the bullet, but Gamay might get away in the confusion. At the worst, they would both be killed.

As Arnaud's finger tightened on the trigger and Trout prepared to make his last-ditch move, there was a sound, half grunt, half cough, from the Indian wearing the Yankees baseball cap. He had dropped the shotgun, and now he looked down in terror at the brown wooden shaft of an oversized arrow that protruded at least two feet from the front of his chest. Its barbed point glistened with red. He made a motion to grab onto the arrow, but the tremendous hemorrhaging from the projectile took its toll, and he crumpled to the ground near Dieter's body.

Another Indian cried out. *"Chulo!"* A giant arrow cut him down as soon as the shout left his lips.

His companions took up the horrified chant.

"Chulo! Chulo!"

There was a strange ululating cry, and a ghastly blue-and-white face appeared in the bushes. Then another, and within seconds the masklike faces seemed to be everywhere. More arrows filled the air. More Indians fell. Torches dropped or were thrown to the ground in panic.

In the darkness and confusion Paul's long arm reached over and grabbed Gamay by the wrist, shocking her out of her trance. Ducking low, they ran toward the river with the same thought. *Get to the boat.* In their frantic haste they almost bowled over the slender figure who stepped out of the shadows and stood in their way.

"Stop!" she said firmly.

It was Dieter's wife, Tessa.

"We're going to the boat," Gamay said. "Come with us."

"No," she said, and pointed to the river. *"Look!"*

In the light of the torches they carried, dozens of blue-faced men could be seen swarming ashore from large canoes.

The woman tugged at Gamay's arm. "This way is safer."

She led the Trouts out of the clearing, and they plunged into the dark forest. Bushes and thorns whipped at their legs and faces. The ululation grew fainter. They could have been at the center of the earth as far as they knew. It was just as hot and dark.

"Where are you taking us?" Gamay said, stopping to catch her breath.

"Can't stop now. Chulo come soon."

Sure enough, the strange war cry began to increase in strength. They kept moving until Dieter's wife stopped after several minutes. They were in a grove of trees, dwarfed by the huge, misshapen trunks that soared for more than a hundred feet. Tessa was barely visible in the moonlight streaming down from openings in the tree canopy. She had raised her hand. The Trouts lifted their eyes to the treetops. They saw only darkness broken here and there by the silver-gray night sky.

The woman detected their confusion, and like a teacher working with blind children, she opened their hands and placed something in them that felt like dead snakes. Thick nylon ropes. Paul remembered the belts Arnaud and his pal wore and Dieter's comment about the zeppelin. He quickly fashioned a loop around Gamay's thin waist. She hauled on the other end of the line and began to rise above the ground. Paul looked around. Dieter's wife had vanished. They were on their own.

"Keep going," he said. "I'm right behind you." He rigged another rope around his own waist and with several strong pulls was yards off the ground. By the hard sound of breathing, Gamay was just ahead.

From below came a burst of the strange warbling cry. The torches of the Chulos appeared. The Indians threw the torches into the air, where they arced and fell like exhausted comets.

Gamay and Paul expected to be skewered by oversized arrows that could easily reach them, but they kept pulling.

Just as they thought they were out of range they looked down and saw two of the Indians lift off the ground. *Of course,* Paul thought. If there were two hauling ropes, there would be others as well.

Gamay yelled from above his head. "I'm at the *top!*"

Paul kept climbing and felt his wife's hand reach down to help him clamber onto a branch thicker than a man's waist. Grunting with effort, he pulled himself onto the limb and reached for another branch. His hand touched a smooth, rubbery surface. The pewter light from a half moon was diffused by a mist that hung over the trees, but he could see a large platform of mesh and tubing draped like a giant spider's web over the canopy. It was an ingenious working platform, Trout thought, but he would have to save his admiration for later. Heavy breathing was coming from under their feet. Paul grabbed for his hunting knife and remembered that one of the Indians had taken it from him at the same time he was relieved of the Colt.

Gamay yelled and pointed at the rotund silhouette of a small blimp floating above their heads. There was a crack of twigs from just under their feet. The Chulos were seconds away. Paul detached himself from the lifting line and walked with some difficulty across the spongy mesh until he reached a mooring rope. He gripped the line and used his weight to pull the blimp down to where Gamay could clamber into the seat hanging under the gas bag. With her weight holding the blimp down, he climbed in next to her.

"Do you know how to operate one of these things?" Gamay said.

"Can't be too hard. Think of it as a boat. First thing you do is cast off."

Gamay had sailed the Great Lakes as a child, so the comparison was reassuring even if she didn't believe it. They quickly untied the other mooring lines. The blimp hesitated, then made up its mind and rose slowly above the trees. They looked down and saw shadows leaping to grab the dangling lines, but the blimp was safely out of reach.

They rose high above the fog-filled valleys that stretched off in every direction and began to drift like a milkweed seed, wondering if they had simply exchanged one set of dangers for another.

11

"SEÑOR? SEÑOR!"

Austin's eyes blinked open to see a white stubble of whiskers covering leathery cheeks and a gap-toothed mouth stretched wide in a jack-o'-lantern grin. It was the face of the Mexican fisherman he and Joe had met on the cliffs the day before. Austin lay on his back in an open wooden boat, his head cushioned by a coil of rope. He was still in his wet suit, but his scuba gear was gone. He pushed himself upright with his hands, a task of no small difficulty because his joints were sore and he was sprawled on a slimy pile of fish.

A fisherman who strongly resembled the first man, right down to the cleft in his dental work, sat at the other end of the boat keeping watch over Zavala. Joe's hair, normally so neatly combed, sprouted in a hundred different directions, and his shorts and T-shirt were dripping wet. He looked dazed but awake.

"You okay?" Austin called out.

A fish flopped onto Zavala's lap. He carefully picked up the creature by the tail and tossed it with the others. "No broken bones. Now I know what it's like to be shot out of a cannon. How about you?"

"A few aches and pains." Austin rubbed the throbbing muscles of his shoulder, then went to work on his legs. "I feel like I've gone through a car wash and a telephone keeps ringing in my ear."

"Your voice sounds like it's still coming over an underwater communicator. Do you know what happened? I was coming to get you in the Brogan when all hell broke loose."

"There was an underwater explosion." Austin glanced at the mirror-flat sea. The boat lay off the cove entrance. The *Sea Robin* was nowhere in sight. Austin couldn't figure it. Contos and his crew would have heard the blast. Why hadn't they come out to investigate?

He turned his attention back to their own predicament. "Would you ask our friends how we got here?"

Zavala questioned the fishermen in Spanish. One of them did most of the talking, speaking in rapid fire as his brother nodded in agreement. Zavala thanked him and translated the exchange.

"This man's name is Juan," Zavala said. "He remembers us from yesterday up on the cliffs. The other guy is his brother Pedro. They were fishing when they heard a big muffled roar and the water bubbled and foamed in the inlet."

"*Sí, sí, la bufadora,*" Juan said. He threw his hands expansively into the air like an orchestra conductor calling for a crescendo.

"What's with the theatrics?" Austin asked

"He says the noise was like the blowhole outside Ensenada where the sea comes into a cleft in the rocks and makes a big boom. Only it was many times louder. The cliff split away behind the tortilla factory. There were big swells, and the boat almost capsized. Then we popped out of the water. They pulled us in like a couple of overgrown sardines, and here we are."

Austin scanned the sea again. "Did they mention seeing the *Sea Robin?*"

"They saw a ship earlier. From their description it must have been the *Robin*. It went around to the other side of the headland, and they haven't seen it since."

Austin was starting to worry about Contos and his crew. "Please thank our benefactors for their kindness and ask if they would mind taking us around the point."

Zavala relayed Austin's request, and the fishermen started the old Mercury outboard in a cloud of blue smoke. Coughing like an asthmatic corn popper, the motor effortlessly moved the boat through the silken sea. With Juan manning the tiller, they rounded the headland and immediately saw why the *Sea Robin* hadn't left its mooring. The NUMA ship wasn't going *anywhere* for a while.

The deck was covered with a small mountain of dirt and boulders, and the vessel listed heavily to the starboard. The A-frame at the stern and the free-standing cranes on the aft deck had been twisted as easily as pretzels by the debris. Above the boat, the steep cliff face was layered with yellow strata exposed by the rockslide. Crew members were attacking the rubble with shovels and crowbars, tossing what debris they could manage over the side. A forklift was moving the bigger rocks.

Juan maneuvered the fishing boat alongside the NUMA vessel. Contos came to the rail and leaned over. His hands and face were caked with dirt, and he looked as if he had crawled out of a mine.

Austin cupped his hands and called out, "Anyone hurt?"

"A few cuts and bruises," Contos yelled back. "Luckily the aft deck was clear. We had heard a loud boom from the cove and were about to check it out. Then the whole side of the cliff came down before we could weigh anchor. Where the hell have you two *been?*"

"I like your new makeup," Austin said.

Joe chimed in, "Is it Estee Lauder?"

Contos's attempt to rub the dirt off his nose only made it worse. "It's evident from your wise-ass comment that you're hale and hearty. When you're through being obnoxious, would you mind telling me what happened?"

"That boom you heard was an underwater explosion," Joe said.

Contos shook his head in disbelief. "I don't know of any volcanic activity along here. What caused it?"

"Best we can say for sure is that it was centered in the underwater installation," Austin said.

He gave Austin a blank look.

"We'll explain later." Austin surveyed the yellowed cliffs. "The explosion shook the slide loose."

Contos furrowed his brow. "Hey," he said as a thought struck him. "What did you do with the Brogan?"

Austin and Zavala looked at each other like guilty children who had broken the cookie jar. Austin was beginning to wonder if he were a Jonah, the name mariners give a seaman who attracts calamity. This was the second craft he had lost in as many days.

"We lost her," Austin said. "Sorry. It couldn't be helped. Juan and Pedro here hauled us out of the water."

"Pleased to meet you," Contos said to the smiling fishermen. "Not much we can do about it now. NUMA will simply have to build me a new one."

Austin swept his eyes over the tilted hull of the *Sea Robin*. "Your vessel has quite a list. Are you in any danger of sinking?"

"I think we'll be okay. No leaks detected so far. We'll see what happens once we get under way. Most of the damage is to the deck and superstructure. The cranes are useless, as you can see. The forklift can move the big stuff. We haven't called for help because we don't want to have to explain what we're doing in Mexican waters."

"Do we have time to check out the cove?"

Contos looked over his shoulder at the rubble still to be removed. "Be my guest. We'll get under way as soon as we're able."

Zavala asked the fishermen to take them back to the inlet. The request started an animated argument between the brothers. Pedro had had enough of the cursed place with its strange explosions and stranger mermen popping out of the sea. He clearly wanted to go home, but his brother prevailed.

The boat made its way around the headland. As they entered the cove they could see smoke coming from the tortilla factory. Like the cliff above the *Sea Robin*, the sheer face behind the factory was layered yellow where the outer rock cover had been dislodged by the explosion. The rock slide had taken with it all traces of the monorail elevator.

The fishing boat cut a path through the debris and dead fish that covered the surface of the inlet. Using a bucket, Austin and Zavala scooped pieces of melted plastic and charred paper from the water. Remembering how a tiny piece of metal had helped track down the source of the TWA jet explosion over Lockerbee, Scotland, Austin figured even the tiniest fragment might be of use.

The work was painstaking, but their persistence paid off. Zavala snagged a metal cylinder bobbing in the water. It was about two feet long and six inches in diameter. Austin found a serial number and the name of its manufacturer etched into the metal.

Joe called his attention to movement at the top of the cliffs. Human specks could be seen lining the bluff. Austin didn't feel like answering questions for the local authorities. The fishermen were happy to head back to the ship. The deck was practically clear as they pulled up next to the *Sea Robin*. The ship was close to its normal pitch. Austin borrowed some money from Contos and tried to pay the fishermen for their services, but the brothers refused the cash. Juan explained through Zavala that showing them the hole in the fence was a service for which he would accept payment, but saving men from the sea was a moral duty. Austin thought about it, then persuaded the fishermen to accept a gift of friendship. After discussing it with Contos, they presented the happy fishermen with an outboard motor soon to be retired from service but in excellent shape.

The engines were started, and the ship slowly headed for open water. No leaks were detected. Contos set a course north. They left just in time. As they cruised along, a dark green helicopter appeared out of nowhere, circled the inlet several times, then dashed off to the north as quickly as it had come. They mingled with the boat traffic around Ensenada, where they spotted a Mexican coast guard boat steaming at full speed in the opposite direction. With the *Sea Robin* safely on its way, the NUMA men hit the showers and got into dry clothes. They rejoined Contos on the bridge. He had a fresh pot of coffee waiting.

"Okay, gentlemen," he said, pouring two hot steaming mugs. "As skipper of this vessel, which you commandeered for what turned out to be a commando mission, I'd appreciate it if you would fill me in."

Austin took a sip of the high-octane brew and decided he had never tasted anything more delicious.

"The explosion was a surprise to us," he said. "Our basic mission was pretty simple. We wanted to check out the source of the heat that may have killed those whales. We think we found it." He described the underwater structure as they first saw it, filling Contos in on the approach, the fake hazard buoys, the fishing net, and the high water temperature. Then he turned the narrative over to Joe.

Putting himself back underwater in the moments before the explosion, Zavala curled his hands as if he were clutching an invisible steering wheel.

"Everything's fine. We figure the high temperature readings are coming from the installation. You set off for a closer look, and I put the sub on the bottom to wait. The temps start to go off the charts, and I suggest you get back to the Brogan."

Austin reached into his memory. "I had just looked through a skylight on the top of the structure when I got your call. There were people and machinery inside. I headed back to the sub. Then *boom!*"

"You said the structure was full of piping," Zavala said. "Some of it would have been high-pressure conduits, hence the potential for explosion."

"I don't know. There could have been a flaw in the piping, but this was a sophisticated operation. They would have had layers of safety valves and shutoffs to prevent a pressure buildup. From what I could see there was nothing out of the ordinary. Nobody was rushing around in a panic. No indication of anything wrong."

"What about the water temperature buildup?"

"Good question, although the satellite photos indicate this isn't the first time there has been a high-temperature water discharge into the cove, so it probably didn't have a direct link to the explosion." Austin had brought a plastic bag with him. He opened it and produced the metal cylinder. "We found this floating in the cove. Any idea what it is?"

Contos examined the object and shook his head. "I'll try to track down the manufacturer when we get back to Washington."

"Guess your instincts were right, Kurt. Remember, back at Hussong's, when you said you had the feeling a big bad-assed *something* was watching us."

Austin's coral eyes hardened. "If you'll remember, I made another astute observation."

"What was that?"

"I said that whatever it is lurking in the shadows, the damned thing is as hungry as hell."

"You two are spooky," Contos said. "It sounds as if you're talking about Godzilla."

Austin said nothing. He stared out at the bow cleaving the waves as if the answers to the questions whirling around in his head could be found beneath the blue-green of the sea.

12

The Hand of God

THE AIRSHIP GLIDED OVER THE rain forest like a huge, elongated Japanese lantern, pulsating with a soft blue-and-orange light as twin tongues of flame from the propane burners heated the air inside the big sausage-shaped envelope. Except for the occasional burner blast, the only evidence of the craft's existence was a silent shadow that blotted out the moon and stars like a passing cloud.

What Paul and Gamay thought to be a blimp was actually a thermal airship, an ingenious cross between a hot-air balloon and a dirigible. Hot-air burners provided lift, but unlike a balloon, which goes where the wind takes it, the thermal airship had an engine and could be steered under power. The more streamlined zeppelin silhouette had replaced the customary pear-shaped air bag known as the envelope. The envelope kept its shape with internal air pressure instead of a rigid blimp skeleton.

The Trouts sat side-by-side at the front of the aluminum-frame gondola, held in their comfortable padded seats by full harnesses. From their perspective, slung under the belly of the envelope, the blimp looked enormous. The polyester fabric bag was one hundred feet long and half that in height. It had a full rudder at the back end for steering and large, thick fins for stability. Behind the passenger seats were the propane tanks that fueled the burners, the fuel containers for the Rotex two-stroke power plant, the engine itself, and the three-blade propeller that provided lateral thrust.

Paul and Gamay had taken turns acquainting themselves with the airship's controls. Both Trouts had ridden in balloons and knew the principles of hot air. The airship's operation was relatively simple. A foot-operated valve controlled the stainless-steel burners that kept hot air flowing through a metal chute into the envelope. The instrument panel had only half a dozen gauges. The Trouts watched the altimeter with gimlet eyes, keeping the airship at about two thousand feet, an altitude that would give them a reasonable safety margin.

Keeping the airship aloft had drained the propane from one tank, and they were operating on reserve. They had been waiting for daylight to use the power plant, so a plentiful fuel supply remained for the propeller drive. A pearl-gray glow in the east announced the coming of dawn. Soon the sky turned rose-petal pink. Even after the sun rose the visibility was obscured by fog. The vapors rising off the tree canopy absorbed the sky's hue, and a roiling, reddish sea of mist stretched off to the horizon. While Paul operated the airship Gamay rummaged around in a storage box between the two seats. "Time for breakfast," she announced cheerfully.

"I'll have mine over easy," Paul replied. "Crisp on the bacon, please, and the home fries burned around the edges."

Gamay offered Paul a choice of granola bars. "You can have raspberry or blueberry."

"I'll try room service." He flicked on the radio, but all they heard was the crackle of static. "Bet Phineas Fogg never had to rough it like this," Paul said with a frown. "Aw hell, I'll take blueberry."

She handed him a bar and a bottle of warm mineral water. "That was quite a night."

"Yes, I would say that having a brush with ruthless biopirates, witnessing a cold-blooded murder, and escaping from savage Indians would certainly qualify as quite a night."

"We owe our lives to Tessa. I wonder how she got hooked up with Dieter."

"She's not the first woman to show poor judgment in men. If you had married a lawyer or a doctor instead of a fisherman's son, you would be floating in your backyard pool instead of being up here."

"How boring." Gamay chewed thoughtfully on her breakfast bar. "Any idea where we are, Mr. Fisherman's Son?"

He shook his head. "I wish my dad were here. He learned how to navigate the old-fashioned way before we started to depend on electronic gear."

"What about the compass?"

"Not much use unless you've got landmarks or navigational buoys to go with it. That's obviously east." He pointed to the sun.

"The Dutchman's settlement was south and west of Ramirez," Gamay said. "What if we aimed this thing northeast?"

Paul scratched his head. "That might work if we were sure we were still at the exact spot where we climbed into this rig. There was a breeze last night. I don't know how far it could have pushed us. Could make a big difference, and we've only got a limited amount of fuel left for the burners. Any decision will have to be the right one. The engine tanks are full, but it won't do much good to go forward if we lose altitude."

Gamay gazed over the ocean of green. "Sure is beautiful."

"Not as beautiful as three eggs over easy and bacon with home fries."

She handed him another granola bar. "Use your imagination."

"I am. I'm trying to imagine how they got this airship into the forest. They could have flown it in, but that's doubtful because this isn't big enough to carry all the supplies and spare fuel it would need. My guess is they launched it from the ground not far from where we found it."

"Since there are no roads," Gamay said, picking up the thread of logic, "they probably came in by water. If we found the river or tributary we could retrace our way back to Dr. Ramirez's camp. Perhaps if we went higher, we'd see more of the forest."

"Brilliant," he said, and goosed the throttle with his foot.

The burners responded with a throaty whisper, and after a pause the aircraft began to rise. As they ascended, the heat of the sun was beginning to burn off the mist. The tree canopy began to appear as ragged patches of green. Reddish flowers grew in patches on the treetops like coral reefs.

At three thousand feet Gamay squinted through the haze. "I see something over there."

Paul started the power plant and turned the steering wheel that controlled the cables running to the rudder until the airship came slowly about. With the water-cooled engine purring quietly, the airship gained speed slowly as it overcame its inertia, and before long the propeller was kicking them along at ten miles per hour. Gamay had found a pair of binoculars and was using them to scope out where they were going.

"Incredible," she said as the mists cleared.

"What do you see?"

Gamay was silent for a second. "The Hand of God," she said with quiet awe.

Paul hesitated. He hadn't slept much and was slow on the uptake. "The Great Falls the Dutchman talked about?"

Gamay nodded. "Even at this distance it's magnificent."

Paul tried to increase their speed. He sensed something peculiar about the controls. The airship seemed to be dragging. He peered down and saw a red triangular object dangling from lines attached to the gondola.

"Hello," he said. "We've got company."

Gamay lowered the binoculars and followed Paul's gaze. "It looks vaguely like a life raft. Made out of rubber tubing and mesh in the middle. They probably used it to drop people and supplies off on the tree canopy."

"Sounds like a reasonable explanation. We'll have to be careful it doesn't catch in the treetops." He lifted his head to check on their course. What he saw sent chills up his spine.

They were approaching a high headland that rose from the forest in the shape of a giant step. A river coursed from the forest toward the precipice of the plateau where rocky formations broke the flow into five waterfalls. With the sunlight sparkling off the white water the streams looked like gems being run through the fingers of a diamond merchant. The falls had the deceptive slow-motion look that water has when it plunges from a great height. A thick cloud of foglike condensation rose from the explosive force of thousands of gallons of water cascading into a lake directly below the steep-sided bluff.

Paul said, "Those falls make Niagara look like a herring brook."

"All that water has to have an outlet." Gamay scanned the perimeter of the lake. "Paul, over there! I can see the river. It's flowing out of the lake. All we have to do is follow it."

"Not unless you see a gas station, too," Trout said with a glance at the propane fuel gauge. The tank was practically on empty. "We're about to drop out of the sky."

"We can still move forward. Get us as close to the river as possible. We'll ditch this thing and use the raft."

Trout did a mental rundown of a water splashdown. The gondola's weight would pull it under the water. Residual air in the envelope might keep the gondola from going down immediately, but the hundreds of square feet of fabric would pose a hazard, trapping them in its folds. They should both be clear of the airship before it hit water and do their best to keep the raft intact. It could be their ticket out of the forest.

Paul quickly outlined his analysis and plan. "I think we should cut the raft loose before we land. Otherwise we could lose it."

Gamay took another look over the side. Nine nylon lines, three at each corner, were attached to the dangling raft.

"There's a Swiss Army knife in the storage box," she said.

Paul tested the sharpness of the blade with his thumb and tucked the knife in the big pocket of his cargo shorts.

"You take us in," he said. "Get us as low to the water as you can. I'll cut the raft free."

"Then I bring this buggy to a hover and we abandon ship and go in for a swim," Gamay said.

"As easy as one-two-three," Paul said with a grin.

Gamay took over the steering wheel and put the airship into a slow turn away from the falls. Sunlight streaming through the mists that rose off the lake created multiple rainbows. Gamay hoped it was a good sign.

The gondola tilted from Paul's weight as he climbed out onto the right side of the framework. He looked down at the red triangle swinging about thirty feet below and made his way to the rear of the gondola behind the tanks and burners. He sawed away at the lines attached to the rear left corner of the raft, then continued across the gondola's framework and repeated his work. Attached to the gondola only by its nose lines, the raft bobbed and twisted in the wind.

Using a light foot on the burner control, Gamay aimed for a spot near the river, bringing the airship down in a long, easy glide. She was starting to think that his crazy scheme might work. Her optimism vanished as the burner went *ploof,* then was silent. They had run out of fuel at an altitude of a thousand feet.

There was no immediate change in the airship's behavior. The heated air maintained the envelope's streamlined shape, and the propeller kept the craft at a shallow angle. The airship continued on its heading. At five hundred feet altitude the situation began to come apart at the seams. As the air cooled, lift was lost, and the angle of descent became steeper. Pressure inside the envelope diminished as well, and the front end developed a dent. The airship assumed the shape of a rotten tomato and swung to the left.

Paul was working a few feet directly in front of Gamay. He had severed two lines and was about to work on the third. He had become overconfident and had released his safety grip on the framework when the blimp swerved. Not expecting the sudden maneuver, he lost his balance and tumbled off. Gamay yelled helplessly.

The gondola was jerked violently and nosed down. Gamay leaned over and saw Paul clutching the line immediately above the dangling raft, which twisted violently, snapping back and forth like a child's swing in the wind. The blimp's forward motion had slowed almost to a stop. She looked up at the envelope, which had become a formless blob, then back under the gondola. Paul was still hanging on. Trout didn't want to be under the blimp when it came down. He cut the line and plunged feet-first into the water from a height of about fifty feet. As he came to the surface the raft hit the water with a great splash.

Gamay was operating on pure adrenaline. She unsnapped her harness, climbed out onto the side of the gondola, took a deep breath, and dove off. Despite the shakiness of the platform and the fact that it was plunging rapidly toward the water, Gamay did a classic swan dive that would have earned her a top score in an Olympic competition. She hit the water with arms outstretched, her body straight, went deep, then kicked her way quickly back to the shimmering surface. Just in time to see the airship come down directly on top of the raft.

The raft disappeared under the layered folds of the envelope along with any hope it could be used to float their way home. She was more concerned about Paul for the moment and was relieved beyond words when she heard his voice calling, although she still couldn't see him.

Pulled under by the gondola, the envelope sank, taking the raft with it. She saw Paul's head bobbing on the other side of the sinking airship. He waved, and they swam toward each other, meeting in the middle. They treaded water for a few moments, gazing with awe at the cascading streams. Then, taking advantage of the push from the water rippling out from the falls, they began to swim for the distant shore.

13

FBI SPECIAL AGENT MIGUEL GOMEZ leaned his beefy wrestler's body back in his swivel chair, laced his fingers behind his head, and gazed in wonderment at the two men sitting on the other side of his desk.

"You gentlemen must like tortillas one hell of a lot to want to see Enrico Pedralez."

Austin said, "We'll pass on the tortillas. We just want to ask Pedralez a few questions."

"*Impossible,*" the agent said flatly, shaking his head for emphasis. His eyes were as dark as raisins, and they had the sad and wary expression cops get when they have seen it all.

"I don't understand," Austin said, a hint of impatience in his voice. "You make an appointment with his secretary. You go in and have a chat. Just like any businessman."

"The Farmer isn't just *any* businessman."

"The *Farmer?* I was unaware he was into agriculture, too."

Gomez couldn't hold back a toothy grin. "Guess you could call it agriculture. Did you hear about the big search for bodies buried at a couple of ranches just over the border?"

"Sure," Austin said. "It was in all the papers. They found dozens of corpses, probably people killed by drug dealers."

"I was one of the FBI field agents the Mexicans allowed to come in on that operation. The ranches were owned by Enrico, or, rather, in the names of guys who worked for Pedralez."

Zavala, who was sitting in the other chair, said, "You're telling us the tortilla king is a *drug* dealer?"

Gomez leaned forward onto his desk and counted on his fingers. "Drugs, prostitution, extortion, kidnapping, Medicaid fraud, purse snatching, and making a public nuisance of himself. You name it. His organization is like any other conglomerate that doesn't put all its eggs in one basket. The bad boys are taking their cue from Wall Street. Diversification is the byword in the Mexican mafia these days."

"Mafia," Austin said. "That might present a little problem."

"Nothing little about it," the agent said. He was on a roll. "The Mexican mafia makes the Sicilians look like choir boys. The old *Cosa Nostra* would whack a guy, but it was hands off the family. The Russian mob will wipe out your wife and kids if you get out of line, but even with them, it's purely business. With the Mexicans, it's personal. Anyone who gets in their way is offending their *machismo.* Enrico doesn't just kill his enemies, he grinds them, their relatives, and their friends into powder."

"Thanks for the warning," Austin said, unfazed by the agent's monologue. "Now will you tell us how we go about seeing him?"

Gomez let out a whooping laugh. He had wondered about this pair since they walked into his office and flashed their NUMA identification. He only knew of the National Underwater & Marine Agency by name, that it was the undersea equivalent of NASA. Austin and Zavala didn't fit in with his preconceived notion of ocean scientists. The bronze-skinned man with the penetrating blue-green eyes and albino hair looked as if he could knock down walls with those battering-ram shoulders. His partner was soft-spoken, and a slight smile played around his lips, but with a mask and a sword he would have been a casting director's ideal choice to play Zorro.

"Okay, guys," Gomez said, shaking his head in defeat. "Since it is still against the law to assist a suicide, I would feel better if you told me what's going down. Why is NUMA interested in a tortilla plant owned by a Mexican crook?"

"There was an underwater explosion in the cove behind the plant Pedralez owns in Baja California. We want to ask him if he knows anything. We're not the FBI. We're simply a scientific organization looking for a few answers."

"Doesn't matter. All feds are the enemy. Asking questions about his business would be considered an aggressive act. He's killed people for less."

"Look, Agent Gomez, we haven't cornered the market on foolhardiness," Austin said. "We tried other avenues first. The Mexican police say the steam pipes caused the blast. Case closed. We thought the owner might have something to tell us, so we called the Department of Commerce. They did an uh-oh, said the plant was owned by Enrico, and suggested that we get in touch with Gomez in the San Diego field office. That's you. Now we'd like to take the next step. Does he have an office in the U.S.?"

"He won't cross the border. He knows we'll grab him."

"Then we'll have to go to him."

"This won't be easy. Pedralez used to be a Mexican federal cop, and half the police are on his payroll. They protect him and turn over informants, competitors, or anyone else who might cause him trouble."

Gomez unlocked a drawer in his desk. He pulled out two thick files and laid them on the desk blotter. "This is the file on Enrico's dirty stuff, and the other has information on his *legal* operations. He has to launder that dirty money somewhere, so he's set up or bought legitimate businesses on both sides of the Mexican-American border. The tortilla business is the leader. Tortillas have become worth millions of dollars since the U.S. market opened up and people on this side of the border started eating the things. A few companies control the business. Just look in your supermarket if you don't believe me. Enrico used his government connections, sprinkled the bribes around to get a piece of the action." He pushed the files across the desk. "I can't let this go out of the office, but you're welcome to read it."

Austin thanked him and took the file into a small conference room. He and Zavala sat on opposite sides of a table. Austin gave Joe the file on the legal businesses, told him to shout if he saw anything interesting, and begin to skim through the other file. He wanted a measure of the man he might be dealing with. The more he read, the less he liked. He hadn't thought so much evil could be poured into one skin. Enrico was responsible for hundreds of murders, and every one of the executions had its own grisly touch. He was glad when Zavala gave him the excuse to halt his reading.

"*Got* it!" Joe said. He rustled a couple of sheets of paper. "These are background and surveillance reports on the tortilla factory. He's owned it a couple of years. The FBI went down to take a peek. Didn't see anything suspicious. Sounds like they took the same tour we did, except for my little side trip. Report says it seems like a legitimate operation."

"Nothing about the underwater facility?"

Zavala frowned. "Nope. Not a word."

"I'm not surprised. The installation could have been floated in at night."

"Plausible. How about your file? Did you learn anything?"

"Yeah, that he's one nasty SOB. We still have to talk to him."

"Gomez says it's impossible. Got any ideas?"

"I might have." He handed Zavala a piece of paper from his file. "This is a list of his hobbies. Wine, women, racehorses, gambling, the usual things. Something caught my eye."

Zavala saw it right away. "He collects antique firearms. Sounds like someone else I know."

Austin smiled. He was a serious collector of dueling pistols. The walls of the old Potomac boathouse where he made his home were covered with the exquisitely fashioned instruments of death. He kept the most valuable pieces in a vault and had one of the finest collections in the country.

"You remember the new pieces I bought for my collection the day before our race? They're a fine pair, but they duplicate a brace I have. I was planning to use them in trade with another collector."

"I think I see where you're going with this. How do you let Enrico know they're available?"

"Every dealer has a client list so buyers can be quickly matched up to acquisitions. You never know when an unusual collectible will come up, or how long a dealer may be able to keep the transaction exclusive. I'll call a couple of dealers and tell them I have to unload the pistols in a hurry. I'll make it sound as if I'm in desperate straits. A crook can never resist the chance to cheat someone."

"What if Enrico has pistols like these?"

"They're relatively rare. But if he does have copies, he might want them for the same reason I did, for future trades. The main thing is having the opportunity to talk to him. He'd still want to see them, hold them in his hands. It's a collector thing."

"Say a dealer gets several anonymous queries. How do we know which is Enrico?"

"We know he doesn't come north of the border. If I am asked to go to Mexico to make the deal, we'll know he's it."

They returned the files to Gomez and told him of their plan.

"Might work. Might not. It's dangerous as hell. No guarantee he's going to talk, even if you do get to meet him."

"We've considered that possibility."

Gomez nodded. "Look, I hate to have something happen to a nice fellow like you. I can't protect you outright because the Mexicans are a little sensitive about *gringo* cops treading on their territory. I *can* make certain that if he does kill you his life won't be worth a plugged *peso*."

"Thanks, Agent Gomez. My survivors will be reassured."

"Best I can do. I'll line up a few assets. Let me know when this thing is happening."

They shook hands, and the NUMA men headed back to the hotel. Austin brought out the dark brown wood case from his duffel bag, opened the lid, and removed one of the pistols.

"These are almost identical to a pair I have in my collection. They were made by a gunsmith named Boutet about the time of Napoleon's Egyptian campaign. He incorporated the Sphinx and the Pyramids into the barrel. These were probably made for an Englishman." He sighted at a floor lamp. "The butt is cut round instead of square like the continental type. But the rifling is multigrooved in the French style." He replaced the pistol in its green baize. "I'd say this is irresistible bait for any collector."

Austin consulted his list of dealers and called around. He made sure the dealers knew he was extremely interested in selling the pistols, even at a loss, and that he was leaving San Diego the next day. Austin believed the best cover stories are at least partially true. He said his boat sank and he needed cash to pay off his bills. Then he and Zavala went over possible eventualities and how best to respond to them.

An hour after he began putting feelers out, Austin received an excited call from a particularly vulpine dealer with a slightly shady reputation. His name was Latham.

"I have a potential client for your pistols," Latham said with excitement. "He's very interested and would like to see them as soon as possible. Can you meet him in Tijuana today? It's not far."

Austin curled his thumb and forefinger and silently mouthed a word. *Bingo.* "No problem. Where would he like us to get together?"

The dealer told him to park on the U.S. side of the border and walk across the pedestrian bridge. The pistol case would identify him. Austin said he'd be there in two hours and hung up. Then he filled Zavala in.

Zavala said, "What if he takes you somewhere we can't help you, like one of those ranches where he likes to plant people?"

"Then I'll keep the conversation on the pistols, and we'll go through with the transaction if he's interested. At the very least it will give me a chance to size him up."

Austin immediately called Gomez. The FBI agent said he'd assembled a team in anticipation. They would watch Austin's back but couldn't get too close because Pedralez would make sure Austin was not followed. A few minutes later the NUMA men were on the way south again in the borrowed pickup.

Zavala left Austin off on the American side and drove into Mexico. Austin waited twenty minutes, then walked across the bridge, the pistol case tucked under his arm. He'd hardly gotten off the bridge when a portly middle-aged man in a cheap suit approached him.

"Meester Austeen?" he said.

"Yes, that's my name."

The man produced a federal police badge. "Police escort for you and your valuables," he said with a grin. "Courtesy of the chief. Lotsa bad people in Tijuana."

He led the way to a dark blue sedan and held the back door open. Austin got in first, making a quick sweep of the parking lot with his eyes. Zavala was nowhere to be seen. Austin would have been disappointed if Zavala were too conspicuous, but he would have felt better knowing that his back was being watched.

The car plunged into the Tijuana traffic, winding its way through a bewildering warren of slums. While the driver was leering at a young woman crossing the street, Austin checked the rear. The only vehicle behind them was a battered old yellow cab.

The police car stopped in front of a windowless cantina whose pockmarked stucco exterior of seasick green looked as if it had been used for target practice by an AK-47. The old cab went speeding by. Austin got out and stood next to a rusty Corona beer sign, wondering if he was expected to go inside the cantina and whether it would be a good idea. A gunmetal-gray Mercedes came around the corner and halted at the curb. A tough-looking young man wearing a chauffeur's cap got out and wordlessly held the door open. Austin got in, and they were off.

The car left the slums and drove into a middle-class neighborhood, stopping in front of an outdoor café. Another young Mexican opened the door and escorted Austin to a table where a man was sitting by himself.

The man extended his hand and smiled broadly. "Please sit down, Mr. Austin," he said. "My name is Enrico Pedralez."

Austin wondered at the banality of evil, how even a monster could look so ordinary. Enrico was in his fifties, Austin guessed.

He was casually dressed in tan cotton slacks and a white short-sleeved shirt. He could have passed for any of the merchants who sold sombreros and blankets in the tourist shops. He had black hair and a mustache that looked dyed and wore a great deal of gold in the form of rings, wristlets, and a chain.

A waiter delivered two tall glasses of cold fruit juice. Austin sipped his drink and glanced around. Eight swarthy men sat two at each table. The men were not talking to each other. They made a pretense of not looking at Austin, but out of the corner of his eye he caught quick glances in his direction. Mr. Pedralez might be a bit cocky about appearing in public, but he took no chances.

"Thank you very much for coming to see me on such short notice, Mr. Austin. I hope it was no trouble." He spoke English with a slight accent.

"Not at all. I was pleased to be put in touch with a potential buyer so quickly. I'm leaving San Diego tomorrow."

"*Señor* Latham said you were involved in the boat race."

"I was one of the losers, unfortunately. My boat sank."

"A pity," Pedralez said. He removed his sunglasses, his small greedy eyes moving to the pistol case. He rubbed his hands briskly together in anticipation. "May I see them?"

"Of course." Austin unsnapped the clasp on the box and opened the cover.

"Ah, truly magnificent," Pedralez said with the eagerness of a true connoisseur. He took a pistol out and sighted it at one of the men at a nearby table. The man smiled nervously. Then the drug lord ran his finger over the oiled barrel. "Boutet. Made in the English style, for a wealthy lord, no doubt."

"That was my assessment as well."

"The workmanship is excellent, as I would expect." He carefully placed the pistol back in its case and sighed theatrically. "Unfortunately I have a similar pair."

"Oh. Well." Austin made a show of trying to hide his disappointment. As Austin went to close the case, Pedralez put his hand on his.

"Perhaps we can still do business. I would like to present these as a gift to a close friend. Have you thought of a price?"

"Yes," Austin said casually. He looked around, hoping Gomez was serious about his backup, and said casually, "I need some information."

The Mexican's eyes narrowed. "I don't understand," he said warily.

"I'm in the market for some property myself. There's a tortilla factory in the Baja. I understand that it might be available in a fire sale."

"You're mistaken," Pedralez said coldly. He snapped his fingers. The men lounging at the surrounding tables came to alert. "Who are you?"

"I represent an organization far bigger than yours."

"You're a policeman? FBI?"

"No. I'm with the National Underwater and Marine Agency. I'm an ocean scientist, and I'm investigating an explosion near your plant. In return for information I'd like to make these pistols a gift."

The avuncular smile had vanished, and Enrico's lips were curled in a humorless and ferocious grin. "Do you take me for a fool? I own this restaurant. These men, the waiters, the cook, they all work for me. You could disappear without a trace. They would swear you were never here. What do I care for your *pistolas?*" he said with contempt. "I have dozens more."

Austin kept his gaze leveled on Enrico's face. "Tell me, Mr. Pedralez, as a fellow collector, what is your fascination with these old weapons?"

The Mexican seemed amused at the question. The heat went out of the fierce glitter in his eyes, but the temperature went down only a few degrees.

"They represent power and the means of power. Yet at the same time they are as beautiful as a woman's body."

"Well said."

"And you?"

"Aside from their fine workmanship, they remind me that

lives and fate can be altered by chance. A trigger squeezed prematurely. A gun raised too quickly. A single shot missing a vital organ by an inch or two. They represent the luck of the draw in its most lethal terms."

The Mexican seemed intrigued by the answer. "You must consider yourself very lucky to place yourself in my hands, Mr. Austin."

"Not at all. I took the chance that you would be willing to chat."

"You made your gamble. I applaud your audacity. Unfortunately this is not your day. You lose," he said coldly. "I don't care who you are or who you represent. You have drawn the death card." He snapped his fingers again, and the men rose from the tables and began to move in. Austin felt like a fox outfoxed by the hunters.

With an ear-splitting roar of its unmuffled exhaust system, the battered yellow cab squealed to a stop in front of the restaurant. The car, an ancient Checker, was still bouncing on worn shock absorbers when the cab driver got out. Except for the soiled seersucker sports jacket over a Hussong's T-shirt, the driver behind the reflecting silver lenses looked suspiciously like Joe Zavala.

Joe stood on the sidewalk and called out in heavily accented English. "Anybody here call a cab?"

One of Enrico's men went over and growled at Joe in Spanish.

"I'm looking for an American," Zavala said in English at the top of his voice, looking past the thug's shoulder. "Sergeant Alvin York."

The man put his palm on Zavala's chest to emphasize his point.

"Okay, okay! Damned *gringos.*" He stalked back to his cab and lurched off, trailing a purple cloud of exhaust fumes.

The thug turned around and laughed.

Austin breathed a sigh of relief. His eyes roved the low rooftops, and he smiled.

Zavala was passing on a message, not very subtle but effective. Sergeant York was the Kentucky sharpshooter who got the

Medal of Honor for capturing German prisoners during World War I.

"An amusing fellow, eh, Mr. Austin?"

"*Very* amusing."

"Good. Now I must go. *Adios,* Mr. Austin. Unfortunately we will not be meeting again."

"Wait."

The Mexican scowled at Austin as if he were a bit of lint on his shirt.

"I wouldn't move if I were you. You're in the sights of a sniper. One wrong move, and your head will explode like a ripe melon. Look up on that roof if you don't believe me, and that one over there."

Pedralez swiveled his head like a praying mantis and scanned the low rooftops. Three snipers, placed at different locations, made no effort to hide. He sat down again.

"It seems you don't believe entirely in the forces of fate. What do you want?"

"I simply want to know who owns the Baja Tortilla factory."

"*I* do, of course. It's quite profitable, really."

"What about the underwater laboratory in the cove? What do you know about that?"

"I'm a busy man, Mr. Austin, so I will tell you the story, and then we will part. Two years ago somebody came to me. A lawyer from San Diego. He had a proposition. Someone wanted to build a factory. They would pay for its construction, and I would take all the profits. There were conditions. It had to be isolated, and it had to be on the water."

"I want to know what was built *in* the water."

"I don't know. A large ship came. There were guards. They brought something into the cove and deliberately sank it. Connections were made to the factory. People came and went. I asked no questions."

"What do you know about the explosion?"

He shrugged. "Someone called afterward and said not to

worry. They would make good on my loss. That's all I know. The police don't care."

"This lawyer who handled the deal, what was his name?"

"Francis Xavier Hanley. Now I must go. I have told you all I can."

"Yes, I know, you're a busy man."

Pedralez waved his hand. The men got up from the tables and formed a corridor to the sidewalk on either side of him. The Mercedes appeared out of nowhere; the door opened with machinelike precision. The bodyguards piled into two Jeep Cherokees ahead of and behind the Mercedes.

"Mr. Pedralez," Austin called out. "A deal's a deal. You forgot the pistols."

Enrico answered with a mirthless smile. "Keep them," he said, and added a few more words. He got into the back of the car, shut the door, and zoomed down the street. Austin was sweating, and it wasn't just from the heat. The junky cab pulled up in front of him and tooted the horn.

Austin slid in the passenger side and looked around in amazement. "Where'd you get this rig?"

"Agent Gomez was nice enough to have it waiting for me. It's got a hot engine and all kinds of radio gear I used to let our friends know where you were. I'm going to hate to give it up. Did Mr. Pedralez say anything?"

Austin held up the pistol case. "Yeah, he told me the next time I came to Tijuana to be sure these things are loaded."

14

THE SCENE WAS SO AWE INSPIRing in its terrible beauty that Trout almost forgot the predicament he and Gamay were in. Paul sat on a rocky ledge about twenty feet above the lake, long legs dangling down, swiveling his head back and forth to take in the whole panoramic sweep. He had to strain his neck to see the tops of the falls. Multiple rainbows arced over the five cascades as the sun caught the droplets of water in the twisting vapor cloud that rose for hundreds of feet. The roar was like that of a hundred distant locomotives at full steam. Trout wasn't a religious man, but if anything was the Hand of God, he was looking at it.

A groan ended his reverie. "What are you doing?" Gamay said with a yawn. She was lying nearby in the shade of a tree.

"Thinking what a great place this would be to build a hotel."

"Ugh," Gamay said with a scowl. She sat up and wiped the sweat from her face. "Make sure you have air conditioning."

It had rained briefly an hour before, and the sun returned with a vengeance. Their perch was well shaded by trees and bushes, and they slept for a time, but there was no way to escape the suffocating humidity. Paul was the first to awake.

"I'll get you some water," Paul said. He fashioned a palm leaf into a cup, climbed down to the lake, and scooped up water in the makeshift container. He spilled half the contents bringing it to Gamay, who was trying to pick blades of grass from her ratty-looking hair. She guzzled the water, her eyes closed in bliss, then passed what was left to Paul.

"Thanks," she said with a smile. "That was refreshing. I hope you won't mind if I take a dip in our water supply." She climbed down to the lake, plunged in, and swam out several strokes.

Paul was thinking of joining Gamay after he had quenched his thirst, when a movement near the river outlet caught his eye. He called out a warning, but Gamay couldn't hear him because of the rumble of the falls. He climbed down, half falling, to the water's edge and dove in. He swam out to Gamay, who was peacefully floating on her back, and grabbed her by her T-shirt.

Gamay was startled at first, then she laughed. "Hey, this is no time to get playful."

"Hush," he said. "Get back to shore. *Hurry*."

The urgency in his voice was unmistakable. Without a further word Gamay swam quickly to shore with Paul right behind her. She started to climb onto the ledge. Paul pulled her down into a bush. He held his finger to his lips and pointed toward the lake.

Gamay squinted through the leaves and tensed as the sun glinted off wet paddles and she saw flashes of blue and white. Chulo. Paul had seen the four canoes emerge from the river into the lake. They would have run right into Gamay. The canoes were moving in single file. Each canoe held three Indians. Two were paddling, and the other was riding shotgun, his bow resting across his lap. They seemed intent on where they were going and unaware that they were being watched.

The Indians passed within a few yards of the hiding place, so close the beads of sweat on their rippling muscles were clearly visible. They moved silently across the lake until foggy tendrils enveloped them. An instant later they disappeared into the vapor cloud.

"That was some vanishing act," Paul said, puffing his cheeks out.

"Now we know why they're called the People of the Mist," Gamay said.

Using his six-foot-eight height to good advantage, Paul stood cautiously and made sure there were no stragglers. "All clear," he said. "We'd better think of getting out of here. I still have the Swiss Army knife. Maybe we could fashion a raft with logs and vines and float our way out."

Gamay was staring toward the mists. "I have a better idea." She paused. "It may be a little risky."

"A *little* risky?" Paul chuckled. "Don't forget I'm well acquainted with the way your mind works. You're about to suggest that we follow those guys and steal a canoe."

"Why not? Look, this is their home turf, so they won't expect it. With all due respect for your talents with a Swiss Army knife, I can't see us fashioning a boat that will carry the two of us God knows how many miles downriver without sinking or running into more of those characters. It was tough enough traveling in an airboat. They can't paddle those canoes all day. They must pull them up somewhere on shore. We just find them, wait until dark, and slip one away. They'll never even miss it, I bet."

Amusement crept into Paul's large hazel eyes. "Do I detect a hint of scientific curiosity in your proposal?"

"Okay, I admit there's more here than simply a matter of survival. Don't tell me you haven't wondered about this high-tech tribe and the talk of a white goddess."

"I was wondering if they have any food," Paul said, patting his stomach. He chewed thoughtfully on a blade of grass. "Seriously, we're in something of a pickle and really don't have many choices. We don't know where we are and aren't sure how to get out of here. We have no supplies. As you pointed out, this is their territory. I suggest that we reconnoiter. We're strangers in a strange land. We go slow, and if the situation looks too dangerous, we get out in a hurry."

"Agreed," Gamay said. "Now, as for food, I'm fresh out of granola bars. I've been watching the birds eating the berries on that bush. I don't see any dead birds, so they're probably not poison."

"Berries it is," Paul said. "They can't be *that* bad."

Trout was wrong. The berries were so bitter it was impossible to eat even one without puckering up. With empty stomachs, the Trouts struck off along the shore of the lake. At one point where the mud looked like quicksand, they climbed to higher ground and stumbled onto a footpath. The trail was overgrown and looked as if it hadn't seen any recent use. Still, they proceeded cautiously, ready to dive into the bushes if they encountered anyone.

They trekked along the path for about a mile until they came to a place where mists from the lake rolled into the forest like vapor from a fog machine. The leafy growth was as wet as if it had been pelted by a rain shower, and the roar of the falls was like the beating of a thousand kettledrums. They were aware that the same noise that muffled their movement could drown out the approach of a marching army. The air became chilly and so damp that they put their hands over their noses so they wouldn't gag. The visibility was only a few feet, and they kept their heads low so their eyes could pick out the path.

Then, suddenly, they were out of the forest. If they were expecting to burst out on a beautiful valley like wayfarers in Shangri-la, they were disappointed. The forest was no different on the other side of the mists. The path no longer led along the lake but instead veered off along a tributary that the canoes must have followed.

After a few minutes Gamay stopped and shook her head. "Notice anything strange about this little river?"

Paul walked over to the edge of the banking. "Yes, it's much too straight to be natural. It looks as if someone has taken an existing stream and marsh and cleared them out with shovel and pick."

"My thoughts exactly." Gamay started walking again. "As I said, the Chulo are most fascinating."

They plodded ahead for several hours. They had fashioned hats from palm leaves and stopped frequently to quench their thirst from the river. At one point they waited out a shower. They became more tense and watchful as the path widened, and they began to see the imprints of a bare foot in the soft, dark earth.

After a short discussion, they decided to follow the river for a while longer, then hide in the forest until dark. They were dog-tired and needed to replenish their energy. As they plodded along they encountered a path coming in from the forest to their right. It was made of thousands of flat stones and reminded Gamay of the Maya or Inca roads. It was as good as anything she had seen on the Appian Way. Their curiosity got the best of them, and they followed the paved path for five more minutes. They were drawn on even farther by a gleam through the trees.

The walkway widened into a perfectly circular clearing about fifty feet in diameter and also surfaced entirely with stones. In the center of the clearing was a large object.

"I'll be damned," they said in unison.

The jet plane was in two sections. The front was intact, but the passenger cabin was virtually gone. The tail section was in fair shape and had been moved directly behind the cockpit, giving the aircraft a short, stubby look. The paint was old and faded and not overgrown by vines or lichen as might be expected.

They peered through the cracked cockpit windows, expecting to see skeletons. The seats were empty. Directly in front of the cockpit was a shallow pit holding the blackened ashes of fires and charred bones of small animals. Carved totems as tall and thick as a man ringed the stone circle. The figures adorning each post were different. Carved in dark wood at the top of each pole was a winged woman with her hands cupped in front of her. It was the same figure carved onto the medallion they had found on the dead Indian.

"It looks like some sort of shrine," Gamay whispered. She went over to the ash pit. "This must be where they burned sacrifices. Mostly bones from small animals."

"That's certainly reassuring," Paul said. He looked up at the sun, then checked his watch. "They've got the plane positioned so that it acts like a sundial. It reminds me of the layout at

Stonehenge, with the concentric rings that acted as a celestial calendar."

Gamay put her hand on the plane's nose. "Does this blue-and-white color scheme seem familiar to you?"

"What do you know? The Chulo national colors."

Gamay's eyes widened as she looked past Paul, who had his back to the forest.

"That's not the *only* thing around here that's blue and white."

Paul turned and saw about twenty Chulo Indians emerge from the trees, their faces and bodies painted the colors of sky and bone. He cursed himself for allowing the plane's discovery to push caution aside. As silently as the ghosts they were reputed to be, the Indians surrounded them. There was no way to run. Paul and Gamay were completely boxed in.

The Indians advanced with their spears held high, but then they did a peculiar thing. They opened the circle. One Indian indicated with his spear that they were to go through the opening. The Trouts glanced at each other for mutual reassurance, then, with the silent Indians flanking them like a military honor guard, they marched from the shrine and followed the path along the river.

The path widened into a road that took them to a stockade palisade. They made their way toward a gate wide enough to drive a truck through. From a distance they had seen on either side of the gate tall wooden staffs that had knobs on the top like flagpoles. As they neared the entrance Gamay squeezed her husband's hand even tighter.

"Paul, look," she said.

He followed her gaze. "Oh, hell."

The knobs were in fact human heads. Their faces had been baked brown like apples in the sun, and the birds and insects had been making inroads, but it was still possible to pick out Dieter's features. He wasn't smiling. Neither was Arnaud or his taciturn assistant, Carlo. The fourth head belonged to their Indian henchman. Trout recognized him by the New York Yankees baseball cap.

Then they were through the gates, past the grisly decorations. Behind the fence were several dozen long thatched huts clustered along the river. No women or children were visible. Their guards had lowered their spears and unstrung their arrows and were using the presence of their bodies to keep the Trouts from trying anything foolish.

Paul said, "Look at that water wheel. We have them like that in New England."

Water had been diverted from the river and was flowing through wooden chutes to turn a wheel. They didn't get the chance for a closer look. Their guards directed them toward a structure at the center of the settlement. It was four times bigger than any of the surrounding huts, and the walls were made of putty-colored clay rather than saplings. They stopped in front of a portal that looked like a large, gaping mouth. Hung over the entrance was the bladed fan from a jet engine. The Indians closed ranks behind them, put their weapons aside, and kneeled with their noses touching the earth.

"*Now* what?" Gamay said with astonishment at the sudden submissiveness of the fierce Indians.

"I wouldn't advise running for it. We wouldn't get ten feet before they nailed us. My guess is they want us to go in. After you, madame."

"We'll go in together."

They walked hand-in-hand through the doorway into the dim interior. They passed through two smaller rooms, then into a large space. At the far end of the hut, visible in a shaft of light coming through a hole cut in the roof, was a seated figure. The figure raised its arm and beckoned for them to approach. They moved ahead slowly. The floor was made of wood, not dirt like the huts they had been in before.

The figure sat on a throne made of what looked like an airplane seat. With the exception of two tanned and shapely legs, most of the body was hidden behind a blue-and-white oval mask that could have come out of a nightmare. It was painted with huge eyes and a wide mouth with sharp-pointed shark's teeth.

The Trouts stood nervously in front of the bizarre figure, not knowing what to do. Then two hands came from behind the mask and lifted it off.

"Whew, this thing is hot," the beautiful woman behind the ugly mask said in English. She set the mask aside, cocked her head at Paul, then at Gamay.

"The Drs. Trout, I presume?"

Gamay was the first to speak through their astonishment. "How do you know our names?"

"We white goddesses see all and know all." She laughed when she saw the puzzlement deepen even more. "I'm a poor host, teasing my guests."

She smiled and clapped her hands lightly. The Trouts were in for another surprise. The beaded curtains behind the throne parted with a rustle, and Dieter's wife, Tessa, stepped out.

15

THE LAW OFFICE OF FRANCIS Xavier Hanley was on the twelfth floor of a blue glass tower that looked out onto San Diego Harbor. Austin and Zavala stepped from the elevator into the office lobby and gave the attractive young receptionist their names. She punched a button on her intercom and after a murmured conversation smiled brightly and told them to go right in. A ruddy-faced man with the body of a nightclub bouncer gone to flab greeted them at the door. He introduced himself as Hanley and ushered them to a pair of Empire-style chairs. Settling his bulk behind a large mahogany desk, he leaned back in his plush swivel chair, tented his fingertips, and contemplated the two men like a wolf drooling over a pair of staked goats.

After crossing back from Tijuana, Austin had called Hanley's office and asked for an appointment. He spread his story on as thick as peanut butter, saying he and his partner "had made a few mil" in the market and wanted a place to spend it. They got an immediate meeting. The predatory gleam in the lawyer's pale green eyes suggested that the bait had done its job well. He looked from one man to the other. "I believe in getting right down to business," he purred. "You said on the phone that you're interested in foreign investment."

"We're primarily interested in Mexico," Zavala explained.

The attorney wore an expensive sharkskin gray suit and had enough gold and diamonds on his fleshy hands to sink the *Ti-*

tanic. All the tailors in the world couldn't hide the brawler's body, and no amount of jewelry could have obscured the coarseness ingrained in his every word and move. The NUMA men were dressed in jeans, T-shirts, and windbreakers. It was a studied casualness. In California, the only ones who look like millionaires are those who aren't.

Hanley took in Zavala's Latin American looks. "You've come to the right place," he said expansively. He smiled in an attempt to exert charm, but the V-shaped mouth in the fleshy face made him look like a fat vulture. "Did you have a specific area in mind?"

"We like tortillas," Austin said with a straight face.

A look of incomprehension appeared on Hanley's florid features. "Pardon me," he said, not certain he had heard correctly.

"You know, tortillas," Austin said, making a circular motion with his finger. "We hear it's a fast-growing business."

Recovering nicely, Hanley replied, "And so it is. A booming sector in the expanding food services area."

Austin had the feeling that the answer would have been the same had they told Hanley they were interested in making mud pies. He and Zavala had decided to use the direct approach that had worked so well in drawing a strong reaction from Pedralez.

Zavala smiled and said, "We've been hearing about a tortilla plant in Baja California, outside Ensenada, that might be for sale real cheap."

Hanley's watery eyes narrowed under the prominent brow ridge. "Where'd you hear that?" he growled.

"Around." The corners of Zavala's lips turned up in a mysterious smile.

"Sorry, gentlemen, I'm not familiar with any Baja tortilla plant."

Zavala turned to Austin. "He says he's not familiar with that one."

Austin shrugged. "We're surprised at your answer. Enrico Pedralez says you're *very* familiar with the property. He gave us your name and said you arranged the deal for him."

Hanley's defenses went on full alert at the mention of the Mexican mob boss. He was uncertain how accountable he had to be to these two strangers. He fast-forwarded through the categories of likely threats: police, IRS, state bureaucrats. These men didn't fit into any pigeonhole. He decided to take the offensive.

"May I see some identification from you gentlemen?"

"That won't be necessary," Austin said.

"In that case, if you're not out of my office in two seconds, I'll throw you out myself."

Austin made no move to rise. "You could try," he said with an icy coldness, "but I wouldn't recommend it. I wouldn't bother calling in your Mexican pals, either."

Seeing that intimidation wasn't going to work, the lawyer reached for the phone. "I'm calling the police."

"Why don't you call the bar association while you're at it?" Austin said. "I'm sure they'd like to hear how one of their members set up a deal with a notorious Mexican mafioso. That framed license on your wall won't be worth the paper it's printed on."

The hand retreated, and Hanley stared across the desk. "Who *are* you gentlemen?" He practically spat out the last word.

"A couple of people who want to know more about that plant in the Baja," Austin said.

Hanley was having a hard time trying to figure out this pair. With their athletic builds and sun-burnished faces they looked like a couple of beach bums, but he detected a hard edge under their genial image.

"Even if you *had* credible authority I couldn't help you," he said. "All discussions on that matter are covered by lawyer-client privilege."

"That's true," Austin said agreeably. "It is also true that you could go to jail for making a dirty deal with a known criminal."

Hanley's mouth widened in an insincere smile. "Okay, you win," he said. "I'll tell you what I can. But let's compromise. Tell me why you are interested in this property. It would be the fair thing to do."

"True," Austin said, "but this is an unfair world." His coral-green eyes bored into Hanley's face. "I'll put your mind at ease. Your slimy dealings are not our concern. Once you tell us who hired you for the Baja job, chances are you'll never see us again."

Hanley nodded and plucked a cigar from a humidor without offering his guests one. He lit up and puffed smoke in their direction. "I was contacted about two years ago by a broker from Sacramento. He had heard about my, ah, connections, south of the border and thought I would be the perfect go-between for a highly lucrative deal with no risk and little work."

"An offer you couldn't refuse."

"Of course. But I was cautious. Everyone in California has a get-rich scheme. He knew about my ties to Enrico. So I had to make sure this guy wasn't working in an official capacity. I had a private detective check him out. He was legit."

Austin smiled faintly at the irony of a crooked lawyer worrying about honesty. "What did he hire you to do?"

"The people he represented wanted to find land in the Baja. It had to be remote and on the coast. Then he wanted me to handle the paperwork and red tape involved in starting a business in Mexico."

"Baja Tortillas."

"Yes. He wanted a Mexican to hold the actual ownership for the plant. He said it would be easier that way. It would be a turnkey operation. He supplied the plant specifications and brought in a construction crew. His clients would require access to the plant after it was built, but they would not interfere in the operation. They said Enrico could keep half the profits, and the plant would be his free and clear after five years."

"Did you ever wonder why anyone would be so generous with what must have been a considerable investment?"

"I am paid substantially because I don't ask questions like that."

"Seems your friends wanted a cover operation," Zavala said.

"That certainly crossed my mind. The Japanese ran into all sorts of flak when they tried to build a salt-producing plant along the coast. A bunch of whale huggers made a big stink with the Mexican government. I assumed the man's clients saw what had happened with the Japanese and didn't want to go through the same headaches."

"Who was this broker?"

"His name was Jones. Oh yes, that's his real name," Hanley added when he saw the skeptical glances. "He's a matchmaker who specializes in buying and selling businesses."

"Who was he representing?"

"He never told me."

Austin leaned forward onto Hanley's desk. "Don't jerk us around, Mr. Hanley. You're a careful man. You would have had your private detective poke into this guy."

Hanley shrugged. "Why deny it? The clients tried to hide their identity behind a web of corporate paper."

"You said *tried.* Who are they?"

"I only got as far as an outfit called the Mulholland Group. It's a closed corporation with ties to companies involved in large-scale hydraulic projects."

"What else?"

"That's all I know." Hanley checked his Cartier wristwatch. "If you'll excuse me, I have an appointment with a *real* client."

"We want the broker's address and phone number."

"It won't do you any good. He died a few weeks ago. His car went off a mountain road."

Austin had been gazing through the floor-to-ceiling window behind Hanley at a helicopter going back and forth across the harbor. It was moving closer with each pass. At the mention of unusual death, he brought his full attention back to Hanley.

"We'd like whatever information you have on him anyway. And your whole file as well."

Hanley frowned. He thought he was through with this annoying pair. "I can't give you the original. I'll have it copied. It might take a couple of hours."

"That would be fine. We'll be back for it in two hours."

Hanley's frown deepened. Then he smiled again, rose from his desk, and showed them to the door.

Back in the elevator, Austin said, "We'll call Hiram Yaeger. Hanley's bound to censor the stuff he gives us, so we might want to conduct our own investigation into this Mulholland Group." Hiram Yaeger was NUMA's computer whiz. The tenth-floor computer complex he called Max was plugged into a vast database of oceanic knowledge from every source in the world. Max routinely hacked into outside databases.

They stepped out of the building lobby into the Southern California sun. As Zavala walked to the curb to hail a cab there was a loud *whup-whup* sound from directly overhead. A green helicopter hovered over the street, about a hundred feet from the glass face of the building. Like the other pedestrians they stared at the aircraft with curiosity. Then recognition flashed in Austin's mind.

He grabbed Zavala's arm. "We've got to go back."

Zavala glanced at the helicopter and bolted for the revolving door behind Austin.

They dashed into an open elevator and punched the button for the lawyer's floor. Halfway up there was a dull thud, and the elevator's sides rattled in the shaft. Austin hit the stop button for the floor below Hanley's office. They ran past startled office workers and raced up the stairway to the next level.

Acrid black smoke filled the stairwell. Austin felt the door to the law-office floor. Unable to detect heat that would indicate a fierce blaze on the other side, he opened the door a crack. More smoke poured out. They opened the door wide enough to pass through, got down on their hands and knees, and crawled through the choking fumes into the receptionist's area. The sprinkler system had been set off, and they were drenched under a cooling spray. The receptionist lay on the rug next to her desk.

"What about Hanley?" Joe shouted. Smoke was billowing from the office door.

"Don't bother. He's gone."

They dragged the receptionist to the stairwell and got her

limp body down to the floor below. She came around after a few minutes of mouth-to-mouth resuscitation. Soon firemen pounded onto the floor, and they turned her over to an EMT. They walked down rather than take an elevator where they would be stuck if the power went off. More firemen poured into the lobby. The police had arrived and were evacuating the building. They joined the crowd milling around outside, but seeing there was nothing they could do, they walked a couple of blocks and hailed a cab.

The driver, a Senegalese from the looks of his ID card, glanced at their soot-covered faces. "You in there? Man, I just heard over the radio. Some kind of explosion."

Zavala looked out the back window at the confusion outside the building where police were stopping traffic and setting up a fire line.

Zavala wiped the soot from his cheek. "How did you know that was going to happen?"

"I didn't. But I noticed the helicopter going back and forth across the harbor when we were talking to Hanley."

"I saw it, too, but didn't pay much attention. I figured it was a traffic chopper."

"I had the same reaction at first. Then we saw it up close, and something clicked. The same chopper or one very much like it did a fly-by after the explosion at the tortilla plant."

"I remember. Dark green. It buzzed the cove, then flew off." Zavala pondered the implication. "Whoever owned that chopper wanted Hanley dead in a bad way."

"Hanley ran with a pretty rough crowd."

"You think it was Enrico?"

"It's possible. He knew we would talk to Hanley. I was surprised he didn't call Hanley to warn him we were coming."

"I've been thinking about Mr. Jones, the guy who brokered the deal," Zavala said thoughtfully. "Maybe his mouth was shut for him as well."

"It would fit in with the Enrico theory until something better comes along," Austin said.

Something better did come along back at the hotel. While Austin went in to clean up and change, Zavala flipped to the TV news. The camera showed shots of smoke belching from the office and fire trucks outside. The fire department spokesman said a number of people were treated for smoke inhalation, but there was apparently only one death. The name would be released pending notice of next of kin. Cause of the explosion was unknown. The report ended, and Zavala was about to turn the TV off when a familiar face appeared on the screen.

"Kurt, you've got to see this," he called.

Austin emerged in time to hear the blow-dried announcer give his report.

"This just in. Alleged Mexican mafia drug figure Enrico Pedralez was killed today when his car exploded in Tijuana. Two men who may have been bodyguards also died in the explosion."

The announcer went on to read the Mexican's law-breaking laundry list.

"Looks like our green chopper people don't like loose ends," Austin observed.

The phone rang, and Zavala picked it up. He listened for a moment, muttered "You're welcome," and replaced the phone in its cradle. "That was FBI Agent Miguel Gomez," he said.

"What did he want?"

Zavala's mouth puckered in a wry smile. "He just wanted to say thanks for making his job a little easier."

16

BRYNHILD SIGURD RAN HER FAR-flung empire from a turret office high above the sprawling Viking edifice she called Valhalla. The windowless room was built in an exact circle, the geometric form closest to perfection. The walls were stark white and unadorned by paintings or wall hangings. She sat in front of a flat-screen monitor and a telephone console of white plastic. It was all she needed to be in instant touch with her operations around the world. The temperature was kept at a cool thirty-eight degrees summer and winter. The few who had been allowed into this aerie compared it to being in a walk-in refrigerator, but it suited her fine.

As a girl growing up on an isolated farm in Minnesota, she had come to love the cold and reveled in the purity to be found in subfreezing temperatures. She would ski alone for hours under the stars ignoring the icy chill that stung her cheeks. As she grew in height and strength she distanced herself even more from humanity, the "little people" as she called them, who saw her as a freak. At school in Europe, her natural brilliance allowed her to excel at her studies even when she seldom attended class. Those times when she couldn't hide and had to suffer the stares of others only drove her ambition, fueled her smoldering resentment, and planted the seeds for her megalomania.

She was talking on the speaker phone: "Thank you for your

support of the Colorado River legislation, Senator Barnes. Your state stands to gain quite handsomely for your key vote, especially when your brother's firm starts picking up contracts for the work we have planned. I hope you've taken advantage of the suggestions I've made."

"Yes, ma'am, I have, thank you. I've had to avoid the conflict-of-interest thing, of course, but my brother and I are quite close, if you know what I mean."

"I do, Senator. Have you talked to the president?"

"Just got off the phone with his chief of staff. The White House will veto any bill that seeks to overturn the privatization legislation we passed. The president is a firm believer that the private sector can always do a better job than government, whether it's running prisons, social security, or pumping water."

"What sort of backing does the Kinkaid bill have?"

"Only a scattering of votes, nothing serious. Damned shame about Kinkaid having that accident. I always liked the man. But without him around to whip up the troops, an override is bound to fail."

"Excellent. How are the other privatization bills faring?"

"They'll do just fine. You'll be seeing publicly run water facilities being privatized all over the country."

"So there are no problems?"

"One maybe. The biggest pain in the butt is the editor of the daily paper in my state capital. He's raising a ruckus, and I'm afraid he might bollix things up."

She asked the editor's name and made a mental note of the senator's answer. Her desktop was free of pen and paper. She committed everything to memory.

"By the way, Senator Barnes, was the contribution to your reelection campaign sufficient?"

"Yes, ma'am, it was very generous considering I'm running unopposed. Having a big war chest discourages the opposition."

A red light was blinking on the phone console.

"We'll speak again. Good-bye, Senator."

She pressed a button, and a door opened in the wall of the room. The Kradzik brothers, wearing their usual black leather, stepped inside.

"Well?" she said.

The thin lips widened in identical metallic smiles.

"We have fired Mexican farmer . . ."

". . . and lawyer as you ordered."

"No complications?"

They shook their heads.

"The authorities will spend little time on the farmer's case," she said. "The lawyer had many enemies. Now to other matters. There have been some developments on the explosion at our Mexican operation."

She touched the screen, and two photos appeared. One of the photos, taken by a surveillance camera, showed Austin and Zavala in the reception area of the tortilla plant. The other picture was an enlarged shot of the two men standing on the deck of the *Sea Robin* off Ensenada. Brynhild's eye went from the wide-shouldered man with the silver-white hair for a moment, then shifted to the handsome dark-haired man.

"Do you know who these men are?"

The brothers shrugged.

"That's Kurt Austin, head of NUMA's Special Assignments Team, and José Zavala, a member of the team."

"When can we . . ."

". . . eliminate them?"

The temperature in the cool room seemed to drop another twenty degrees.

"If they were responsible for the destruction of the Baja facility, they will pay with their lives," Brynhild said. "But not now. There's a minor problem to be taken care of." She gave them the name of the newspaper editor and said, "That's all. You can go."

The brothers hastened from the room like a pair of dogs sent to fetch a bone, and Brynhild was alone again. She sat there brooding about the Baja facility. All that work wasted. Even worse, the supply of the catalyst was destroyed in the blast. She stared with hate-filled eyes at the faces of the two men on the computer monitor.

"*Little* people," she snarled.

With a wave of her hand the screen went blank.

17

PAUL TROUT TURNED THE SHOWER off and again examined its workings with scientific admiration. Water flowed through a wooden pipe and sprayed out through tiny holes in the hardened shell of a hollowed-out gourd. A simple wooden valve controlled the flow. The water disappeared through a drain hole in the hardwood floor. He stepped from the wooden stall, dried himself with a cotton towel, wrapped his body in another, and went through a doorway into an adjacent room lit by clay lamps.

Gamay was stretched out on a comfortable grass-filled mattress placed on a platform bed. She had fashioned her towel into a toga, had combed and braided her dark red hair, and was sampling fruit from a large bowl like a woman of ancient Rome. She eyed Paul, whose towel looked ridiculously small on his tall figure. "What do you think of all this, nature boy?"

"I've seen worse plumbing back in the so-called civilized world."

"Did you know a civilization can be measured by the sophistication of its plumbing?"

"I can't say much for the uncivilized habit the locals have of sticking heads on sharpened poles, but this whole village is a miracle. Look at the workmanship in these walls," he said, running his fingers over the white plastered surface. "I've got a million questions. Any word from our hostess?"

"She sent Tessa by and said she would see us after we've had a chance to rest. Talk about pulling a rabbit out a hat. I thought the Chulo grabbed Dieter's wife."

The goddess had offered no explanations. After greeting the Trouts by name and producing Tessa, she simply said, "Please be patient. I'll explain everything in time."

At a clap of her hands two young Indian women had emerged with heads lowered from behind the curtain. The bare-breasted ladies-in-waiting led the Trouts to their bedroom, demonstrated the workings of the shower, and left them with a bowl of fruit.

"I know better than to disobey a white goddess," Paul said, sitting alongside his wife. "What do you make of her?"

"Let's deal with the obvious." Gamay tallied her conclusions on her fingers. "She didn't grow up in these parts. She speaks English with a slight accent. She's smart. She's friendly. And certainly knows her fruit. Here, try one of these little yellow ones. It tastes like an orange sprinkled with cinnamon."

Trout sampled the plum-sized blob and agreed with the assessment. Then he stretched out on the bed, his feet sticking out over the end. They only intended to rest a little while, but exhausted from the long trek in the sun and relaxed by the shower, they fell asleep.

When they awoke they saw an Indian lady-in-waiting sitting cross-legged on the floor watching them. Seeing them stir, she slipped silently from the room. Lying on a table were their clothes, which had disappeared when they were in the shower. Their shorts and shirts had been washed clean of sweat and grime and were neatly folded. Trout checked his watch. They had slept three hours. They dressed quickly, hastened by the aroma of cooking food.

Tessa arrived and beckoned for them to follow. She led them along a passageway to a large chamber. A dark wood table and three covered stools occupied the center of the room. An Indian woman was tending to clay pots bubbling on a ceramic stove whose exhaust was carried through the ceiling by pipes.

The white goddess arrived a moment later, her barefoot presence announced by the soft jingle of her metal bracelets and anklets. A pendant similar to that worn by the dead Indian hung from her neck. She was wearing a two-piece suit of jaguar skin which hugged the contours of her bronzed body nicely. She had Oriental eyes and high cheekbones. Her hair, bleached to a honeyed blond by the sun, was combed back and cut in bangs the way the native women wore theirs.

Taking a seat at the table, she said, "You look more rested."

"The shower helped immensely," Gamay said.

"That's a remarkable setup," Paul added. "As a native New Englander, I was intrigued by your Yankee inventiveness."

"It was one of my first projects, thank you. The water is pumped by windmill into a holding tank to maintain pressure. It ties in with a ventilated system of pipes that runs through these walls and keeps this place cool even on the hottest days. It was the best air conditioning I could come up with given the materials I had to work with." Anticipating their curiosity, she said, "First we'll eat, and then we'll talk."

The cook brought over a vegetable and meat stew served with salad greens in blue-and-white bowls. Questions were forgotten as Gamay and Paul plunged into their food, washing their meal down with a refreshing faintly alcoholic beverage. Sugar-sweetened cakes were served for dessert. The goddess looked on, amused at their hunger.

When the dishes were cleared, the goddess declared, "Now it is time to pay for your dinner." She smiled. "You must tell me what has been going on in the outside world for the past ten years."

"That's a cheap price for a meal like that," Paul said.

"You may not think so when I'm through. Start with science if you will. What advances, great or small, have come about in the last decade?"

They took turns, describing the advances in computers, the widespread use of the Internet and wireless communication, the space shuttle missions, the Hubble telescope, unmanned space probes, discoveries by NUMA in the field of oceanography, and advances in medicine. She listened with fascination, her chin resting on her folded hands. Occasionally she asked a probing question that indicated her own scientific background, but mostly she absorbed the information with the dreamy look of an addict inhaling opium fumes.

"Now tell me about the political situation," she requested.

Again they pored through the events in their memory: American presidential politics, relations with Russia, the Persian Gulf wars, the strife in the Balkans, droughts, famines, terrorism, the European Union. She asked about Brazil and seemed pleased when they said the country had become a democracy. They talked about movies and plays, music and art, about the deaths of well-known figures. Even Paul and Gamay were surprised at the incredible busyness of the past decade. Their jaws were getting tired from the litany of events.

"What about cancer? Have they found a cure?"

"Unfortunately no."

"What about fresh water? Is it still a problem for many countries?"

"Worse than ever, between development and pollution."

She shook her head sadly. "So much," she said in a faraway voice. "I've missed so much. I don't know if my parents are still alive. I miss them, my mother especially." A tear gleamed in her eye, and she wiped it away with her napkin. "I must apologize for being so demanding, but you have no idea how awful it is to be isolated here in the forest, with no communication to the outside world. You have been very kind and patient. Now it is time for you to hear my story." She called for tea to be served, then dismissed the Indian women so that there were only the three of them.

"My name is Francesca Cabral," she began. For an hour the Trouts listened raptly to the goddess's story, starting with her family, going through her education in Brazil and America, up to the time of the plane crash.

"I was the only survivor of the crash," she said. "The copilot was a scoundrel, but he knew how to fly. The jet skidded into muddy wetlands near the river. The mud cushioned the landing and prevented fire. When I woke up I found myself in a hut where the Indians carried me. I was in terrible pain from my cuts and bruises, and my right leg was broken. A compound fracture, the worst kind. As you've heard, the rain forest medicines can be potent. They set my leg and treated me with potions that dulled the suffering and promoted healing. I learned later that the plane had landed on top of their chief's house and killed him. They held me no ill. In fact, it was just the opposite."

"They made you their goddess," Gamay said.

"You can see why. The Chulo retreated from the onslaught of the white man a long time ago. They've been completely cut off from the world. Then I come like a comet flaming from the sky. Gods are supposed to behave that way to keep people in line. They figured the chief had angered the gods. I became the center of their religion."

"A cargo cult?" Gamay offered.

Paul said, "Back during World War II, natives who saw planes overhead for the first time built replicas on the ground to worship."

"Yes," Gamay said. "Remember that movie *The Gods Must Be Crazy?* A Coke bottle dropped from an airplane became an object of religious veneration and started all sorts of trouble."

"Precisely," Francesca said. "Think of how those natives would react if they had an actual plane in their possession."

"That explains the shrine with the plane at its center."

She nodded. "They hauled the pieces of the jet there and did a fairly good job of reassembling it. Sort of a 'chariot of the god.' We have to sacrifice an animal now and then so the gods won't wreak more destruction on the tribe."

"The plane was blue and white," Gamay said. "The natives paint themselves with the same color scheme. No coincidence?"

"They believe it will give them protection against their enemies."

"How did Tessa come to be here?"

"Tessa is half Chulo. Her mother was captured during a raid

by a neighboring tribe and traded to a European who was Tessa's father. He was killed during a tribal dispute, and Tessa became Dieter's property. He knew of the Chulo and married Tessa when she was still a girl, erroneously thinking it would give him entree to the tribe and its medicinal herbs, which he trafficked in."

"Why did she stay with Dieter?"

"She thought she had no choice. Dieter reminded her constantly that she was a half-breed, spoiled goods. An outcast."

"What about the Indian whose body we found?"

"Tessa wasn't the first child born to her mother. She had a half-brother who lived here. He was determined to find his family and began to make explorations beyond the falls. He learned that his mother had died but that he had a sister. Tessa. He went to bring her back. The Chulo take family honor very seriously. The plant pirates working with Dieter captured him. They wanted him to show them where to find blood root."

"Arnaud mentioned the plant."

"It's the miraculous species that was used to help me after the plane crash. The tribe considers it to be sacred. He refused to tell them where to find it, so they tortured him. He was shot trying to escape, and you found him. Dieter stole the specimens. I sent a search party to look for Tessa's brother. She was trying to get back here when they ran into her, and she told them the story. I sent her back to Dieter's with instructions to keep us informed about what was going on. Then you showed up unexpectedly. Tessa tried to warn you off. When that didn't work she helped you escape. Or so she thought. You reappeared on our doorstep."

"We're in one piece. That's more than I can say for Dieter and his friends."

"The men of the tribe brought the heads back as gifts to me." She glanced around the dining room which was hung with colorful tapestries of village life. "Shrunken heads would clash with my decor, so I suggested they put them outside the village."

"Were you also responsible for our welcoming committee?"

"Oh, yes. You must admit that big orange-and-blue balloon

you were flying was not inconspicuous. The men reported that you had almost flown into the falls. I had ordered that if you were seen you would be observed but not harmed. They were tracking you from the start. I was surprised when you started this way. You couldn't have been lost."

"We thought we might borrow a canoe."

"Ah. How audacious! You wouldn't have stood a chance. The reputation these people have is well deserved. They tracked you for miles. Sometimes I think they truly are the ghost people. They can melt through the forest like the mists the other Indians say they are made of."

Paul had been pondering Francesca's story. "Why would someone want to hijack the plane and kidnap you?"

"I have an idea why. Come, I'll show you."

Francesca rose from the table and led the way through torch-lit hallways to a large bedroom. She reached into a chest and pulled out a battered and scarred aluminum case. She set it on top of her bed, then opened it. Inside was a jumble of broken wires and circuits.

"This was a model of the experiment I was carrying to Cairo. I won't go into the technical details, but if you pour seawater in on this end, the salt is extracted and fresh water comes out here."

"A desalting process?"

"Yes. It was a revolutionary approach unlike any devised before. It took me two years to perfect. The problem with desalination has been its cost. This process would transform hundreds of gallons for only pennies. At the same time it produces heat which can be transformed into energy." She shook her head. "It would have turned deserts into gardens and allowed people the benefits of power."

"I still don't understand," Paul said. "Why would someone want to prevent a boon like this from being made available to the world?"

"I've asked myself that question many times in the past ten years and still have no satisfactory answer."

"Was this your only model?"

"Yes," she said sadly. "I took everything with me from São Paulo. All my papers were burned in the plane crash." Brightening, she said, "I was able to put my hydraulic engineering skills to work here. It can be boring just sitting around being adored all day. I'm virtually a prisoner. They hid me from search parties after the crash. The only place where I am truly alone is this palace. Only those who are invited can enter. My servants were handpicked for their loyalty. Outside the palace I'm watched by my Praetorian guard."

"Being a white goddess isn't all it's cracked up to be," Paul said.

"An understatement. Which is why I'm so happy you dropped out of the sky. Tonight you rest. Tomorrow I will give you a tour of the village, and we will start planning."

"Planning for what?" Gamay said.

"Sorry, I thought that was obvious. Planning to escape."

18

AUSTIN HAD A QUICK BREAKFAST of ham and scrambled eggs on the deck of his boathouse below the Potomac palisades in Fairfax, Virginia. He stared longingly at the slow-moving river, thinking that a brisk row in his scull would be far preferable to morning traffic on the Beltway. But the events of the last few days gnawed at him. Having narrowly missed being killed twice had injected a personal note into the case.

Driving a turquoise NUMA-issue Jeep Cherokee, Austin headed south and then east across the Woodrow Wilson Memorial Bridge into Maryland, where he left the Beltway. In suburban Suitland he pulled off the road at a complex of metal buildings so boringly nondescript that they could only have been built by the federal government.

A docent in the visitor center took his name and made a call. Minutes later a trim middle-aged man arrived carrying a clipboard. He wore paint-splattered jeans, a denim work shirt, and a baseball cap with the Smithsonian National Air and Space Museum logo. He gave Austin a firm handshake and introduced himself.

"I'm Fred Miller. We talked on the phone," he said.

"Thanks for seeing me on such short notice."

"No problem." Miller raised a quizzical brow. "Are you the same Kurt Austin who found the Christopher Columbus tomb in Guatemala?"

"That's me."

"That must have been some adventure."

"It had its moments."

"I'll bet. I have to apologize. Aside from what I read in the papers of NUMA's undersea exploits, I don't know a lot about your agency."

"Maybe we can both learn something about our respective work. I don't know much about the Paul E. Garber Preservation, Restoration, and Storage Facility. Your Web site says you restore historical and vintage airplanes."

"That's only the tip of the iceberg," Miller said, showing the way to the door. "C'mon, I'll give you a tour."

He led Austin outside and continued his narrative as they walked past a row of identical buildings, all with low roofs and big sliding doors. "Paul Garber was a plane nut, which was fortunate for us. When he was just a kid he saw Orville Wright fly the world's first military aircraft. Later he worked for the Smithsonian and was instrumental in creating the National Air Museum. The Air Force and Navy had collected examples of the planes that won World War II and some of the enemy planes they beat. They wanted to get rid of them. Garber did an aerial survey and found twenty-one acres owned by the federal government out here in the sticks. There are thirty-two buildings at the center." They stopped in front of one of the larger structures. "This is Building Ten, the workshop where we do the restorations."

"I saw some of your work on the live Web cam."

"You might have spotted me. I just came from there. I worked for years as a project manager for Boeing in Seattle, but I'm originally from Virginia, and when I had a chance to come to the center I jumped at it. At any given time we've got several projects going. We've been finishing up a Hawker Hurricane restoration. It's been a little delayed because of a parts problem. We're restoring the fuselage of the *Enola Gay,* the B-29 that carried the A-bomb over Hiroshima. There's a nifty little biplane called Pitt's special 'Little Stinker' that's getting its fabric skin painted. It's not just planes. We've had a Russian air-to-surface missile, plane engines, even the spaceship model they used in that movie *Close Encounters.* We can stop in for a look on the way back."

"I'd like that. Sounds like an eclectic collection."

"Oh, it *is.* We've got aircraft from all over the world that we're getting ready for exhibition. Three buildings are devoted to exhibition restoration alone. This is a high-class club. The artifacts have to have a story behind them to qualify for a makeover. Something historical or technological, or maybe they're the last of their kind. Here, this is what you're interested in."

They entered a building laid out like a warehouse. High metal shelves ran from one end to the other. Stacked neatly on the shelves were hundreds of taped cardboard boxes of all sizes. "Storage is our third most important function, along with restoration and preservation," Miller explained. "We've got more than one hundred and fifty aircraft and tons of other artifacts spread throughout the complex. This is mostly parts in here."

Consulting a computer printout on a clipboard, he walked down one of the aisles with Austin trailing.

"How do you find what you're looking for?" Austin asked with bewilderment.

Miller chuckled. "It's not as bad as you might think. Every important part from every plane in the world has something stamped on it. We've got complete records of serial numbers, registration numbers, or letter codes. Here, this is what we're looking for."

Using a pocket knife, he slit the sealing tape on a cardboard box. After reaching inside, he pulled out a metal cylinder about two feet long. Austin thought it was the part he had sent from California, but it was too shiny, and its surface was free of dents and nicks.

"This is identical to the artifact you sent us." He extracted Austin's cylinder from the box. "We matched the two objects through their serial numbers. This first is from a plane that was decommissioned and taken apart, which is why it's in such good condition."

He handed the cylinder to Austin, who hefted it. Like the other, it was lightweight aluminum and weighed only a few pounds.

"What was this used for?"

"It was a water- and airtight storage container. This one is pristine because the plane never went into active service. We examined the interior of yours, but the seawater leaked in through the hole and contaminated the residue of what, if anything, was inside. We *can* tell you what aircraft these things came from."

"Anything would be a help."

Miller nodded. "You've heard of the Northrop flying wings?"

"Sure, I've seen pictures of them. They were the original delta-winged aircraft."

"Jack Northrop was way ahead of his time. Take a look at the stealth bomber and fighter, and you'll know he was onto something."

"What does the flying wing have to do with these cylinders?"

"They both come from flying wings. Where'd you get this, if you don't mind my asking?"

"It was found in the water off the coast of Baja California."

"Hmmm. That makes the mystery of our phantom plane even deeper."

"Phantom?"

Miller lay the cylinders side-by-side on the shelf. "*Our* artifact comes from a plane that was junked after the war. With the numbers on this thing we can trace its history right back to the assembly line." He tapped the battered artifact with his finger. "The numerical designation on this part doesn't match up to any plane we have record of. It came from a plane that didn't exist."

"How could that be? A mistake?"

"Possible, but not likely. Taking a long shot, I'd say that the government ordered up a plane, but maybe it didn't want anyone to know about it."

"Could you be more specific about the type of plane?"

Miller carefully replaced both cylinders in the box and retaped it. "Let's go for a walk."

Building 20 was crammed with aircraft, bombs, and plane parts. They stopped in front of an odd-shaped single-passenger plane with a broad swept-back wing. Two propellers faced backward from the trailing edge.

"This is the N1-M, Jack Northrop's first project. He wanted to prove a flying wing could fly without all the drag-producing surfaces like engine housings and tail sections."

Austin walked around the plane. "Looks like an overgrown boomerang."

"Northrop called it the Jeep. He built it in 1940 basically as a flying mockup. It had some real problems during the tests, but it performed well enough for Northrop to talk the Air Force into building the B-35 bomber."

"Interesting, but what does this have to do with the cylinder?"

"Northrop used this model to talk General Hap Arnold into funding bigger wings, right up to bomber size. After the war they converted a couple of big propeller-powered B-35 wings to jet power and called them the B-49 series. The plane broke every speed and distance record on the books. It had eight jet engines that gave it a cruising speed of four hundred miles per hour at forty thousand feet. Even after one crashed during a test flight, the Air Force ordered thirty with various airframes. The pilots liked the plane. They said it handled more like a fighter than a big bomber. Then in 1949, only months after making its big order, the Air Force canceled the flying wing program in favor of B-36, even though that was an inferior plane. A six-engine wing survived and was broken up. It was the plane our cylinder comes from. Yours came from another bomber."

"The plane that doesn't exist."

Miller nodded. "A lot of crazy stuff went on after Germany surrendered. The cold war was getting revved up. People were seeing commies under their beds. All sorts of secret stuff going on. The government got even worse after the Russians developed the bomb. My guess is that they built your plane with a mission in mind and didn't tell anyone about it."

"What *kind* of mission?"

"I don't know, but I'd hazard a guess."

"Hazard for all it's worth, my friend."

Miller laughed. "The Northrop bomber was the original stealth plane. Radar was still comparatively primitive back then, and it had a hard time picking up the slim silhouette. In 1948 they took a wing out into the Pacific and flew back to the mainland at five hundred miles per hour on a direct line toward the Coastal Command radar at Half Moon Bay, south of San Francisco. The plane wasn't detected by radar until it was overhead."

"A characteristic like that would come in handy if you wanted to get in and out of hostile territory."

"That's my guess, but I have no evidence to substantiate it."

"What could have happened to the plane?"

"Even with its low radar profile it could have been shot down. More likely, though, it was scrapped like the others or crashed during a test or a mission. They were still working out the bugs in the design."

"Neither possibility explains how a piece of the plane ended up in the sea off Mexico."

Miller shrugged.

"Maybe I can find something in the records," Austin suggested.

"Good luck. Remember what I said about crazy stuff happening after the war? After the Air Force canceled its contract for the last batch of wings, it went into the plant, cut up all the planes being built, and carted them away as scrap metal. They refused the Smithsonian's request for a plane to put on exhibition and ordered all production jigs and dies destroyed. All the official records on the flying wing were 'lost,' supposedly under direct orders from Truman."

"That was convenient." Austin stared at the flying wing as if the answers to the puzzle were locked in its aerodynamic fuselage, but like the plane, his thoughts refused to get off the ground. "Well, thanks for all your help," he said finally. "It looks like a dead end."

"Wish I could have been of more help," Miller said. "I've got a suggestion. It's a long shot. A widow of one of the test pilots lives not far from here. She showed up one day looking for information about her husband. He died while they were testing one of the big wings. She was compiling a scrapbook to pass on to the kids and grandchildren. We gave her some pictures, and she was happy with that. Her husband could have said something to her. Maybe he didn't know about our missing plane, but there are always rumors."

Austin glanced at his watch. He hadn't planned to be back at his NUMA office until after lunch. "Thanks for the tip. I'll see if I can track her down."

They returned to the visitor center and looked up the woman's name and address. She had made a substantial donation to the center in her husband's name. Austin thanked Miller and headed south beyond the suburbs that ring Washington until the countryside began to look more rural. The address was a big two story gingerbread Victorian on a back road. A car was parked out front. Austin went up to the front door and rang the bell. An athletically built man in his fifties answered the door.

Kurt introduced himself. "I'm looking for Mrs. Phyllis Martin. Do I have the right house?"

"Yes, this is the Martin house. But I'm afraid you've come a little too late. My mother passed away several weeks ago."

"I'm very sorry to hear that," Austin said. "Hope I haven't bothered you."

"Not at all. I'm her son, Buzz Martin. I'm taking care of some things around the house. Perhaps I can help you."

"Possibly. I'm with NUMA, the National Underwater and Marine Agency. I'm doing some historical research on flying wings and was hopeful your mother might like to talk about your father."

"Doesn't NUMA deal with the ocean sciences?"

"That's right, but this might have a connection with NUMA's work."

Buzz Martin gave Austin a long look. "It's no bother, really. I'd be happy to talk to you. Have a seat on the porch rocker. I've been working in the cellar and could use some fresh air. I just made a pot of ice coffee."

He went inside and returned a few minutes later with two tumblers that clinked with ice. They sat in a couple of Adirondack chairs. Martin looked out at the oak trees shading the big lawn.

"I grew up here. I haven't been around much with the demands of job and family. I run an air charter service out of Baltimore." He sipped his drink. "But enough about me. What can I tell you about my father?"

"Anything you can remember that might help clear up a mystery having to do with the flying wing he piloted."

Martin's face lit up like a streetlight. He smacked his hands together. "*Aha!* I knew the cover-up would unravel one day."

"Cover-up?"

"That's right," Martin said bitterly. "This whole crummy deal with my father and the phony crash."

Austin sensed that he'd learn more by saying less. "Tell me what you know," he said.

The suggestion was hardly necessary. Martin had been waiting for years for a friendly ear to listen to his tale.

"Excuse me," he said with a deep sigh. "This stuff has been building up for a long time." He stood and paced the length of the porch. His face was contorted by anguish. He took several deep breaths to get his emotions in check. Then he sat on the railing, arms folded, and began to tell his story.

"My father died in 1949. According to my mother, he was testing one of the new flying wings. There were bugs in the design, and they were always tinkering with one thing or another. On one flight the plane supposedly rolled; he couldn't get it under control. He died in the crash. I was seven years old."

"It must have been devastating for you."

"I was pretty young," he said with a shrug, "and the whole thing was exciting, what with the Air Force brass and the president sending messages. I never saw my father much anyway. During the war he was away a lot." He paused. "Actually, it really hit me when I discovered he wasn't dead."

"You're saying your father *wasn't* killed in a crash?"

"He looked quite healthy when I saw him at Arlington Cemetery."

"You're talking about seeing him in the coffin, you mean."

"No. He was watching the funeral from a distance."

Austin scrutinized Martin's face, not sure what he was looking for.

Detecting no sign of dementia, he said, "I'd like to hear about it."

Martin broke out into a broad grin. "I've been waiting more than forty years to hear somebody say those words." He stared into space as if he could see the scene playing out on an invisible screen. "I still remember the little things. It was in the spring, and robins were flitting around. I can recall the way the sun reflected off the buttons on the Air Force uniforms, the smell of new-cut grass and earth. I was standing by the casket, next to my mother, holding her hand, squirming in my suit because it was so hot and the collar was tight. The minister was going on and on in this droning voice. Everyone had their eyes on him." He took a deep breath as his memory drifted back in time. "I saw a movement, a bird maybe, and looked beyond the crowd. A man had stepped away from a tree. He was dressed in dark clothes. He was too far away for me to see his face, but there was no mistaking him. My father had a funny way of standing on one leg, kinda crooked. Old football injury."

"What was he doing?"

"Nothing. He just stood there. I knew he was staring at me. Then he raised his right arm a little, as if he were about to wave. Two men came up beside him. They talked. It looked as if they were arguing. Then they all walked away. I tried to get my mother's attention, but she shushed me."

"You're sure it wasn't the wishful thinking of a distraught boy?"

"Yes. I was so certain that after the funeral I told my mother what I had seen. It only made her cry. I'll never forget those tears. I never brought it up again. She was young enough and remarried. My stepfather was a nice guy. He was successful in business, and they had a good life. They were very happy for many years." He laughed. "I was my father's kid. My mother tried to talk me out of flying, but I became a pilot. This thing has burned in me all that time. I made inquiries but never got anywhere. I was convinced the truth would never come out. Then you show up and start asking questions."

"What do you know about your father's job?"

"He was a veteran pilot. He was hired by Avion Corporation, the company Northrop set up to manufacture flying wings, although he was still in the Air Force. Dad had several close calls. The wing design was a great concept, but with the materials and the know-how at the time, flying the prototypes was risky business. That's why nobody was surprised when his plane crashed."

"You were very young, but do you remember anything he said?"

"Not much. My mother told me he loved to fly those contraptions, that he said they were going to revolutionize aviation. He seemed quite excited about his assignments. At one point he disappeared for a period of weeks. No communication, no contact except in the direst emergency. Mom said that when he came home she said something about his sunburn. He laughed and said it was more like *snow* burn, but he never explained what he meant."

"Did he leave any papers, a journal or diary?"

"Nothing I know of. I remember after he died that a bunch of Air Force people came to the house. They might have taken whatever he had written. Does any of this help?"

Austin thought about his conversation with Fred Miller at Garber, particularly the mention of early stealth aircraft technology. "My guess is that your father was training for a secret mission in the north."

"That was fifty years ago. Why still keep it secret?"

"Secrets have a way of justifying themselves beyond the point of necessity."

Miller looked out over the shady yard. "The worst thing is knowing that my father could have been alive all those years." He turned back to Austin. "Maybe he's *still* alive. He'd be in his eighties."

"It's possible. It also means that there might be someone out there who knows the real story."

"I'd like the truth to come out, Mr. Austin. Can you help me?"

"I'll do what I can."

They talked further. Before parting they exchanged phone numbers. Austin vowed he would call if he learned anything. He started back for Washington. Like any good detective he had knocked on doors and used up some shoe leather, but this puzzle was too old, too complex for ordinary methods. It was time to see NUMA's computer whiz, Hiram Yaeger.

19

THE INDIAN VILLAGE WAS A MARvel of city planning. Strolling along the network of hard-packed earthen paths that connected the thatched huts, the Trouts could almost forget that their entourage included a mysterious and beautiful white goddess in a jaguar-skin bikini and a silent escort of six armed Chulo Indians painted the color of an executive jet.

Francesca led the procession. The warriors, three on either side, kept pace a respectable spear's length away. Francesca stopped near the big well in the village center. Indian women were filling pots with water while gangs of naked children happily chased each other around their mothers' legs. Francesca beamed with obvious pride.

"Every improvement you see here is part of an integrated scheme," she said with a sweep of her hands. "I planned the project as if I were building a new infrastructure for São Paulo. I worked for months before one spadeful of earth was turned, putting everything in place, right down to the allocation of capital, sources of supply, and labor. I had to establish a subsidiary to manufacture the specialized tools that would be needed to produce wooden pipe, valves, and fittings. At the same time it was necessary to keep the village functioning without interrupting hunting and harvesting."

"Remarkable," Gamay said, looking around at the neatly ordered huts. She couldn't help comparing the village with the squalor of Dieter's empire or the relatively civilized settlement where Dr. Ramirez had his house. "Absolutely remarkable," Gamay repeated.

"Thank you, but once I had the preparations in place it wasn't as difficult as it looks. The key was water flow. It's just as essential to life and living here as it is back in the so-called civilized world. I assigned digging crews to divert the river. We had the same problems as any project. The shovel makers complained that we were pushing them too hard and that quality was suffering." She laughed. "It was exhilarating. We made a canal to open a tributary from the lake. Once we established the water supply, it was a simple matter to divert it to the public wells. The gristmill was basic time-proven technology."

"The water wheel is as good as anything I've seen in the old industrial towns in New England," Paul said, stopping in front of a hut no bigger than a one-car garage. "But I am really impressed with the plumbing in these public commodes. Back where I come from they used outhouses right into the twentieth century."

"I'm particularly proud of the public water closets," she said as they continued their tour. "When I finally admitted to myself that my desalination process would never see the light of day, I turned my efforts to improving the life of these wretched savages. They lived at a Stone Age level. Their hygiene was pitiful. Mothers routinely died in childbirth. The infant mortality rate was incredible. The adults were the targets of every parasite that grows in the rain forest. Their traditional medicinal plants were simply overwhelmed. Diet was of little nutrition. Producing a clean and reliable water flow not only protected the people from their usual ailments, but it allowed them to grow the crops that would keep them healthy."

"We were wondering whether your talents extended to surgery," Gamay said. "Tessa's brother had a peculiar scar on his body."

She clapped her hands like a delighted child. "Oh, the appendectomy! He would have died if I hadn't acted. My training was limited to first aid. I had the Chulo pharmacology to thank. They dip their blowgun darts in the sap from a plant. They use it to paralyze game, but even a small amount can incapacitate a human. I smeared it on a large leaf and placed it on the skin. It functioned as a local anesthetic. The stitches used to close the wound were made with fibers from another plant that seems to resist infection. The knife had an obsidian point, sharper than a scalpel. Nothing high-tech, I'm afraid."

"I wish I could say the same for those weapons your guards are carrying," Paul said, eyeing the steel tips of the short throwing spears their guards carried. Each man also carried a bow and a quiver of long-shafted arrows.

"Those bows and spear tips were made with aluminum from the plane. The shortened bow is easier to carry through the forest, and the design makes the arrow fly farther."

"If Arnaud and his men were still alive they could vouch for their effectiveness," Paul said.

"I'm truly sorry about those men, but they brought their fate upon themselves. The Chulo are a comparatively small tribe, and they've always preferred flight to fight. Oh, they'll shrink a head or eat an enemy, but they rarely go out and catch someone in a raid. They just want to be left alone. The white man drove them further into the forest. They thought they were safe once they went beyond the Great Falls, but white exploiters continued to press them. They would have been destroyed if I hadn't helped them improve their defenses."

"I've been noticing the arrangement of the village," Gamay said. "The layout reminds me of the architecture I've seen in old walled cities."

"Very perceptive. Anyone who got past the stockade fence would be in a most uncomfortable position. The village is full of cul-de-sacs and blind alleys that offer prime opportunities for ambush."

"What if the intruders were coming to rescue you?" Paul said. "Wouldn't these preparations be self-defeating?"

"I gave up hope of rescue a long time ago. My father would

have made sure search parties scoured the forest. He must have become convinced that I was dead, which is just as well. Three men died in the plane crash, and the tribal chief was killed because of me. I wouldn't want to be responsible for additional deaths."

"It's ironic," Gamay mused. "The more you do for these people, the less likely they are to release you."

"True, but they would have kept me captive even if I just sat around making goddess sounds and getting fat. As long as I *had* to be here, it would have been sinful not to use my talents to improve their lot. When white men finally come, I hope the Chulo will use their knowledge rather than their arms to deal with civilization's impact. Unfortunately in the meantime I have little control of the tribe's more murderous instincts. Once Arnaud and his friends showed hostile intent they were doomed. There was no way I could save them. In your case it was easier. You were so helpless in the forest, they never saw you as a threat until now."

Gamay's ears perked up. "A *threat?*"

"Try not to look alarmed," Francesca said. A smile played on her lips, but her eyes were deadly serious. "They don't understand what we're saying, but they sense things." She stopped to demonstrate a water pipe that served as a fire hydrant, then resumed her casual walk. "They're worried. They think you are flawed gods."

"If we're so insignificant, why are they concerned?" Gamay said.

"They're afraid you're here to take me back into the sky where I came from."

"They *told* you that?"

"They don't have to. I know these people intimately. In addition, Tessa's been picking up whisperings. They're talking about burning you. The smoke from your bodies will take you back into the sky. Problem solved."

Paul ventured a sidelong glance at the guards, but he failed to detect any change in their stony expressions.

"I can't argue with their logic, but that solves the problem for *them,* not for us," he said.

"I agree. It makes it all the more urgent that we escape as soon as possible. Come with me. We'll be able to talk about a plan without the palace guard peering over our shoulders."

They had arrived at the white stone walkway that led through the forest to the shrine. With the Trouts following, Francesca walked to the circular clearing with the plane at its center and sat down on a polished wooden bench facing the nose of the Learjet. The Trouts sat cross-legged on the tiled ground.

"I come here to be alone. Only the priests are allowed at the shrine otherwise. The warriors will be in the forest watching our every move, but we'll be able to talk about our escape plans."

Gamay glanced toward the jungle where the warriors had melted out of sight.

"I hope you've got something up your sleeve, because we don't," she said.

"Your original instincts were on the mark. Our only way out is by water. Up the tributary and canal to the lake, then follow the main river. We would never make it through the forest. They would catch us in an instant, or we'd become lost."

"I've seen your boys handle a canoe," Paul said. "We'd need a substantial jump on them."

"We would have a few hours. But they are skilled and strong paddlers. They would be getting their strength just as we were tiring."

"What would they do if they caught us?" Paul asked. "Theoretically speaking."

"No theory about it," Francesca said. "They would kill us."

"Even *you,* their goddess?"

She nodded. "Leaving them would constitute a demotion in my status, I'm afraid. My head would be up there on the stockade fence along with yours."

Paul involuntarily rubbed his neck.

All at once they were no longer alone. An Indian had stepped into the clearing followed by eight armed warriors. He was taller than the other Chulo by a few inches, and unlike the flat facial features typical in the tribe, his profile was almost Roman. His muscular body was painted red rather than blue and white. He stepped over to Francesca and spoke, gesturing from time to time at the Trouts. Francesca stood like a rearing cobra and cut him short with a dagger-sharp reply. He glared at her, then bowed his head slightly. His companions followed suit. They backed up several steps, turned, and quickly strode away from the shrine. Francesca watched them go, her eyes blazing with heat.

"This is not good," she said.

"Who were those people?" Gamay said.

"The tall man is the son of the chief I killed in the plane crash. I have named him Alaric after the Visigoth king. He's quite intelligent and a natural leader, but he tends to be a bully. He would like to depose me and has gathered a group of young Turks around him. The fact that he set foot on the forbidden shrine shows that he has become bolder. He is obviously exploiting the questions raised by your arrival. We must get back to the palace."

As they left the shrine the guards materialized from the forest and took their places alongside. Francesca walked briskly, and they were back at the compound within minutes. Something was different inside the stockade fence. Knots of Indian men stood around. They averted their eyes when the procession passed. There were no friendly smiles as on the way out.

About twenty armed warriors were gathered in front of the palace with Alaric at their center. They parted with sullen looks at a wave of Francesca's hand, but Gamay noticed that they took their time doing it. Tessa greeted them inside the door. Her eyes were wide with fright. She and Francesca talked in their language for a minute, then the white goddess translated for the Trouts.

"The priests have made a decision. You're to be killed in the morning. They'll spend the night getting their courage up and building the pyres to burn you."

Gamay's mouth hardened. "Sorry we can't stay for the barbecue," she said. "If you would point us to the nearest canoe, we'll be saying good-bye."

"Impossible! You wouldn't get ten feet now."

"Then what do we do?"

Francesca mounted her dais and sat on her throne, her eyes glued to the chamber door. "We wait," she said.

20

THE ANCIENT SHIP HUNG IN SPACE as if suspended from invisible cables, its multi-decked hull outlined by shimmering spiderweb lines of gossamer blue. The great square sails were bowed full, and ghostly pennants fluttered at the masthead as if tossed by a freshened breeze.

Hiram Yaeger leaned back in his chair and studied the spectral image hovering over a platform in front of his horseshoe-shaped console. "It's *beautiful,* Max," he said, "but the detail needs sharpening."

A soft and disembodied feminine voice filled the room from a dozen speakers set in the walls. "You only asked for a blueprint, Hiram." There was the hint of petulance in the tone.

"That's right, Max," Yaeger said, "and you've gone far beyond that. But now I'd like to see how close we can get to the finished product."

"Done," said the voice.

The ship's hull solidified like a specter materializing from ectoplasm. Its hull blazed with gold that highlighted the elaborate carvings covering the sides from stem to stern. Yaeger's eyes lingered on the beak head, crowned by a wooden image of King Edgar, the hoofs of his charger trampling the seven fallen monarchs whose shorn beards bordered his mantle. Then he studied the astronomical panels that represented the glories of the

Olympic gods, going back to the high stern, embellished with biblical figures. Every detail was perfect.

"Wow!" Yaeger said. "You didn't tell me you had programmed the full picture. All it needs now is a couple of dolphins."

Instantly, simulated seas appeared under the ship, and at her bow a pair of dolphins leaped and splashed. The three-dimensional image spun slowly as the whistles and twitters of the dolphins filled the air.

Yaeger clapped his hands and laughed like a child with delight.

"Max, you're brilliant!"

"I should be," the voice replied. "You created me."

Not only had Yaeger created the vast artificial intelligence system, but he had programmed his own voice into the original program. He didn't like talking to himself, so he modified it into Max's female tones. The computer system had developed a feminine personality all on its own.

"Flattery will get you everywhere," Yaeger said.

"Thank you. If you're through I'll take a break to allow my circuits to cool down. Holograms always exhaust me."

Yaeger knew Max was prone to exaggerate and that the ship represented only a tiny fraction of the capacity in her circuits. But along with a feminine version of his own voice, he had programmed in some human traits, including the need to be appreciated. He waved his hand. The ship, the roiling seas, the leaping dolphins vanished in a blink of the eye.

Yaeger turned to the sound of applause and saw Austin standing there clapping his hands.

"Hi, Kurt," he said with a grin. "Have a seat."

"Quite a show," Austin said, easing into a chair next to Yaeger. "Right down to the vanishing act. I doubt even David Copperfield could make a full-blown English capital ship disappear."

Yaeger was truly a magician, but his sleight of hand was performed with computers rather than a top hat and wand. He was an unlikely-looking magus, dressed with a studied scruffiness in

Levi's jeans and denim jacket over a plain white T-shirt. Beat-up cowboy boots adorned his feet. Yet he presided like a master sorcerer over the vast computer network that covered nearly the entire tenth floor of the NUMA building. The National Underwater & Marine Agency oceans center stored and processed the most enormous amount of digital data on oceanography and related sciences ever assembled under one roof.

"That was nothing," he said with boyish delight. Excitement danced in the gray eyes behind wire-rimmed granny glasses perched on his narrow nose. "Wait until you see the treat Max and I have planned for you."

"I can hardly wait. That was *Sovereign of the Seas?*"

"Right. Launched in 1637 at the orders of Charles I. One of the largest seagoing vessels constructed up to that time."

"Also one of the most top-heavy, as I recall. She had her top deck cut down, which was appropriate, given that Charles lost his head."

"I'll add the modifications later. The new program will be available for the nautical archaeology department of any university that wants it. Max has been making a list of hundreds of old vessels. We feed their plans, architect's renderings, dimensions, history, everything we know about a vessel, into the computers. Max pulls it all together into a holographic reconstruction. She'll even fill in missing details when information is incomplete. Max, would you mind telling Kurt what you found with the material he gave us?"

The face of a lovely woman appeared on the huge monitor just beyond the platform. Her lips parted in a white smile.

"I'd come off my coffee break *any* time for Mr. Austin," the voice said flirtatiously.

The air above the platform shimmered with blue light at the nexus of lasers scattered in the walls. Stud by stud, beam by beam, but with lightning speed, the flashing lasers assembled a long open ship with a single square sail.

"C'mon." Yaeger got up, and they walked onto the platform. Austin's vision blurred for a second. When it cleared they were standing on the deck of the vessel looking toward the gracefully upturned bow. Circular wooden shields adorned the sides.

"This is the next evolution in the program. Not only will you be able to *see* the ships in our inventory, you'll be able to walk around on the decks. The virtual perspective changes as you move. The simplicity of design made this one fairly easy."

"I'd say I'm standing on the deck of the Gogstad ship."

"Correct. Built in Norway between A.D. 700 and 1000. The original ship was seventy-nine feet long and was constructed entirely of oak, something a bit more substantial than light beams. This is a half-scale model."

"It's beautiful," Austin said, "but what does it have to do with the material I gave you?"

"I'll show you what I found."

They walked through the shimmering walls back to the console.

"It wasn't hard getting some data on the Mulholland Group," Yaeger said. "As your dead lawyer friend told you, the company is involved in hydraulic projects. I had to dig around, but I found that it was part of a larger corporation called Gogstad. The logo of the parent company is the ship you see before you." The hologram disappeared, and a stylized version of the ship appeared on the monitor.

"Tell me more."

"I asked Max to start playing around with Gogstad. I didn't get much on the company, but apparently it's a huge transnational corporation involved in all kinds of stuff. Finance. Engineering. Banking. Construction."

He handed Austin a computer disk. "This is what I found. Nothing startling. I'll keep trying."

"Thanks, Hiram. I'll review it. In the meantime I've got another favor to ask of you and Max." He related his visit to the Garber center and his interview with the pilot's son. "I'd like to know if this plane was ever built and what happened to the pilot."

Max had been attentive again. A photograph of a large wing-shaped craft appeared on the screen.

"This is a picture from the Smithsonian files of the YB-49A, the last Northrop flying wing bomber to take to the air," the low voice purred. "I can give you a three-D rendering, like the ships."

"This is fine for now. The designation etched on the cylinder was YB-49B."

The photograph was replaced by a drawing. "This is the YB-49B," Max said.

"What's the difference between this model and the one you just showed us, Max?"

"The designers ironed out the oscillation problem that bothered the bombardiers. In addition it would have flown faster and farther than the earlier model. It was never built."

Austin knew better than to argue with Max. Instead, he watched the statistical and performance figures roll under the picture. Something in the data bothered him.

"Wait," he said. "Go back. See there, it says the cruising speed was five hundred and twenty-five miles per hour. How would they have known the speed if they hadn't conducted field trials?"

"It may be an estimate?" Yaeger ventured.

"Maybe. But it doesn't say that it's estimated."

"You're right. They would have to have conducted field trials back then because they didn't have smart machines like Max to simulate flying conditions."

"Thank you for the compliment, although it does state the obvious," Max said. "Kurt has a point, Hiram. While you were talking I checked and found that in every instance where a plane was designed but not actually built, its speed was *estimated.* Except for this one."

Yaeger knew better than to argue with Max. "It seems that maybe this plane *did* exist? But what happened to it?"

"This may be as far as we get for now," Austin said. "The Northrop and Air Force records were lost. What can Max tell us about the pilot, Frank Martin?"

"Do you want the quick economy search or the full-blown probe?" Max asked.

"What's the difference?"

"The quick tour goes to the Pentagon's armed services registry, which contains the name of everyone, living or dead, who served in the armed forces. The full monte digs additional information from the Pentagon's classified files. I'll throw in the National Security Council, the FBI, and the CIA just for ha-has."

"This is a mere technicality, but isn't it illegal to hack into those databases?"

"*Hack* is such an ugly word," Max said. "Let's say I'm simply paying social calls on fellow computer systems so we can exchange gossip."

"In that case, do all the socializing you want to," Austin said.

"Interesting," Max said after a moment. "I've tried to open several doors, but in every case Harry has put a lock on them."

"Who's Harry, another computer?" Yaeger said.

"No, silly. Harry Truman."

Austin scratched his head. "Are you saying that all the files on this pilot were sealed by order of the president?"

"That's right. Aside from the most basic information about Mr. Martin, everything else is still classified." There was an uncharacteristic pause. "That's peculiar," Max said. "I just got a trace. It was as if someone opened a door that was locked. Here's your boy." A picture of a young man in an Air Force uniform appeared. "He lives in upstate New York near Cooperstown."

"He's still *alive?*"

"There seems to be some disagreement on that. The Pentagon says he died in a plane crash in 1949. This new information says just the opposite."

"A mistake?"

"I wouldn't be surprised. Humans are fallible. I'm not."

"Does he have a phone?"

"No. But I have an address."

A printout came out of a slot on the console. Still puzzled,

Austin looked at the name and address as if they were in vanishing ink. He folded the paper and tucked it into his pocket. "Thanks, Hiram and Max. You've been a great help." He started for the door.

"Where you off to now?" Yaeger said.

"Cooperstown. This may be my one and only chance to get into the Baseball Hall of Fame."

21 ACROSS THE POTOMAC AT THE NEW

CIA headquarters building in Langley, Virginia, an analyst in the Directorate of Intelligence was wondering if his computer was having the hiccups. The analyst, an eastern European specialist named J. Barrett Browning, stood up and peered over the partition into the adjacent cubicle.

"Say, Jack, do you have a second to look at something really weird?"

The sallow-faced man at the cluttered desk put aside the Russian newspaper he had been marking up and rubbed his deep-set eyes.

"Sex, crime, and more sex. I don't know what could be weirder than the Russian press," said John Rowland, a respected translator who had joined the CIA after the agency's dark Nixon days. "It's like U.S. supermarket tabloids on hormones. I almost miss the tractor production statistics." He rose from his work station and came around into Browning's cubicle. "What's the problem, young man?"

"This crazy message on my computer," Browning replied with a shake of his head. "I was scrolling some historical material on the Soviet Union, and this popped up on the screen."

Rowland leaned forward and read the words: "PROTOCOL ACTIVATED FOR SANCTION WITH EXTREME PREJUDICE."

Rowland tugged his pepper-and-salt goatee. "Extreme prejudice? *Nobody* uses language like that anymore."

"What's it mean?"

"It's a euphemism. Goes way back to the cold war and Vietnam. It's a polite way of referring to a hit."

"Huh?"

"Don't they teach you *anything* at Yale?" Rowland said with a grin. "*Sanctioning* someone is setting him up for assassination. Real James Bond stuff."

"Oh, I get it," Barrett said, looking around the room at the other cubicles. "Let's guess which of our esteemed colleagues is the practical joker."

Rowland was in deep thought and didn't reply. He slid into Browning's chair and studied the underlined file number at the end of the message. He highlighted the number and hit the enter key. A series of digits appeared.

"If this is a joke, it's a good one," he muttered. "No one has used this encoding since Allen Dulles was agency director after World War II."

Rowland hit the print button and took the copy of the message to his cubicle with his puzzled colleague right behind him. He made a quick phone call, then fed the code into his computer and tapped the keys. "I'm sending this down to a pal in the decoding division. It's pretty antiquated stuff. He can decipher it in a matter of minutes with the programs available today."

"Where do you suppose it came from?" Browning said.

"What were you reading when the message appeared?"

"Archives material. Mostly diplomatic reports. One of the Senate staff guys needed it for his boss who's on the armed services committee. He was looking for patterns of Soviet behavior, probably so he could jack up the defense budget."

"What was the context of these reports?"

"They were from field agents to the director. It had to do with Soviet nuclear development. They were in the old files that Clinton ordered declassified."

"Interesting. That tells us that that the material was meant for eyes only at the highest level."

"Sounds plausible. But what's this business with the protocol?"

Rowland sighed. "I don't know what the agency is going to do when old war horses like me get put out to pasture. Let me tell you how the protocols worked back in the old covert action days. First a policy would be approved, usually at the highest levels, with the director, NSA, joint chiefs all signing on. The president would be kept out of the loop officially, for purposes of deniability. The policy would generate a course of action in response to a given threat or threats. That was the protocol. The action was distilled into an order. The order was broken down into a number of parts."

"Makes sense. That way those who carried out the order only knew their small part of it. You preserve secrecy."

"Aha, I guess they *did* teach you something in the halls of Eli, even if it's all wrong. Those nutty plans like whacking Castro or Iran-contra were set up that way, and they all fell apart."

"So why have a protocol at all?"

"The *prime* reason is so the guys at the top can disallow responsibility. A protocol was usually reserved for the most serious type of action. In this case, we're talking about a political assassination. It was not something taken lightly. Heads of state are not supposed to plot the demise of other heads of state or people in their own government. It makes for bad precedent. So the order would be multilevel. It was designed not to leave fingerprints. No one gave orders that could be traced back. A number of predetermined circumstances had to come about for the command to be followed through to its end."

"It sounds like the fail-safe system they used with the nuclear bombers. There were several steps involved, and the mission could be aborted up until the very last."

"Something like that. Let me give you another analogy. A threat is perceived. One hand takes out the gun. The threat grows. Another hand loads the bullet. The threat escalates. A third hand cocks the hammer. Next, the trigger is pulled and the threat is eliminated. All those action-reaction steps would be necessary for the gun to fire."

Browning nodded. "I understand what you're saying, but I can't figure out how the bloody thing got onto my computer."

"Maybe that's not as mysterious as it seems." Most of Rowland's days were spent in the boring task of reading and analyzing newspapers, and he relished the chance for intellectual exercise. He leaned back in the chair and stared at the ceiling.

"The protocol originally would have been recorded on paper, probably broken down into parts. It is never carried out. Then the agency goes from paper to computers. The protocol becomes encoded in the agency's database. It sits there for decades, until all the triggering mechanisms are in place to activate it. The director is supposed to be notified automatically, only the files have been declassified and the computer doesn't know that a lowly analyst will be reading a file meant only for the director."

"Brilliant," Browning said. "Now we have to figure out what could have set a fifty-year-old protocol in motion. I was looking at these same files yesterday. This was not there."

"That means the protocol was activated in the last twenty-four hours. Wait—" The e-mail was blinking. Rowland retrieved the message.

"Dear Rowland. Here's your message. Ho-hum. Please send something more challenging next time."

The words on the screen simply said, "Sanction under way."

"It's a coded reply from the hit man," Rowland said. Browning shook his head. "I wonder who the poor bastard was."

"I don't think we have to worry about the past; it's the *future* I'm concerned about."

"Hey, c'mon, Jack, it's been half a century since this protocol was approved. Everyone involved must be long dead. Hit man and victim alike."

"Maybe," Rowland said. "Maybe not." He tapped the words on the screen. "This reply has just been sent. It means the hit man is still alive, and so is his victim. At least for now."

"What do you mean?"

Rowland reached for the phone, a grave expression carved into the usual cheery face.

"The director didn't countermand the order, so it goes to the next step. The *killing.*" Rowland held his hand up to cut off Browning's question. "Please put me through to the director," he barked into the phone. "Yes, it's urgent," he said, his voice rising in a rare display of emotion. "*Damned* urgent!"

22

THE BLAZE HAD BEEN EXTINguished and the firefighters were mopping up when Zavala returned to Hanley's office building. Zavala bluffed his way past the yellow police tape with officious flashes of his NUMA identification card. He waved the laminated card with his picture close to the arson investigator's nose, then quickly tucked it back into his billfold. He didn't want to explain why someone from a federal ocean science agency was at a San Diego disaster scene.

The investigator, whose name was Connors, said witnesses had told him about the hovering helicopter and described a strange flash of light before the explosion, but he hadn't eliminated the possibility that the detonation was internal. Zavala couldn't blame him. It's not every day an armed helicopter attacks an office building in San Diego.

"How is the injured woman?" Zavala asked.

"Okay last I heard," Connors said. "A couple of guys dragged her out of her office before the fire got going."

Zavala then thanked Connors and walked to the next block to catch a taxi. As he raised his hand to hail a cab, a plain black Ford sedan pulled up to the curb. Agent Miguel Gomez was behind the wheel. The FBI man leaned across the seat and opened the door. Zavala got in.

Gomez gave Zavala his world-weary look. "Things sure have gotten busy since you and your partner arrived in town," the agent said. "A few hours after you walk into my office the Farmer *and* his sleazeball lawyer go up in smoke. Why don't you stick around a few more days? The whole Mexican mafia and their pals will self-destruct, and I'll be out of a job, which will suit me fine."

Zavala chuckled. "Thanks again for watching our backs in Tijuana."

"In return for risking an international incident by bringing a sniper team across the border, maybe you'll tell me what in God's name is going on."

"I wish I knew," Zavala said with a shrug. "What's the story on Pedralez?"

"He was in his armored car going through Colonia Obrera, a cutthroat neighborhood west of Tijuana. He's got bodyguards in SUVs in front and behind. The lead vehicle gets hit first. A second later Pedralez's car explodes. It must have been slammed real hard because that thing was built like a tank. The driver of the third vehicle does a quick U-turn and gets the hell out."

"An antitank missile would have done the job."

Gomez affixed Zavala with dark, probing eyes. "The Mexican police found the loader for a Swedish Gustav antitank missile in an alley."

"The Swedes are attacking Mexican drug lords?"

"I *wish.* The hardware is available on the world arms market. They're probably giving them away on the backs of cereal boxes. You can fire the thing from the shoulder. They tell me two guys can get off six rounds a minute. What do you know about this thing with Hanley?"

"Kurt and I had just left the building when we saw a green helicopter hovering outside Hanley's office. We went back inside and heard the blast while we were in the elevator. Some witnesses saw a flash of light. It could have been from a missile launcher."

"How many missiles does it take to wipe out a shyster? Sounds like a lawyer joke."

"I don't see Hanley laughing."

"Guy never did have a sense of humor. Talk about *overkill.* Someone really wanted him dead real bad to go through all that trouble." He paused. "Why did you go *back* into the building?"

"Kurt thought the helicopter looked like one he had seen after the explosion in the Baja."

"So you already talked with Hanley?"

Gomez might look sleepy, but he didn't miss a trick, Zavala thought.

"We asked him about the tortilla plant. He said a Sacramento business broker contacted him for a client who wanted to get a cover operation going in Mexico. Hanley hooked his client up with Pedralez."

"What was the broker's name?"

"Jones. Save your dime. He's dead."

Gomez smirked. "Don't tell me. His car blew up."

"He drove off a cliff. It was supposedly an accident."

A man in a dark blue suit came over and tapped on the car window. The agent nodded and turned back to Zavala. "They want me inside. Let's keep in touch." He switched to Spanish. "We Mexican-American chili peppers have to stick together."

"Definitely," Zavala said, opening the door to get out. "I'll be heading back to Washington. Call me at NUMA headquarters if I can be of help."

Zavala had been truthful with Gomez up to a point. He purposely hadn't mentioned Hanley's disclosure about the Mulholland Group. He doubted the FBI would blast its way through the front door warrant in hand, but he hadn't wanted to complicate his investigation. On his return to the hotel he called Los Angeles directory asssistance and tried the number he was given for the Mulholland Group. The pleasant-sounding receptionist who answered the phone gave him directions to the office. He asked the hotel concierge to arrange a rental car, and before long he was driving north to Los Angeles.

Later that morning he pulled off the Hollywood Freeway into a typical California maze of close-built residential blocks interspersed with commercial plazas. Zavala wasn't sure what he expected, but after the explosion in Baja and the bizarre deaths of Hanley and Pedralez, he was surprised to find a well-marked office in a professional building sandwiched between a Staples office supply store and a Pizza Hut.

The lobby was open and airy. The cheery receptionist who greeted him was the same one who had given him directions on the phone. He didn't have to exert his Latin charm. She readily answered questions about the company, showered Zavala with brochures, and said to call if he ever needed hydraulic engineering services. He went back out to his rental car and sat behind the wheel staring at the unassuming façade, wondering what to do next. His cell phone buzzed. Austin was calling from his office at NUMA headquarters.

"Any luck at your end?" Kurt said.

"I'm sitting outside the Mulholland Group as we speak," Zavala said. He filled him in on his findings. Austin in turn told Joe about his visit to the Garber center, his conversation with Buzz Martin, and the revelations from Max.

"You've accomplished a hell of a lot more than I have," Zavala said.

"All blind alleys so far. I'm heading to upstate New York this afternoon to see if I can clear up the mystery of the flying wing pilot. While you're in L.A. maybe you can poke around on Gogstad."

They agreed to compare notes back in Washington the next day. Zavala hung up and called information for the *Los Angeles Times.* He got through to the newsroom, where he gave his name and asked for Randy Cohen in the business section.

Moments later a boyish voice came on the phone.

"Joe Zavala, what a nice surprise! How are you?"

"I'm fine, thanks. How's the best investigative reporter west of the Mississippi?"

"Doing what I can with the limited brain cells left from our tequila sunrise days. Are you still keeping NUMA afloat?"

"As a matter of fact I'm in town on NUMA business and wondered if you could give me a hand."

"Always ready to do what I can for an old college pal."

"I appreciate that, Randy. I need some information on a California-based company. Have you ever heard of the Gogstad Corporation?"

The other end of the line went silent. Then Cohen said, "You *did* say Gogstad?'

"That's right." Joe spelled the name so there would be no mistake. "Does it ring a bell?"

"Call me back at this number," Cohen said, and abruptly clicked off. Zavala did as he was told. Cohen answered. "Sorry to cut you off. We're talking on my cell phone. Where are you?"

Zavala described his location. Cohen was familiar with the neighborhood and gave him directions to a nearby coffee bar. Zavala was sipping on his second espresso when Cohen walked in. The reporter saw Zavala sitting at the counter and gave him a big grin. He strode over and pumped his hand.

"God, you look great, Joe. Haven't changed a bit."

"Neither have you." Zavala was telling the truth. The reporter looked much the same as when they had worked together on their college newspaper. Cohen had put a few pounds on his lean frame, and his black beard was tinged with flecks of gray, but he still walked like a giant crane, and the blue eyes blinking from behind horn-rimmed glasses were as intense as ever.

Cohen ordered a double latte and herded Joe to a table removed from the others. He took a sip, pronounced the coffee a ten, then leaned forward and said in a low voice, "So tell me, old friend, what's NUMA's interest in Gogstad?"

"You probably heard about the pod of gray whales that was found dead off San Diego." Cohen nodded. "We've tracked the possible cause of death to an operation on the Baja peninsula. There was a link to the Mulholland Group. Gogstad is the parent company."

Cohen's eyes narrowed. "What *kind* of operation?"

"Don't laugh. It's a tortilla plant."

"I don't laugh at *anything* having to do with this outfit."

"Then you know it."

"*Intimately.* That's why I was stunned when you called. I've been on an investigative team digging into Gogstad for almost a year. We're going to call the story series 'The Water Pirates.' "

"I thought piracy went out with Captain Kidd."

"This is bigger than Kidd could ever have imagined."

"What turned you on to the story?"

"Dumb luck. We were looking into corporate mergers, the quiet ones that don't always make the headlines but have just as much impact on the average citizen. We started crisscrossing the same faint trail. It was like a hunter coming across snow-blown tracks in the woods again and again."

"The tracks were Gogstad's."

Cohen nodded. "It took us months to pin it down, and we still only have a partial picture. Gogstad is enormous! With holdings in the hundreds of billions, it may be the biggest worldwide conglomerate in history."

"I'll admit I don't read the *Wall Street Journal* every day, but I'm surprised I never heard of this outfit if it's as big as you say."

"Don't feel bad. They've spent millions to keep their dealings a secret. They use back-room deals, straw and dummy corporations, every trick in the book. Thank God for computers! We fed the stuff through a Geographic Information System. The GIS connects the info in the database to points on a map. The cops use the same system to keep tabs on gang connections. We've got some great graphs that show Gogstad's holdings around the world."

"Who's behind this super-corp?"

"We're pretty sure the reins of power are held by one person. Her name is Brynhild Sigurd."

Zavala had a deserved reputation as a ladies' man, so his ears perked up at the mention of a woman. "Tell me about Ms. Sigurd."

"There isn't much I *can* tell. She's never made the *Fortune* magazine list of most powerful women, although she deserves to be at the top. We do know she was born in the U.S. of Scandinavian parents, that she went to school in Europe and later started an engineering company called the Mulholland Group."

"I was just there. I should have asked to see the lady."

"It wouldn't do you any good. She's still listed as company president, but nobody sees her."

"I'm not clear on the company name. The office isn't on Mulholland Drive."

Cohen smiled indulgently. "Have you ever heard of the Owens Valley scandal?"

"It had to do with the Los Angeles water system, I believe."

"That's right. It's hard to believe today, but L.A. was just a small desert town back in the 1920s. The city needed water to grow. The nearest major source of fresh water was sleepy little Owens Valley two hundred miles to the north. L.A. quietly sent guys to the valley to buy out the water rights to the river. By the time the valley people figured out what was going on it was too late to do anything. Their water was on its way to Los Angeles."

"What happened to the Owens Valley?"

"Drained dry." He chuckled evilly. "Most of the water the taxpayers paid for went to the San Fernando Valley, not the city. A bunch of local businessmen bought land cheap there. Prices skyrocketed when water came in and made the speculators millions. The man who engineered the coup was William Mulholland."

"Interesting. How does the Mulholland Group fit in with Gogstad?"

"Mulholland was the seed company for Gogstad. Now it's a subsidiary that provides engineering services for the parent corporation."

"What exactly does Gogstad do?"

"At first they acquired interests in pipeline, energy, and construction companies. Since then they have branched out into financial institutions, insurance, media. For the last several years they've concentrated on one product: blue gold."

"I'm only familiar with the fourteen-karat stuff."

Cohen lifted the tumbler in front of him.

"Blue gold is *water?*"

"Yep." Cohen held the glass to the light like a fine wine, then took a hearty gulp. "Water is no longer a natural right, it's a commodity that can fetch a higher price than refined gas. Gogstad is the dominant player in the world water business. It has the controlling interest in water companies in one hundred and fifty countries on six continents and distributes water to more than two hundred million people. Their biggest coup was engineering passage of the Colorado River privatization bill."

"I've read something about that. Fill me in."

"The Colorado River is the main source of water for the western and southwestern states. The system has always been operated by the feds, the people who brought you the big dams and reservoirs, working with the states and cities. The bill took control away from the government and placed it in the hands of private companies."

"Privatization is pretty common these days. You've got private companies running prisons. Why not water systems?"

"Exactly the argument advanced for the bill. The states have been fighting over water rights for years. Tons of money have been spent on lawsuits. The proponents said privatization would end this. Water would be distributed more efficiently. The investors would shoulder the costs of big capital improvements. What pushed it into the win column was the drought. Cities are running out of water, and people are scared."

"Where does Gogstad fit in?"

"The way it was set up, the Colorado River system would be run by a bunch of separate companies working together."

"Spreading the wealth?"

"That was the idea. Only problem is, every one of these companies is secretly owned by Gogstad."

"So Gogstad has control of the Colorado River?"

He nodded. "They've been doing the same thing on a smaller scale all over the country. They've got contracts to extract glacier water in Alaska. They've expanded their reach into Canada, which has the major sources of water in North America. They've nailed down control of most of British Columbia's water. Before long the Great Lakes will become Gogstad reservoirs."

Zavala let out a low whistle. "That's scary, but it fits right in with globalization, the concentration of economic power in fewer hands."

"Sure. Taking ownership of a country's most precious resource is entirely legal whether we like it or not. But Gogstad doesn't play by the rules, and that's even scarier."

"What do you mean?"

"I'll give you one example. Congressman Jeremy Kinkaid fought the Colorado River bill tooth and nail and was threatening congressional hearings to rescind the legislation. He died in an accident."

"Lots of people die in accidents."

The reporter extracted a map of the world from his pocket and unfolded it on the table. Speaking almost in a whisper, he said, "See these red squares? Don't bother counting them. There are dozens."

"Gogstad acquisitions?"

"In a manner of speaking. As Gogstad expanded it ran into established players, the companies and municipalities that controlled the water in other countries. In many cases a rival resisted Gogstad's overtures." He tapped the map. "We correlated the data on the acquisitions with information on company personnel. Every place where you see a red square the acquisition coincided with fatal 'accidents' among the corporate hierarchy. Sometimes top executives simply disappeared."

"Either Gogstad is using street gang methods or it is very lucky."

"You figure it out. In the past ten years it has assimilated transnational water companies in France, Italy, Britain, and South America. It's like the Borg, that alien race in *Star Trek* that grows in power by absorbing other species into its collective. It's acquired water concessions in Asia and South Africa—" Cohen stopped his breathless recitation. His eyes darted to the door. He relaxed when a woman and a child walked in.

Zavala raised a brow, but he said nothing.

"Sorry," Cohen said. "This whole thing has me as paranoid as hell."

"A little paranoia can be a healthy thing, my friend."

Cohen dropped his voice to a whisper again. "We may have a mole in the news department. That's why I had you call on my cell phone." He fidgeted nervously with his spoon. "A lot of weird stuff has been happening at the paper."

"What kind of stuff?"

"Nothing I can put my finger on. Files out of the order you put them in. Strangers in the building. Odd glances."

"Are you sure it's not your imagination?"

"Others on the team have noticed the funny stuff, too. Hell. Are my jitters *that* obvious?"

"You're even making *me* nervous."

"Good, I *want* you to be nervous. I don't think Gogstad would think twice about getting rid of anyone standing in the way of its goal."

"Which is?"

"It's clear to me that they want to control the world's fresh water supply."

Zavala pondered the pronouncement. "That's a tall order. What they've done in North America and Europe is pretty impressive, but can any one company corner the world's fresh water?"

"It's not as hard as you might think. Fresh water is less than one half of one percent of the world's total water stock. What remains is seawater, or it's locked up in ice caps or in the ground. A lot of our water is too polluted to use, and the world needs more of it every day."

"But isn't most of that water still controlled by all sorts of people and governments?"

"No more. Gogstad locates a likely water source, then offers to run it, making all sorts of generous concessions. Once it has its foot in the door it uses bribery, extortion, or more to convert it to private ownership. In the past five years Gogstad has stepped up the pace of privatization tremendously. It's been helped by the fact that under the new international trade agreements, a country no longer owns its water. For Godsakes, Joe, this is Owens Valley all over again, but it's happening worldwide!"

"Your megacompany sounds like a very big octopus."

"Nice analogy even if it is a little cliché." He took a red grease pencil from his pocket and drew lines and arrows on the map. "Here are your tentacles. Water will flow from Canada and Alaska to China. From Scotland and Austria it will go to Africa and the Mideast. Australia has contracts to export water to Asia. On the surface separate interests are involved. But Gogstad calls the shots through its shadow corporations."

"How do they intend to move all that water?"

"A Gogstad company has already developed the technology to transport millions of gallons across the oceans in huge sealed bags. In addition, Gogstad shipyards have been building fifty-thousand-gross-ton tankers that can serve double duty hauling oil and water."

"That's got to be pretty expensive."

"They say water flows uphill to money. The customers will pay any price. Most of it won't quench the thirst of some poor bastard scratching a living in a dust bowl. It's for high tech, one of the biggest polluters, incidentally."

"The whole thing is incredible."

"Hold on to your seat, Joe, because that's only part of it." He tapped the map of North America with his finger. "Here's the big market. The U.S.A. Remember what I said about Gogstad controlling the Canadian water supply? There's a plan to divert massive quantities of water from Hudson Bay through the Great Lakes to the U.S. Sun Belt." His finger moved to Alaska. "California and the other desert states have sucked the Colorado River practically dry, so another scheme would take glacier water from the Yukon and move it to the American West through a vast system of dams, dikes, and giant reservoirs. A tenth of British Columbia would be flooded, and there would be massive natural resource and human disruptions. The new hydroelectric plants would garner huge amounts of energy. Guess who is strategically placed to benefit from the energy and construction money?"

"I think I know the answer."

"Uh-huh. They'll reap billions! The plans for this boondoggle have been around for years. They've never advanced because they're so destructive and expensive, but they are getting some powerful support, and there's a chance they'll go through."

"Gogstad again?"

"*Now* you're getting it," Cohen said. He was becoming more excited. "This time the opposition won't be there. Gogstad has bought up newspapers and TV stations. It can create a drumbeat that won't be easy to resist. The political clout Gogstad can bring to bear is phenomenal. They've got ex-presidents, prime ministers, secretaries of state on their boards. There's no way to fight it. You put that kind of political and financial clout in the hands of someone willing to use street gang methods, and you'll know why I'm so damned nervous."

He stopped to catch his breath. His face was flushed with excitement. Beads of sweat glistened on his forehead. He stared at Zavala as if daring him to argue with him.

Then Cohen's whole body seemed to deflate. "Sorry," he apologized. "I've been close to this mess for too long. I think I'm on the verge of a nervous breakdown. This is the first chance I've had to get it out of my system."

Zavala nodded. "The sooner the story is published, the better. How soon before you run it?"

"Soon. We're putting the final pieces in place. We want to know why Gogstad has built so many supertankers."

"That certainly fits in with their plans to ship bulk water."

"Yes, we know they have the contracts in place to move glacier water from Alaska, but we've crunched the numbers. There are far too many tankers for the existing market, even if you add China."

"It takes a while to build a ship. Maybe they want to be ready. They'll mothball the ships until the time is ripe."

"That's the strange thing. These ships aren't being mothballed. Each tanker has a captain and a crew. They're just sitting in Alaskan waters as if they're waiting."

"Waiting for *what?*"

"That's what we would like to know."

"Something's going on," Zavala murmured.

"My reporter's nose for news says the same thing."

Zavala got a cold feeling as if one of those slimy tentacles they talked about had tapped him on the shoulder. He recalled the conversation he had had with Austin about the unseen fears that sometimes come beneath the sea. As usual, Kurt's intuition was on the mark. Zavala's own instincts were telling him that a big, hungry something lay hidden in the blue shadows, watching and waiting. And its name was Gogstad.

23

CIA DIRECTOR ERWIN LEGRAND beamed proudly as his fourteen-year-old daughter, Katherine, trotted over on the back of her chestnut gelding. She slipped out of the saddle and presented her father with the trophy for first place, English style.

"This is for your office, Dad," she said with excitement in her cornflower-blue eyes. "It's for being the best father in the world. You're the one who bought me Val and paid for all those expensive riding lessons."

LeGrand took the trophy and put his arm around his daughter's shoulders, thinking how much she looked like her mother. "Thank you, Katie, but I wasn't the one who worked so hard to show Valiant who's boss." He smiled. "I'll only take it on the condition that it's on loan. As soon as I've bragged to everyone at the agency, it's going back in your trophy case with the others."

LeGrand's pride was mixed with guilt. True, he had supported his daughter's love for riding financially, but this was the first event he had attended in years. The country club photographer came over, and LeGrand posed with his daughter and her horse, wishing as he did that his wife were still alive to make the picture complete.

Katie led Val back to the stable, and LeGrand ambled across the field, chatting with his assistant, a plain but extremely intelligent woman named Hester Leonard. LeGrand was sometimes likened in press reports to a beardless Lincoln, a comparison based on his reputation for honesty and his resemblance to the sixteenth president. He was tall and homely, but there was no mistaking the character etched into his large features. He had earned a reputation for integrity in running the world's largest intelligence-gathering organization, and in another age with no TV and sound bites, he would have been considered seriously as a candidate for president.

Leonard's cell phone buzzed, and she put it to her ear. "Sir," she said hesitantly, "call for you from Langley."

LeGrand scowled, muttering under his breath about no peace for the wicked. He made no motion to take the phone. "Didn't I ask that I *not* be disturbed for two hours while I was in McLean unless it was extremely urgent?"

"It's John Rowland, and he says it *is* of utmost importance."

"Rowland? Well, in that case . . . " He took the phone and stuck it in his ear. "Hello, John," he said, frown changing to a smile. "No apology needed. You're just in time to hear the good news. Katie won first place in English riding at the country club. . . . Thank you. Now, what's so important that it interrupts possibly the most important moment of Katie's life?"

LeGrand's brow furrowed. "No, I've never heard of it . . . yes, of course . . . wait for me in my office."

He handed the phone to his aide, looked at the trophy, and shook his head. "Tell the car to come around and pick me up immediately at the stable. We've got to get back to Langley immediately. Then put a call in to my office and tell them to render any assistance that John Rowland asks for. I've got to say my good-byes and make amends. Hell, this will probably cost me another horse." He loped off to offer his apologies to his daughter.

Twenty minutes later the black limo squealed to a halt in front of CIA headquarters. LeGrand got out, striding through the lobby on his long legs. An assistant met him inside the door. He snatched the folder from his aide's hand and scanned the material in the elevator. Moments later he stepped into his office. John Rowland was waiting with a nervous young man he introduced as a fellow analyst named Browning.

Rowland and the director shook hands like the old friends they were. Years before, both were at the same level in the agency. But LeGrand had political ambition and the drive to climb to the top of the ladder. Rowland was content to stay in his post where he was known as a mentor for the young analysts coming through the ranks. LeGrand put unquestioning faith in Rowland, who on more than one occasion had saved his boss from stepping into a cow flap.

"I just read the material you got off the database. What's your take on it?"

Rowland lost no time outlining his analysis.

"This thing can't be stopped?" LeGrand said.

"The protocol has been activated. The sanction will be carried out to the end."

"*Damn!* Heads are going to roll when I'm through. Who's the target?"

Rowland handed him a sheet of paper. LeGrand read the name on it, and the color drained from his face.

"Call the Secret Service. Tell them we've learned of an assassination plot against the speaker of the House. He needs protection immediately. Dear God," he said. "Can anyone tell me how something like this happens?"

"We're going to have to do some digging to get all the details," Rowland said. "We only know that the protocol was triggered by simultaneous queries to the intelligence-gathering community that came from the National Underwater & Marine Agency."

"*NUMA?*" The air over LeGrand's head crackled blue as he gave an impressive demonstration of his renowned skill for inventive expletive. He slammed his big hand down on the desk with enough force to topple the pen from its holder and yelled at the nearest assistant. "Get James Sandecker on the phone."

24

"WE'RE ABOUT TWENTY MINUTES from Albany," Buzz Martin said.

Austin looked out the window of Martin's two-engine Piper Seneca. The visibility was as unlimited as when they had left Baltimore earlier that afternoon. Austin could practically read the names on the boats dotting the upper reaches of the Hudson River.

"Thanks again for the lift. My partner Joe Zavala usually chauffeurs me around on these junkets, but he's still in California."

Martin gave Austin a thumbs-up sign. "Hell, I'm the one who should be thanking *you*. I'm sure you could have got up here on your own."

"Probably, but my motives are not unselfish. I need you to identify your father."

Martin glanced off at the Catskill Mountains to the west. "I wonder if I'll even recognize him after all these years. It's been a long time. He could have changed a lot." A cloud passed over his sunny features. "Damn, ever since you called and asked me to fly you up here, I've been trying to figure out what I'm going to say to him. I don't know whether to hug him or hit the old bastard."

"You might shake his hand for starters. Taking a swing at your long-lost father is no way to start a family reunion."

Martin chuckled. "Yeah, you're right. But I can't stop being angry with him. I want him to tell me why he left my mother and me and why he stayed hidden all these years, making us think he was dead. Good thing my mother is gone. She was an old-fashioned girl, and it would have killed her to think she had married while her first husband was still alive. Hell," he said with a catch in his voice, "I just hope I don't start bawling."

He picked up the microphone and called the Albany control tower for landing instructions. Within minutes they were on the ground.

The car rental counter had no lines, and before long they were driving out of the city in a four-wheel-drive Pathfinder. Austin headed southwest on Route 88 toward Binghamton through rolling hills and small farms. About an hour from Albany he left the main highway and drove north to Cooperstown, an idyllic village whose neat main street looked like a set from a Frank Capra movie. From Cooperstown they headed west on a winding two-lane country road. This was James Fenimore Cooper's Leatherstocking country, and with a little imagination Austin could picture Hawkeye skulking through the wooded valleys with his Indian companions. Towns and houses grew even farther apart. In this part of the world the cows outnumbered the people.

Even with a map it was hard to find the place they were looking for. Austin stopped at a gas station–general store, and Buzz went in for directions. When he came out he was clearly excited.

"The old-timer in there says he's known Bucky Martin for years. 'Nice fella. Pretty much keeps to himself.' Go up this road a half a mile and turn left. The farm is about five miles from there."

The road became narrow and bumpy, the tarmac almost an afterthought. The farms alternated with thick patches of woods, and they almost missed the turnoff. The only marker was an aluminum mailbox with no name or number on it. A dirt drive ran past the mailbox into the woods. They turned onto the driveway and passed through a copse of trees that shielded the house from the highway. Eventually the trees gave way to pastures where small herds of cows grazed. Finally, at least a half a mile from the road, they came upon the farmhouse.

The big two-story building was built in an era when three generations lived together to work a farm. The decorative windows and stained glass indicated that the owner had been successful enough to afford extra touches. A porch ran across the front. Behind the house was a red barn and silo. Next to the barn was a corral with two horses in it. A fairly new pickup truck was parked in the yard.

Austin swung into the circular driveway and parked in front of the house. No one came out to greet them. There was no curious face in the windows.

"Maybe you should let me go first," Austin suggested. "It might help if I do a little prep work before you meet face-to-face."

"That's fine," Buzz said. "I'm losing courage fast."

Austin squeezed Martin's arm. "You'll be fine." He didn't know what he would have done in the man's place. He doubted he would have been as calm. "I'll check him out and break it to him gradually."

"I appreciate that," Martin said.

Austin left the car, went up to the front door, and knocked several times. No one answered. Nor was there a response when he twisted the knob of the old doorbell. He turned around and threw his hands apart so Martin could see. He descended the porch and walked behind the house to the barn. The only sound was the soft clucking of chickens and the occasional grunt from a rooting pig.

The barn door was open. He walked inside, thinking that barns smelled the same the world over, an unmistakable combination of manure, hay, and big animals. A horse snorted as he walked by its stall, maybe thinking he was bringing it sugar, but there was no sign of Martin. He called out a hello and when there was no response walked out the back door. The chickens and hogs came over to their fences, thinking he had food for them. A lone hawk wheeled in the sky. Austin turned and stepped back into the barn.

"Can I help you?"

The figure of a man was framed in silhouette.

"Mr. Martin?" Austin asked.

"That's me. Who're you?" the man said. "Speak loud, son. My hearing isn't what it used to be."

The man took a few steps closer. Unlike his shorter, compact-built son, Martin was a big man with a hard-looking body. He could have posed for a tractor ad. He was dressed in tan shirt and pants, thick-soled workboots, and a soiled Caterpillar baseball hat that covered snow-white hair. His face was dark from the sun and deeply creased. Blue eyes looked out from under frosty brows. Austin guessed that he was in his well-preserved seventies or eighties. He was chewing on the stub of a cigar.

"My name is Kurt Austin. I'm with the National Underwater and Marine Agency."

"What can I do for you, Mr. Austin?"

"I'm looking for Bucky Martin, who was a test pilot back in the late fifties. Might that be you?"

The blue eyes seemed to gleam with amusement at a secret joke. "Yep, that's me."

Austin wondered if he should get right to it and tell the old man his son had come to see him. The old man spoke.

"You come alone?" Martin said.

It was an odd question, and it set an alarm bell off in Austin's brain. Something about this guy wasn't right. The old man didn't wait for an answer. He went outside, where he had a view of the rental car. Apparently satisfied at what he saw, he dropped the cigar and ground it with the heel of his boot, then came back into the barn. Austin wondered what had happened to Buzz.

"Gotta be careful with smokes around all this dry hay," he said with a grin. "How'd you find me?"

"We went through some old government files, and your address popped up. How long have you run this farm?"

Martin sighed. "Seems like it's been forever, son, and maybe it has been. There's nothing like tilling the land and taking care of livestock to let you know why people got off the farm as fast as they could in the old days. Damned hard work. Well, looks like my sentence is about to end, though I didn't think you'd come this soon."

Austin was puzzled. "You were *expecting* me?"

Martin stepped to one side and reached behind the gate of a stall. He pulled out a double-barreled shotgun and leveled it at Austin's midsection. "I got a telephone call just like the protocol said I would. I wouldn't move if I were you. My sight isn't what it used to be, but I can see you real well from here."

Austin stared at the shotgun's yawning black muzzle. "Maybe you should put that thing down before it goes off accidentally."

"Sorry, son, I can't do that," Martin said. "And don't try for the pitchfork stuck in that bale, I'd cut you in half before you took one step. Like I said, it's that damned protocol calling the shots, not me."

"I still don't understand what you're talking about."

"Of course you don't. The protocol's been around probably since before you were born. Don't suppose it will do any harm to let you know what it's all about before I kill you."

Austin's heart ratcheted up a beat. He was defenseless. All he could do was stall for time. "I think you've made a mistake."

"No mistake. That's why I asked what you were doing here. I didn't want to shoot some tourist who just dropped by to buy some eggs. The fact that you were looking for Martin shows you're here to stop me."

"Stop you from *what?*"

"Carrying out my contract."

"I don't know anything about any contract, but are you telling me you're *not* Martin?"

"Heck no. I killed him a long time ago."

"Why? He was just a test pilot."

"Nothing personal, just like with you. I worked for the OSS

under Wild Bill Donovan. I was what they'd call a hit man today. I pulled a few assignments after the war, then told them I wanted to retire. The boss said there was no way they could let me do that. I knew too much. So we worked out a deal. They'd keep me active for one more job. The only problem was, they didn't know when the order would be carried out. It could be five months or five years." He chuckled. "No one figured it would go on this long, especially me."

Austin noticed that Martin had lost his folksy farm accent.

"Who were you supposed to kill?"

"The government had this big secret they didn't want anyone to know about. They devised a system so that if anyone started snooping and got too close, the protocol would be activated. Here's the real clever thing. They would make potential opposition come to *me.* They set me up here in the middle of nowhere. When you started poking around, it triggered a series of commands. One would tell you where I was. The last would tell me to carry out the original sanction against the speaker of the House. Seems he heard about the government's secret and was going to blow the whistle."

"This protocol you're talking about must be fifty years old. The congressman you were supposed to kill has been dead for years."

"That doesn't matter," he said with a shake of his head. "I'm still under orders. Sad thing, that secret's so old it probably doesn't make a difference one way or the other." He lapsed back into his farm accent, and the blue eyes grew hard and cold. "Sure glad you came, son. I'm officially retired after this."

The gun came up. Austin braced himself for the deafening blast. He tensed his stomach muscles as if by sheer will he could prevent the slug from tearing into his rib cage. Had he time to think about it, he would have ruminated on the irony, after surviving countless near-fatal assignments, of dying at the hands of a half-deaf, near-blind, octogenarian assassin.

A figure suddenly materialized behind Martin. It was Buzz. The old man's sight was still keen enough for him to detect an involuntary change in Austin's expression. He whirled around as Buzz cried out in surprise.

"You're not my father!"

The old man's body had shielded the shotgun, but now Buzz's eyes dropped from Martin's face to the weapon in his arms. The farmer brought his gun up to his shoulder, but his reflexes were dulled by the years. Austin had to make a split-second decision. He could put his head down and crash into the man's backside like an enraged bull. Not enough time, he decided

"Martin!" he yelled, at the same time yanking the pitchfork from the bale.

The farmer turned back to Austin, who whipped the pitchfork at him like a javelin. He was aiming for Martin's shooting side, but the old man stepped into the oncoming pitchfork and the tines perforated his heart and lungs. He cried out in pain, and the shotgun went off, barrel pointed toward the roof. The horse went crazy and tried to kick down its stall. The gun fell from Martin's fingers. His eyes rolled into his head, and he crumpled to the wooden floor.

Austin kicked the shotgun out of reach more out of habit than necessity. Buzz had been frozen with shock, but now he came over and knelt by the body. Austin turned it over so they could see the face.

Buzz studied the man's features for a moment and, to Austin's relief, softly said, "No, he's definitely not my father. He's too tall, to begin with. My father was stocky like me And the face is all wrong. Who in God's name is he?"

"He called himself Martin, but that's not his real name. I don't know what it is."

"Why was he trying to kill you—I mean, both of us?"

"He didn't really know. He was like one of those trick bombs the Germans used to drop. They'd go off when the bomb squad tried to defuse them. By the way, I thought you were going to wait in the car."

"I tried, but I had to get out and walk. I went behind the

house, didn't see anybody, so I came into the barn looking for you."

"I'm glad you did." Austin cocked his ear. "I think I hear something." He took a last look at the body. "Happy retirement, Bucky," he said, and walked toward the door.

Buzz followed him out into the yard as a black-and-white car with blue roof dome flashing burst from the woods and squealed to a stop in a cloud of dust. Printed in big letters on the car door was the word SHERIFF. Two men in blue uniforms got out. One was burly and young, and the other was slim and gray-haired. The younger man came over with his hand on his holster. His badge signified he was a deputy sheriff.

"Which one of you is Austin?" he said.

"That's me," Kurt said.

The deputy must have been prepared for an evasion because he didn't seem to know what to say next.

The older man gently pushed his deputy aside. "I'm Sheriff Hastings. Either one of you seen Bucky Martin?"

"He's in the barn," Austin said.

The deputy hustled into the barn, and when he came out a moment later his face was white.

"Jeezus," he said, fumbling for his sidearm, "Old Bucky is dead. Stuck with a pitchfork. Which one of you two did it?"

Hastings gestured for his deputy to calm down and call the county homicide team. "Could you tell me what's been going on, Mr. Austin?"

"Martin tried to kill us with that shotgun next to the body. I had to kill him. I was trying to slow him down, but that's not the way it worked out."

"Thanks, but I mean what's *really* going on with this whole thing, me getting calls from Washington and all."

"Washington?"

"You bet. First the governor's office calls and tells me to hold, then they patch through this maniac Admiral Sandecker. He says his man Austin is in danger and I'd better get out to Martin's place or there will be a killing. When I asked what makes him think somebody's going to be killed, he promises to rip me a new belly button if I don't stop asking dumb questions and get on my way." He grinned. "Guess he was right." He turned to Buzz. "What's your name?"

"Buzz Martin."

The sheriff blinked in surprise. "Any relation to the deceased?"

Austin and Martin looked at each other, not sure how to answer the question.

Finally Austin shook his head and said, "Hope you've got time, sheriff, because that's a long, long story."

25

THE DRUMS HAD BEEN BEATING steadily for an hour. The sound was cadenced at first, coming from a lone drum at the same throbbing tempo as a human heartbeat. Then other drums had joined in. The hollow thumping accelerated in pace, and a monotonous chanting could be heard in the background. Francesca paced back and forth in the throne room like a caged lion, her hands clasped behind her, head bent low in thought. The Trouts sat next to the throne, waiting patiently for Francesca to speak. Tessa had pulled her vanishing act again.

Something caused a commotion at the entrance. Seconds later Francesca's two handmaidens rushed into the throne room, threw themselves on their knees, and babbled excitedly. Calming the young Indians with her soft voice, Francesca gently lifted them to their feet and brushed their disheveled hair away from their faces. She listened to the women speak in turn, then took two bracelets made of airplane parts and slipped them onto their wrists. She kissed her attendants on the tops of their heads and sent them on their way.

Turning to the Trouts, Francesca said, "Events are moving faster than I anticipated. The women say Alaric has talked the tribe into moving against us."

Gamay frowned. "I thought they wouldn't enter your palace."

"I've always said Alaric was intelligent. He sent my servants to tell me his plans, evidently to exert psychological pressure. The drums are his work." She pointed to the ceiling. "The palace walls are clay, but the roof is made of dry grass. They will light the place on fire. He says the true gods will rise from the ashes. If we run outside to escape the flames it will prove that we're the frauds he says we are, and they will cut us down."

"Would they really harm their queen?" Gamay asked.

"It wouldn't be the first time royalty has fallen fatally out of favor. Have you forgotten Mary Queen of Scots or Anne Boleyn?"

"I get your point," Gamay said. "What do we do now?"

"We escape. Are you ready?"

"Since all we have are the clothes on our backs, we're ready when you are," Paul said. "But how are we going to get past that unruly crowd out there?"

"I still have a few white goddess tricks up my sleeve. Ah, good, Tessa is back." The Indian woman had materialized as silently as a shadow. She spoke a few words in her native language to Francesca, who answered with a nod. Tessa took one of the torches flanking the throne.

Francesca said, "Dr. Paul, if you would be so kind as to help Tessa." Trout went over and hoisted Tessa up by the waist. She was as light as a feather. Tessa tucked the torch in at an angle where the clay met the thatch. The torch had only to burn a few inches before the flame touched the ceiling. They repeated the procedure with another torch on the opposite wall.

"I don't count arson among my talents, but this crude time delay will create a distraction when we need it," Francesca said. She looked around the throne room. "Good-bye," she said sadly to no one in particular. "In some ways I'll miss being a queen." She turned to Tessa, and they talked heatedly. When the discussion was ended Tessa had a satisfied look on her face. Francesca sighed heavily. "You see what's happening? My subjects are already rebelling. I ordered Tessa to stay, but she wants to go with us. We don't have time to argue further. Follow me."

Francesca led the way along the dim passageways to her bedroom. The two woven bags on the bed explained Tessa's temporary absence. She had been packing for their escape. Francesca removed her battered aluminum suitcase from the wooden chest. It had been rigged with a strap which she threw over her shoulder. Handing one bag to Paul and the other to Gamay, Francesca said that the containers held food and supplies and "a few essentials."

Gamay looked around the windowless room. "Where do we go from here?" The sound of drums was muffled, but the beating was more frenetic.

"We take a shower, of course," Francesca said.

She lit a small clay lamp from the torch, went over to the shower stall, and pulled up the polished wooden floor to reveal a rectangular opening.

"There's a ladder. It's very steep. Be careful."

She descended first so the others could climb down by lamplight. They were crowded together in a small space, standing on the gravel drain that had been used to catch water from the shower. A passage led off into the darkness.

"My apologies to you, Dr. Paul. I wasn't expecting someone as tall. We've been digging this tunnel for years, carrying the dirt out in small amounts and secretly disposing of it. This passageway runs into a covered trench I had the men build years ago for future waterworks."

With Paul stooping low to keep from bumping his head, they half walked, half crawled along the passageway. The floor and walls had been smoothed, and evenly spaced beams supported the ceiling. Francesca extinguished the light because of the smoke in the tight confines, and they traveled in darkness. After about fifty feet the tunnel angled into another, slightly bigger passageway.

"This is the water works," Francesca said in hushed tones. "We must be silent. The tunnel is only a couple of feet below ground, and the Chulo have sharp ears."

Using a primitive fire starter similar to the one carried by Tessa's half-brother, Francesca got the lamp going again and they forged ahead. They made slow progress, but after about fifteen minutes the tunnel came to an end. Francesca motioned for Paul to squeeze up beside her. She pulled a small spade from her bag and chopped away at the blank dirt wall until the blade hit something with a thud.

"I'll need your strength again, Dr. Paul. Push against this hatch. I don't think anyone is at the river, but be cautious."

She backed off to give Paul more room. He put his shoulder against the wood, braced himself, and shoved, gradually increasing the pressure until he felt the wood give. He pushed harder. The circular cover opened a few inches. Paul peered through the narrow space with one eye and saw water. With a final shove he popped the hatch off.

The opening was in the side of a grassy embankment. He slithered through the hole, then helped the others climb out. Moving from the cool, dark tunnel into the hot sunlight was a shock, and they blinked their eyes like moles. Paul replaced the hatch. While the others covered the opening he slid on his stomach to the top of the bank and peered over the edge.

The stockade fence and its grim decorations were a short distance away. The tunnel had passed right under it. A tall, billowing plume of black smoke rose from beyond the fence. What sounded like a flock of wild birds could be heard. As he listened the bird cries became human voices. He slid back down.

"It looks like they're having a *queenie* roast," he announced with a grin. Turning to Francesca, he added, "Don't ever tell me you don't have a talent for arson."

Francesca responded by motioning for the others to follow her along the edge of the river. They stayed low, hidden by the embankment, and after a few minutes came upon a dozen dugout canoes. They hauled two dugouts aside. Trout thought of scuttling the others, but their hulls were thick and not easily damaged.

"Anybody got a power saw?" he said. "Even a hatchet would do."

Francesca reached into her sack and came out with a covered

pot. Using a flat stone from the riverbed, she smeared the blackish yellow contents of the pot onto the other canoes. She lit the substance on fire. The wood flared into smoldering flames where she had daubed the unctuous mess.

"Greek fire," she said. "It's a combination of resin from local trees. It will burn hotter than napalm. If someone tries to put it out with water, it only makes the fire spread."

The Trouts looked on with wonder as the flames began to eat through the hulls. They knew the sabotage would help, but once the natives had discovered their scuttled craft, they could race along the well-maintained pathway that bordered the river.

They paired the stronger paddlers with weaker ones. Gamay and Francesca got in one craft. Paul and Tessa took the other. They shoved off into the river and paddled for their lives. After an hour they pulled over to the shore for a drink of water and five minutes of rest, then set off again. The paddles raised blisters on their palms as they pushed the canoes against the river current. Francesca passed around a medicinal ointment from her amazing bag, and it numbed the pain in their hands. They kept on, trying to put as many miles between them and the village as possible before daylight failed.

Darkness came all too soon. Travel on the river became difficult, then impossible. The canoes became tangled in thick grass or ran aground on sandbars. They were quickly exhausting themselves and getting nowhere. They gave up and paddled closer to shore, where they dined on jerky and dried fruit. They tried unsuccessfully to sleep, but the dugouts served poorly as beds, and they were happy to see the gray light of morning.

With bleary eyes and stiff joints they set off again. The sound of drums spurred them on and made them set aside their aches and pains. The ominous drumming seemed to come from everywhere and echoed through the forest.

The canoes glided through the curtain of mist rising off the river. The smokescreen hid them from Chulo eyes, but they had to move slowly to avoid obstacles. As the sun rose it baked the mists off to a translucent haze. With the river ahead once more visible they paddled furiously until the sound of drums faded. They kept moving for another hour, not daring to stop. Before long they began to hear a different sound.

Gamay cocked her ear. "Listen," she said.

From a distance came a low roar, as if a train were speeding through the forest.

Francesca, whose serious expression had not changed since they left the village, ventured a slight smile. "The Hand of God beckons."

With spirits renewed, they forgot they were tired and hungry and that their buttocks were numb and dug their paddles in once more. The roar grew louder, but it didn't obliterate another sound, a quick *whirr* as if a river bird had taken flight, followed by a solid *tunk.*

Paul looked down in disbelief. A three-foot-long arrow was embedded in the side of his canoe. A few inches higher and it would have pierced his rib cage. He looked toward the shore. Flashes of blue-and-white-painted bodies could be seen darting between the trees. The ululating war cry filled the air.

"We're being attacked!" Paul yelled unnecessarily.

Spurred by the arrows chunking into the water around them, Gamay and Francesca were bent low over their paddles. The canoes shot forward out of range.

Their pursuers had quickly caught up, making good time following the path along the river. At one point the trail turned inland to cut through the forest. The natives had to fight their way through thick growth to get a clear shot at the canoes. They made several attempts. Each time the canoes passed beyond the range of their arrows. Even the high-tech weapons Francesca helped forge had their limitations.

It was obvious that the cat-and-mouse game soon would turn in favor of the hunters. The paddlers were bone-weary. They were missing strokes and no longer paddled in a unified rhythm. When it seemed they could go no farther, they were out of the river and onto the lake. They paused for a minute to reconnoiter and to firm up their plan. They would cross the open expanse as quickly as possible, aiming for the outlet to the main river. The impenetrable forest growth along the river would protect them from Chulo arrows.

Heartened by the straightforward scheme, they paddled with renewed vigor, staying midway between the shore and the falls. The thunder of thousands of tons of water plummeting from the five cascades was unimaginable. The canoeists could barely see each other in the fine mist that was thrown up at the base of the falls. Paul vowed to tell Gamay that he had changed his mind about building a hotel there. They came out of the mist cloud into the open lake. Four pairs of eyes scanned the dense forest looking for the outlet.

Gamay, who was in the lead canoe, pointed with her paddle toward the shore. "I see it over there, where the tree line is broken. Oh, hell—"

They all saw the source of Gamay's agitation: the flicker of blue and white as three canoes had come out of the river.

"It's a hunting party," Francesca said, squinting against the sun's reflection. "They've been away and won't know we're escaping. I'm still their queen as far as they know. I'll try to bluff my way. Head right at them."

Gamay and Paul put their misgivings aside and kept the dugouts pointed toward the newcomers. The men in the oncoming canoes showed no sign of hostility, and a couple of them even waved. There was shouting from shore. Alaric and his men had burst from the forest. They were calling and beckoning to the hunting party. The canoes hesitated, then, as the yelling grew louder, they pointed the dugouts toward land. The craft had barely touched shore when the hunters were ejected and the chase party took their place.

Their prey had taken advantage of the slight pause and paddled madly for the river, but their pursuers quickly cut down the angle.

"We can't make it to the river!" Gamay yelled. "They'll cut us off."

"Maybe we can lose them in the mists," Paul replied.

Gamay spun the dugout around and pointed the bow toward the falls. Paul and Tessa were right behind. The water became choppy as they neared the falls. The Indians doggedly kept in pursuit. With their strength and skill they were rapidly closing the gap. The falls loomed closer and the mists enveloped them, but it became apparent that they would be pounded to pieces by the falls if they got closer to the torrents.

Paul shouted over the roar. "Francesca, we need help from your bag of tricks."

Francesca shook her head.

Tessa picked up on Paul's frantic plea. "I have something," she said. She handed over the sack that had rested between her knees. Paul reached into the bag, and his fingers closed on a hard object. He pulled out a 9mm pistol.

"Where did *this* come from?" he said with astonishment.

"It was Dieter's."

Paul looked back at the oncoming canoes, then at the cascading falls. He had little choice. Regardless of Francesca's wishes that her former subjects not be hurt, they were between the devil and the deep blue sea. Arrows were flying in their direction.

Paul plunged his hand into the bag again, looking for extra rounds. This time he came out with a GlobalStar satellite phone. Dieter must have used it to keep in touch with his buyers. He stared at it a moment before the significance of the find sank in. He yelled with joy.

Gamay had moved closer and saw the phone. "Does that thing work?"

He pushed the ready light, and the phone was on. "I'll be damned." Paul handed Gamay the phone. "Give it a try. I'll see if I can scare those guys off."

Gamay punched a number out on the phone. Seconds later a familiar deep voice answered.

"Kurt!" Gamay yelled into the phone. "It's me."

"Gamay? We've been worried about you. Are you and Paul okay?"

She glanced at the oncoming canoes and swallowed hard. "We're in a hell of a mess, and that's an understatement." She had to shout over the roar of the falls. "Can't talk, I'm calling on a GlobalStar. Can you get a fix on our position?"

Crack!

Paul had laid a shot across the bow of Alaric's canoe, but it failed to slow him down.

"Was that a gun?"

"That was Paul shooting."

"Hard to hear you with that background noise. Hold on."

The seconds ticked by like years. Gamay had no illusions about her call. Even with a position fix it could be days before someone came to their aid. At least Austin would know what happened to them. Austin's voice came back on, calm and reassuring. "We've got a lock on you."

"Good. Gotta go!" Gamay answered, ducking low as an arrow whizzed past like an angry bee.

With Gamay and Paul busy, their canoes had drifted sideways to the waves. They dug their paddles in and got the boats around. Both dugouts rocked dangerously, but they moved closer to the falls where the mists might hide them.

The Indians hesitated, then, sensing the end was near, began their strange ululation. The archers were kneeling in the bow. They could stand off and let arrows fly at their helpless targets.

Paul had lost all patience. He raised the handgun and took a bead on Alaric. If he killed the leader the others might run for it. Francesca yelled. He thought she was trying to spoil his shot, but the white queen was pointing toward the top of the falls.

What looked like a huge insect flew over the crest of the falls and descended rapidly through the rainbows and the cloud of mist until it was a hundred feet above the lake. The helicopter hovered for an instant, then swooped low and buzzed the war canoes. The archers dropped their bows, grabbed their paddles, and stroked madly for shore.

Paul lowered the pistol and grinned at Gamay. They began to

paddle back toward the quieter waters of the lake. The helicopter circled around the lake, then came back and hovered above the dugouts. A smiling figure with a bushy silver mustache and deep-set eyes leaned out a side door and waved. It was Dr. Ramirez.

The phone rang. It was Austin. "Gamay, are you and Paul all right?"

"We're fine," she said, laughing with relief. "Thanks for sending the taxi. But you're going to explain how you pulled this one off. This is something, even for the great Kurt Austin."

"Tell you about it later. See you tomorrow. I need you back here. Be ready to work."

A ladder was being lowered out of the chopper.

Ramirez signaled for Francesca to go first. She hesitated, then grabbed the lower rung and, as befitting a white goddess, began to climb into the sky from which she had descended ten years before.

26

SANDY WHEELER WAS GETTING INto her Honda Civic when the strange man approached and asked in accented English how to get to the *Los Angeles Times* advertising department. Instinctively she hugged her purse close to her body and glanced around. She was relieved to see other people in the newspaper's garage. She had grown up in L.A. and was used to freaks. But she was jumpy lately handling this crazy water story, and even the cute, pearl-handled .22-caliber pistol in her pocketbook wasn't totally reassuring. The stranger looked as if he could chew the barrel off her gun with his metal teeth.

Wheeler had the reporter's ability to take in people at a glance, and what she saw was someone who looked as if he played the bad guy for the WWF. He was her height and would have been taller if he had a neck. The dark green sweatsuit was a couple of sizes too small for a square, powerful body that looked as if it had been assembled from refrigerator parts. The roundish, grinning face framed by the Prussian-cut dirty blond hair reminded her of one of the monsters in Maurice Sendak's *Where the Wild Things Are.* Only uglier. But it was the eyes that got her. The irises were so black that the pupils were practically invisible.

After giving the man hurried directions, Sandy got into her car and instantly locked the doors. She didn't care how unfriendly the gesture looked. As she backed out of her space he seemed to be in no rush to go to the advertising department. He stood there staring at her with eyes as hard as marbles. She was in her thirties, with long chestnut hair, an athletic body from jogging and working out. Her nut-brown face was taut and angular but not unattractive, dominated by large sky-blue eyes. She was pretty enough to attract occasional attention from the odd characters who seemed to drop from the palm trees around town. She was street-smart and had gained a layer of emotional calluses working as a police reporter before being assigned to the investigative team. She didn't spook easily, but this creep gave her the shivers. It went beyond appearances. There was something of the grave about him.

She checked her rearview mirror and was surprised to see that the man had disappeared. Easy come, easy go, she thought. She scolded herself for letting him sneak up on her. Growing up in L.A., she had learned early on to be aware of her surroundings at all times. This damned water story had preoccupied her, taken the edge off her alertness. Cohen had promised only a couple more days before they ran the story. Not soon enough. She was getting sick of taking the file disks home. Cohen was positively paranoid about leaving them in the building. Every night he cleaned the files off the computer and put them on backup disks. In the mornings he would load them back on.

Not that Sandy blamed him for being paranoid. There was something special about this story. The team had talked Pulitzer Prize. Cohen coordinated the work of the three reporters. Her area was the Mulholland Group and its mysterious president, Brynhild Sigurd. The other two reporters concentrated respectively on domestic acquisitions and international connections. They had access to an accountant and a lawyer. The secrecy was tighter than the Manhattan Project. The editor was aware of the story but not its scope. She sighed. The story would be out in a few days, and she could take that long vacation in Maui.

She swung out of the garage and headed to her condo in Culver City. She stopped off at a shopping plaza and picked up a bottle of California Zinfandel. Cohen was coming over later to talk about wrapping up loose ends, and she had promised to whip up a pot of penne. As she was paying the cashier she noticed someone standing in front of the window looking into the store. It was that damned metal-tooth creep, and he was smiling. This was no coincidence. The jerk must have followed her. She glared at him as she exited the store, then strode purposefully toward her car. First she dug the pistol out of the purse and tucked it in her belt. Then she called Cohen on her cell phone. He had told her to report anything unusual. Cohen wasn't there, but she left a message on his recorder saying she was on her way home and that she thought she was being followed.

Starting the car, she pulled slowly out of the plaza, then gunned the engine and shot through an intersection just as the light changed to red. The cars behind her all stopped. She knew the neighborhood well and cut through a couple of motel parking lots, then down a side street in a circular route to her apartment. Her heart was beating rapidly as she drove, but her pulse slowed to normal when she pulled up in front of the sanctuary of the condominium building. She buzzed herself into the five-story apartment building and took the elevator up to the fourth floor. She stepped out of the elevator and almost dropped her groceries in surprise. The creep was at the far end of the hallway. He stood there with that insane grin, staring at her. That did it. She put the bag on the floor, pulled her pistol from her belt, and pointed it at him.

"You come any nearer, and I'll blast your private parts off," she said.

He made no motion. If anything, the grin got wider.

She wondered how he had got there ahead of her. *Of course.* He must have known her address. While she was zigzagging in an attempt to lose him, he had simply driven directly to her apartment. That didn't explain how he had got into the building. The management was going to get an earful about the lack of security. Maybe she'd even do a story on it.

Still keeping the pistol leveled, she fumbled in her purse for her keys, opened the door, and quickly shut it. Safe at last. She put the pistol on a small table, snapped the deadbolt and chain lock, and put her eye to the peephole in the door. The creep was standing just outside, his face distorted even more grotesquely by the lens. He was holding her bag of groceries as if he were a delivery boy. The *nerve* of him. She swore lustily. She wasn't going to screw around with Cohen this time. A straight call to 911 to report she was being stalked.

She suddenly had the odd feeling that she wasn't alone.

She turned from the door and stared with unbelieving eyes, frozen with fear.

The man with the metallic teeth was standing in her way. *Impossible.* He was out in the hall. Then the answer came to her in a flash.

Twins.

The epiphany came too late. As she backed against the door he began to walk slowly toward her, his eyes glittering like black pearls.

Cohen sounded frantic on the phone.

"Joe, for Godsakes, I've been trying to reach you for an hour!"

"Sorry, I was out," Zavala apologized. "What's wrong?"

"Sandy's disappeared. The bastards have got her."

"Calm down for a minute," Zavala said evenly. "Tell me who Sandy is and these bastards you're talking about. Start from the beginning."

"Okay, okay," Cohen replied. There was a pause as he pulled himself together, and when he spoke again it was with his normal composure, although it was clear from the tenseness of his voice that panic lurked close to the surface.

"I went back to the paper. I just had a funny feeling. All our source material is missing. We kept it in a locked file. Empty."

"Who had access?"

"Just the members of the team. They're all solid. The only way someone could get them to open the files is if they had a gun at their head. Oh, God," Cohen said as the implication of his statement sank in.

Zavala could sense that he was losing Cohen.

"Tell me what happened next," he said.

Cohen took a deep breath and let it out. "Okay. Sorry. Next I checked the computer disks. Nothing. You needed a password to get into them. Everybody on the team was aware of it. We backed everything up at the end of each working day. We took turns. Sandy Wheeler, one of the reporters, took the disks home with her today. I got a message saying some guy was following her. She was in a parking lot near her condo. We were supposed to have dinner tonight, go over some material for the first installment of the story. I called when I heard her message. There was no one home. I came over. Sandy had given me a key. The grocery bag was on the table. The wine was still in it. She always puts her wine into the rack. She's compulsive about that."

"There's no sign of her?"

"Nothing. I got the hell out of there as soon as I could."

A thought came to Zavala. "What about the other reporters on your team?"

"I tried to call them. No answer. What should I do?"

Cohen probably saved his own life by going to Sandy's apartment and then leaving quickly. Those who were rolling up the investigative team had already been there, but they might check back.

"Where are you calling from? I hear music in the background."

"I'm in a leather bar near Sandy's condo." Cohen nervously laughed through his fear. "I ducked in here when I thought someone was following me and wanted to be in a public place."

"Anyone follow you inside?"

"I don't think so. This is pretty much a biker crowd. They'd stand out."

"Can you call me back in five minutes?" Joe asked.

"Yeah, but make it fast. There's a tall transvestite giving me the eye."

Zavala looked up the number Gomez had given him. Gomez answered the phone on the third try. Zavala brushed off the usual greetings.

"I'm in L.A.," he said. "I've got someone who needs to be out of circulation. Can you help? No questions now, but I promise to fill you in as soon as I can."

"Does this happen to have anything to do with the business you were involved in down here?"

"That and more. Sorry to be so mysterious. Can you help?"

Pause. Then Gomez's voice came back, all business. "We maintain a safe house in Inglewood. There's a caretaker there. I'll call and let him know to expect a package." He gave Zavala directions to the safe house.

"Thanks. Talk to you later," Joe said.

"I hope so," Gomez replied.

The phone rang as soon as he put it down. He rattled off the address Gomez had given him and told Cohen to take a taxi there. "Leave your car," he cautioned. "It might have a transmitter on it."

"*Of course.* I never thought of anything like that. Oh, jeez. I knew this thing was big. Poor Sandy and the others. I feel responsible for them."

"There was nothing else you could have done, Randy. You didn't know you were playing well out of your league."

"What the hell is going on?"

"You had it right the first time we talked," Zavala said. "Blue gold."

27

THE BLACK RUBBER BALL WAS only a meteor blur, but Sandecker had anticipated the bounce, and his light wooden racket flicked out like a serpent's tongue. The quick backhand sent the ball speeding with a sharp *thwack* against the right wall. LeGrand lunged, but he had misjudged the spin and his racket swiped clumsily at thin air.

"That's the game, I believe," said Sandecker, deftly scooping up the bouncing ball. Sandecker was a fitness and nutrition fanatic, and his strict regimen of jogging and weightlifting gave him a competitive edge over men much younger and bigger. He stood with legs wide apart, the racket resting easily in the crook of his arm. Not one drop of perspiration beaded his forehead. Nor was a single red hair out of place on his head or the precisely trimmed fiery red Van Dyke beard.

By contrast, LeGrand dripped with sweat. As he removed his eye protectors and toweled his face dry he remembered why he had stopped playing with Sandecker. The CIA director had the height and muscle advantage over Sandecker, who stood a few inches over five feet, but as he learned each time he stepped onto the court with Sandecker, squash was a game of strategy, not power. Under normal circumstances he would have put the admiral off when he called the day after the incident in New York State.

"I've reserved a court at the club," Sandecker said cheerfully. "How'd you like to bat the little black ball around for a bit?"

Despite the genial tone there was no doubt in LeGrand's mind that this was a command performance. LeGrand canceled his morning appointments and stopped at the Watergate complex to pick up his gear. Sandecker was waiting at the squash club. He was wearing a designer sweatsuit of navy blue with gold piping. But even in his casual outfit it took little imagination to picture Sandecker pacing the deck of a man o' war in a bygone day, barking commands to trim sail or unleash a broadside against a Barbary pirate. He ran NUMA the same way, keeping one eye on the changes in the wind and the other on his adversaries. Like any good commander he took a keen interest in his crew's welfare.

When he learned Austin had been put in harm's way by a cockeyed intelligence scheme he erupted in an explosion that would have put Krakatoa to shame. The CIA's involvement added to the violence of his reaction. He was fond of LeGrand, but in Sandecker's uncompromising view the Company was pampered and overfunded.

While he relished the chance to put the CIA director in the hot seat, he saw it as more than an opportunity to vent his spleen. Sandecker wasn't above political chicanery. He was quite adept at it, in fact. One of his more valuable talents was the ability to stay ahead of his anger and use it to get his way. Targets of his rage had no idea that behind his laser-hot fury he was often serene, even joyful. His ability served him well. Presidents of both parties deferred to him. Senators and congressmen went out of their way to cultivate his acquaintance. Cabinet members instructed their staff to put through his phone calls without question.

LeGrand had readily accepted the admiral's invitation for a match because he was drenched with guilt over the incident in New York and welcomed the opportunity to make amends, even if it meant being humiliated on the squash court. To his surprise, Sandecker had greeted him with a smile and hadn't mentioned the incident throughout their play. He even offered to buy the first round at the juice bar.

"Thanks for the match on such short notice," Sandecker said with his famous alligator smile.

LeGrand sipped his papaya juice and shook his head. "One of these days maybe I'll beat you."

"Your backhand needs some work first," Sandecker offered. "By the way, while I have your ear, I'd like to thank you for averting a potential tragedy involving my man Austin."

This might not be as bad as he expected, LeGrand thought.

Sandecker maintained his disconcerting smile. "Pity you didn't get someone to respond more quickly," he said. "You might have been able to save your asset." He put heavy emphasis on the first syllable of the last word.

LeGrand groaned inwardly. It was obvious Sandecker was going to worry this one like a puppy with a bone.

Ignoring the play on words, the director said, "I'm sorry about that regrettable episode. The full extent of this, er, problem wasn't apparent at first. It was a very complex situation."

"So I hear," Sandecker said lightly. "Tell you what I'm going to do, Erwin. I will forget for the time being that a screwball scheme hatched by the OSS and carried out by the CIA went awry, almost killing the head of the NUMA Special Assignments Team and an innocent bystander and placing the speaker of the House in jeopardy."

"You're very gracious, James," LeGrand said.

Sandecker nodded. "No details of this schoolboy spy prank will ever go beyond the walls of NUMA."

"The Agency appreciates your discretion," LeGrand said.

Sandecker raised a red eyebrow. "You're not entirely off the hook," he said archly. "In exchange I want a full accounting of this sordid affair."

LeGrand knew there would be a quid pro quo. There always was with Sandecker. He had already decided to lay his cards out on the table.

"You're certainly justified in demanding an accounting," he agreed.

"I think so," Sandecker said agreeably.

"It was quite a task to piece this story together, especially on such short notice, but I'll do my best to explain what happened."

"Or thankfully in this case," Sandecker said, "what *didn't* happen."

LeGrand smiled wanly. "The end of World War II is the beginning of the story. With Germany defeated, the Allied coalition fell apart. Churchill came out with his Iron Curtain speech, and the stage was set for the cold war. The U.S. was still complacent because it was the only country that had the bomb. That smugness was eroded when the Soviets exploded their own nuclear device, and the arms race was on. We gained headway with the hydrogen bomb. But the Russians were breathing down our necks, and it was clearly a matter of time before the Soviets gained parity. As you know, the hydrogen bomb utilized a different process to create an explosion."

"The thermonuclear bomb uses fusion rather than fission," said Sandecker, who was well versed in atomic physics, having served on nuclear-powered submarines. "Atoms are joined rather than split apart."

LeGrand nodded. "The hydrogen atom was fused with the helium atom. The sun and other stars use the same process to create their energy. Once it became known that the main Soviet fusion lab was in Siberia there was talk in our government of sabotage. Hubris was still strong after defeating the Axis, and some people talked nostalgically of the commando raid on the heavy-water plant in Norway. You're familiar with that mission, of course."

"You mean the plant that was producing an isotope needed for the production of a German A-bomb," Sandecker said.

"That's right. The raid delayed the German effort."

"A similar commando raid in Siberia would have been an ambitious undertaking, to say the least."

"As a matter of fact, it would have been *impossible,*" LeGrand said. "The Norway raid was incredibly difficult to launch, even with accessibility and strong partisan support. There was another consideration as well."

Sandecker, who tended to see situations from a global perspective, said, "Germany was at war with the Allies at the time of the Norway raid. The U.S.S.R. and the U.S. had not declared open hostilities. Both sides were careful to avoid direct military confrontation. A raid on a Soviet laboratory would be considered an overt act of war that could not be ignored."

"That's correct. It would be no different from the Russians destroying a lab in New Mexico. It could have provoked a shooting war."

Sandecker was not exactly innocent when it came to making end runs around politically dicey situations. "A raid might be feasible, but it would have to be an ironclad secret with no way to trace it."

LeGrand nodded. "That was precisely what the president said when the situation was presented to him."

"A tall order indeed," Sandecker noted.

"Granted, but these were not ordinary men. They had created the greatest military industrial machine in history virtually from scratch and ruthlessly used it to squash two formidable foes on several continents and seas. But even all their determination and resourcefulness wasn't up to this challenge. Fortunately for them, two unconnected developments intersected and showed them the way. The first was the development of the aircraft that came to be known as the flying wing. The design had its problems, but there was one unplanned characteristic that made it very attractive. Stealth technology. The plane's slim silhouette and clean surface meant that under the right circumstances it could slip undetected past radar."

"My guess is that you're talking about *Russian* radar," Sandecker said.

LeGrand smiled mysteriously. "Supposedly all flying wings, including those still in production, were destroyed by the Air Force. But the president gave the go-ahead for a modified version to be built in secret. It had even greater range and speed than any of the original models. In short, here was a delivery system that could get in and out of Siberia without being detected."

"In my experience the Russians are not a dull people," Sandecker said. "If their lab went up in smoke they would surmise the U.S. was behind it."

"Undoubtedly, which is why the second part of the equation was crucial," LeGrand said. "That was the discovery of anasazium. It was a by-product of the work at Los Alamos. The scientist who discovered the substance was an amateur anthropologist. He was fascinated by the old Pueblo culture that once lived in the Southwest. He named his discovery after the Anasazi. The material has a number of interesting properties. The one that attracted the most interest was its ability to change the hydrogen atom in subtle ways. If anasazium could be secretly introduced into a Soviet weapons lab, it might mess up the fusion research. Estimates were that it would hamstring their bomb project by several years. The U.S. would gain time to build an intercontinental bomber and missile fleet so advanced that the Soviets would never catch up. The plan was to float bombs down on parachutes. They would explode, and release the substance in liquid form, which would get into the lab's ventilation systems. By itself the substance is not any more harmful than water to humans. Those under attack would think they heard a very strange thunderstorm of extremely short duration."

"It doesn't sound exactly like pinpoint bombing."

"It wasn't. As they say, desperate times call for desperate measures."

"What if the plane crashed for some mechanical reason?"

"That possibility was taken into account. There was no poison pill like the one Francis Gary Powers *didn't* take after his U-2 crash. They wanted no talkative survivors. No parachutes were packed for the crew. In fact, it would have been impossible to parachute from the plane. Ejection seats had not yet been developed, and the pilot's canopy could not be jettisoned. If wreckage were found it could always be said that this was an experimental plane tragically gone off-course."

"The crew knew this?"

"They were highly motivated volunteers with no sense of failure."

"Too bad the plan failed," Sandecker said.

"To the contrary," LeGrand said. "The mission was an unqualified success."

"How so? The Soviets built a hydrogen bomb close on our heels, as I recall."

"Quite true. They exploded their first thermonuclear device in 1953, two years after the U.S. Remember what I said about hubris. Our people couldn't imagine that an ignorant peasant like Stalin could outsmart them. He was extremely suspicious of everyone. He ordered Igor Kurchatov, the Soviet equivalent of our man Oppenheimer, to set up a duplicate hydrogen research lab in the Ural Mountains. Their research was successful. Stalin thought the Siberian lab had failed on purpose and ordered its technicians liquidated."

"I'm surprised a strike wasn't ordered into the Ural operation."

"A raid was contemplated, but the mission was canceled. Maybe it was considered too dangerous, or perhaps the flying wing had insurmountable technical problems."

"What happened to the plane?"

"It was sealed in its hangar with the cargo. The Alaskan base it flew from was abandoned. The men at the base were scattered all over the globe. None of them had a complete picture of the operation. That was almost the end of it."

"*Almost*. You mean the protocol and the killing of the pilot?"

LeGrand stirred uncomfortably in his chair. "That and more. Actually the entire flight crew was killed," he said quietly. "They were the only nonpolitical types who knew the mission and the target intimately. Four men died. Their families were told they were in an accident. They were buried with full military honors at Arlington."

"A lovely gesture."

LeGrand nervously cleared his throat. "You all know that I've done my best to clean things up at the Agency. Sometimes I'll scrape off one layer of dirt to reveal another even more filthy. Unfortunately much of the good work we've done has gone unheralded for obvious reasons. But the intelligence community did some things that are nothing to be proud of. This sad episode was one of them."

"Austin filled me in on his findings. The pilot was at Arlington attending his own funeral. I understand his son saw him."

"He insisted that he be allowed one more look at his wife and child," the director said. "He was told he was going into protective custody for an indefinite time. Of course it was only a ruse. Shortly after he was placed under protection, he was killed by his protector."

"The man who lived in upstate New York."

"That's right."

Sandecker's blue eyes hardened. "Sorry I don't feel any sadness for the assassin. He was a cold-blooded killer at an age when we supposedly attain wisdom. And he would have murdered Austin. What was the reason for the protocol? Wasn't murdering those crewmen enough?"

"The brass who decided this thing didn't want the faintest chance the secret would get out. They thought it could start another war. Relations were bad enough as it was between us and the Soviets. The protocol was set up to react blindly to any attempt to unravel the secret. They thought any spy snooping would come from abroad. No one dreamed the threat would come from the U.S. congress. It was all totally unnecessary. The speaker of the House was defeated for reelection, and his exposé never got off the ground. It was probably assumed that the little land mine they left to blow up in the face of anyone following their trail would deactivate itself. They never thought it would still be dangerous fifty years later."

Sandecker leaned back in his chair and tented his fingers. "So this ancient scheme cooked up by a bunch of macho cowboys is what almost got my man killed. I understand that the assassin had his bags packed ready to go with a sniper's rifle and explosives. Apparently planning quite a retirement party for himself. Too bad we can't let the American public know what tomfoolery their tax dollars were used for in the name of democracy."

LeGrand said, "That would be a mistake. It is *still* extremely sensitive. Reducing Russia's nuclear arsenal has been a struggle. If this story got out it would strengthen the hand of the nationalists who say the U.S. can't be trusted."

"They would think that anyhow," Sandecker said dryly. "In my experience there is one thing powerful people fear the most: embarrassment." He smiled. "I trust there are no more protocols waiting out there to ambush the unwary?"

It was a veiled warning.

"I've already ordered a complete examination of our computer files to prevent exactly such a possibility," LeGrand said. "No more surprises."

"Let's hope so," Sandecker said.

28

AUSTIN POURED HIMSELF A HOT mug of Jamaican Blue Mountain coffee straight, took a sip of the high-octane brew, and picked the aluminum cylinder off his desk. He hefted it in his big hand, staring at the battered convex surface as if it were a crystal ball. The object yielded no secrets, only a distorted reflection of his bronzed features and pale hair.

Setting the cylinder aside, he returned to the map of Alaska spread out on his desk. He had been to Alaska several times, and the sheer immensity of the fiftieth state never failed to boggle his mind. Searching for the old flying wing base in some of the most rugged territory on earth would be like trying to find a single grain of sand on Malibu beach. Compounding the problem, the base would have been built in a way to keep it from prying eyes. He ran his finger from Barrow deep inside the Arctic Circle south to the Kenai Peninsula. The phone rang as the seed of an idea was beginning to sprout.

Eyes glued on the map, he grabbed the phone, stuck it in his ear, and snapped a perfunctory hello. Sandecker's crisp voice came on the line.

"Kurt, can you come up to my office?"

"Can this wait, Admiral?" Austin said, trying to hold on to his thought.

"Of *course,* Kurt," Sandecker said magnanimously. "Is five minutes sufficient?"

The notion withered and died like a flower in the sun. Sandecker must have been the original irresistible force. The admiral's mind operated at warp speed, and consequently his sense of time tended to be compressed.

"I'll be there in two minutes."

"Splendid. I think you'll find it worth your while."

When Austin walked into Sandecker's tenth-floor office he expected to see the director of NUMA behind the immense desk made from a hatch taken from a Confederate blockade runner. Instead the admiral sat off to the side in one of the comfortable dark leather chairs reserved for visitors. He was chatting with a woman who sat with her back to Austin. Sandecker, who was wearing a navy blazer with gold anchors embroidered over the breast pocket, rose to greet Austin.

"Thank you for coming, Kurt. There's someone here I'd like you to meet."

The woman stood, and Austin's preoccupation with his Alaskan puzzle evaporated in a single glance.

She was tall and slim, with Eurasian high cheekbones and almond-shaped eyes. In contrast to her exotic looks she was dressed conservatively in a long burgundy skirt and matching jacket. Her dark blond hair was tightly woven into a single braid down to her shoulder blades. Something about her went beyond natural beauty. She had the erect carriage of someone born to royalty, but at the same time she walked with the lithe easiness of a panther as she came over to shake hands. The deep brown eyes with gold flecks seemed to radiate a tropical heat. Maybe it was his imagination, but her musky scent made Austin think of the throb of distant drums. It suddenly dawned on him who the woman was.

"You're Dr. Cabral?"

Austin would not have been surprised if she had answered with a soft purr. In a low, mellow voice she said, "Thank you for coming to see me, Mr. Austin. I hope I haven't interrupted anything important. I asked Admiral Sandecker if I might have the chance to thank you personally for your help."

"You're very welcome, but Gamay and Paul did all the hard work. I simply answered the phone and pushed a couple of buttons."

"You are far too modest, Mr. Austin," she said with a smile that could have melted ice cubes. "If not for your quick action I'm afraid my head and those of your colleagues would be decorating a village thousands of miles from these comfortable surroundings."

Sandecker stepped between them and guided Francesca back to her chair. "On that happy note, Dr. Cabral, would you mind if we imposed and asked you to tell us your story from start to finish?"

"Not at all," she replied. "Talking to someone about my experience has therapeutic value, and I also find myself remembering details I had forgotten."

Sandecker motioned for Austin to sit, then slipped into his desk chair and lit up one of the ten custom-made cigars he smoked each day. He and Austin listened with rapt attention as Francesca narrated the gripping tale of the hijacking, the crash and her brush with death, her ascension as a white goddess. She went into great detail about the public works projects in the Chulo village that she took so much pride in. She ended with an account of the arrival of the Trouts, their mad flight, and their rescue by helicopter.

"Fascinating," Sandecker said, "absolutely fascinating. Tell me, what became of your friend Tessa?"

"She stayed on with Dr. Ramirez. Her knowledge of medicinal plants will be invaluable in his research. I talked by phone to my parents to make sure they are well. They wanted me to come home, but I decided to stay in the U.S. I need more of a decompression time before I insert myself back into the São Paulo social whirl. Beyond that, I am determined to carry on the task that was interrupted ten years ago."

Sandecker contemplated the stubborn set of Francesca's jaw. "I firmly believe past is not only present but also future. It would help to know what lies ahead if you told us something about the events that led to your plane trip."

Francesca stared into the distance as if she could see through time. "It goes back to my childhood. I became aware at a very early age that I come from a privileged background. Even as a girl I knew I lived in a city with appalling slums. As I grew older and traveled I learned that my city was a microcosm for the world. Here in one place were the haves and the have-nots. I also discovered that the difference between rich and poor nations is the earth's most plentiful substance: water. Fresh water lubricates development. Without water there is nothing to eat. Without food there is no will to live, to raise one's standard of living. Even the oil-rich countries use much of their petroleum revenues to buy or produce water. We take it for granted that when we turn on the tap water will flow, but that will not always be the case. The competition for water has become greater than ever."

"The U.S. is no stranger to water disputes," Sandecker said. "In the old days range wars were fought over water rights."

"That will be nothing compared with the troubles of the future," Francesca said darkly. "In this century wars will not be fought over oil, as in the past, but over water. The situation is becoming desperate. The world's water is strained by the population growth. There is no more fresh water on the earth than two thousand years ago when the population was three percent of its current size. Even without the inevitable droughts, like the current one, it will get worse as demand and pollution increase. Some countries will simply run out of water, sparking a global refugee crisis. Tens of millions of people will flood across international borders. It means the collapse of fisheries, environmental destruction, conflict, lower living standards." She paused for a moment. "As people who deal with the ocean you must see the irony. We are facing a shortage on a planet whose surface is covered two-thirds with water."

"Water, water, everywhere, nor any drop to drink," Austin said, quoting the Samuel Taylor Coleridge poem.

"Precisely. But suppose the Mariner had a magic wand he could wave over a bucket of seawater, changing it into fresh."

"His ship would have survived."

"Now extend that analogy to millions of buckets."

"The global water crisis would be over," Austin said. "Nearly seventy percent of the world's population lives within fifty miles of the ocean."

"Exactly," Francesca said, her mood lightening.

"Are you telling me you *have* this magic wand?"

"Something almost as good. I have developed a revolutionary means to extract salt from seawater."

"You must know that desalting is hardly a new concept," Sandecker said.

Francesca nodded. "The extraction of salt from seawater goes back to the ancient Greeks. Desalination plants have been built around the world, including many in the Middle East. There are several methods, but all are costly. In my doctorate I proposed a radically *new* approach. I threw out all the old methods. My goal was a process that would be efficient and cheap, available to the poorest farmer trying to scratch a living from the dust. *Think* of the implications. Water would be nearly free. Deserts would become centers of civilization."

"I'm sure you thought of the undesirable consequences," Sandecker said, "the fact that cheap water would stimulate development, population growth, and the pollution that goes with them."

"I thought long and hard about that, Admiral Sandecker, but the alternatives were even more unpalatable. I would make orderly development a requirement before allowing a country to use my process."

"It goes without saying then that your experimentation was a success," Austin said.

"Very much so. I was bringing a working model of the process to the international conference. Seawater would go in one end, fresh water come out at the other. It would produce energy and little to no waste products."

"A process like that would have been worth millions of dollars."

"No doubt. I had offers that would have made me immensely

rich, but I planned to give my process to the world free of charge."

"That was quite generous of you. You say you had offers. Then someone knew of your process and plans?"

"Once I contacted the United Nations to attend the conference it became an open secret." She paused. "Something has always puzzled me. Many people knew about my process. The people who tried to kidnap me would be immediately exposed if they tried to profit from my work."

"There's another possibility," Austin suggested. "Maybe they wanted to *bury* your work and keep the process a secret from the world."

"But why would *anyone* try to stop a boon to humanity?"

"Perhaps you're too young to remember," said Sandecker, who had been listening intently. "Years ago stories circulated about the inventor who supposedly built a car engine that could go a hundred miles on a gallon or burn water. The details aren't important. The oil companies reportedly bought the secret and buried it so they could continue to make profits. The stories were apocryphal, but do you see my point?"

"Who would prevent the poor nations from enjoying cheap water?"

"Our investigations have given us an advantage over you, Dr. Cabral. Let me ask you a theoretical question. Suppose you controlled the world's supply of fresh water. How would you greet the arrival of a process that suddenly makes cheap water available to all?"

"My process would end your theoretical water monopoly. But this is a moot point. It is simply not *possible* for someone to control the world's water."

Sandecker and Austin exchanged glances.

Taking over from Sandecker, Austin said, "A lot has been happening in the past ten years, Dr. Cabral. We can fill you in on the whole story later, but we've discovered that a huge pan-national organization called the Gogstad Corporation is very close to acquiring a monopoly over the world's fresh water."

"Impossible!"

"I wish it were."

Francesca's eyes hardened. "Then this Gogstad must be the one who tried to kidnap me, who stole those ten years from my life."

"We have no solid proof," Austin said. "There is certainly strong circumstantial evidence pointing in that direction. Tell me, what do you know of a substance called anasazium?"

Francesca's mouth dropped open in surprise. Recovering quickly she said, "Is there anything you people at NUMA do *not* know?"

"Quite a bit, I'm sorry to say. We know very little about this stuff other than the fact that it can affect the hydrogen atom in strange ways."

"That's its most important property. It's a very complex relationship. This material is at the heart of my desalting process. Only a few people know of its existence. It's extremely rare."

"How did you come across it?"

"By chance. I read an obscure paper written by a former Los Alamos physicist. Rather than try to improve on the existing methods of desalting, I wanted to deal with it at a molecular or even nuclear level. A solution had eluded me until I heard about this substance. I contacted the scientist who wrote the article. He had a small amount of the material and was willing to part with it when I told him why I needed it."

"Why is it so rare?"

"Several reasons. With no apparent economic use for it, the demand was nonexistent. Then, too, the refinement process is quite complicated. The main ore source is in a troubled part of Africa that is constantly at war. I had several ounces, enough for a working model. I would have proposed that the nations of the world pool their resources to produce enough anasazium to set up pilot projects. Working together we could have viable quantities of this substance within a short time."

"Gogstad was running an installation off the coast of Mexico. It was destroyed in a tremendous explosion."

"Tell me more about this installation."

Austin gave her a quick summary, starting with the death of the whales. He described the storage cylinder after the explosion and how he traced it to the flying wing. Sandecker filled her in on the cold war mission to Siberia.

"A fantastic tale. It's too bad about the whales," she said sadly. "My process produces heat which can be turned into energy. The material can be unstable and under certain circumstances becomes a powerful explosive. These people must have been trying to replicate my desalination process and were unaware of the material's instability. Where would they have acquired the anasazium?"

"We don't know," Austin said. "We are aware of a large source but don't know its exact location."

"We must find it so I can resume my research," Francesca insisted.

"There's an even more important reason," Sandecker interjected.

"I know no more important reason than to continue my work," she said defensively.

"In time, Dr. Cabral, in time. Your work will have little meaning if Gogstad succeeds in its plans. Whoever controls the world's water controls the world."

"It sounds as if you're talking about global domination, Admiral Sandecker."

"Why not? Napoleon and Hitler failed, but their attempts were made through force of arms. In each case they came up against somebody with a bigger stick." He took a smooth puff on his cigar and watched the cloud of smoke. "The people protesting globalization, all that business with the World Trade Organization and the International Monetary Fund, were onto something. The danger is not in these entities but in the fact that it is easier now for someone to exert total control over an economic sector."

"A sort of global Al Capone?" Austin offered.

"There are similarities. Capone was ruthless about exterminating the competition and had a fine instinct for organization. His economic power gave him political clout. Bootleg booze is a far cry from water. The world can't do without water. Those who control its flow will have the *ultimate* political power. Who will stand up against someone whose word can condemn you and your country to die of thirst? That is why I say with all due respect, Dr. Cabral, that there are more important matters to be taken care of first."

"You're right, Admiral Sandecker," Francesca conceded. "If this Gogstad finds the main supply of anasazium, it will control my process as well."

"Intelligence and beauty are such a welcome combination," Sandecker said with unveiled appreciation. "The young lady has stated my fears exactly. It's imperative that we find that long-lost cache before Gogstad does."

"I was trying to figure out how to pinpoint the location when you called. I'm going to need some help."

"That's not a problem. Use any NUMA resource that you need, and if we don't have them we'll find them elsewhere."

"I think Joe and I should leave as soon as possible for Alaska."

"Before you go dashing off to the Yukon there's something else we have to discuss. This buildup of tankers that Joe's reporter friend told him about has me worried. What do you make of it?"

"At the very least Gogstad is expecting to move lots of water from Alaska to someplace that needs it. There has been talk of transporting water to China."

"Perhaps," Sandecker said, unconvinced. "I'll talk to Rudi Gunn. Maybe he and Yaeger can shed light on this mystery. While you and Joe are trying to nail down this flying wing, they can see what they can find about the tankers."

Austin rose and said, "I'll start things moving." He shook hands with Francesca and said, "I'll show you out, Dr. Cabral."

"Thank you, and please call me Francesca," she said as they strolled to the elevator.

"I will if you call me Kurt. Tell me, do you prefer Korean, Thai, Italian, or just plain old American cooking?"

"I beg your pardon."

"No one told you?" he said with mock amazement. "Dinner is part of the Austin rescue package. I hope you won't refuse. Who knows how long I will have to subsist on whale blubber and walrus steaks after today."

"In that case, I would be happy to accept your invitation. Would seven o'clock be convenient?"

"That's fine. It will give me plenty of time to start making preparations for our trip to Alaska."

"I'll see you then. As you know I am staying with the Trouts. And Korean would be fine."

Austin bid Francesca good-bye near the huge globe that rose from the center of the sea-green floor in the NUMA lobby, an atrium surrounded by waterfalls and aquariums filled with colorful and exotic sea life. Then he went back to his fourth-floor office, called Zavala to let him know of his meeting with Sandecker, and lined up transportation for their trip.

Francesca was ready when he arrived at the Trouts' Georgetown house to pick her up. He chatted with Paul and Gamay long enough to be polite, then drove to his favorite Korean restaurant, housed in an unpretentious building in Alexandria.

Austin recommended that they order *belogi,* thin strips of marinated beef cooked on a hot plate on the table. Ordinarily it was one of his favorite meals, but he hardly tasted it; he was too busy looking at Francesca. She was dressed simply in a stonewashed denim dress whose light blue color set off her dark complexion and long luxurious hair that seemed to have captured the light of the sun. It was hard for Austin to reconcile the picture of this cultured and beautiful woman, who was clearly delighted over the simple pleasure of a civilized meal, with the tale he had heard of her reign as a white goddess among savage Indians. She seemed relaxed and entirely at ease, but even as they laughed over her inept use of chopsticks, Austin couldn't shake the feeling he experienced when they first met. Despite the civilized veneer, the jungle had seeped into her blood. He saw it in the feline gracefulness of her movement, and the watchfulness in her dark eyes. It was a quality that fascinated and attracted Austin, and he vowed to see more of Francesca when he returned from his mission.

Which was why it was all the more painful when Austin apologized for calling it an early night. He had much to do before leaving for Alaska, he explained. As he dropped her off on the Trouts' doorstep, he asked if she would like to go out again when he returned.

"Thank you. I'd like that, very much," she said. "I plan to be in Washington for some time and hope we can get to know each other better."

"Until then," Austin said. "At a time and place to be announced."

She smiled and pecked him lightly on the lips. "It's a date."

29

WITH SANDECKER'S BACKING, AUS-tin had no trouble commandeering a NUMA jet. Streaking across the country at five hundred miles per hour, the turquoise Cessna Citation Ultra had refueled at Salt Lake City before pushing on to Anchorage. After the all-night trip they arrived as the morning light cast a rosy glow over the Chugach Mountains on the outskirts of Alaska's big city, which some of the locals call Los Anchorage. They were airborne within minutes, pushing on to their destination in Nome.

Shortly after the NUMA jet took off from Anchorage, Zavala came back from the galley with a couple of steaming mugs of coffee. Austin was studying an old map spread out on the table that folded down between the seats. He was directing his attention to a fist of land whose knuckles jabbed at the former U.S.S.R. a few miles across the Bering Strait.

Settling into the chair opposite Austin's, Zavala sipped his coffee and looked out the window at the vast land mass below. Black mountains edged by rivers and heavy forests were visible through a scattering of whiskered cirrus clouds.

"That's big country," Zavala said lazily. "Any idea of our next port of call after Nome?"

Austin leaned back, laced his fingers behind his head, and stared into space. His broad mouth curled in a wry smile. "More or less," he said.

Zavala knew his partner wasn't trying to be mysterious. Austin simply didn't like surprises. When time allowed he cautiously collected the facts before making a move. Zavala pointed downward. "I'm sure it doesn't come as any surprise to you that there is *more* down there than less."

"Something like six hundred thousand square miles, last I heard. I have no illusions about the formidable task we're up against. We could search until we became eligible for NUMA pensions and not find a thing." Austin's brow furrowed in thought. "That's why I decided to work my way backward from what we know, not what we *don't* know."

Zavala swiftly grasped the premise. "We know what the target was in the Soviet Union." He pointed on the map to the northwest coast of Alaska where blunt fingers of the ragged coastline, all that remained of the old land bridge, reached toward Asia. "What was the flying wing's statistical range?"

"Around three thousand miles cruising at around five hundred miles per hour. I'm assuming that its fuel storage capacity would have been beefed up to extend the range as much as possible for this mission."

"There's always the possibility of midair refueling," Zavala said.

"I've taken that into consideration. I'm guessing that they would have kept the operation simple and short to avoid detection."

Taking a sharp pencil in hand, Austin drew an arc from Barrow to the Yukon Delta.

Zavala let out a low whistle. "You're talking about a trip that could be more than a thousand miles from target. That's still a lot of territory to cover."

"It's bigger than some states," Austin acknowledged. "So I made an educated guess. The cloak-and-dagger boys wanted to keep this crazy scheme as hush-hush as possible. Building a new base would be costly and time-consuming, and most important, it might attract unwanted attention."

Zavala snapped his fingers. "They would use an *existing* base."

Austin nodded. "During World War II, Alaska bristled with gun emplacements and airfields because of fears Japan would invade. Each red dot on the map denotes an airstrip from World War II."

Zavala pondered the problem. "What if the base were secret?"

"It *was* secret, at least up to now." Austin jabbed the map with his pencil at Nome and drew a wide circle around the dot. "We'll find what we're looking for here, although I must admit that with all the suppositions I've made, it's still a crapshoot."

Zavala studied the map, and his lips twitched up at the corners in his trademark smile. "How can you be certain this is the right area? The plane could have taken off from dozens of places."

"I had a little help from a ghost." Austin reached into his jacket pocket and produced a small spiral-bound notebook. The brown cover was worn, but it was still possible to read the words "U.S. Army Air Force" and the name inked just below. He handed the notebook to Zavala. "This is the diary of Buzz Martin's father, the pilot who flew the wing on its last mission."

Zavala laughed with delight. "You should have been a magician. You couldn't have done better pulling a rabbit out of a hat."

"This rabbit jumped into my lap. After Sandecker met with LeGrand, the CIA poked around and came up with Martin's personal effects. They must have been in a hurry to get rid of incriminating evidence and didn't vet the stuff thoroughly. Buzz found the notebook tucked into his father's uniform. He thought it might contain something of importance and gave it to me just before we left Washington."

Zavala thumbed through the curling pages. "I don't see a detailed map to follow."

"You didn't think this was going to be easy, did you?" Austin took the book back and opened to a page where he had placed a yellow sticky tab. "Martin was a good soldier. He knew that loose lips sink ships. Most of the diary is devoted to how he missed his wife and kid. But he let a few things sneak in. Here, let me read you the first paragraph:

"To my dear wife Phyllis and son Buzz. Maybe someday you will read this. I had a lot of time on my hands and started this diary on the way to No-Name. If the brass knew I was taking notes, I'd be in hot water. This thing is even more secret than the Manhattan Project. As the spooks frequently reminded me, I'm just a dumb sky jockey who's supposed to follow orders and not ask questions. Sometimes I feel more like a prisoner. I'm kept under close supervision with the rest of the crew. So I guess this journal is a way of saying, hey, I'm a person. They're feeding us well, Phyllis, I know how you worry about the way I eat. Lots of good fresh meat and fish. The Quonset hut was not made for the frozen north. The snow slides off the roof, but metal is a lousy insulator. We keep the wood stove going day and night. We'd be better off in an igloo. The plane gets the first-class accommodations in its hidey-hole. Sorry to complain. I'm lucky to be flying this baby! I can't believe an aircraft as big as this can maneuver like a fighter plane. It's definitely the aviation wave of the future."

Austin stopped reading. "He goes on to say how homesick he is and how glad he'll be to get back."

"Too bad Martin didn't get to enjoy that future. He had no idea he was not only a prisoner but a condemned man as well."

"Martin wasn't the first or last patriot thrown to the dogs in the interests of what the higher-ups said was the greater good. Unfortunately he can't have the satisfaction of knowing his little diary will show us the way to No-Name."

"That's even more obscure than the dateline they used to use during the war: 'Somewhere in the Pacific.' "

"I thought so, too, until I remembered a story I heard years ago. Seems a British Navy officer sailing off Alaska in the 1850s saw land that wasn't on the chart so he wrote in '?Name.' The Admiralty draftsman who recopied the chart thought the question mark was a *C* and that the *a* in *Name* was an *o. No name* became *Cape Nome* which became *Nome.* Here's something else:

"Uneventful trip from Seattle. Plane handles like a dream. Touched down thirty minutes past No-Name."

"What was the cruising speed of the wing?" Zavala asked.

"About four hundred to five hundred miles per hour."

"That would put them two hundred to two hundred fifty miles beyond Nome."

"My calculations exactly. Here's where it starts to get interesting:

"Got my first look at our destination. Told the guys it looks like Doug's nose from the air."

"A dog's nose?"

"No, the proper name, Doug,"

"That narrows it down to a few million guys," Zavala said wearily.

"Yeah, I know, I had the same reaction until I read the rest: *All it needs is a corn cob pipe to look like old Eagle Beak."*

"Douglas MacArthur. Who could forget that profile?"

"Especially someone who had come out of the Big War. In addition, Nome is only one hundred and sixty one miles from Russia. I thought it was worth ordering up some satellite pictures. While you snoozed your way over the continental United States, I was going over the photos with a magnifying glass."

He handed the satellite views to Zavala, who examined them for a few minutes and shook his head. "I don't see anything that resembles an eagle's beak."

"I didn't find one, either. I told you it wasn't going to be easy."

They were still going over the photos and map when the NUMA pilot announced that the plane was starting its descent to Nome Airport. They gathered their gear in a couple of bags and were ready when the plane rolled to a stop on the tarmac of the small but modern airport. A taxi took them to town along one of Nome's three two-lane gravel roads. The bright sun did little to relieve the monotonous terrain of flat, treeless tundra, although the Kigluaik Mountains could be seen in the distance. The cab took them onto Front Street, which bordered the blue-gray waters of the Bering Sea, past the turn-of-the-century city hall, terminus for the Iditarod dogsled race, dropping them off at the barge port and fishing harbor where their leased float plane awaited with a full tank of fuel.

Zavala was more than pleased with the plane, a single-engine Maule M-7 with short takeoff and landing capability. While Joe checked out the plane Austin picked up some sandwiches and coffee at Fat Freddie's diner. They were traveling light. They brought clothing mostly, although Austin had packed his trusty Bowen revolver. Zavala had brought along an Ingram machine pistol capable of firing hundreds of rounds a minute. When Austin asked why he needed such lethal firepower in the desolate northland, Zavala had muttered something about grizzly bears.

With Zavala at the controls the Maule headed northeasterly along the coast. The plane stayed low, cruising at a hundred and seventy-five miles per hour. The day was cloudy but with none of the rain the Nome area is noted for. They quickly settled into a routine. Austin called out a promising-looking piece of real estate, and Zavala circled it a couple of times. Austin pencil-shaded the areas they covered on his map. Their excitement at being on the hunt quickly faded as the plane droned over mile after mile of ragged coastline. The barren land was broken only by lacy rivers and shallow ponds created by melted snow.

Austin kept them amused by reciting poems of Robert Service which Zavala translated into Spanish. But even "The Shooting of Dan McGrew" didn't dull the monotony of their quest. Zavala's usual good humor was beginning to wear. "We've seen parrot beaks, pigeon beaks, and even a turtle beak, but no eagle," he grumbled.

Austin studied the shaded portions of his map. A substantial amount of coastline had yet to be covered.

"We've still got a lot of territory to check out. I'd like to keep on going. How are you doing?"

"I'm fine, but the plane is going to need fuel before long."

"We passed what looked like a fishing camp a short while back. How about breaking for lunch while we tank up old Betsy here?"

Zavala responded by putting the plane into a banking circle. Before long they picked up the river they had flown over earlier and followed it for about ten minutes until they sighted a cluster of plywood shacks. Two float planes were tied up in the river. Zavala scoped out a straight stretch of water. He brought the plane down, skimmed the surface in a near perfect landing, and taxied the plane up to a weather-beaten pier. A stocky young man with a face as round as a full moon saw them coming and threw out a mooring line.

"Welcome to Tinook Village, population one hundred and sixty-seven, most of them related," he said with a smile as dazzling as sunlight on new snow. "My name is Mike Tinook."

Tinook didn't appear surprised to have a couple of strangers drop out of the sky to visit his remote village. With vast distances to cover Alaskans will fly a hundred miles just to have breakfast. Perhaps it has something to do with the scarcity of human contact outside Anchorage, but most Alaskans spin out their stories about how they came north within five minutes of making an acquaintance. Mike related how he grew up in the village, worked as an airplane mechanic in Anchorage, and came back home to stay.

Austin explained they were with the National Underwater & Marine Agency.

"Had you figured for some kind of government guys," Tinook said knowingly. "Too clean for oil men or hunters and too sure of yourselves to be tourists. We had a NUMA team drop by a few years ago. They were doing research in the Chukchi Sea. What brings you to the Land of the Midnight Sun?"

"We're doing sort of a geological survey, but I must confess that we're not having much success," Austin said. "We're looking for a point of land that sticks out into the water. It's shaped like an eagle's beak."

Tinook shook his head. "That's my plane out there. I do a lot of flying when I'm not fishing or helping to tend the reindeer herd, but it doesn't ring a bell. C'mon up to the store. We can look at a map." They climbed a rickety staircase to the plywood building. It was the typical Alaskan general store, a combination of grocery, pharmaceutical, hardware, gift shop, and wilderness outfitter. Customers could take their pick from insect repellent, canned goods, snowmobile replacement parts, and TV videos.

Tinook checked a wall map of the area. "Nope. Nothing like an eagle's beak." He scratched his head. "Maybe you should talk to Clarence."

"Clarence?"

"Yeah, my grandfather. He used to get around a lot and likes visitors."

Austin's eyes glazed over. He was impatient to get in the air again. He was trying to think of a diplomatic way to put Tinook off without hurting his feelings, when he noticed a rifle hung on the wall behind the counter. He walked over for a closer look. It was a Carbine M1, the workhorse rifle carried by American infantrymen in World War II. He had seen M1s before, but this was in exceptionally mint condition.

"Is that your rifle?" he asked Tinook.

"My grandfather gave it to me, but I use my own gun for hunting. That thing has got quite a story behind it. Sure you wouldn't want to talk to Clarence? Might be worth your while."

Zavala saw Austin's newfound interest. "I wouldn't mind stretching my legs for a while longer. At least we don't have to worry about getting home before dark."

Joe's point was well taken. Daylight was more than twenty-two hours long, and even after the sun set, technically, night was only a short period of dusk.

Mike guided them along a muddy street past more shacks, gangs of round-faced children, sleeping huskies, and racks where crimson strips of salmon dried in the sun. He went up to the door of a shack smaller than the others and knocked. Someone inside told them to come in. They stepped into the one-room house. It smelled of wood smoke and something meaty cooking on a camp stove. The house was sparsely furnished with a bunk bed in one corner and a table covered with a red-and-white checkered oilcloth. A man who looked as old as a glacier sat at the table carefully painting a wooden polar bear figure about six inches high. Several others figures of wolves and eagles had been painted and lined up.

"Grandpa, these men would like to hear the story about your rifle."

Dark Oriental eyes sparkled with intelligence and good humor from a face creased in a thousand wrinkles. Clarence wore dark-framed glasses, and his thick silvery hair was neatly parted on one side. His mouth widened in a grin that seemed to take over his whole jaw. Although he must have been in his eighties, he shook hands in a bone-crunching grip and looked as if he could still wrestle a sea lion to the floor. Yet the voice that should have been amplified by the powerful frame was as soft as wind-blown snow.

His grandson said, "I have to go back to the shop. I'll have the plane refueled by the time you get back."

"I make these for the gift shops in Anchorage," the old man said, putting the polar bear and paints aside. "Glad you dropped by. You're just in time for lunch." He indicated a couple of rickety chairs, and, refusing the protests of his guests, he spooned the stew from the stove pot into some chipped willow-pattern china bowls. He took a big spoonful as if to show there was no harm in his cooking. "How is it?"

Austin and Zavala tentatively sampled the stew and pronounced it quite good.

The old man beamed with pleasure.

"Is it caribou?" Zavala asked.

The old man reached into a trash bucket and pulled out a can of Dinty Moore beef stew.

"Mike's a good boy," Clarence said. "He and his wife buy me stuff so I won't have to cook. They worry that I'm lonely since my wife died. I like visitors, but I don't want to bore you men."

Austin looked around the room. The walls were decorated with primitive harpoons and Eskimo folk art. A Norman Rockwell print with the boy sitting in the dentist's office was hung incongruously next to a fierce walrus mask. There were family pictures, including many of a stout, handsome woman who could have been the old man's wife. The most out-of-place object was a computer tucked in the corner. Grandpa Tinook saw Austin's amused gaze and said, "It's amazing. We've got the satellite so the kids can learn about the rest of the world. I can talk on that machine with anyone, so I'm never alone."

Clarence was no old blubber-chewing windbag, Austin deduced. He was sorry he had been in such a rush to avoid meeting him. "If you don't mind, we'd very much like to hear your story," he said.

Grandpa Tinook noisily scooped up the last of his stew, put the bowls in the sink, and sat down again. He squinted as if the memory were hard to recall, but when he started to talk it was clear he had spun this tale before.

"One day many years ago I was out hunting. There was some good trout and salmon fishing, fox to trap, and herds of caribou. I always got something. I had this little aluminum skiff and a fine motor. Got me around pretty good. It was too far to come home after the hunt, so I used to stay over a couple of nights at the old airfield."

Austin glanced at Zavala. Alaska is dotted with airfields hardly worth the name.

"Where was this airfield?" he asked.

"Up north a ways. Left over from the Big War. They used to ferry planes to Russia and used it as a stopoff. Blimps there used to look for subs. Not much left. There was a hut where I could light a fire and keep warm and dry. I could store game and smoke it there 'til it was time to come home."

"How long ago was that?"

"Oh, fifty years ago or so. My memory ain't what it used to be. I remember when they said I had to stop going there, though."

"They?"

The old man nodded. "For months I never seen anybody. Then one day two men come by in a plane just as I'm cooking up some trout. Hard-lookin' white men. They flash their badges, say they're with the government and want to know what I'm doing. I give them some fish, and they're a lot nicer. They say there's going to be a big secret at the base and I can't come there anymore. But they will buy any fresh meat and fish I can get them. One of them gave me that gun you saw so I could shoot game. I took them lots of game and fish, never to the base, though. I'd meet them halfway."

"Did you see any planes?"

"Sure, lots coming and going. Once I was hunting and I heard one that sounded like a hundred rushing rivers. Big as this whole village and crazy shape."

"What kind of shape?"

He went to the wall and took down a harpoon. Touching the sharp metal point with his finger, he said, "Something like this."

Austin's gaze was unwavering. "How long did you hunt game for these men?"

"'Bout six months, I think. One day they showed up, said they didn't need any more. They told me to stay away from the airfield. Didn't want me to step on a mine. Said I could keep the rifle. They left in a big hurry."

Zavala said, "We've been looking for an old airfield supposed to be on a piece of land that looked like an eagle's nose, but we can't find it."

"Oh, sure, this place used to be like that. Things have changed from ice and wind. In the summer the water comes in from rivers and floods the land. Doesn't look the same as it did back then. You got a map?"

Kurt pulled the map from his jacket and unfolded it.

Grandpa Tinook's thick finger came down on a section of coast under the pencil shading. "Right here," he said.

"We must have flown right over it," Zavala said.

"Tell me," Austin said, "those men, did they give you their names?"

"Sure, Hewy and Dewy, they said."

Zavala chuckled. "I suppose Lewy was busy."

The old man shrugged. "I read Donald Duck when I shipped out on merchant ships out of Anchorage. They figured I musta ate whale blubber all my life. I let them think that."

"It was probably a good thing that you did."

"Like I said, they were hard men, although we became pretty good friends. I went back to the old base after the war. I think they just said that about the mines to scare me off. Felt like something had been poisoned and left to rot." He paused thoughtfully. "Maybe you can tell me. One thing I always wondered. What was the big secret? We weren't fighting the Japanese. The war was over."

"Some men can't live without war," Austin replied. "If they don't have one they find another."

"Sounds crazy to me, but what do I know? Well, that was years ago. Why do you men want to go to that old placc?"

For once Austin was at a loss for words. He could have said how important it was to find an odd substance named anasazium before Gogstad got its hands on it and made worldwide mischief. But he suspected his real reasons were more visceral. The story of Buzz Martin's father had smoldered in him and offended his sense of right and wrong.

The best answer he could muster was, "There was a boy once who went to his father's funeral, only his father wasn't dead."

The old man nodded solemnly as if Austin had been the soul of clarity.

Austin's mind was already racing toward the task ahead. "Thank you very much for telling us your story," Kurt said, rising. "And for lunch, too."

"Wait," Clarence said. He perused the wooden figures he'd

carved, picked out two, and gave one to each of the NUMA men. "Take these. The bear for strength and the wolf for cunning."

Austin and Zavala thanked the old man for his generosity.

"Makes me feel better to give you some luck after telling you how to get to that place. You go back to that old base, I got the feeling you're going to need it."

30

THE SUN'S BLINDING REFLECTION on the mirrored surface of the water had prevented a good look at the Eagle's Beak on the first pass. Only a thin, ragged crescent of tundra could be seen, part of an inundated coastal plain extending into a pear-shaped bay. Zavala angled the plane so that the dark outline of General MacArthur's nose was visible under the translucent covering of water. Austin gave Zavala the thumbs up. *This is it.* The thumb pointed down. *Land.*

Zavala brought the plane around in a low sweep and flew the length of the peninsula at an altitude of about two hundred feet. The crooked finger of land was more than a mile long and less than half as wide. Blackwater marsh had encroached on its borders and added to the ravages of wind and ice that had distorted its original shape.

"See how close you can get us to those moraines," Austin said, pointing to the low, glacier-carved mounds that began where the peninsula joined the mainland.

Zavala tapped the brim of his NUMA baseball cap. "No sweat. This baby can land on the head of a pin. Stand by for a picture-perfect landing."

Austin had every bit of confidence in his partner's flying ability. Zavala had logged hundreds of hours flying every conceivable type of aircraft. There were times, though, when Austin had visions of Snoopy pretending his doghouse was a

World War I Sopwith Camel. He pushed the thought out of his mind as Zavala circled the strip again, dropped into a long glide, and reduced speed until the plane's floats skimmed the shallow water.

The plane was about to set down smoothly when they heard a loud thump under their feet followed by the tortured sound of metal tearing. The plane snapped around like an amusement park ride. The two men were flung against their seatbelts like rag dolls. The spinning plane came to rest at a drunken angle. Zavala had the wind knocked out of him but managed to kill the engine.

As the propeller spun to a stop Austin felt his head to make sure it was still attached to his shoulders. "If that was picture-perfect, I'd hate to see a *rough* landing. What happened to the head of a pin?"

Zavala adjusted his baseball cap and straightened his reflecting sunglasses on his nose. "Sorry," he said with uncharacteristic humbleness. "They must be making pins bigger than they used to."

Austin shook his head and suggested they inspect the damage. They climbed out onto the pontoons to be met by the local welcoming committee. A cloud of condor-sized Alaskan mosquitoes thirsting for human blood drove them back into the cockpit. After liberally dousing themselves with Cutter's industrial-strength bug repellent, they ventured out again. They stepped off the plane into about two feet of water and examined the twisted metal around the right-hand float.

"We'll have some 'splaining to do at the plane rental place, but we'll be able to take off," Zavala said. He sloshed back along their landing path. Moments later he bent over and said, "Hey, check this out."

Austin came over and examined a metal post covered by a few inches of water. Metal gleamed brightly where the top was sheared off and copper electrical wires dangled out.

"Congratulations," Austin said. "I think you found a landing beacon."

"The unerring Zavala homing instinct never fails," Joe said as if he had hit the landing light on purpose. He expanded his search and within minutes located another light. This one had the glass lens and bulb socket still intact.

Austin surveyed their surroundings and tried to get his bearings. It was easy to see why the remote spot was picked for a secret airstrip. The terrain was naturally as flat as an aircraft carrier and would have needed little grading. He looked toward the hills where the sun sparkled off a lacework of streams that pooled into the lake that hid the strip.

They unloaded the plane, slung their packs over their shoulders, and waded toward the hills less than a quarter of a mile distant. Although they wore boots that kept their feet dry, the water sloshed onto their waterproof Gore-Tex pants, and they were glad the temperature was in the fifties. The water became shallower and turned into spongy bog, then they were crunching on permafrost as they made their way through patches of buttercup, wild crocus, and poppies. They spotted more landing lights, all leading in a line toward the hills. At one point they stopped and looked off at a huge flock of eiders floating over the marsh like a dark plume of smoke. With the unearthly quiet they could have been on the surface of another planet.

Continuing their hike they came to the foot of an escarpment that angled sharply up from the ground. The elongated hill was round at the top and shaped vaguely like a loaf of Italian bread. Patches of black rock splotched with lichens and moss were visible through the thick vegetation that covered much of the hill. Austin thought it peculiar that the mound stood by itself, isolated from the nearest hills by several hundred yards. He mentioned his observation to Zavala.

"Notice how the land here is flat except for this bump?"

"If I were a geologist I might be able to make something of it."

"I was thinking more of the landing lights. They lead right to the face of this hill."

He stared at an exposed section for a moment, then put his

face inches away and ran his fingers over the shiny surface. Using the large blade on his Swiss Army knife he poked at the rock and chipped off a thin piece about as big as his palm. He examined the material, then grinned and handed it to Zavala.

"Paint," Zavala said with wonder. He ran his hand over the shiny area exposed by Austin's knife. "Sheetmetal and bolts. Someone went to a lot of trouble to keep this thing hidden."

Austin took several steps back and raised his eyes to the top of the mound. "I remember Clarence Tinook saying something about an old blimp base. Maybe there's a dirigible hangar under this stuff."

"That makes sense and goes with our theory that they used an existing base. The next question is how we get inside."

"Try saying 'open sesame' and hope for the best."

Zavala stood back and bellowed the famous command from *Ali Baba and the Forty Thieves.* When nothing happened he tried again in Spanish, also to no avail.

"You know any more magic words?" he asked Austin.

"You just exhausted my entire repertoire," Kurt said with a shrug.

They walked around behind the hangar. Sticking out of the permafrost were the foundations of several small buildings that could have been Quonset huts. A dump area revealed piles of rusty tin cans and broken glass, but no entrance to the mound presented itself.

It was Zavala who stumbled, literally, on the entrance.

Austin was walking several steps ahead of his partner when he heard a yell. He turned quickly. Joe had vanished as if the earth had swallowed him up. Confirming this possibility, Zavala's disembodied voice, swearing in the tongue of his ancestors, issued eerily from the ground. Austin carefully backtracked and found Zavala in a cellar hole that had been covered over by vegetation. Austin had walked right by the hole without seeing it.

"Are you okay?" Austin called out.

More mutterings. "Yeah, the brush that covered this damned

hole cushioned my fall. C'mon down. There's a short set of stairs."

Austin joined Zavala at the bottom of the hole, which was about eight feet deep. Joe was standing in front of a partially open door of heavily riveted steel.

"Don't tell me," Austin grunted. "The unerring Zavala homing instinct."

"What else?" Zavala said.

Austin pulled a small but powerful halogen light from his pack. The door noisily opened with some persuasion from his shoulder. He stepped inside with Zavala close behind. A blast of cold and fetid air hit them in the face as if they were standing in front of an air conditioner for a mausoleum. The beam of light showed a corridor whose concrete walls and ceiling were inadequate insulation against permafrost and seemed to amplify the cold. Pulling their jacket collars tight around their necks, they started along the corridor.

Several doors led off the main hallway of the underground bunker. Austin flashed his light inside the rooms. Rusty bed frames and mattresses rotting with decay testified to the use of one space as a bunkroom. Farther along was a kitchen and pantry. The last chamber was a communications room.

"They left in a rush," Zavala said. The smashed vacuum tubes and radio cabinets looked as if they had been attacked with a sledgehammer.

They continued along the passageway, skirting a large rectangular hole in the floor. The metal grating that once covered it had mostly rusted through. Austin pointed the flashlight down the deep shaft. "Some sort of ventilation or heating, maybe."

"I've been thinking about what Clarence Tinook said about mines," Zavala said.

"Let's hope it was a concocted story they hoped would scare off hunters and fishermen," Austin said. "Maybe he actually said *mimes.*"

"Now that would certainly scare me," Zavala replied.

The corridor eventually ended in a short set of stairs that led to another steel door. They guessed that they were under the hangar. Not entirely convinced of his own argument against booby traps, Austin took a deep breath, opened the door, and stepped through. Austin immediately sensed a change in atmosphere. The cold was less biting and musty than in the concrete bunker. The staleness of the air was overpowered by the smell of gasoline, oil, and heated metal.

On the wall to the right of the door was a switch. A stenciled sign read "Generator." Austin gave Zavala the go-ahead, and Joe yanked the switch down. Nothing happened at first. Then there was a click from somewhere in the darkness and a series of sputtering pops as a motor coughed reluctantly into life. High above, lights glimmered dimly then glowed brightly, illuminating the vaulted ceilings of a huge artificial cave. Zavala was too awestruck to speak. Illuminated at center stage was what looked like a black-winged avenger from a Norse myth.

He walked over behind the scimitar-shaped craft, reached up, and tentatively touched one of the vertical fins extending down from the trailing end of the fuselage.

"Beautiful," he whispered as if he were talking about a lovely woman. "I've read about this thing, seen pictures, but I never dreamed it would be so magnificent."

Austin went over and stood beside him, taking in the broad sweep of sculpted aluminum. "Either we've stumbled into the Bat Cave or we just found the long-lost phantom flying wing," he said.

Zavala walked under the fuselage. "I did some reading about the plane. These fins were added later for stabilization when they went from prop to jet power. She's about a hundred seventy feet from wing tip to wing tip."

"That's half the length of a football field," Austin said.

Zavala nodded. "It was the largest plane of its day even though she's only about fifty feet from front to back. Check out these jet engines. In the original all eight were built into the fuselage. They slung these two underneath the wing to free up fuel space. Fits in with what you said about modifications to increase range."

They walked around to the front of the plane. The swept-back aerodynamic lines were even more impressive from this angle. Although the plane weighed more than two hundred thousand tons, it seemed to balance lightly on its tripod landing gear.

"Jack Northrop really had something when he designed this lady," Austin replied.

"Absolutely. Look at that slim silhouette. There's hardly any surface for radar to bounce off. They've even painted it black like the stealth planes. Let's go inside," Zavala said eagerly.

They climbed up a ladder through a hatchway in the plane's belly and made their way along a short ramp. Like the rest of the plane, the flight deck was unconventional. Zavala sat in the rotating pilot's seat and used a hand-operated mechanism to pump the seat four feet higher into a Plexiglas bubble. He peered through the cowling, which was to the left of the wing's center line. The conventional switches and instruments were located between the pilot and the copilot, who sat at a lower level. The throttle controls were suspended from the overhead, similar to Navy flying boats such as the *Catalina.*

"Fantastic visibility," Zavala said. "It feels like being in a fighter plane."

Austin had settled into the copilot's seat on the right. He could see through window panels in the wing's leading edge. While Zavala ran his fingers lovingly over the controls, Austin went to explore the rest of the plane. The flight engineer sat in front of an impressive array of instrument gauges about ten feet behind the copilot facing the rear. He would have been unable to see out. Austin thought the layout was awkward, but he was impressed by the headroom and the small bunkroom, head, and kitchen that indicated the plane was built for long-range missions. He sat at the bombardier's seat and stared out the window, trying to picture himself high above the bleak Siberian landscape. Then he crawled into the bomb bays. Zavala was still in the pilot's seat, hands on the controls, when Austin returned to the cockpit.

"Find anything back there?" he asked Austin.

"It's what I *didn't* find," Austin said. "The bomb bay racks are empty."

"No canister bombs?"

"Not even a water balloon." He smiled at Zavala. "Fallen hopelessly in love with the old girl, have we?"

Zavala grinned lasciviously. "A case of love at first sight. Older women have always appealed to me. I'll show you something. There's still life in this baby." His fingers played over the instrument console. The bank of dials and gauges in front of them glowed red.

"She's all gassed up and ready to go," Austin said with disbelief.

Zavala nodded. "She must be hooked up to the generator. There's no reason this stuff wouldn't still work. It's been cold and dry here, and she was maintained in mint condition until they deserted this joint."

"Speaking of the joint, let's take a look around."

Zavala reluctantly left the cockpit. They climbed down from the plane and walked around the interior perimeter of the hangar. The space was obviously planned to service the plane efficiently. Within easy reach of the aircraft were hydraulic lifts and cranes, test equipment, fuel and oil pumps. Joe stopped to marvel at a wall hung with tools. They were as clean as surgical instruments. Austin poked his head into a storage room. He glanced around and called for Zavala.

Stacked from floor to ceiling inside the room were dozens of shiny cylinders like the one they had discovered floating in the water off the Baja. Austin carefully lifted a cylinder from the stack and felt its weight.

"This is much heavier than the empty can back in my office."

"Anasazium?"

"The unerring Austin homing instinct," Kurt said with a

smile. "You'll have to admit this is what we *really* came all this way to find."

"I suppose so. But I can see why Martin fell in love with that plane out there."

"Let's hope it isn't a similar case of fatal attraction. We're going to have to figure out what to do next."

Zavala eyed the contents of the storeroom. "We'll need something bigger than the Maule to move this stuff."

Austin said, "It's been a long day. Let's get back to Nome. We can call in for reinforcements. I'm not crazy about the way we came in. Let's see if we can find another door."

They walked around in front of the flying wing again. The plane was positioned so that it pointed toward the broad side of the hangar, facing onto the airstrip. They tried a door that would have led to the outside, but it was overgrown with vegetation and wouldn't open. A big section of wall apparently moved up and down like a garage door. Austin saw a wall switch marked "Door." Since they had good luck with the generator, he gave it a yank. The hum of motors filled the air, then came loud creaks and rattles and the squeal of metal against metal. The motors strained to move the door against the vegetation that had taken over on the outside, but finally it ripped free and rumbled to a clanking stop in fully open position.

It was near midnight, and the sun had partially set, casting the tundra in a leaden light. The two men walked outside and turned around. As they gazed at the strange craft resting in what Buzz Martin's father had called its hidey-hole, they heard an intrusive clatter from behind them. They turned to see a large helicopter dropping out of the sky like a raptor.

The helicopter made a pass over the float plane, then stopped and hovered a short distance away. It did a three-hundred-sixty spin in place. There was a flash of light from the front of the chopper, and the float plane disappeared in a blinding explosion of yellow and red flames. A cloud of black smoke billowed from the funeral pyre that had been an aircraft seconds before, and the tundra was lit up for hundreds of yards.

"I think we just lost the deposit on our leased plane," Zavala said.

Finished with its first line of business, the chopper swiveled so that its nose pointed toward the hangar. Austin and Zavala had been dumbfounded in the seconds since the helicopter arrived and began its deadly work. Now Austin realized how vulnerable they were. They dashed for the open door as the chopper leaped forward. White bursts of flame flowered from the guns on either side of the speeding aircraft, and the bullets threw up geysers of water and mud as they stitched their way toward the two running figures.

They ducked inside, and Austin hit the door switch. There was another grinding of motors and machinery, and slowly the door began to close. The chopper landed a few hundred yards away. Armed men in dark green uniforms spilled out and advanced on the hangar with automatic weapons.

Unfortunately Zavala had left his machine pistol in the plane. Austin's Bowen revolver filled his hand, and he let off a couple of shots to give the attackers something to think about. Then the door clanked shut, and the gunfire became barely audible.

"We'd better bolt the back door," Austin said, sprinting for the rear of the hangar where they had come in.

They ran along the corridor to the cellar hole. The bolt was rusted away, and they couldn't secure the door. Hoping their attackers were as stupid as they were bold, they dragged one of the mattresses out of a bunkroom and covered the ventilation hole in the floor in a makeshift pitfall. Then they dashed back and secured the door leading directly into the hangar. All was silent, but they had no illusions about their security. It was obvious that the attackers didn't want to damage the flying wing, but a few well-placed rockets or explosives could peel back the hangar's metal walls like a sardine can.

"Who *are* those guys?" Zavala said, trying to catch his breath.

There was a sharp hammering on the metal skin of the hangar as if someone were testing it for weakness. Austin's coral-green eyes swept the hangar from one end to the other.

"If I'm not mistaken, we're about to find out."

31

THE SIEGE WAS ANNOUNCED WITH an ear-splitting explosion that echoed off every square inch of steel, as if the metal-enclosed space were a huge bell. Shards of hot metal and pieces of burning vegetation rained down from a hole high in the front face of the hangar. A patch of daylight opened, but the thick cushion of vegetation and earth that had grown up around the hangar over the decades had dampened the explosion.

Austin looked up at the ragged hole and said, "They're aiming high so they won't hit the plane. Probably hoping to spook us."

"They're doing a good job," Zavala said. "I'm spooked."

In fact, Zavala looked anything but spooked. He would have retired from the Special Assignments Team long before if he succumbed easily to panic. His eyes calmly scanned the interior of the hangar looking for something that would give them even the slightest edge.

The reverberations from the blast had barely faded when there was a loud hammering on the steel door at the rear of the hangar.

"So much for our pitfall," Austin said.

They raced behind the plane and grabbed tool chests, benches, and storage lockers, anything they could move, stacking them against the door. The makeshift barricade would stall determined attackers only a few minutes. They were more concerned with the front of the hangar, where the main firepower appeared to be concentrated. As they darted under the plane's fuselage Zavala glanced up at the jet engines. The yawning black exhausts protruding from the rear of the wing resembled cannon barrels lined up on a fort. He grabbed Austin by the arm.

"Look, Kurt, those jets are pointed right at the rear wall. If we got the engines started, we could give those guys coming in the back door a warm welcome."

Austin calmly walked under the plane's fuselage, seemingly oblivious to the steady thumping from the rear of the hangar. He stood in front of the plane, where the wing's thin edge came to a point, his hands on his hips, and gazed up at the cockpit.

"Even if we somehow made it out of the hangar, we'd have no place to go. Maybe I've a got better idea," he said thoughtfully.

Working with Austin had given Zavala insight into the unorthodox way his partner's mind functioned. He caught Austin's drift instantly. "You're *kidding,*" he said.

Austin's eyes were deadly serious.

"You said the systems are working. If we can crank up the engines, why waste fuel toasting a few bad guys when we can simply leave them in the dust? Admit it," he said, catching the gleam in Zavala's eye. "You've been itching to fly this thing."

"There are a lot of ifs here. The engines may not start, or the fuel could have gone sour," Zavala said. He listed a few more undesirable possibilities, but from the way the corners of his mouth were turned up in a smile it was clear he was discounting disaster. Austin had tapped into Joe's desire to fly every type of aircraft that had ever been built.

"I know it won't be easy. Those trucks over there were probably used to tow the plane outside where it could take off. We won't have that luxury. We're going to have to make a running start."

"I'd be happy if we could make *any* kind of start. Those engines haven't been cranked over in fifty years," Zavala said.

"Just keep thinking about the scene in that Woody Allen movie, where the Volkswagen starts right up after centuries in a cave. Should be a piece of cake."

Zavala grinned. "This isn't exactly a Volkswagen," he protested, although it was clear from his excitement that the idea had gone beyond a matter of life and death. It was now a challenge. "First I'll have to see if I can get this old buggy cranked up. We're not going anywhere with those flat tires. We'll have to get air into them."

"I saw some air hoses, but we don't have much time."

"We'll start with the two outside tires under the fuselage and the nose wheel. We'll get to the inside tires if we can."

They quickly uncoiled the air hose and fed the air into the tires. The rattle of the compressor was slightly slower than their heartbeats. Austin stopped pumping air and listened. The pounding had stopped although the back door was still firmly secured. Austin didn't like it. The halt could mean the attackers were preparing to blow the door. He didn't have time to worry. Another horrendous explosion came from the front of the hangar. The blast sent them both sprawling face-first onto the oil-soaked concrete floor. A second rocket had been fired to open up the gap below the first hole. Smoke from burning vegetation hovered near the ceiling.

"We're out of time!" Austin yelled. "We'll have to stop for air at a gas station. Leave the belly hatch open. As soon as I hear the engines cranking I'll hit the wall switch. While the door's on its way up I'll run for the plane."

"Don't forget to detach the plane from its power umbilical," Zavala said as he ran for the belly hatch.

Austin took up his post next to the wall with his hand on the switch. He knew the odds were against them but hoped American wartime engineering would prove its worth.

Zavala scrambled into the pilot's high seat and peered through the plastic cowling. The dials blurred as he stared at the strange instrument panel. This was going to be a fast learning curve. He blinked his eyes and relaxed, trying to remember the procedure he used to fly the *Catalina,* trying not to look at every dial, only for needles that indicated trouble. All systems checked out fine. The center-line console between the two pilot stations contained the radio and the fuel and air speed gauges. His fingers flew over the switches, and the dials lit up like a pinball machine display.

Holding his breath, he hit the ignition switches for the engines one at a time. The turbines began with a throaty rumble and worked themselves up to a high pitch. Satisfied that the engines were working, he waved at Austin, who stood next to the wall. Austin waved back.

As Zavala jumped into the copilot's seat and adjusted the fuel feed, Austin hit the wall switch. A thin line of daylight began to shine under the rising door. Kurt dashed beneath the plane and disconnected the umbilical. Then, using the sledgehammer he had set aside for the task, he knocked the wooden wheel chocks away. Austin groped his way through the smoke, pulled himself into the plane, and battened the hatch.

The hot exhaust from engines blasted the rear of the building. Anything not nailed down was blown against the wall by the tremendous force or melted by the intense heat. The noise was so loud it was almost impossible to think, and hot, choking fumes and smoke filled the hangar.

Austin crashed, gasping for breath, into the copilot's seat. "She's all yours, pal."

Zavala gave him the thumbs-up sign. "She's a little cranky but not bad for an old gal."

Zavala's eyes were glued on the rising door. He kept the brakes set and pushed each throttle forward until they were at full power. If they had the luxury of a full crew, Zavala would have relied on a flight engineer to tell him if the engines were running the way they should, but the best he could do was rely on his experienced ear. It was impossible to distinguish individual engines, but the unbroken roar was a good sign.

The door seemed to catch for an instant, then it pulled free. He released the brakes, and the plane lurched forward. Zavala pushed the throttle levers smoothly forward and let out a rebel yell as the power from thousands of pounds of thrust pushed the plane out into the open, but his jubilation was short-lived.

The big green helicopter was directly in the line of takeoff.

The helicopter had landed after blasting the second hole, and now it sat on the tundra about a half mile away. Men in dark green uniforms were outside the hangar preparing for an assault when the wing emerged like a monstrous black bird hatching from its egg. Their surprise quickly turned to terror, and they scattered like leaves before the wind.

The helicopter pilot was leaning against the chopper smoking a cigarette when he saw the monstrous aircraft bearing down in his direction. He jumped back into the helicopter, where he was faced with an immediate decision. He could stay where he was and be rammed. He could fire his rockets or guns at the oncoming wing and hope that his hurried shots would hit the slim fuselage. Or he could head for the sky.

Austin was distracted by the sound of a giant woodpecker rapping on the fuselage. Zavala thought it was one of the engines falling apart and was only partially relieved when Austin said, "They're shooting at us. Are you going to fly this rig or drive it all the way to Nome?"

Because of the unusual position of the instrument panel, Zavala could not see all the gauges. Aiming for the helicopter to keep the plane on a straight line, Zavala shouted at Austin to call out the air speed.

"Forty!" Austin yelled.

Zavala was surprised at how quickly the plane accelerated, despite its huge mass and the partially deflated tires. He had to maintain a firm hand on the controls to keep the nose from lifting.

"Sixty!"

The landing gear hit the water of the shallow lake, but the plane's speed continued to increase.

"Eighty!"

Even as Austin called out, Zavala felt the lightness on the wheel indicating that the plane was near takeoff speed.

"One *hundred!*"

Zavala counted to ten, then pulled back on the wheel. Both men practically drove their feet through the floorboards as they pressed on imaginary accelerators. The massive plane seemed to leap into the air. Zavala had assumed that they would easily clear the helicopter, but once the plane was up at an angle all he could see was blue sky.

The helicopter pilot had finally chosen a course of action, but it was the wrong one. He mistakenly assumed that the huge bat-shaped aircraft lumbering across the permafrost in his direction would hit the chopper on the ground. He lifted off about the same time Zavala got the wing airborne.

From his level in the copilot's seat, Austin had a clear view of the chopper rising into the path of the flying wing. Unaware of the impending collision, Zavala had been concentrating on the takeoff. From his reading Zavala knew that the wing's rapid acceleration would blow the covers off the slow-moving landing gear. The gear had been designed for slower-moving propeller-driven planes and took too long to retract. Pilots compensated by retracting the gear while the plane was only a few hundred feet off the ground and pulling the nose up at a fairly steep angle.

If not for the unusual maneuver the aircraft would have collided. Instead they missed by several feet, but there was a horrendous metallic crunch as the landing gear grazed the whirling rotors. The rotors disintegrated, and the helicopter seemed to hang for a moment before it plummeted back to the ground, where it exploded in a ball of flame. The wing wobbled from the impact, but Zavala got it back under control. He kept climbing before he leveled off at five thousand feet.

Zavala realized he had forgotten to breathe. He puffed out his cheeks and gulped air into his lungs so quickly the effort made him dizzy. Austin asked him to do a damage check. He did a visual inspection of the plane from his perch. The fuselage was riddled with bullet holes. Scraps of aluminum continued to peel off, and a second engine was starting to smoke.

"She looks like a wedge of Swiss cheese, but she's a tough old bird."

He put the flying wing on a course that would take them into the vicinity of Nome. There was no need for altitude, and he kept the plane at a few thousand feet. After a while he started laughing.

"What's so funny, *compadre?*" Austin called out from his perch, where he was fiddling with the radio.

"I was just wondering what they're going to say when we come tooling in all shot up with a fifty-year-old stealth bomber."

"Simple. We'll say we were flying a mission and were kidnapped by a UFO."

Zavala shook his head. "That's almost as unbelievable as the *real* story," he said.

The arrival of the bullet-riddled flying wing had been the biggest event to hit Nome since the original Iditarod. Word of the odd-shaped black plane that had landed without landing gear on a sheet of foam had spread like wildfire, and before long it was surrounded by curious townspeople. Austin had called Sandecker from the airport to report his findings and to request some muscle power. Sandecker got in touch with the Pentagon and learned that a Special Operations team was on maneuvers at Elendorf Air Force Base outside Anchorage. The team was ordered to fly into Nome. After Austin briefed the Special Ops leaders at a strategy session, they decided to send the helicopter ahead to scope the situation out, with a quick followup by the main assault force.

It was something of a coincidence that Austin and Zavala returned to the secret blimp base in a Pave Hawk helicopter. The sixty-four-foot-long aircraft was the same kind of helicopter that patrolled Area 51, the top-secret location that UFO buffs say holds alien remains and a spaceship that crashed in Roswell, New Mexico. The helicopter had come in alone at a speed of a hundred and fifty miles per hour, flying low over the tundra to avoid detection. As it came up on the base, it made one pass over the water-covered airstrip, scouring the ground with its motion and vibration sensors. Finding no signs of life, the chopper went into a wide circling pattern. On board was a crew of three, eight heavily armed Special Operations troops, and two passengers, Austin and Zavala, who scanned the skies expectantly. They didn't have long to wait.

A fixed-wing plane appeared from the direction of the sea and passed over the base. The four-engine turboprop Combat Talon was especially designed for inserting a Special Operations Team under any conditions. Dark objects dropped from the fuselage and within seconds blossomed into twenty-six parachutes. The paratroopers floated down into the low hills behind the flying wing hangar.

The helicopter continued to circle. The plane brought in the first contingent as part of a one-two punch. If the initial assault group ran into trouble the chopper would blast the opposition from the air with its twin 7.62mm guns and land the backup force where it was most needed.

Several tense minutes passed. Then the voice of the team leader on the ground crackled over the chopper's radio.

"All clear. Okay to come in."

The Hawk darted in over the scattered wreckage of the ski plane and the blackened hulk of the chopper that had been dispatched by the flying wing. It landed directly in front of the hangar whose massive door gaped wide open like a patient in a dentist chair. A contingent of camouflage-clad Special Ops troops armed with M-16A1 assault rifles and grenade launchers, each man a killing machine of formidable power, guarded the outside while another squad explored the hangar's cavernous interior. The helicopter troops poured out of the side doors as soon as the wheels touched the ground and joined their comrades.

Then the two NUMA men got out and walked into the hangar. The space seemed even more enormous now that it no longer housed the flying wing. Blackened and charred debris left over from their takeoff was scattered throughout the hangar. The rear walls, which had felt the full force and heat of the jet-engine exhaust, were scorched and the paint blistered. They picked their way around the smoldering rubble and went directly to the storeroom. The door was open. The canisters were gone.

"Empty as a bottle of tequila on a Sunday morning," Zavala said.

"I was afraid of this. They must have brought in another chopper."

They walked outside to get away from the choking smoke inside the hangar. The Talon had found a flat, dry strip of land and was landing about a quarter of a mile away. They headed toward the wreckage of the helicopter, hoping it could provide clues to the attack. Blackened corpses were visible in and around the charred hulk. The officer who had led the first wave came over and shook hands.

"I don't know why you wanted us to come along," he said, jerking his thumb at the downed chopper. "You boys did fine on your own."

"We didn't want to press our luck," Austin said.

The officer grinned. "This place is as clean as a whistle. We checked the underground bunker as you suggested. Found a couple of dead guys at the bottom of the shaft you told us to watch out for. You know anything about that?"

Austin and Zavala exchanged a surprised glance.

"Joe and I set up a little tiger trap for our guests. We never expected it to work."

"Oh, it *worked.* Remind me never to come in your back door without knocking."

"I'll remember. Sorry you had to go through all this trouble for nothing," Austin said.

"You can never be too careful. You know what happened on Atka and Kiska."

Austin nodded. He knew the story of the two Aleutian Islands occupied by the Japanese. After U.S. troops were bloodied in the invasion of one island, they planned a massive invasion of Kiska, only to find the Japanese had quietly slipped away the night before.

"The same thing happened here. The chickens have flown the coop."

The officer surveyed the twisted wreckage again and let out a low whistle. "I'd say you clipped their wings."

Austin shook his head. "Unfortunately there was something

back in that hangar they took with them. Thanks anyway for all your help, Major."

"My pleasure. Drills are fine, but there is no substitute for a mission where people might actually be shooting at you."

"I'll see if I can arrange that next time."

The officer smiled a tight smile. "From the looks of that old bomber you brought into Nome, I'd say you're probably a man of your word."

With that operation a bust, Austin and Zavala accepted the offer of a ride to Elendorf, where they might be able to catch a flight to Washington. When the planes stopped at Nome to refuel, Zavala volunteered to use his considerable charm and the NUMA bank account to soothe the owner of the leased Maule that had been destroyed. He was coming out of the lease office after agreeing to buy the company a new plane when he saw Austin striding toward him with a serious expression on his face. He handed Zavala a piece of paper.

"This just came in."

Zavala scanned the message from NUMA: "Gamay and Francesca kidnapped. Trout injured. Come home immediately. S."

Without exchanging a word they hustled across the tarmac toward the waiting Talon.

32

PAUL TROUT LAY IN HIS HOSPITAL bed with his chest and nose wrapped in bandages, cursing himself repeatedly for not being more alert to danger. When he and Gamay were dodging the arrows of headhunters their survival instincts were at their sharpest. But their return to the so-called civilized world had dulled their senses. They had no idea that the eyes watching from the van parked outside their Georgetown townhouse were far more savage than any they had encountered in the jungle.

The letters painted on the van's doors, identifying it as belonging to the District of Columbia department of public works, were still tacky to the touch. Inside the vehicle was the latest in communications and electronic snooping equipment. Bent over the TV monitors and speakers that probed the brick walls of the house were the Kradzik brothers. Watching and waiting did not come easily to the twins. In Bosnia they used a brutally simple routine. They picked their target of choice. Then they and a couple of truckloads of paramilitary troops pulled up to the house in the dead of night, bashed the door in, and dragged the terrified occupants from their beds. The men were taken away and shot, the women raped and murdered, the house systematically looted.

Getting into the Trouts' townhouse presented a different problem. The house was on a back street, but it was well traveled with pedestrians and car traffic. The street had been even busier than usual since the Trouts returned. The discovery of a white goddess by two NUMA scientists and their dramatic escape from bloodthirsty savages was the stuff of an adventure movie. After CNN released the story a number of journalists had tracked down the Trouts. Enterprising reporters and photographers from the *Washington Post,* the *New York Times,* the national television networks, and a handful of disreputable supermarket tabloids had gathered outside their door.

Gamay and Paul took turns politely telling them that they were trying to catch up on their rest and would answer all questions at a press conference to be given the next day at NUMA headquarters. They referred inquiries to the NUMA press section. The photographers took pictures of the house, and the TV people gave reports with its façade as a backdrop. Eventually the river of attention dribbled to nothing. The same news coverage that had fascinated people around the world drew interest from more malignant sources.

Paul was in his second-floor office typing a summary of their experiences into a report for NUMA. In the downstairs study Francesca and Gamay discussed how to put the desalting project back on track as quickly as possible. After Francesca announced that she had delayed her return to São Paulo the Trouts had offered her a haven from the hordes of media attention. When the doorbell rang Gamay sighed heavily. It was her turn to answer the summons from the fourth estate. The TV crews were the most persistent, and as Gamay expected she was greeted at the door by a reporter with notebook in hand and a cameraman with his Steadicam balanced on a shoulder. A third man carried a flood lamp and a metal suitcase.

Gamay resisted her first urge, which was to tell these characters to buzz off. Instead she forced a smile and said, "You evidently haven't heard about the press conference tomorrow morning."

"Excuse please," said the reporter. "No one tell us about conference."

That's funny, Gamay thought. The public affairs people at NUMA were well plugged into the press scene. They were well respected by reporters for being up front with the amazing stories that came out of NUMA. This guy in the ill-fitting suit was nothing like any of the coiffed pretty boys who read the news. He was short and stocky, his hair cut down to the scalp. Although he was grinning, his face was feral and thuggish. Besides, since when had the networks been hiring news readers with thick eastern European accents? She looked past him, expecting to see a TV truck with disk antennas sprouting from the roof, but saw only a city work van.

"Sorry," she said, and went to close the door.

The grin disappeared, and he shoved his foot in. Startled at first by the move, Gamay quickly recovered from her surprise. She put her weight against the door until the man winced with pain. She drew her elbow back, preparing to stiff-arm the intruder in the face with the palm of her hand, but the other two men lunged forward and threw their shoulders against the door. She was knocked aside and went down on one knee. She quickly regained her footing. By then it was too late to run or fight. She was looking down the barrel of a pistol in the hand of the so-called reporter. The cameraman had put his video gear aside. He came over and grabbed her by the neck until she could barely breathe. Then he slammed her up against the wall so hard that a nineteenth-century gilded mirror crashed to the floor.

Anger surged in Gamay's breast. The mirror had cost weeks of hunting and thousands of dollars. She put her fear aside and brought her knee up into the man's crotch. The grip on her throat loosened for a second before he came at her again with a killer's gleam in his eyes. She braced herself, but the reporter yelled something and the attacker retreated. He drew his finger across his Adam's apple in an unmistakable gesture. Gamay glared at him, which was all she could do, but the significance of his sign language was not lost on her. She knew instinctively that he'd slit her throat in an instant.

Her instincts were right on the mark. Although the Kradziks preferred to work on their own, from time to time they needed help from some old compatriots. When Brynhild Sigurd had eased the exit of the Kradzik brothers from Bosnia, they had insisted that she do the same for ten of the most loyal and cold-blooded of their followers. Together they called themselves the Dirty Dozen, after the American movie of the same name. But this group made the movie misfits look like Cub Scouts. Collectively they had been responsible for the death, maiming, torture, and rape of hundreds of innocent victims. The men were scattered around the world, but could be assigned to an assassination or called in for an operation within hours. Since going to work for Gogstad they had approached their work with unbridled enthusiasm.

Francesca had heard the mirror crash and come from the study into the narrow front hall. The man in the suit barked a command, and before Francesca could make a move she was seized and shoved against the wall next to Gamay. The man who had been carrying the suitcase popped it open and drew out two Czech-made Skorpion machine pistols. The phony reporter opened the front door, and a moment later another man stepped inside. Gamay's first thought was that he looked like an overgrown troll. Although the day was warm he wore a long black leather jacket over a black turtleneck and slacks and a black military-style cap on his head.

He surveyed the situation and said something to the others that must have pleased them because they leered in response. Gamay had been around the world for her work, and she guessed that the language he spoke was Serbo-Croatian. He barked an order, and one of the men armed with a Skorpion moved down the hallway, the folding wire butt tight against his biceps. The man peered cautiously into the rooms leading off the hallway, which went to the back of the house, then continued on. His comrade climbed the stairs that led from the first level to the second floor.

The leather-clad man walked over to the mirror, surveyed the broken glass, then turned to Gamay.

"Seven years bad luck," he said with a grin that looked as if it had been forged in a foundry.

"Who are you?" Gamay said.

He ignored the question. "Where is husband?"

Gamay truthfully told the leather man that she didn't know where her husband was. He nodded, as if he knew something she didn't, and spun her around to face the wall. She expected a blow to the head or a bullet to the back. Instead there was a sharp bee-sting in her right arm. A needle. *Bastards!* They had jabbed her with a hypodermic. She looked over in time to see the syringe plunge into Francesca's arm. She tried to go to the aid of the other woman, but her arm went dead. Within seconds the numbness spread to the rest of her body. The room whirled, and she felt as if she were hurtling into an abyss.

Paul heard the mirror crash to the floor and from the top of the stairs saw the man throttle Gamay. He was about to spring from the staircase when the creep in the leather coat came in. Paul went back into his office and tried to call for help. The phone was dead. The lines must have been cut. He crept silently down a narrow back stairway to the kitchen. He kept a revolver in the study, but the only way to get to it was along the hallway. He saw the two armed men split off, one heading upstairs, the other coming his way, and ducked back into the kitchen.

He looked around for a weapon. Knives were obvious, but they were messy and wouldn't stand a chance against the machine pistol. Even if he got the upper hand the others would come running to finish him off at the slightest noise. He needed someplace where he could dispatch the man with a minimum of racket. The last time he and Gamay remodeled the house they had sunk a year's salary into the kitchen. All-new oak cabinets had been installed along with a restaurant-type stove. The biggest change was a walk-in cooler whose ceiling was high enough for Paul to go inside without bumping his head.

Seeing no alternative, he slipped into the cooler and left the door ajar about six inches. He unscrewed the light bulb, placed it just inside the door, and plastered himself into the recess next to the heavy door. *Just in time.* Through the frosted glass he saw the man come into the kitchen, his gun ready. He stopped and looked around, and the open door caught his attention. He approached it warily, pushed it open with his elbow, and stepped inside. The toe of his shoe sent the bulb skittering noisily across the wooden floor. The gun barrel swung around, and his finger tightened on the trigger. Then the roof fell in on his head. His knees buckled, and he crashed to the floor.

Trout put down the frozen smoked Virginia ham he had used as a club. He grabbed the machine pistol and stepped out into the kitchen, well aware that he and the women weren't home free. First he checked the stairs that led from the kitchen to the second floor. He could hear the other man moving around upstairs. He'd deal with that after he made sure Gamay and Francesca were safe. He slowly eased himself into the hallway. The machine pistol only gave him limited leverage. He didn't want to catch the women in the pistol's scattershot spray.

As he stepped into the hall he saw the other men bending over the prone figures of his wife and Francesca. He brushed caution aside and moved forward, so intent on the scene that he never saw the man come up behind him.

He felt the cold steel of a knife between his ribs and tried to turn to face his attacker only to have his legs turned to scrambled eggs. He fell to the floor, smashing his face on the rug and breaking his nose.

Melo had been covering the back door for a possible escape when he saw Trout emerge from the cooler. Seeing blood pool around Paul's body, he stepped over him and went over to pat his brother on the back.

"Your suggestion to cover the rear was a good one, brother."

"It seems so," the other twin said, looking at the sprawled figure. "What should we do with him?"

"Leave him to bleed to death."

"Agreed. We can take the women out the back way without being seen."

He called to the man upstairs to come back down. Then they carried the unconscious women to a waiting Mercedes four-wheel drive, stuffed them in the back, and drove off, followed a few minutes later by the fake DPW truck. The initial shock of the knife wound had turned to pain, and Paul regained consciousness for a few moments. Using every bit of strength at his command he dragged himself to the study, where he had a cell phone, and called 911. He awoke in a hospital bed.

His cursing wore him out, and he fell asleep again. When he awoke he was aware someone else was in the room. Through gluey eyes he saw two figures standing by his bed. He grinned feebly.

"What took you so damned long?"

"We hitchhiked with a couple of fighter planes out of Elendorf and came east as fast as we could," Austin said. "How do you feel?"

"The right half of my body isn't so bad, but the left feels as if it's being pinched by red-hot pliers. And my nose doesn't feel great."

"The knife missed your lung by this much," Austin said, pinching his thumb and forefinger. "It will take a while for the muscle to heal. Good thing you're not a southpaw."

"Figured it was something like that. Any word on Gamay or Francesca?" he said apprehensively.

"We think they're still alive, but they were kidnapped by the goons who did this to you."

"The police have checked airports and stations, the usual stuff," Zavala said. "We're going to start our own search."

The pain in Paul's blue eyes was replaced by a look of steely determination. He swung his long legs out of the bed and said, "I'm coming with you." The painful effort made him dizzy, and he stopped as his stomach roiled for a few seconds. He jiggled the IV tube. "I may need a hand here, fellas. Don't try to talk me out of this," he said, catching Austin's concerned expression.

"The best thing you can do is spring me from the joint. Hope you've got some pull with the floor nurse."

Austin knew Paul well enough to realize he would drag himself from the hospital if he had to. Austin glanced at Zavala, who was smiling, and knew he'd get no help from that quarter.

"I'll see what I can do." He shrugged. "In the meantime, Joe, maybe you can get our friend here something more modest than that hospital johnny," he said. Then he turned and headed for the nurses' station.

33

THE MOOD IN THE TENTH-FLOOR NUMA conference room was as somber as a crepe hangers' convention. Admiral Sandecker hadn't expected Trout to attend the emergency meeting, given the dire reports from the hospital. The lanky ocean geologist looked like warmed-over spit, but Sandecker kept his thoughts to himself. Nothing he could say would dissuade Paul from joining the hunt for Gamay and Francesca.

Sandecker flashed Trout a reassuring smile and looked around the table. Flanking Paul in case he fell out of his chair were his NUMA colleagues Austin and Zavala. The fourth figure at the table, a slightly built, narrow-shouldered man whose heavy horn-rimmed glasses gave him a professorial air, was NUMA operations director Rudi Gunn, second in command to the admiral.

Sandecker checked his watch. "Where's Yaeger?" His voice carried a hint of impatience.

Yaeger's special computer skills bought him latitude with the NUMA dress code, but not even the president would dare show up late for a Sandecker meeting. Especially one as important as this.

"He'll be along in a few minutes," Austin explained. "I asked Hiram to check out something that might have a bearing on our discussion."

A thought had been fluttering around like a butterfly inside

Austin's skull. He had allowed himself a few hours of sleep after coming in from Alaska. The rest must have refreshed his mind. On his way in from Virginia he caught the elusive notion in an imaginary net. Seconds later he was talking to Yaeger on his cell phone. The computer whiz was driving in from the fashionable section of Maryland where he lived with his artist wife and two teenage daughters. Austin quickly outlined his idea, asked Yaeger to follow through, and said he would cover for him at the meeting.

Sandecker got right down to business. "We have a mystery on our hands, gentlemen. Two people have been kidnapped and one attacked by unknown assailants. Kurt, would you bring us up to date?"

Austin nodded. "The D.C. police are investigating every possible lead. The city van was found abandoned near the Washington Monument. The vehicle had been stolen a few hours earlier. No trace of fingerprints was found. All the airports and train stations are being watched. With help from Paul, the FBI put together a composite of the leader of the gang, and it's being circulated with Interpol."

"I suspect they will get nowhere," Sandecker said. "The people we're dealing with are professionals. The job of finding Gamay and Dr. Cabral will be up to us. As you know, Rudi has been out of the country on assignment. I've kept him current as best as I could, but it might help if you quickly gave us a chronological summary of the situation."

Austin was prepared for the question. "This thing began ten years ago with the failed attempt to kidnap Francesca Cabral. Her plane crashed in the Venezuela rain forest, and it was assumed she was dead. Fast-forward ten years. Joe and I, quite literally, run into a dead pod of gray whales off San Diego. The whales died after being exposed to extreme heat emanating from an underwater facility off Baja California in Mexico. The facility blew up while we were investigating it. I talked to a Mexican mobster who was a front for the real owner, a California consulting firm called the Mulholland

Group. The mobster's lawyer confirmed that Mulholland in turn is part of a transnational conglomerate named the Gogstad Corporation. The mobster and his lawyer were assassinated shortly after they talked to us."

"Rather spectacularly, as I recall," Sandecker noted.

"That's correct. These weren't exactly drive-by shootings. The murders were well planned, and the hit men used sophisticated weaponry."

"That would suggest well-organized assassins with extensive resources," said Gunn, who had once served as director of logistics at NUMA and was well acquainted with the difficulties in pulling together any operation.

"We came to the same conclusion," Austin agreed. "It was the kind of organization and resources that could be provided by a big corporation so motivated."

"Gogstad?"

Austin nodded.

"I'm not sure I understand the significance of the name Gogstad," Gunn said.

"The only connection I could find was the company logo. It shows the Gogstad Viking ship that was discovered back in the 1800s. I asked Hiram to see what he could dig up on the company. There isn't a lot. Even Max had problems finding information, but basically it's a huge conglomerate with holdings worldwide. It's run by a woman named Brynhild Sigurd."

"A *woman,*" Gunn noted with surprise. "Interesting name. Brynhild was a Valkyrie, one of the Norse maidens who carry the fallen heroes from the battlefield to Valhalla. Sigurd was her lover. You don't suppose that was her real name, do you?"

"We don't know much about the woman."

"I know megacorporations can be ruthless in their business dealings," Gunn said with a shake of his head, "but we're talking about gangland methods here."

"That's the way it seems," Austin said. He turned to Zavala. "Joe, could you fill Rudi in on your findings?"

"Kurt called me in California with the Gogstad lead," Zavala said. "I talked to a newspaper reporter from the *Los Angeles Times.* He knew Gogstad quite well. In fact, he was heading an investigative team looking into the corporation. He told me they were doing a story on what he called the water pirates. It would reveal how Gogstad is cornering the world's supply of water."

"I can't believe it's possible for one company to control the world's water," Gunn said.

"I was pretty skeptical, too," Zavala replied. "But from what the reporter told me it's not that far-fetched. Gogstad's companies have legally taken over the privatization of the Colorado River. Water is going from public to private ownership on every continent. Gogstad has muscled out the competition. The reporter said that there have been deaths and disappearances worldwide over the past several years. The missing or dead were all people who competed with Gogstad or opposed Gogstad takeovers."

Gunn whistled softly. "That story should cause quite a stir when it hits the headlines."

"That won't happen any time soon. The paper killed the Gogstad story for no reason. The other three members of the investigative team have disappeared, and my friend has gone into hiding."

"You're sure there's no mistake," Gunn said with alarm.

Zavala slowly shook his head. There was silence in the room, then Gunn spoke.

"There's obviously a pattern, then," he said. "Let me think about this." Gunn's unprepossessing appearance was misleading. His graduation at the top of his class in the Naval Academy was no accident. He was a sheer genius, and his analytical skills were uncanny. He cradled his chin between his thumb and forefinger and lost himself in deep thought for a moment. "Something has changed," he said abruptly.

"What do you mean, Rudi?" Sandecker said.

"Their methodology has shifted gears. Let's assume that our basic premise is right and Gogstad is behind all this murder and mayhem. According to Joe, they have acted quietly. People quite simply vanished or were killed in so-called accidents. This changed with the murders of the Mexican and the crooked lawyer. I believe the word the admiral used to describe them was *spectacular.*"

Austin chuckled. "Those were love pats compared with the attack in Alaska. Joe and I had to contend with an all-out military assault."

"The attack on my house was on the heavy-handed side, too," Trout added.

"I think I see where you're headed with this, Rudi," Sandecker said. "Paul, how soon did word get out that Dr. Cabral was alive?"

"Almost immediately," Trout said. "Dr. Ramirez called Caracas from the helicopter that rescued us. The Venezuelan government lost no time making the news public. I would guess that CNN was broadcasting the story around the globe while we were still in the rain forest."

"Events accelerated shortly thereafter," Sandecker said. "The situation is clear to me. The catalyst was the news that Francesca Cabral was alive. Her emergence from the grave meant that her water-desalting process was again within the realm of possibility. With her expertise once more available, all that was needed was the rare substance that makes her process work. Dr. Cabral again planned to give her discovery to the world. The people who opposed this simply picked up where they left off ten years ago."

"Only this time they succeeded," Austin said.

"Okay, that explains Francesca's kidnapping," Trout said. "But why did they take Gamay?"

"This outfit does nothing at random," Austin replied. "Gamay may have been lucky. She might have been killed if they didn't have need of her. Is there anything else you can remember about the kidnapping, Paul?"

"I didn't see much after the first few minutes they were in the house. The leader, the guy in black leather, spoke with an accent I can't place. His pals had heavier accents."

Sandecker had been sitting back in his chair, fingers tented in front of him, listening to the conversational byplay. He snapped upright.

"These hoodlums are the small fry. We must go right to the top. We must find this woman with the Wagnerian name who runs Gogstad."

"She's a ghost," Austin said. "Nobody even knows where she lives."

"She and Gogstad are the key," Sandecker said firmly. "Do we know where their headquarters are?"

"They have offices in New York, Washington, and the West Coast. There must be a dozen scattered across Europe and Asia."

"Quite the hydra," Sandecker said.

"Even if we knew where their central office was, it wouldn't do much good. To outward appearances, Gogstad is a legitimate business. They'll deny any accusations we make."

Hiram Yaeger slipped quietly into the room and settled into a chair. "Sorry," he said. "I had to run some stuff off for the meeting." He looked expectantly at Austin, who took the cue.

"I was thinking about something Hiram showed me earlier. It was a hologram of a Viking ship. The same ship is the centerpiece of the Gogstad corporate logo. I reasoned that this ship must have some significance to be given such a prominent place. I asked Hiram to start playing around with Gogstad, to go beyond the scant corporate stuff Max dug up for us."

Yaeger nodded. "At Kurt's suggestion I asked Max to go back and brush over the historical and maritime links I had pretty much ignored before. Tons of material on the subject exist, as you might imagine. Kurt had said to look for a California connection, perhaps with the Mulholland Group. Max picked up an interesting newspaper story. A Norwegian designer of antique ships had come to California to do a replica of the Gogstad ship for a wealthy client."

"Who was the client?" Austin asked.

"The article didn't say. But it was easy to track down the Norwegian designer. I called him a few minutes ago and asked about the job. He had been sworn to secrecy, but it was years ago, and he didn't mind saying he built the replica for a big woman in a big house."

"Big woman?"

"He meant *tall.* A giantess."

"Sounds like a Scandinavian folktale. What's this about the house?"

"He said it was like a modern-day Viking compound on the shores of a large lake in California surrounded by mountains."

"Tahoe?"

"That was my conclusion."

"A big Viking house on the shores of Lake Tahoe. Shouldn't be too hard to find."

"Already done. Max linked up to a commercial satellite." Yaeger passed around copies of the satellite photos. "There are some big places around the lake, trophy homes, resorts and hotels. But nothing like this."

The first picture showed the icy blue waters of Lake Tahoe viewed from a high altitude as if it were a puddle. In another photo the camera had zoomed down on a dot alongside the lake, enlarging the details so that the sprawling building and the nearby helicopter pad were clear.

"Does this hovel have an owner?" Austin said.

"I was able to tap into the local assessor's office and tax database." Yaeger grinned. If he had a tail he'd be wagging it. "It's owned by a realty trust."

"That doesn't give us much to go on."

"How about this, then? The trust is part of the Gogstad Corporation."

Sandecker looked up from the photos. He had kept his famous temper in control throughout the meeting, but he was furious at the kidnapping of one of his favored staffers and the wounding of another. He was enraged, too, after all she had suffered, at the abduction of the lovely Dr. Cabral. Once again a discovery with lifesaving implications was being kept from the world.

"Thank you, Hiram." He glanced around the table with cold, commanding blue eyes. "Well, gentlemen," he said with a voice as sharp-edged as a razor. "We know what we have to do."

34

THE MEN WATCHING FRANCESCA were either twins or some mad cloning experiment gone bad. The most terrifying thing was not their repulsiveness. It was their absolute silence. They sat a few yards away, one on either side, leaning on the backs of chairs that had been turned around. They were identical in every way, from their troll-like ugliness to their preference for black leather.

She tried not to look at the dark, red-rimmed eyes under beetling brows, the metallic dental work, and the bloodless pallor of the psychopathic faces. They were looking at her hungrily, but there was nothing sexual in their leers. This was not the ignorant savagery she was used to with the Chulo. This was pure animal lust, hunger for blood and bone. She glanced around the strange circular white room with the plain walls and uncomfortably cool temperature. At its center was a computer console. She was thinking how absurdly big the furniture was and wondered whether the outsized chairs, like the low temperature, were a psychological ploy to make people brought there feel small and inadequate. She could be anywhere in the world.

Francesca had no idea how she had come to this sterile chamber. She was vaguely aware of being moved from one place to the other. At one point she thought she heard jet engines, but she was injected with drugs again and slipped off into black unconsciousness. She had seen no sign of Gamay, and that worried her, too. She had felt a pinprick in her arm and awakened quickly as if she had been injected with a stimulant. As her eyes fluttered open she saw the twins. No one had spoken for several minutes. She was grateful when the door hissed open and the woman entered and waved the grotesque twins away.

Francesca wondered if she had blundered into a freak show or the set of a Fellini movie. She knew the reason for the outsized furniture. The woman dressed in the dark green uniform was a giantess. Settling into a big sofa, she smiled pleasantly but without warmth. "Are you well, Dr. Cabral?"

"What did you do with Gamay?"

"Your NUMA friend? She is comfortably quartered in her room."

"I want to see her."

The woman lazily reached over and tapped her computer screen, and Gamay appeared on the monitor, lying on her side on a cot. Francesca held her breath. Then Gamay stirred, tried to rise, only to fall back onto the cot.

"She has not been given the drug antidote as you were. She will sleep it off and awaken in a few hours."

"I want to see her in person to make sure she is all right."

"Later perhaps." The answer was uncompromising. The woman touched the screen, and it went dark.

Francesca looked around. "Where exactly *is* this place?"

"That's not important."

"Why have you brought us here?"

The woman ignored her question. "Did Melo and Radko frighten you?"

"Do you mean the human mushrooms who just left?"

She smiled at the comparison. "A clever metaphor, but you would do better to compare them to poisonous toadstools. Despite your bravado, I can see the fear in your eyes. Good. They *should* frighten you. During the ethnic cleansing campaign in Bosnia the Kradzik brothers personally killed hundreds of people and planned the deaths of thousands. They destroyed entire villages and engineered numerous massacres. If not for me they would be sitting in the prisoners' dock at the World Court in the Hague, charged with crimes against humanity. There is no war crime they did not commit. They have absolutely no conscience, no morals, no sense of remorse for anything they do. Maiming and killing are second nature to them." She paused to let her words sink in. "Am I making my point?"

"Yes. That you have no scruples yourself about hiring murderers."

"Exactly. Their murderous character is precisely *why* I hired them. It is no different from a carpenter buying a hammer to drive nails into a board. The Kradzik twins are my hammer."

"People aren't nails."

"Some are. Some aren't, Dr. Cabral."

Francesca wanted to change the subject. "How do you know my name?"

"I have known and admired your work for years, Dr. Cabral. In my opinion, your fame as one of the world's leading hydro-engineers easily eclipses your more recent notoriety as a white goddess."

"You know who I am, but who are you?"

"My name is Brynhild Sigurd. Although your name is better known than mine, we are both accomplished in our chosen field, the movement of the earth's most precious substance, its water."

"You're a hydro-engineer?"

"I studied at the finest technological institutions in Europe. After I finished my studies I moved to California, where I started my consulting company, now one of the biggest in the world."

Francesca shook her head. She thought she knew everyone in the water engineering fraternity. "I've never heard of you."

"I prefer it that way. I've always operated behind the scenes. I'm nearly seven feet tall. My stature makes me a freak, subject to derision from those very much inferior to me."

Despite her predicament, Francesca felt a slight pang of empathy. "I had my share of harassment from idiots who don't like the idea of a woman excelling in their field. I never let it bother me."

"Perhaps you *should* have. In the long run my resentment at having to hide from the public has been an asset. I directed my anger, retooling it into an unstoppable ambition. I acquired other companies, all with an eye toward the future. There was only one fly in the ointment." The cold smile again. "*You,* Dr. Cabral."

"I've never considered myself an insect, Ms. Sigurd."

"My apologies for the label, but the analogy is precise. Some years ago it became clear to me that in time the demand for the world's water would exceed the supply, and I wanted to be the one with her hand on the tap. Then I heard about your revolutionary desalting process. If you were successful it would torpedo my carefully laid plans. I couldn't allow that to happen. I considered making you an offer, but I had studied your personality and knew I could never get through your impractical altruism. I resolved to prevent you from giving the process to the world."

Francesca felt the heat rising in her cheeks. Her voice came out in a hiss. "*You* were the one behind my attempted kidnapping."

"I had hoped to persuade you to work for me. I would have set you up in a laboratory to perfect your process. Unfortunately my plans went awry, and you disappeared into the Amazon. Everyone thought you were dead. Then I read with admiration about your adventures among the savages, how you became their queen. I knew that we were both survivors in a hostile world."

Francesca had gotten her initial fury under control, and her reply was in measured tones. "What would you have done with the process if I *had* given it to you?"

"I would have kept it secret while I consolidated my grip on the world's water."

"I was going to *give* my findings to the world free of charge," Francesca said disdainfully. "My goal was to *relieve* suffering, not profit by it."

"Laudable but self-defeating. With you apparently dead, I set up a plant in Mexico to duplicate your work. It was destroyed in an explosion."

Francesca almost laughed. She knew the reason for the blast and was tempted to throw it in this woman's face. Instead she said, "I'm not surprised. Working with high pressure and extreme heat can be tricky."

"No matter. The main lab here was working on another aspect of the process. Then came the happy announcement of your escape from the Amazon. Again you disappeared, but I knew of your ties to NUMA. We've been watching the Trouts since they returned."

"Too bad you're wasting your time once again."

"I don't think so. It's not too late to put your talents to work for me."

"You have a strange way of recruiting employees. Your first kidnapping attempt was the reason I spent ten years in the wilderness. Now you drug and kidnap me again. Why would I want to do *anything* for you?"

"I can offer you unparalleled support for your research."

"A dozen foundations would be glad to fund my work. Even if I were inclined to work for you, which I'm not, there is a major obstacle. The desalting process involves a complex molecular metamorphosis that works only in the presence of a rare substance."

"I know about anasazium. My supply of the material was destroyed in the blast at the Mexican facility."

"Too bad," Francesca said. "The process can't work without it. So if you'll be so kind as to allow me to leave . . ."

"You'll be pleased to know that I have all the anasazium you'll need to develop your process. When I heard of your return I acquired a substantial amount of the refined material. Just in time, I might add. NUMA had dispatched part of its Special Assignments Team on a similar mission. Now I can carry out my full plan to control the world's fresh water. You alone would appreciate the simple brilliance of my scheme, Dr. Cabral."

Francesca feigned a reluctant agreement, as if she were secretly pleased at the compliment. "Well, of course, as a water scientist I would be curious about such an ambitious endeavor."

"The world is entering one of the most serious droughts in its history. This dry spell could last a hundred years if the past is any indication. The first impacts have been felt in Africa, China, and the Middle East. Europe is beginning to experience a thirst that cannot be quenched. I simply plan to accelerate the process of drying out the world."

"Excuse my skepticism, but that's absurd."

"Is it?" Brynhild replied with a smile. "The United States is not immune. The great desert cities of the Southwest, Los Angeles, Phoenix, Las Vegas, draw their water from the Colorado River, which is now under my control. They rely on a tenuous network of dams, reservoirs, and river diversion. The water supply hangs by a thread. Any disruption in the water supply would be disastrous."

"You're not going to blow up a dam?" Francesca said with alarm.

"Nothing so crude. With their regular water supply at the breaking point, the cities have been depending more and more on private sources. Gogstad's straw corporations have been buying up water systems everywhere. We can create a water shortage wherever and whenever we want to simply by turning the handle of the tap. Then we will sell only to the places that can afford it, the big cities and the high-tech centers."

"What of those who *can't* afford it?"

"There's an old saying in the West: 'Water flows uphill to money.' The wealthy have always been assured of a cheap water source at the expense of others. Under my plan water will no longer be cheap. We will be doing this on a worldwide scale, in Europe and Asia, South America and Africa. It will be capitalism at its purest. The market will determine price."

"But water isn't a commodity like pork bellies."

"You've been in the jungle too long. Globalization is nothing more than the promotion of monopolies in communication, agriculture, food, or power. Why not water? Under the new international treaties, no one country owns its water resources anymore. They go to the highest bidder, and Gogstad will be the highest bidder."

"You will deny water to thousands who will be forced out of the market. There will be famine and chaos in countries that can't afford to buy water."

"Chaos will be our friend. It will prepare the way for Gogstad's political takeover of weakened governments. Think of it as water Darwinism. The strong will survive."

The icy blue eyes seemed to bore into Francesca's skull. "Don't think this is retribution for all the slights I have received because of my stature. I am a businesswoman who realizes the proper political climate is necessary to do business. This has required no small investment on my part. I have spent millions building up a fleet of water tankers that would transport water from places that have it, towing it behind them in huge ocean-going bags. I have been waiting years for this moment. I have not dared to move because I feared your process. It could destroy my monopoly within weeks. Now that I have you and the anasazium, I can strike. Within days the entire western half of the country will run out of water."

"That's impossible!"

"*Is* it? We will see. Once the Colorado River is finished as a supplier, the rest of the pieces will fall rapidly into place. My company controls most of the fresh water supplies in other parts of the world. We will simply turn the faucet off, so to speak. Gradually at first, then more forcefully. If there are any complaints, we will say that we are producing as much water as possible."

"You know the results," Francesca said levelly. "You're talking about turning much of the world into desert. The consequences would be terrible."

"Terrible for some, but not those who control the world's water. We could get any price we ask."

"From desperate people. You would soon be exposed as the monster you are."

"To the contrary. Gogstad will say that we are ready to move water from Alaska, British Columbia, and the Great Lakes to other parts of the world in the tanker fleet I have been building. When Gogstad's beautiful tankers appear off the coast we will be hailed as heroes."

"You're already apparently rich beyond the dreams of many. Why do you need more wealth?"

"This could benefit the world in the long run. I will prevent wars from being fought over water."

"A pax Gogstad, imposed by force."

"Force will not be necessary. I will reward those who bend to my will, punish those who don't."

"By letting them wither and die."

"If that's necessary, yes. You must wonder where your desalination process fits in."

"I assume you would never allow it to spoil your mad plot."

"To the contrary, your process is an important part of my scheme. I don't intend to keep my tankers at sea forever. They are only a stopgap measure while the world builds the fantastic infrastructure that will run water down from the polar ice cap. Vast agricultural areas that have gone to desert will have to be invigorated with huge-scale irrigation."

"No country could afford that. Whole nations will go bankrupt."

"All the better to snatch them up at a fire sale. Eventually I will build desalting plants using the Cabral process, but I alone will control their output."

"Again to the highest bidder."

"Of course. Now let me present my new offer. I will place you in a lab with everything you need at your command."

"If I say no?"

"Then I will turn your NUMA friend over to the Kradzik brothers. She will not die quickly or pleasantly."

"She's an innocent. She has no part in this."

"Nonetheless she is a nail that must be hammered down if necessary."

Francesca was silent for a moment. Then she said, "How do I know I can trust you?"

"You *can't* trust me, Dr. Cabral. You should know that you can never trust anyone. But you are intelligent enough to see that you are far more valuable to me than your friend's life and that I am willing to trade. As long as you cooperate, she lives. Do you agree?"

This woman and the deeds hatched in the dark recesses of her brilliant mind revolted Francesca. Brynhild was obviously a megalomaniac and, like so many of her ruthless predecessors, was impervious to the sufferings of the innocent. Francesca had not survived ten years among savage headhunters, blood-sucking bats, and stinging insects and plants without inner resources. She could be as Machiavellian as the most devious. Living in the jungle had given her the quiet ferocity of a stalking jaguar. Since her escape she had been consumed with the desire for revenge. She knew it was wrong and misplaced, but it sustained and helped maintain her grip on her sanity. She pushed her thirst for vengeance aside for the moment. This woman must be stopped.

Suppressing a smile, she bowed her head in submission and with a feigned catch in her voice said, "You win. I will help in developing the process."

"Agreed. I'll show you the facility you'll be working in. You'll be quite impressed."

"I want to talk to Gamay to make sure she is all right."

Brynhild punched a button on the intercom. Two men in dark green uniforms appeared. Francesca was relieved to see that they were not the Kradziks.

"Take Dr. Cabral to see our other guest," Brynhild ordered. "Then bring her back to me." She turned to Francesca. "You have ten minutes. I want you to get to work immediately."

Flanked by the guards, Francesca was led through a labyrinth of passageways to an elevator that dropped several levels. They stopped in front of an unmarked door opened by punching out the code on a keypad. The guards stood outside while Francesca entered the small windowless room. Gamay was sitting on the edge of her cot. She looked groggy, like a fighter who has taken one too many punches. She brightened and smiled when she saw Francesca. She tried to rise, but her legs buckled and she had to sit again.

Francesca sat on the cot and put her arm around her friend's shoulders. "Are you all right?"

Gamay brushed her straggly hair aside. "My legs are wobbly, but I'll be fine. What about you?"

"They gave me a stimulant. I've been awake for some time. Your drugs will wear off soon."

"Did anyone mention what happend to Paul? He was upstairs when the kidnappers broke in."

Francesca shook her head. Putting aside her worst fears, Gamay said, "Do you have any idea where we are?"

"No. Our host didn't tell us."

"You mean you've spoken to someone I can thank for these glorious accommodations?"

"Her name is Brynhild Sigurd. Those were her men who kidnapped us."

Gamay started to reply, but Francesca pursed her lips and shifted her eyes from left to right. Gamay caught the hint. They were being bugged and probably watched.

"I only have a few minutes. I just wanted you to know I've agreed to work with Ms. Sigurd on my desalting process. We'll have to stay here until the project is complete. I don't know how long it will take."

"You're going to work with the person who kidnapped us?"

"Yes," Francesca replied with a stubborn tilt of her chin. "I wasted ten years of my life in the jungle. There's a great deal of money to be made, but beyond that I believe Gogstad has the best chance of bringing my process to the world in an orderly and controlled fashion."

"Are you sure this is what you want to do?"

"Yes, I'm absolutely sure," she said.

The door slid open, and one of the guards motioned for Francesca to leave. She nodded, then leaned over and gave

Gamay a hug. Then she stood quickly and went off with the guards. Alone once more, Gamay pondered what had just happened. As their eyes met briefly, Francesca had winked. There was no mistake about it. Gamay was pleased to think there was more to Francesca's startling announcement that she was working for the enemy, but there were more immediate concerns. She lay back on her cot and closed her eyes. Her first priority was to give her body and brain a rest. Then she would try to figure out how to escape.

35

THE MAN FLOATED HIGH ABOVE the cobalt-blue waters of Lake Tahoe, suspended from the parasail under a red-and-white canopy that billowed over his head like an old-fashioned round parachute. He sat in a reclining Skyrider chair attached by a towline to the moving winch boat two hundred feet below.

The rider clicked on his handheld radio. "Let's go around for one more pass, Joe."

Zavala, who was at the wheel of the boat, waved to show that he had heard Austin's instruction. He put the ParaNautique winch boat into a big, slow turn that would take them back along the lake's California side.

The maneuver gave Austin a sweeping view of the lake. Lake Tahoe is on the California-Nevada border in the Sierra Nevada about twenty-three miles southwest of Reno. Ringed by rugged mountains that are covered with snow in the winter, Tahoe is the largest alpine lake in the United States. It is more than a mile high, more than sixteen hundred feet deep. The lake is twenty-two miles long and about a dozen miles wide and lies in a fault basin created by ancient forces deep in the earth. Two-thirds of its two-hundred-square-mile area is in California. At the north end it empties into the Truckee River. At the south end a river of money empties into the coffers of the high-rise gambling casinos at Stateline. The first white man to discover the lake was John C.

Freemont who was on a surveying mission. To English speakers the Washoe Indian name for the lake, *Da-ow,* which means "much water," sounded like Tahoe, and the pronunciation stuck.

As the parasail brought Austin around in a wide arc he concentrated his attention on a particular stretch of shoreline and the dark forest rising behind it, imprinting the image on his mind. He would have preferred to use a video or still camera instead of his imperfect memory, but traffic this close to Gogstad's lair was sure to come under close scrutiny. Any undue interest on his part, such as pointing a camera lens in the wrong direction, would set off alarms.

He drifted past a long pier that jutted from the rocky shore. A powerboat was tied up at the pier. Behind a boathouse or storage shed, the black rocks rose at a sharp angle, then leveled off into a heavily wooded natural tableland. Several hundred yards back from shore the land rose again in thick forest. The towers, roofs, and turrets peeking above the tall trees reminded Austin of the castle ramparts in a Grimm fairy tale.

Austin's eye was drawn by sudden movement. Several men in dark clothes had run out to the end of the pier. He was too far away to see details, but he wouldn't be surprised if pictures of him parasailing wound up in a Gogstad family album.

The pier disappeared in his wake as the winch boat towed him another mile south. When they were safely out of view he gave Zavala the okay to haul him in. The winch pulled the Skyrider in like a boy reeling in a kite. The reclining chair splashed down and floated in the water. Austin was grateful he wasn't using the old harness-style rig which would have dunked him in the lake. Even in summer the water temperature was in the sixties.

"See anything interesting?" Zavala asked as he helped Austin back into the winch boat.

"There's no welcome mat on the doorstep, if that's what you mean."

"I think I saw a welcoming committee on the dock."

"They came charging out the minute we did our second fly-by. We were right about the tight security."

They had assumed the compound would be well guarded and that there would be no point sneaking around. Reasoning that the obvious was often the most innocuous, they had flashed a wad of bills and their NUMA IDs and persuaded the owner of the parasail and the winch boat to spare his equipment for a few hours. They implied that they were investigating the Mafia, which was not implausible given the nearness to the gambling casinos. Since business was off and he stood to make more in the deal than he earned in a week, he went along with the deal.

Austin helped Zavala stow the Skyrider and parasail, then he opened a waterproof bag and dug out a sketch pad and pen. Apologizing for his draftsmanship, which was really quite good, he drew several sketches of what he had seen from the air. He had brought along the satellite photos Yaeger provided and compared the sketches to them. At the top of the bluff the staircase from the dock connected with a walkway. This in turn widened into a road that led to the main complex. A spur from the road shot off to a helicopter pad.

"A full frontal waterborne assault is out of the question," he said.

"Can't say I'm disappointed. I haven't forgotten our shootout in Alaska," Zavala said.

"I had hoped to see down into the water. In the old days the lake was as clear as crystal, but the runoff from all the development around the shores has clouded up the water with algae growth."

Zavala had been studying another photo. After their strategy meeting at NUMA headquarters, Austin called up a NOAA satellite photo of Lake Tahoe. The shot showed the water temperature of the lake in colors. The lake was almost entirely blue except for one spot along the western shore where the red shade denoted high temperatures. The heated water was practically under the Gogstad pier. It was similar to the heat pulse in the ocean off the Baja coast.

"Pictures don't lie," Zavala said. "There's always the possibility of a hot spring."

Austin frowned.

"Okay, say you're right, that there's an underwater facility like the one in the Baja. There's one thing I don't understand. We're talking about a *desalting* plant. This is a freshwater lake."

"I agree, it doesn't make sense. But there's only one way to find out for sure. Let's head back and see if our package has arrived."

Austin started the engine and pointed the winch boat toward South Lake Tahoe. They skimmed over the intense blue waters, and before long they were pulling into a marina. A lanky figure stood at the end of a finger pier waving at them. Paul had stayed on shore. His wound was still too tender to allow him to bounce around in a boat. As they pulled up to the slip he grabbed the line with his good hand and tied them off.

"Your package has arrived," he announced. "It's in the parking lot."

"That was fast," Austin said. "Let's take a look." He and Zavala set off toward the parking lot.

"Wait," Paul said.

Austin was eager to check out the delivery. "We'll fill you in later," he said over his shoulder.

Paul shook his head. "Can't say I didn't try to warn you," he muttered.

The flatbed truck was pulled up off to the side. The object on the trailer was about the shape and size of two cars, one behind the other. It was covered with padding and dark plastic. Austin had moved in for a closer look when the passenger door of the truck opened and a familiar figure stepped out. Jim Contos, skipper of the *Sea Robin,* strolled over with a grin on his face.

"Uh-oh," Zavala said.

"Jim," Austin said. "What a nice surprise."

"What the hell is going on, Kurt?" The grin had vanished.

"It was an emergency, Jim."

"Yeah, I figured it was an emergency when Rudi Gunn called in the middle of sea trials and told me to ship the SeaBus out to Tahoe ASAP. So I just tagged along on the ride in from San Diego to see who was on the receiving end."

Austin noticed a picnic table and suggested they sit down. Then he laid out the situation, using the photos and drawings as visual aids. Contos sat silently through the entire explanation, his dark features growing graver with each added detail.

"So there you have it," Austin said. "When we saw that there might be only one way in, we checked on the nearest submersible to do the job. Unfortunately it happened to be the one you were testing."

"Why play Blind Man's Bluff?" Contos said, referring to daring covert underwater operations during the cold war. "Why not just go in?"

"First of all, the place has better security than Fort Knox. We checked on land access. The complex is surrounded by razor-wire fence rigged to set off alarms if you so much as breathe on it. The perimeter is heavily patrolled. There is only one access road in and out. It runs through dense forest and is heavily guarded. If we send a SWAT team in with guns blazing it's likely someone would get hurt. Beyond that, what if we're wrong about the whole thing, that the women are not being held there, and what's behind all those fences is perfectly legal?"

"You don't think that's the case, do you?"

"No, I don't."

Contos gazed out at the sailboats peacefully gliding across the lake, then turned to Paul, who had joined them at the table.

"Do you think your wife is in there?"

"Yep. I have every intention of getting her out."

Contos noted Trout's arm in its sling. "I'd say you could use an extra hand. And your friends here will need some help launching the SeaBus."

"I designed it," Zavala said.

"I'm well aware of that, but you haven't been the one testing it, so you don't know the quirks. For instance, the batteries are supposed to be good for six hours. They barely make it past four. From what you say, this facility is quite a way from here. Have you given any thought to how you're going to get it to the launch point?"

Austin and Zavala exchanged an amused glance.

"As a matter of fact, we have already lined up a delivery system," Austin said. "Would you like to see it?"

Contos nodded, and they got up from the table and walked through the parking lot to the dock. The closer they got to the water the more puzzled was the expression on Contos's face. Used to NUMA's state-of-the-art equipment, he was looking for something like a high-tech barge fitted out with cranes. There was nothing like that.

"Where's your delivery system?" he said.

"I think I see it coming in now," Austin said.

Contos looked out at the lake, and his eyes grew wider as the old-fashioned paddle-wheel tour boat made its way in their direction. The vessel was painted red, white, and blue and decorated with bunting and fluttering flags.

"You're *kidding,*" he said. "You're going to launch from *that?* It looks like a waterborne wedding cake."

"It is pretty festive. The old girl makes the trip from one end of the lake to the other every day. No one gives it a second look anymore. It's the perfect cover for a covert operation, don't you think, Joe?"

"I've heard they serve a pretty good breakfast aboard," Zavala said with a straight face.

Contos stared grimly at the approaching vessel. Then, without warning, he wheeled about and headed for the parking lot.

"Hey, captain, where are you going?" Austin called after him.

"Back to the truck to get my banjo."

36

FRANCESCA STOOD ON THE DECK of the Viking ship taking in its long, sweeping lines, its graceful, upturned bow and stern, the painted square sail. Even with the thick planking and massive keel it seemed almost delicate in its construction. She looked around at the huge chamber, with its vaulted ceiling, the flaming torches, and high stone walls hung with medieval weapons, and she wondered how anything so beautiful could be in a setting so bizarre and ugly.

Standing by the tiller, Brynhild Sigurd mistook Francesca's silence for appreciative awe.

"It's a masterpiece, isn't it? The Norsemen called this a *skuta* when they built the original nearly two thousand years ago. It was not the biggest of their boats, like the dragon ship, but it was the fastest. I have had her duplicated in every way, from the oak planking to the spun cow's hair that was used as caulking. She is more than seventy-nine feet long and sixteen feet wide. The original is in Oslo, Norway. An earlier replica actually sailed across the Atlantic. You must be wondering why I went through the trouble to have her built and placed in the great hall."

"Some people collect old stamps, others old cars. There's no accounting for tastes."

"This goes beyond a collector's whim." Brynhild took her hand off the tiller and came over to stand before Francesca, who shuddered at their physical proximity. Although Brynhild's towering body was hard and muscular, the menace she projected went beyond the physical. She seemed capable of reaching up and wringing the power from a lightning bolt. "I chose this ship as the symbol of my vast holdings because it embodies the Viking spirit. It was sailed by those who seized what they wanted. I come here often for inspiration. So shall it be with you, Dr. Cabral. Come, I will show you where you will be working."

Francesca had been escorted back to Brynhild's aerie after the brief visit with Gamay. Brynhild had led the way through a bewildering maze of passageways that reminded Francesca of being on a cruise ship. They were unguarded at all times, but the thought of escape never crossed Francesca's mind. Even if she were able to disable the giant woman, an unlikely prospect, she would have become lost in minutes. And she suspected the guards were not far away.

Now they got into an elevator that dropped with knee-bending swiftness. The door opened on a room where a monorail car awaited. Brynhild motioned for Francesca to get into the front, then got in the back, sitting in a space especially made for her tall form. Their weight activated the accelerator. The tram went through an opening and sped along a lighted tunnel. When it seemed the car would go rocketing out of control the computers controlling its speed decelerated it to a comfortable stop in a room very much like the one they had just left.

This room, too, had an elevator, but unlike the more conventional box on a cable, its transparent plastic walls were egg-shaped. There were seats for four people of ordinary stature. The door hissed shut, and the elevator passed through blackness, then descended into a deep blue. Watching the fluid interplay of light and shadow through the transparent walls, Francesca realized they were sinking into water. The blue became darker until, all at once, it was as if they were caught in the beam of a searchlight.

The door opened, and they stepped out. Francesca could hardly believe her eyes. They were in a brightly lit, circular space hundreds of feet across. A curving roof arched overhead. The exact size of the room was difficult to estimate because it was filled with thick pipes, coils, and vats of all sizes. A dozen or so white-frocked technicians moved quietly among the conduits and tanks or were bent over computer monitors.

"Well, what do you think?" Brynhild said with obvious pride.

"It's *incredible.*" The awe in her voice was real. "Where are we, at the bottom of the sea?"

The giantess smiled. "This is where you'll do your work. Come, I'll show you around."

Francesca's scientific mind quickly made order out of her chaotic first impression. Although the pipes went off at different angles, there was definitely a scientific organization to the madness. No matter which way the pipes went, they eventually led toward the center of the room.

"This controls the various conditions that affect the core material," Brynhild said, pointing to the blinking lights on a control board. "This underwater facility stands on four legs. Two of the support legs double as intake pipes, and the other two as outflow. Since we are on a fresh body of water, we first infuse the liquid we pump in with salt and sea minerals from those containers. It is indistinguishable from actual seawater."

They walked toward the center of the chamber. It was occupied by a massive cylindrical tank some twenty feet across and ten feet high.

"This must contain the anasazium," Francesca said.

"That's right. The water is circulated around the core, then returned to the lake through the other two supports."

They walked back to the master control console.

"Well, how close are we to duplicating the Cabral process?"

Francesca examined the gauges. "Refrigeration, electrical current, heat monitoring, all good. You were close, very close."

"We have subjected the anasazium to heat, cold, and electrical current, but with only limited success."

"I'm not surprised. The sonic component is missing."

"Of *course.* Sound vibrations."

"You have the right idea, but the process won't work unless the material is subjected to a certain level of sound waves in concert with the other forces. It's like removing the cello from a string quartet."

"Ingenious. How did you come up with that technique?"

"It was simply a matter of thinking in unconventional terms. As you know, there have been three main methods of desalting before this. In electrodialysis and reverse osmosis, electrified water passes through membranes that remove the salt. The third method is distillation, which evaporates the water the way the sun's heat turns the ocean to vapor. All require tremendous expenditures of energy that made the cost of desalting prohibitive. My method changes molecular and atomic structure. In the process it *creates* energy and becomes self-sustaining. The combination of forces must be exactly right. The process won't work if it is off by a hair."

"Now that you've seen it, how long do you think it would take to modify this facility to your standards?"

She shrugged. "A week."

"Three days," Brynhild said flatly.

"Why the time limit?"

"The Gogstad board of directors is due to meet here. I am bringing people in from all parts of the world. I want to give them a demonstration of your process. Once they have seen it work they will go home and we can implement the greater plan."

Francesca thought about it a moment and said, "I can have it working for you within twenty-four hours."

"That's quite a difference from a week."

"I work faster with incentive. There is a price."

"You're in no position to bargain."

"I realize that. But I want you to let your prisoner go. She was drugged. She has no idea where she is or how she got here. She could never identify or cause you any trouble. You keep her prisoner to make sure I make this plant work. Once the process is working you have no need of her."

"Agreed," Brynhild said. "I will let her go as soon as you show me the first ounce of pure water."

"What guarantees can you give me that you will stand by your word?"

"None. But you have no alternative."

Francesca nodded. "I will need certain equipment and unquestioning assistance."

"Anything you want," Brynhild said. She waved over several technicians. "Dr. Cabral is to have whatever she requests, do you understand?" She barked an order, and another technician came over carrying a battered aluminum suitcase. Brynhild took it from the man and handed it to Francesca. "I believe this belongs to you. We found it at your friends' house. I must leave you now. Call when you are about to run a test."

As Francesca ran her hand lovingly over the suitcase that contained the original working model for her process, Brynhild strode off toward the elevator. Within minutes she was back in her turret room. She had summoned the Kradzik brothers on a portable phone, and they were waiting for her when she returned.

"After all these years of waiting and disappointments, the Cabral process will soon be ours," she announced with triumph.

"How long?" one of the twins asked.

"It should be up and running within twenty-four hours."

"No," said the other twin, the light glittering on his metal teeth. "How long before we can have the women to play with?"

She should have known. The brothers were programmed like malevolent computers to carry out torture and murder. Brynhild had no intention of letting Francesca live after she had delivered the process. Part of her treachery stemmed from her envy of Francesca's scientific prowess and beauty. Part was pure vindictiveness. The Brazilian woman had cost her in time and money. She had nothing in particular against Gamay. Brynhild simply didn't like loose ends.

Her smile brought the already low temperature in the room down another ten degrees.

"Soon," she said.

37

THE NIGHT SHIFT GUARD WAS HAVing a cigarette at the end of the Valhalla pier when his relief man arrived and asked for a report. The swarthy ex-Marine squinted out at the sun-sparkled lake and flicked the butt into the water. "It's been busier'n a one-legged man at a kick-ass contest," he replied in an Alabama drawl. "Choppers coming and going all night."

The relief guard, a former Green Beret, looked up at the *whup-whup* sound of an approaching helicopter. "Looks like more guests are arriving."

"What's going on?" the Alabaman said. "I don't hear much working nights and sleeping days."

"Bunch of big shots are coming in for a meeting. We got the full crew on, and security around the compound's tight as a tick's ass." He glanced toward the lake. "There's the ol' *Tahoe Queen,* right on time."

He brought his binoculars up and focused on the stern wheeler as it crawled toward the north end of the lake. The *Tahoe Queen* looked like something out of *Showboat.* The boat was painted white, like vanilla frosting, with light blue trim that marked the divide between the enclosed first and second decks. Two tall black smokestacks were located at the front. The paddle wheels that churned up the placid lake water and gave the boat its forward motion were painted fire-engine red. The top deck rail was overhung with red, white, and blue bunting. Flags fluttered in the breeze.

"Hmm," the guard said, surveying the deck. "Not many tourists aboard today."

The guard would have been less sanguine if he knew the same coral-green eyes that had scrutinized him the day before from the parasail were watching him again. Austin stood inside the pilothouse that was perched like a cigar box on the top forward deck. He was studying the guards and assessing their state of alertness. Austin could see that the men were armed, but their lackadaisical posture suggested a bored attitude.

The boat's captain, a weathered lake veteran from Emerald Bay, was at the helm. "Want me to drop the *Queen*'s speed down a couple of knots?" the captain asked.

The paddle wheeler was a charming anachronism built more for comfort than for speed. Any slower and it would stop, Austin thought. "I'd keep it steady, captain. Launch shouldn't be a problem." He checked out the pier again and saw that one of the guards was leaving and the other ducked into the shade of a shelter. Austin hoped the man would take a nap.

He extended his hand. "Thanks for your cooperation, captain. Hope we didn't disappoint your regular customers by chartering your boat at the last minute."

"I just drive this old girl back and forth no matter who's on it. Besides, this is a lot more exciting than a boatload of day-trippers."

The captain's excitement had come at a price. The boat line was reluctant to lose a day's revenue, and it took deep pockets and high-level calls from Washington to persuade it to charter the paddle wheeler for official business.

"Glad to help make your day," Austin said. "Got to go. Just keep steaming after you drop us off."

"How will you get back?"

"We're working on that," Austin said with a grin.

Austin left the pilothouse and descended to the spacious salon on the lowest deck. On a normal day the salon would be crowded with tourists eating and drinking as they took in the magnificent scenery. Only two people were in the salon, Joe and

Paul. Zavala was already in his black-hooded Viking Pro military dry suit, and Trout was going over a checklist. Austin lost no time suiting up. Then he and Zavala went through an opening in the side of the boat that was used to let passengers on and off.

They would have stepped directly into the lake if not for a wooden platform slung alongside the stern wheeler. The raft floated on ocean salvage tubes, elongated pontoons made of tough nylon fabric and capable of lifting several tons of weight. The assembly had been cobbled together in the late hours of the morning. Contos was on the raft making sure they hadn't made any major mistakes in hastily putting the thing together.

"How's she look?" Austin said.

"Not quite as good as the one Huckleberry Finn used on the Mississippi," Contos said with a shake of his head. "But she'll do in a pinch, I think."

"Thanks for your unqualified endorsement of our building skills," Zavala said.

As he stepped off the raft, Contos rolled his eyes. "Look guys, please try *not* to lose the SeaBus. It's tough as hell to run a test program without something to test."

Without its protective covering, the SeaBus looked like a fat plastic sausage. It was a small workhorse version of a tourist sub working in Florida, designed to take crews to and from underwater jobs of moderate depth. It carried up to six passengers and their gear in a transparent pressure hull of acrylic plastic. The hull rested on fat, round skids that carried the hard ballast, trim, drop weights, and thrusters. Higher on the sides were additional ballast tanks and compressed air containers. The external structures were attached to the pressure hull by a tough ring frame. The two-seat cockpit was at the front. In the aft section was the electrical, hydraulic, and mechanical heart of the sub and an airlock that allowed divers to go in and out while the SeaBus was submerged.

Trout stuck his head out of the stern wheeler. "We're coming up on target," he said, checking his watch. "Three minutes to launch."

"We're as ready as we'll ever be," Austin said. "How about you, Paul?"

"Finest kind, cap," he said with a lopsided grin.

Trout was far from fine. Despite his stolid Yankee façade, he was worried about Gamay and desperately wanted to go on the mission. He knew that with his bad arm he would just get in the way. Austin convinced Trout that they needed someone with a level head above water to call in the troops in case the situation got dicey.

A crane had been brought in to lift the submersible from the truck onto the raft. The stern wheeler left early in the morning before the waterfront got busy. The boat hunkered offshore until it was time to make its usual crossing. Even with its heavy load the raft pitched and yawed as it was towed along. Austin and Zavala had to brace themselves as they knelt at the rear, each man above one of the lift bags. On signal they simultaneously stabbed the rubber pontoons with their dive knives. The air shot out in a loud hiss that rapidly turned to a flatulent bubbling. Squeezed between the water and the raft, the pontoons rapidly deflated. As the back of the raft settled into the water, they unhooked the tie lines securing the SeaBus. Then they scrambled through the aft hatch, made sure all was tight, and settled into the cockpit.

The front of the raft tilted upward at an angle. Then, as the lift bags deflated, it leveled out and began to sink. It was a primitive launching system for such a sophisticated craft, but it worked. The SeaBus maintained its buoyancy as the raft sank and was pulled out by the forward motion of the paddle wheeler. The submersible danced in the larger boat's wake and sank into the foam kicked up by the stern paddles. As they gained depth the water changed from blue-green to blue-black.

Austin adjusted the ballast, and the sub attained neutral buoyancy at fifty feet. The battery-driven motors whined as Zavala goosed the throttle and pointed the submersible toward shore. They were lucky to have no current pushing against the round, almost blunt bow of the submersible and could keep it at a steady ten knots. Within half an hour they had covered the five miles to land.

As Zavala steered, Austin consulted the sonar screen. The rocky shore continued its vertical drop into the water for more than a hundred feet before jutting out in a wide ledge. The sonar picked up an extremely large object resting on the ledge directly under the floating pier. Moments later they looked up and saw the long shape of the pier and its floats silhouetted against the shimmer of surface light. Austin hoped his earlier assessment was correct, that the guard was too numb from boredom to notice any disturbance the submersible might cause. Zavala took the SeaBus down in a shallow spiral while Austin alternated between radar and visual checks.

"Level out. *Fast,*" Austin said.

Zavala responded instantly, and the submersible circled like a hungry shark.

"Were we getting too close to the ledge?"

"Not exactly. Take her out and go down another fifty feet."

The SeaBus moved away from the shore and spun around so they were facing a ledge.

"Madre de Dios," Zavala said. "Last time I knew, the Astrodome was still in Texas."

"I doubt you'll find any Dallas Cowgirls inside that thing," Austin said.

"It's similar to the one that went *ka-pop* in the Baja. Hate to admit it, but you were right as usual."

"Just lucky."

"I don't know how lucky you are. We've got to get inside that thing."

"There's no time like the present. I suggest we take a look at the underside."

With a nod of his head, Zavala cranked up the throttle and put the SeaBus into a glide that took them directly under the massive structure. The surface was made of a translucent green material that emitted a dull glow. Zavala's hyperbole notwithstanding, the facility would have been an impressive engineering feat even on dry land. Like the Baja operation, this structure also rested on four cylindrical legs around the perimeter.

"There are openings in the outside legs," Austin said. "Probably like the ones in Mexico, used for intake and exhaust."

Zavala brought the submersible in close to a fifth support at the very center of the structure. He switched on the sub's twin spotlights. "No duct openings. Hello. What have we here?" He nudged the SeaBus closer to an oval depression in the otherwise smooth surface of the support. "Looks like a door. Still no welcome mat, though."

"Maybe they forgot it," Austin said. "What say we park the bus and pay a neighborly social call?"

Zavala dropped the SeaBus lightly onto the ledge next to the support leg. They pulled on their air tanks and the headsets for their Divelink communicators. Austin tucked his big Bowen and some spare ammunition into a waterproof fanny pack. The pack held a 9mm Glock to replace the machine pistol Zavala lost in Alaska.

Austin crawled into the snug airlock first, flooded the chamber, then opened the outer hatch. Minutes later, Zavala joined him outside the SeaBus. They swam to the support leg and rose up the thick cylinder, where they hung on to hand bars on either side of the door. To the right of the tight seam was a panel. Encased in clear plastic were two large buttons, one red and the other green. The green one was glowing.

They hesitated.

"She might be connected to an alarm," Zavala said, echoing Austin's own thoughts.

"I was wondering the same thing. But why would they bother? The neighborhood around here isn't exactly swarming with burglars."

"We don't have a lot of choice," Zavala said. "*Go* for it."

Austin pushed against the glowing button. If an alarm went off, they didn't hear it. A section in the support leg slid silently aside to reveal an opening shaped like a mouth wide open in a yawn. Zavala gave Austin the okay sign and swam in first.

Austin was right on his fins. They were in a chamber shaped like the inside of a hat box. A metal ladder hung down from the ceiling. On the wall was a duplicate of the switch that opened the door. Austin pushed the glowing green button. He accidentally nudged the pack with their weapons, and it fell through the opening in the air lock.

"Forget it," he said, anticipating Zavala's question. "We don't have time."

The outer door closed, and a ring of lights flicked on inside. The chamber was quickly pumped dry, and a circular hatch popped open in the ceiling. Still no sign that their presence had been noted. All was quiet except for the hum of distant machinery.

Austin pulled himself up the ladder and poked his head through the hatch. Then he motioned for Zavala to follow and climbed the rest of the way. They were in another, larger circular room. Several dark green dry suits hung from the wall. Air tanks were stacked on shelves. A large cabinet held various specialized tools.

Austin removed his headset, mask, and tank and picked up a long-handled brush with stiff steel bristles. "They must use this stuff to clean the intake ports out there. The openings would get clogged up with algae otherwise."

Zavala went over to a door in the curving wall and pointed to another red-green switch. "I'm beginning to feel like a monkey in one of those intelligence tests where the chimp presses a button for food."

"Not me," Austin said. "A chimp would be too smart to be in a place like this."

On Austin's signal, he hit the green button. The door opened, and they stepped into a room with four walls. The room contained shower stalls and shelves. Austin removed a plastic-wrapped packet from a shelf and opened it. Inside was a white two-piece suit made of a light synthetic material. Without further conversation they got out of their dry suits and quickly pulled the white uniforms over their thermal underwear. Austin's distinctive silver-platinum hair made him stand out from the crowd, so he was glad to see that each packet held a tight-fitting plastic cap.

"How do I look?" he said, aware that the suit wasn't made to accommodate his wide shoulders.

"Like a large and unsavory white mushroom."

"Exactly the image I was trying for. Let's go."

They were in a cavernous chamber with a high, curving roof. Pipes and conduits of varying widths crossed the space. The hum they heard earlier was so loud it almost hurt their ears. The sound seemed to be coming from everywhere.

"Bingo," Austin murmured softly.

Zavala said, "Reminds me of a scene from that movie, *Alien.*"

"I wish these *were* aliens," Austin said.

A white-clad figure unexpectedly emerged from behind a fat vertical duct. They tensed and groped for their missing weapons, but the technician, who was carrying a portable gauge, hardly gave them a glance before disappearing into the maze. The huge room had two levels divided from each other by metal scaffolding and catwalks. They decided to climb above the main floor, where they would have a better view of the entire facility and have less chance of running into other technicians. They ascended the nearest stairs and made their way toward the center. The technicians below were intent on their work, and no one looked up. From their elevation the facility was even more impressive. It looked like a futuristic hive filled with drones.

"We could spend all day searching this place," Austin said. "Let's see if we can find a guide."

They descended stairs that took them back onto the main floor and hid behind a large pipe. Standing before a large console were three technicians. The figures had their backs turned, obviously engrossed in their task.

Two technicians moved off, leaving the third alone. With a quick glance to make sure he was unobserved, Austin swiftly closed on the unsuspecting figure and hooked his thick arm around the person's throat.

"Don't make a sound, or I'll snap your neck," he growled, then dragged his catch back behind the pipe. "Meet our new guide," he said.

Zavala stared at the technician. "We've already met."

Austin spun the technician around. *Francesca.* The terror in her face turned to relief. "What are you *doing* here?"

The pleasure at seeing Francesca overcame Austin's surprise. "We had a date, remember?" he said with a grin. "Time and place to be announced."

Francesca smiled through her nervousness. Calmer now, she glanced around and said, "We can't stay here. Follow me."

They wound their way through the labyrinth into a small room furnished with a plain plastic desk and chair. "I asked for this space so I could work quietly. We'll be safe for a few minutes. If anyone comes, pretend you know what you're doing." She shook her head in wonder. "How in God's name did you get in here?"

"We took the bus," Austin said. "Where's Gamay?"

"This is the desalting facility. She's in the main compound. They have her in a heavily guarded cell on the first level."

"How do we get there?"

"I'll show you. There's an elevator that takes you from the lab. It goes to a tram. The car goes through a tunnel to the main compound. Then an elevator will take you up to her level. Do you think you can rescue her?"

"We won't know until we try," Zavala said with a slight smile.

"It will be very dangerous. You may have a chance, though. The guards are preoccupied. There's some kind of meeting planned. You must move quickly before people start coming here."

"What kind of meeting?" Zavala asked.

"I don't know, only that it's extremely important. I have to have this facility up and working by then, or they'll kill Gamay."

She glanced out of the office to see if the coast was clear. Then she led them to the elevator. Austin thought that she looked exhausted. There were black circles under her red-rimmed eyes. She wished them well and disappeared into the network of pipes.

Wasting no time, they stepped into a strange egg-shaped elevator. The elevator rose through the water to the tram room Francesca had described. They got aboard the tram car and sped along the tunnel to its terminus. From the tram room they stepped into a passageway. The elevator door was a few paces away. The light over the door indicated that the elevator was moving down.

"Do we go naughty or nice?" Zavala asked.

"See if nice works."

The door opened, and a guard stepped out. A machine pistol was slung from his shoulder. He looked at Zavala suspiciously, then at Austin.

"Pardon me," Zavala said politely. "Could you tell us where to find the woman from NUMA? Can't miss her. Tall with red hair."

The guard began to raise his machine pistol. The move brought Austin's ham-sized right fist crashing into the man's midsection. He made a sound like a deflating balloon, and his legs went limp.

"I thought we were going to try nice," Zavala said.

"That *was* nice," Austin replied. He grabbed the man's arms, and with Zavala holding the feet, they dragged the guard into the elevator. Zavala brought the elevator halfway to the next floor and locked it in place. Austin kneeled and lightly patted the guard's cheek. The man's eyes rolled, then popped wide open when he saw Austin's face.

"We're feeling generous today. You get a second chance. Where's the woman?"

The guard shook his head. Austin wasn't in the mood for stalling. He brought the gun muzzle to the bridge of the guard's nose, so close that the man looked cross-eyed at it.

"I'm not going to waste any time," Austin said quietly. "We know she's on the first level. If you don't tell us where she is, we'll find someone who can. Understand?"

The guard nodded.

"Good," Austin said. He pulled the man to a standing position by the scruff of his neck, and Zavala hit the button for the next floor. Nobody was waiting for the elevator. They pushed the guard out into the deserted hall.

"What's the security like ahead?"

The guard shrugged. "Most of the guards are upstairs taking care of the big shots coming in for the meeting."

Austin was curious about the purpose of the meeting and who the VIPs were, but he was more concerned about Gamay. He stuck the gun in the guard's ribs. "Fetch," he said.

The guard reluctantly led the way down a corridor and stopped in front of a door with a keypad lock. He hesitated, wondering if he could stall by saying he didn't know the combination, but one look at the thunder and lightning on Austin's brow told him he'd better not try. He punched out the code, and the door opened. The room was empty.

"This is her room," the guard said. He looked worried.

They pushed him inside and looked around. The small room was evidently used as a cell because it could only be opened from the outside. Zavala went over to the bed, plucked something off the pillow, and grinned.

"She *was* here." The dark red strand he held in his fingers was unmistakably Gamay's.

Austin turned back to the guard. "Where did they take her?"

"I don't know," the guard answered sullenly.

"Make believe that the next thing you say may be your last words, and think very carefully about it."

The guard knew that Austin would shoot him without hesitation.

"I'm not protecting those creeps," he said.

"What are you talking about?"

"The Kradzik brothers. They had her taken to the Great Hall."

"Who are these guys?"

"Couple of killers who do the boss's dirty work," he said with obvious disgust.

"Tell us how to get there."

The guard gave them the directions. Austin told him to expect a return visit if he sent them on a wild goose chase. They left him in the room and locked the door, then bolted down the hall to the elevator. They didn't know who the Kradzik brothers were, and they didn't care. One thing they could be certain of. Whatever was planned for Gamay couldn't be good.

38

THE FIFTY MEN GATHERED AROUND the table on the deck of the Gogstad ship were dressed in dark business suits rather than cloaks and armor, but the scene could have been taken from a thousand-year-old pagan celebration. Torchlight glinted off the sharp metal edges of the medieval armaments lining the walls and cast flickering shadows on the men's faces. The theatrical effect was not accidental. Brynhild had designed the entire chamber as an elaborate stage set with herself as director.

The Gogstad board of directors was made up of some of the most prominent individuals in the world. They came from many countries and every continent. Their ranks included the chief executives of multinational corporations, trade representatives whose secret negotiations gave them more power than some governments, and politicians, past and present, who owed their careers to the plutocracies that were the real ruling class in the countries they came from. The men represented every race and color, but despite the differences in their physical stature and skin complexion, they were bound together by a common denominator: their insatiable avarice. With every disdainful facial expression and gesture, they projected the same polished arrogance.

Brynhild stood on the deck of the Viking ship at the head of the table. "Welcome, gentlemen," she said. "Thank you for coming on short notice. I know many of you traveled a long way, but

I assure you, the journey will have been worth it." She looked from face to face, glorying in the greed she saw lurking behind the practiced smiles and the knifing eyes. "We in this room represent the heart and soul of Gogstad, an invisible government more powerful than any the world has ever seen. You are more than a corporate elite; you are priests in a secret society, like the Knights Templar."

"Pardon me for interrupting your stirring pep talk right at the start," said a fish-eyed English arms dealer named Grimley. "You're not telling us anything new. I hope I didn't just fly six thousand miles to hear you tell us what an extraordinary group this is."

Brynhild smiled. The directors were the only people on earth who could talk to her as equals.

"No, Lord Grimley, I called you together to inform you that our plans have been drastically accelerated."

The Englishman was still unimpressed. His long nose sniffed the air as if he smelled an unpleasant odor. "You were originally talking of years to gain the monopoly on the world's water suppy. That has been changed to months, I take it?"

"No, Lord Grimley. I'm talking a target date of *days.*"

There was a low murmur around the table.

An unctuous smile crossed Grimley's face. "Disregard my earlier comment," he said. "Please go on."

"I'd be happy to," Brynhild said. "As you know from my monthly reports, our plans have been moving smoothly but slowly. Every day we have acquired another water source, but it has taken time to build up our tanker fleet. The huge storage bags that would be used to transport water across oceans have been a problem. Only now has the technology to construct the bags been achieved. And most recently our project has elicited interest from the National Underwater and Marine Agency."

An American real estate baron named Howes was the first to pounce on the significance of her last sentence. "*NUMA?* How did they come to know about us?"

"It's a complicated story. You will all be provided with reports detailing NUMA's interest. Suffice it to say for now that their people are very persistent and lucky."

"This is serious," said the American. "First the newspaper investigation, now this."

"The newspaper will not be running the story, nor will anyone else. All the investigative records have been destroyed. In regard to NUMA, that situation, too, has been neutralized."

"It's still damned worrisome," Howes said. "We've spent millions keeping our activities secret. This whole thing could unravel in no time."

"I agree wholeheartedly," Brynhild replied. "We have done everything possible to preserve our privacy, but an operation of this size and duration could not go undetected forever. The façade we erected to hide our activities from public view is beginning to crack. It was only a matter of time, so I'm not surprised, but it did suggest the need for haste."

"Are you saying that you are rushing our plans because of NUMA?"

"No. Only that there has been a fortunate turn of events."

A German banker named Heimmler was the first to catch on. "There is only one way the plan can be advanced so dramatically," he said with the expression of a boa constrictor presented with a live rabbit. "You have perfected the Cabral desalting method."

Brynhild waited for the buzzing around the table to die down. "Better still," she said triumphantly. "Dr. Cabral is perfecting the process for us."

"Cabral," the German said. "I read press reports that she was still alive, but—"

"Alive and quite well. She has agreed to work with Gogstad since we control the only supply of anasazium. At this moment she is in our laboratory where she is preparing a demonstration. In a short time I will show you this miracle. I spoke to Dr. Cabral before our meeting. She said she would be ready in an hour. In the meantime you are invited to enjoy the refreshments we have prepared for you in the dining room. I must check on transport arrangements and will see you shortly."

As the directors filed out of the Great Hall, Brynhild went to the front entrance of the main complex. Several dark green Suburbans were lined up in front of the spacious porch. A driver and armed guard stood next to each vehicle.

"Is everything ready?" she asked the guard standing by the lead vehicle.

"Yes, ma'am, we can move the guests whenever they are ready to go."

The underground tram was the fastest way to get to the lab, but it was built mainly to shuttle small parties of technicians back and forth. It was quicker to transport a large group, such as the board of directors, in vehicles. Brynhild left nothing to chance. She got in the passenger side of the lead vehicle and ordered the driver to take her to the lake. A few minutes later the SUV pulled up at the edge of the low hill that overlooked the water. She descended a short stairway to the pier and went inside the boathouse. The structure was actually a cover for the elevators that serviced the lab. She walked past the fast egg-shaped lift and into the large freight elevator. Moments later she was striding across the lab toward the main core. There was a discernible air of excitement in the dome-shaped structure.

Francesca was working at the control console. When she saw Brynhild she said, "I was just about to call you. I can perform the demonstration earlier than I anticipated."

"You're absolutely sure it will work?"

"I can give you a preview now if you'd like."

Brynhild considered the offer, then said, "No, I can't wait to see their faces when they observe how our process works."

Francesca ignored the use of the plural possessive in describing ownership of the process. "I'm sure they will be surprised."

Brynhild used her small belt phone to order the shuttles to start transporting the directors. In less than half an hour the entire board was gathered in the lab around the core container. Brynhild introduced Francesca. There was a murmur of admiration when the lovely Brazilian scientist stepped forward. Even as she smiled at the hard-faced men gathered around her, Francesca thought how much they resembled hungry reptiles gathered around a water hole. She didn't have to remind herself that their quest for more power and money was responsible for her years in the rain forest. While she lived with the Chulo awaiting rescue, possibly millions of people who could have benefited from her work died from thirst.

Francesca had never seen so much evil gathered in one room, but she covered her loathing well. "I don't know how many of you have a scientific background, but technical knowledge is not necessary to grasp the basic principle behind what you are about to see. While my process is difficult in execution, it's rather simple in concept. Desalting methods have been around since the time of the ancient Greeks. But those techniques always used a physical process, heating the water to steam, treating it with electricity, pushing it through membranes to screen out the salt the way a child sifts through shells at the beach. I reasoned that it might be easier in some respects to change the molecular structure of the chemicals in salt water at an atomic and subatomic level."

The smooth-faced German banker said, "Your process sounds somewhat like alchemy, Dr. Cabral."

"That's a very appropriate analogy. Although alchemy never achieved its goal, it set the stage for the science of chemistry. Like the alchemists, I, too, was trying to transform a base metal into gold. In my case it was *blue* gold. Water. More precious than any mineral on earth. I needed a sorcerer's stone that would make that possible." She turned to the anasazium core. "Contained here is the catalyst that makes the process work. The salted water is brought into contact with this material which purifies the water."

"When will we get a demonstration of this miracle?" said Lord Grimley.

"If you would step this way," she said, leading the way to the console. Her hands danced over the keyboard. There was a muffled growl of pumps and the sound of rushing water. "That's the salt water coming through the main over your heads. It is flowing into the container. It takes a few minutes."

Francesca herded the group to the other side of the catalytic container. She said nothing for several moments as the suspense built. Then she checked a gauge and pointed to another main. "This is the outtake pipe that carries the fresh water. You can feel the heat produced during the transformation."

The American said, "As I understand it, that heat can be used to produce energy."

"That's correct. Right now the water is being pumped into the cold waters of the lake where the heat is dissipated, but with a few adjustments this facility could be modified so the heat comes back as power to run the plant. There would even be surplus energy that could be exported."

There was a murmur from the board. Francesca could almost feel the aura of greed that emanated from the men as they tallied the billions to be made, aside from the water, by producing cheap energy.

She went over to a vertical set of coils that hung down from the freshwater pipe. At the base of the coil was a tap and beside it a stack of paper cups. "This is a cooling unit that removes heat from the water," she explained. Turning to a technician, she said, "What has been the quality of the water produced by the process before today?"

"Brackish at the very best," the technician said.

Francesca opened the tap and filled one of the cups. She held the cup to the light like a wine connoisseur, took a sip, then downed the contents. "A little warm still, but quite comparable to any spring water I've had."

Brynhild stepped forward, poured herself water, and drank it. "Nectar of the gods," she said triumphantly.

The directors pushed their way to the tap like thirst-crazed steers. There were cries of amazement with each cup sampled. Before long everyone was talking at once. While the directors gathered around the tap as if it were the fountain of youth, Brynhild guided Francesca away from the babble of voices.

"Congratulations, Dr. Cabral. It seems that the process is a success."

"I knew that ten years ago," Francesca said.

Brynhild's thoughts were on the future, not the past. "You've instructed my technicians so they can make the process work?"

"Yes. I had to make only a few adjustments in the procedure. You were quite close to perfecting the process, you know."

"Then we would have developed it in time?"

Francesca thought about it a moment. "Probably not. Your process and mine were like parallel lines. No matter how close they come they never touch. Now that I have done what I said I would, it is time for you to fulfill your side of the bargain."

"Ah, yes, the bargain." Brynhild took the radio from her belt and switched it on. She smiled, her cold blue eyes boring into Francesca's, and said, "Tell the Kradzik brothers that the NUMA woman is all theirs."

"Wait!" Francesca grabbed Brynhild's muscular arm. "You promised—"

Brynhild easily shook the smaller woman off. "I also reminded you that I could not be trusted. Now that you have demonstrated your process, your friend is of no use to me." She brought the phone up to her ear again. Her smile suddenly vanished, replaced by a frown. "What do you mean?" she snapped. Storm clouds gathered on her wide brow. "How long ago?"

She tucked the radio in her belt. "I'll deal with you later," she promised Francesca. With a military heel spin she marched for the staff elevator.

Francesca was frozen in shock. Then, as Brynhild's treachery sank in, the fiery anger that had sustained her for ten years was rekindled. If Gamay were dead, it would only make her decision easier to live with. With her jaw set in renewed determination, she headed back into the labyrinth of pipes.

39

GAMAY WAS ALMOST RELIEVED when the pair of husky guards came to take her away. She was bored to pieces, having concluded that the cell was escape-proof unless she could figure a way to blow the door off its hinges. She resolved to talk to someone at NUMA about coming up with James Bond gadgets. But that would have to wait. Her only option now was to watch for a chance to run for it once she was out of the cell.

Her heart sank as the guards ushered her through a maze of corridors. She would become lost before she went ten feet. They stopped in front of a pair of heavy bronze doors at least eight feet high. The surface of the doors was cast with mythological scenes. The theme was heavy on skulls, but for variety there were giants and dwarfs, strange monsters, fierce horses, twisted trees, runes, and lightning around a central motif, a sleek double-ended sailing ship.

One guard pressed a button on the wall, and the doors swung in noiselessly. The other guard prodded her into the room with his gun.

"This isn't our idea," he said in what sounded like an apology. The doors clicked shut, and she looked around to get her bearings. "Charming," she murmured under her breath.

She was in an enormous chamber bigger than a football field. She could trace its outline by the torches lining the walls of the cavernous space. In the center of the room, illuminated by four tall braziers, was a ship, its one square sail unfurled, that looked like the twin of the vessel carved on the doors.

Before becoming a marine biologist Gamay had been a nautical archaeologist, and she knew immediately that it was a Viking ship or a very good replica of one. She wondered if she were in a museum. No, she decided, it was more like an elaborate crypt. Maybe the ship served as a sepulchre as was the custom of the Norsemen. Partly out of curiosity, but mostly because there was no alternative, she began to walk toward the vessel.

As she made her lonely way across the great hall two pairs of red-rimmed eyes observed her progress from the shadows. The same eyes had hungrily watched her earlier on a TV monitor as she languished in her cell. The Kradzik twins had spent hours in front of the screen. They had taken in her every physical feature, from the distinctive dark red hair to the long, slim legs. There was nothing sexual in their voyeurism; that would have been too natural. Their interest was purely in inflicting pain. They were like a dog trained to balance a treat on its nose until the owner gives the okay to swallow. With Gamay enticingly within their reach, their sadistic urges surfaced. Gamay and the other woman had been promised to them. With Brynhild busy in the lab, they decided to claim their toy.

They ordered Gamay brought to the Great Hall. The guards obeyed with some reluctance. The small army that protected Gogstad and occasionally projected its reach, as in Alaska, were all ex-military men, plucked from elite services around the world. In their ranks were former French Legionnaires, U.S. Special Forces, SEALs, Red Army infantry, British paratroopers, and other assorted mercenaries. It was jokingly said in their barracks that a dishonorable discharge was a minimum requirement to work for Gogstad, and jail time was worth a bonus. They would shoot to kill on order, but they considered themselves professionals simply doing their job. The Kradziks were different. Everybody knew the stories of massacre and murder in Bosnia, and there were rumors of their special assignments for Gogstad. The men also knew of their close ties to Brynhild. When they were ordered to deliver the prisoner, they did so without argument.

Gamay was halfway to the ship when she heard the unmistakable sound of motors starting up. The staccato snarl was made even more intense as it echoed off the hard stone walls. Single headlights appeared to the right and left of the ship and began to move slowly in her direction.

Motorcycles.

She could see the silhouettes of the riders. Gamay felt like a deer caught crossing a highway. Then the motors revved up to a high-pitched whine, and the motorcycles came at her like twin rockets.

Her eyes went to the sharp-pointed lances resting on the handlebars.

The riders came at her like grotesque caricatures of jousting knights. Just when it seemed the spears would penetrate her midsection, the motorcycles swerved off. They quickly reversed course and came in behind her. She whirled as they flashed by in a precision criss-cross. They spun around, their motors idling, and once more the headlights faced her on either side like the glowing eyes of a huge purring cat.

The Kradziks were riding the Yamaha 250 dirt bikes that the security guards used to patrol the perimeter of the giant compound. The lances had been borrowed from the weapon collection decorating the Great Hall. The twins were not imaginative men, and their activities, whether the victim was a teenage girl or an elderly man, always followed the same formula: intimidate, terrorize, inflict pain, and kill.

A voice came out from the darkness on the left: "If you run fast . . ."

Then from the right, ". . . maybe we won't catch you."

Fat chance, Gamay thought. She could tell from the voices that she was dealing with the same metal-mouthed morons who had broken into her house. It was obvious to her they simply wanted a little challenge in their sport. She called out, "Let me see you."

The only sound was the popping idle of the motors. The Kradziks were accustomed to having victims cower and beg for their lives. They didn't know how to deal with questions, especially from a defenseless woman. Curious, they edged their bikes closer and stopped a few yards away.

"Who are you?" she said.

"We are death," they said as one.

The short reprieve was over. The motors revved. The motorbikes reared up on their back wheels. The front wheels came down and, with a double shriek of burning rubber, the bikes shot forward, did another criss-cross, then began to circle. They wanted Gamay to spin until she became dizzy and collapsed into a helpless, blubbering heap. She refused to play their game. Instead she stood her ground with her eyes straight ahead, arms tight by her side. The wind created by their passes blew choking exhaust fumes in her face. It took every measure of self-control not to bolt for it. They'd be on her in a second and use their spears to cut her legs out from under her.

When they saw she had no intention of running, they angled in. A spear tip came so close that it lacerated the front of her shirt. She sucked her stomach in. This wouldn't do. She began to walk. She moved deliberately with measured steps so she wouldn't throw their timing off. Delighted at the new challenge, the riders took turns cutting in front of her, pulling their spears away at the last possible second. She kept on going, her ears filled with the whine of motors. She refused to break her stride. Gamay knew they could kill her any time they wanted to.

She heard a bike coming in from the right. Taking a big chance, she stopped suddenly. The rider misjudged and went wide. The bike skidded around in a tight turn, but the move threw off the uncanny communication the riders seemed to have, and they wheeled around in confusion. She ran past the upturned bow of the boat, intending to vault onto the deck, but she encountered a barrier of overhanging round shields that protected the side above the oar ports. She saw why the Kradziks had let her get this close to the boat. They knew there was no way she could easily climb over the shields.

The only access to the deck was a ramp near the stern. They probably hoped she would run for it. She made a motion in that direction, and they shot over to cut her off. She grabbed one of the shields off the side of the boat, then turned and held it in front, her back to the boat. The twins spun around and came at her with lances leveled. The heavy shield, made of thick wood braced with iron, was designed more for a brawny Norseman than a slim woman. Fortunately Gamay was tall and athletic and managed to get her left arm through the straps and hold the shield in front of her.

Just in time.

Tunk!

The spears hit the front of the shield as one. The force drove her back against the side of the boat and knocked the wind from her lungs.

The bikes peeled off to the left and the right, did quick turns, and headed back. Gamay put the shield down on the floor, braced her foot against it, and pulled out the spears. In contrast to the shield they were surprisingly light, with thin wooden shafts and slender bronze tips. They were probably designed more for throwing than for jousting.

She held the spears vertically and the shield at ready. With their weapons gone, she assumed the brothers were making a feint, but there was a blur of motion as a spiked ball whirled at the end of a chain slammed into the shield. Even with her legs braced she was thrown back and went down on her right knee. She managed to keep the shield high in a move that saved her life as a punishing blow from the second rider crunched into the shield and splintered the outer layer of protective wood.

The brothers had exchanged their spears for maces, the weapons developed to smash their way through armor. The bikes swooped down on her before she had the chance to stand. Again the spiked iron balls crashed into the shield. The wood protected her from the main shock but disintegrated after the second blow until all that was left were the leather straps and useless framework.

She grabbed for a spear and held it at an angle. The bikes held off their attack and went back and forth. Then one attacker came in. The spear spun in his direction like a compass needle. Gamay held her breath. At the last second he turned away. The other came in from her left. She pivoted quickly to face him only to be distracted by another attack on the right. It was a classic flanking tactic. They were not ready for a full press yet, probably just testing to see her reaction.

One bike passed directly in front of her, its rider thinking he was safely beyond the reach of the spear. Instead of jabbing, Gamay brought the spear back on her shoulder and hurled it at the rider. He was moving fast. Her aim was too low. The spear hit the spokes of the front wheel. The force of the wheel shattered the shaft, but not before the skinny, knobbed tire turned at a sharp angle. The bike jackknifed, and the rider flew over the handlebars. The bike skidded along the floor leaving a trail of red and white sparks. Gamay saw him hit the floor and lie still.

The second motorcycle halted its attack, and the rider pointed his headlight at the still form. He dismounted, but he knew even before he crouched down beside the twisted body that his brother was dead. He had felt his brother's fear and pain as his neck snapped. Then came a moan that rose to an agonizing scream. A chill went up Gamay's spine as the remaining Kradzik brother began to howl like a wolf. She edged toward the rear of the boat, hoping that if she made it to the deck she'd find another weapon. The brother saw her move. He straddled his bike in an instant. She held her spear out straight. As he came in from the side she felt the spear jerk, then heard a clink of metal. He had chopped the spear tip neatly off with a short-handled battle-ax. He stopped and held the ax high above his head with both hands. Then he came for her.

She ran for the stern of the boat. He caught up in an instant and crashed his motorcycle into the back of her legs, knocking her down. Pain shot up from her knees and elbows as they smashed against the hard floor, but she had more to worry about. A figure was standing over her.

"My brother . . . is dead . . ."

He spoke haltingly, as if he were waiting for a cadenced answer from his twin.

"You killed . . . now I will kill you. I will start . . . with legs. One by one. Then your arms."

With his black leather pants and sleeveless jacket, he looked like an executioner. His teeth gleamed as he grinned in anticipation. Gamay tried to roll out of the way, but he put his boot on her ankle and she cried out.

As the ax came up there was a whirring sound, and he grunted in surprise. His free hand reached up to feel the shaft of a crossbow bolt protruding from the side of his head, but he was already dead by then. The gleam disappeared from the red-rimmed eyes, and he keeled over. Gamay rolled out of the way as the falling ax clanked onto the floor. She heard quick footsteps, strong arms were picking her up, and she saw Zavala's familiar grin. Then Austin appeared. He was holding an old crossbow in his hands.

"Are you okay?" Austin asked.

"Nothing a good skin transplant won't cure." She saw that Joe was carrying the gun he had borrowed from the guard. "Not that I'm ungrateful, but why play William Tell when you had that thing?"

"This throws quite a spray of bullets," Zavala said. "It's great for cutting down a full assault but not very good for a precision sniper shot. I would have backed Kurt up if he missed." He knelt beside the dead twin. "You were supposed to hit the apple on *top* of his head."

"Next time I'll aim higher," Austin said, tossing the crossbow aside.

She gave them each a peck on the cheek. "Nice to see you even if I have to endure your dumb wisecracks."

Austin inspected the dead man near the motorcycle. "It looks like you were doing pretty well on your own."

"I was about to go to pieces," Gamay said, wondering how she could joke about her near dismemberment. "Where are we?"

"Lake Tahoe."

"Tahoe! How did you find me?"

"We'll explain after we pick up Francesca. Can you walk?"

"I'll crawl on my knees to get out of this dump. Nice outfits," she said, eyeing their white caps and suits. "Is that what got you past the guards at the door?"

"There weren't any guards."

"I guess they didn't want to be responsible for Daryll and Daryll."

"Truth is, we blundered in here. We saw you playing a losing game of tag with your friend. I grabbed a crossbow off the wall and watched as you set him up beautifully for a shot." Austin took a pistol from one of the dead men. "What say we saddle up before the posse comes?"

Gamay nodded and started to limp toward the doors, protectively flanked by the two men. The doors opened, and Brynhild stepped in. She was alone, but that didn't make her any less imposing as she strode across the hall. She barely glanced at the dead bodies as she came over and stood before them, muscular legs spread wide apart like tree trunks, her hands on her hips.

"I take it this is your handiwork," she said.

Austin shrugged. "Sorry about the mess."

"They were fools. If you hadn't killed them, I would have. They disobeyed my orders and defiled this sacred place."

"Still, I know how hard it is to get good help these days."

"Not as hard as you think. There's no shortage of people who like to kill. How did you get in here?"

"We walked in the front door. What is this place?"

"It's the heart and soul of my empire."

"You must be the elusive Brynhild Sigurd," Austin said.

"That's correct, and I know who you are, Mr. Austin, and your friend, Mr. Zavala. We've been watching you since you visited our facility in Mexico. It was thoughtful of you to honor us with your visit."

"Don't mention it. You must let us know who your interior decorator is. What do you think, Joe, early Addams Family or late Transylvanian?"

"I was thinking more like Munster modern. The boat-shaped coffee table is a nice touch."

"You will learn," the woman said. "That boat symbolizes the past, the present, and the glorious future."

Austin laughed. "An appropriate symbol. That boat isn't going anywhere, and neither is your empire."

"You NUMA people are becoming tiresome."

"I was just telling Joe the same thing before you arrived. We don't want to wear out our welcome. If you'll excuse us, we'll be on our way. Saddle up, guys."

Zavala, who was in the lead, tried to step around Brynhild. Out of habit he flashed his trademark smile. Brynhild was a freak, he reasoned, but she was still a female. The famous Zavala charm was lost on the giantess. She reached out and grabbed him by the shirt, shook him like a terrier with a rat, then with her great strength threw him onto the floor. Zavala quickly regained his feet. Ever the gentleman when it came to women of any size or age, he smiled again. "I know how you feel, but this isn't a good way to end our relationship."

Brynhild replied with a backhand slap across his face. Joe staggered back a few steps and wiped the blood that was trickling from a corner of his mouth. Brynhild cocked her right fist for another blow. Austin moved in to protect Joe. He was watching Brynhild's hands, so when she lashed out to the left leg in a classic kickboxing maneuver he was caught by surprise. Her boot smashed into his chest. He felt ribs crack from the tremendous force even before he slammed against the floor with an impact that rattled his teeth.

Seeing Austin fall removed all of Zavala's inhibitions against striking a woman.

"That makes two sucker punches," he said softly.

Joe had financed his way through the New York Maritime College by boxing professionally as a middleweight. He won most of his fights, many by knockouts. He had gained weight since college but still managed to keep down to a fighting trim of one hundred seventy-five pounds. He was five foot ten, which gave Brynhild a height advantage of about a foot. She probably outweighed him by fifty pounds, none of it fat.

Brynhild's kick had put her in a good position to unload a roundhouse right aimed at removing Zavala's head from his shoulders. Zavala's old ring instincts were coming back. He saw the punch coming and ducked as the right fist grazed the top of his head, and then he drove a left hard into Brynhild's midsection. The effort almost cost him a broken wrist, but it threw off his opponent's timing. She threw a long, loose left that caught air. Tucking his chin in and bringing his hands up, he tried a three-punch combo that had decked more than one opponent in his college days. He followed up a quick left jab with a short right cross and a left hook.

The right missed, but the left hook caught Brynhild solidly in the jaw. Her eyes went glassy, but only for a second. She stepped back as he moved in and shot a hard overhand right to the heart that took his breath away. While he sucked in air she got past his lowered guard and clouted him in the midsection. Zavala absorbed the blow with his hard stomach muscles and swung a right and a left aimed at her jaw. Both missed. Brynhild had been surprised by Joe's quick and skillful reaction, but now that she had his measure she stood off and used her superior height and reach to pound him with the long artillery.

Zavala guessed her strategy and tried to move in for an uppercut to her chin, but each time she lobbed haymakers at him while staying safely out of reach. His left eye was partially closed, and his nose was bleeding. He threw a long overhand left that caught Brynhild in the throat, but it cost him another stinging punch to the head in return. In spite of her size, she was as fast as any middleweight he had ever seen. The old ring aficionados used to say that a good big man can beat a good small man any day. Zavala hoped the same truism didn't apply to a big *woman.*

He kept doggedly on, his timing completely off, throwing soggy punches that caught air. He'd only last another minute. Then she'd finish him off with a couple of neck-snapping kicks.

Quite unexpectedly, Brynhild lowered her guard. Before Zavala's weary reflexes could take advantage, the giant woman collapsed in a heap. Joe stood there stupidly and wiped the sweat out of his eyes. He saw Gamay standing over Brynhild, holding one of the wooden shields from the ship in both hands.

"There's more than one way to swat a Viking bitch," she said with fury in her eyes.

Austin had managed to get to his feet. Holding his cracked ribs, he looked at the others and said, "I hope we feel better than we look."

"I'll feel a hell of a lot better when we're out of here," Zavala said through puffy lips.

"Wait," Austin said, looking around. "We need a diversion."

Without hesitation he went over to one of the braziers near the boat. He picked it up by the metal legs and dumped the burning coals onto the boat's deck. Then he went on board and tossed the shields into a pile. The flames from the impromptu bonfire flared up the mast and licked the bottom of the hide sail. Within seconds the square sail was a sheet of fire. Black, noxious smoke from the blaze curled up to the roof and began to move horizontally along the ceiling.

With his work done, Austin led the way to the doors. They waited off to the side as the chamber filled with smoke. Within minutes the big doors swung open, and a group of shouting guards piled into the hall. The new supply of fresh air fueled the fire and sent the black clouds billowing throughout the Great Hall. The guards who ran directly to the boat never saw the three shadowy figures slip through the open portal.

40

INSIDE THE DOMED UNDERWATER facility Francesca was becoming increasingly frantic. One more piece in place, and her plan would be complete. She didn't dare make her move until she knew the others were safe, especially after Brynhild's hurried exit. She glanced around. The technicians were busy currying favor with the directors who milled around tossing back cups of purified water as if it were Moët champagne. The party wouldn't last forever. Someone was bound to notice her continued attention to the control panel.

The babble of conversation stopped suddenly, and Francesca turned to see three bizarre figures step out of the staff elevator. She gasped at the sight of her friends. They were almost unrecognizable. Gamay was limping, her beautiful dark red hair looked as if it had been caught in an egg beater, and her arms and legs were marked with angry bruises. The white coveralls Austin and Zavala wore were streaked with blood and soot. Zavala's face was puffy, and he had adopted a Popeye squint.

They shoved their way through the crowd and came up to Francesca. Austin managed a grin. "Sorry we took so long. We ran into a few, uh, obstacles."

"Thank God you're here."

Austin put his arm around her shoulders. "We don't plan to stay. We've got a taxi sitting under this thing. Can we offer you a lift?"

Francesca said, "There is one more thing I have to do." She went over to the control panel and punched a series of numbers into the computer keyboard. She watched the digital gauges for a moment. Satisfied all was going as planned, she turned and said, "I'm ready."

Zavala had been keeping the Gogstad people cowed with his weapon in the event someone had an unexpected attack of courage. Austin inspected the board of directors with curiosity. They returned his gaze with glares of pure hatred. At one point the Englishman named Grimley stepped forward. He stuck his nose in Austin's face and said, "We demand that you tell us who you are and what you want here."

Austin laughed unpleasantly, put his hand on the man's bony chest, and shoved him back with the others. "Who is this clown?" he asked Francesca.

"He and his friends are a symbol of all that is wrong with the world."

As an amateur philosopher Austin had long been intrigued by questions of good and evil, but metaphysical discussions would have to wait. He ignored the Englishman and took Francesca's arm, guiding her toward the exit that would take them down to the air lock and the submersible. Gamay followed, then Zavala, who covered their rear.

They had taken only a few steps when the freight elevator doors flew open and about twenty guards spilled out into the lab. They quickly surrounded the fugitives and relieved Zavala of his gun.

Brynhild strode from the elevator, and the guards stepped aside to let her through. Her blond hair was disheveled as a result of the encounter with Gamay's shield, and her pale face was smudged with soot. But her disarray didn't diminish her imposing physique and the malevolence in her pale blue eyes. Quivering with rage, she pointed to the NUMA crew as if she were about to unleash a bolt of lightning.

"*Kill* them," she ordered.

The Gogstad directors murmured with pleasure at the turn of

events, and their eyes glittered in anticipation of the slaughter of the upstarts. But as the guards raised their weapons and prepared to unleash a lethal volley, Francesca stepped in front of her battered friends. In a voice whose strength and tenor evoked her reign as a white goddess, she shouted, "Stop!"

"Get out of the way, or they'll kill you as well," Brynhild ordered.

Francesca thrust her chin out. "I don't think so."

Brynhild seemed to grow another foot. "Who are *you* to defy *me?*" she snarled.

In reply, Francesca walked over and stood before the controls. The panel was lighting up like a pinball machine. Numerical phalanxes marched across the computer screen. There was no mistaking the fact that something was dreadfully out of kilter.

Brynhild swooped down on Francesca like an avenging angel. "What have you done?"

"See for yourself," Francesca said, and stepped aside.

Brynhild stared at the colorful display. "What's happening?"

"The instrumentation is having a nervous breakdown as it tries to deal with the equivalent of a chain reaction."

"What do you mean? Tell me, or I'll—"

"You'll kill me? Go ahead. I'm the only one who can stop the reaction." She smiled. "There's something you never knew about anasazium. Left alone, it's no more dangerous than iron. But its atoms become highly unstable when the material is subjected to certain conditions."

"What *kind* of conditions?"

"Exactly the combination of temperature, power, and sonic vibration that the core is being subjected to at this minute. Unless I alter the instructions the core will explode."

"You're bluffing."

"Am I? See for yourself. The heat levels are going off the charts. Still not convinced?" she said. "Think about the mysterious explosion at your Mexican facility. The moment you told me about the blast I knew exactly what had caused it. Only a few pounds of material destroyed your facility. Think of what will happen when hundreds of pounds reach critical mass."

Brynhild turned to the technicians who had gathered around and shouted for someone to stop the reaction. The head technician had been watching the insane pattern on the computer screen with fascination. He stepped forward, sweat beading on his forehead, and said, "We don't know how. Anything we do might make it worse."

Brynhild yanked a machine pistol out of the hands of the nearest guard and pointed it at Gamay.

"If you don't stop this I will kill your friends one by one. Her first."

"Now who's bluffing?" Francesca replied. "You plan to kill them anyhow. This way we'll all die together."

Brynhild's white skin grew impossibly paler. She lowered the gun.

"Tell me what you want," she demanded, her voice taut with anger.

"I want these people safely out of here."

Brynhild had been trained as an engineer to assemble the facts before making a decision. If the reaction were not stopped the resulting explosion would destroy the plant. Francesca was the only one who knew how to defuse the situation. Brynhild would let the NUMA people go. As soon as the reaction was stabilized she would order her security forces to round them up. Then she would deal with Francesca. She wanted revenge for the destruction of her ship, but she could be patient. It had taken her years to get to this moment.

She handed the machine pistol back to the guard. "Agreed," she said. "But you must stay."

Francesca heaved a sigh of relief and turned to Austin. "You said you came by water?"

"Yes. We have scuba gear and a submersible waiting for us directly under the lab."

"You won't be able to go that way," Francesca said. "The heat levels have already built up too far. You'd be boiled before you got to your submarine."

"We'll try to take the elevator up to the pier. There's a boat there."

"That's your best course."

"We can't leave you."

"It's all right. They won't hurt me as long as I'm of use to them." She smiled beguilingly. "I'll look forward to being rescued by NUMA once again." She turned to Brynhild. "I'll see them to the elevator."

"No tricks," she snarled. She ordered two guards to escort the group.

Francesca pressed the button that opened the door on the egg-shaped lift. "You're injured. I'll help you in." When they were all seated she leaned in and whispered, "Does anyone have a gun?"

The guards who relieved Zavala of his machine pistol assumed that because Austin didn't have a gun in his hand he wasn't carrying one. But he still had the revolver he had taken from one of the Kradzik brothers tucked under his shirt.

"I have one," Austin said, "but it would be suicide to try to shoot your way out of here."

"I don't intend to. The gun, please."

Austin reluctantly handed the gun over. In return she reached under her smock and handed him a manila envelope.

"It's all here, Kurt. Guard this with your life," she said.

"What is it?"

"You'll see when you give it to the world." She gave Austin a long and lingering kiss. "I'm sorry, but we'll have to postpone our date," she said with a smile. Then she turned to the others. "Good-bye, my friends. Thank you for everything."

The finality in her voice was unmistakable. Austin suddenly realized that she had no intention of being rescued.

"Get in!" Austin yelled, and made a grab for her arm.

She stepped easily out of reach and glanced at her watch. "You have exactly five minutes. Use them well."

Then she punched the Up button. The door slid shut, and the elevator quickly shot out of sight. The guards diverted their attention to watch the elevator. Francesca eased the gun from under her smock and shot out the elevator controls. Then she did the same with the freight elevator and tossed the gun aside. As Brynhild rushed over with the other guards, a loud klaxon began to sound from loudspeakers set around the dome.

"What have you done?" Brynhild shouted.

"That's the five-minute warning," Francesca yelled back. "The reaction has been locked into place. Nothing will stop it now."

"You said you would stop the reaction if I let your friends go."

Francesca laughed. "I lied. You told me never to trust anyone," flinging Brynhild's words back at her.

The technicians had realized the danger before anyone, and while attention was diverted they silently slipped off to climb a narrow emergency staircase that spiraled in a separate waterproof shaft that led to the surface. The directors saw them trying to flee and tried to follow. The discipline of the guards quickly dissolved under the influence of fear. They used their gun butts to drive the directors back, then opened up on those who wouldn't yield. Bodies piled up in front of the portal that led to the stairway. Guards scrambled over the heap of corpses only to be stuck in the narrow space. None would give way, and others pushed from behind. Within seconds the only way out was clogged with crushed bodies.

Brynhild couldn't believe how quickly her world had deteriorated. She focused all her anger on Francesca, who had made no move to get away. Scooping Austin's handgun from the floor, she aimed it at Francesca.

"You will die for this!" she screamed.

"I died ten years ago when your mad plan sent me into the rain forest."

Brynhild's finger squeezed the trigger and let off three shots. The first two went wild, but the third caught Francesca in the chest. Her knees buckled, and she fell to the floor, landing in a sitting position with her back to the wall. As a black curtain fell over her eyes she smiled beatifically. Then she was dead.

Brynhild threw the gun aside and walked over to the control panel. She stood helplessly in front of the computer screen as if she could make the reaction stop through sheer force of will. She bunched her fists and held them high over her head. Her howl of rage mingled with the hoarse bray of the klaxon.

Then the tortured atoms and molecules trapped within the core material broke free, unleashing a tremendous burst of energy. Blasted by the internal pressures, the core container turned to molten metal. Brynhild was incinerated instantly in the white-hot explosion, and a giant fireball turned the lab into an inferno.

Superheated smoke reared up the elevator shafts, along the tram tunnel, and into the complex, where it filled every passageway, then into the Great Hall. The smoke burst into billowing flames that boiled the air, touched off the banners hanging on the walls. The smoldering gray ashes of the Gogstad ship in the heart of Valhalla vanished in a final firestorm.

41

THE BOSTON WHALER STREAKED across the lake with its bow up on plane, Austin pushing the twin Evinrude 150 outboard motors for all they were worth. His face was a bronze mask of anger and frustration. He had tried to go back to the lab, but the elevator had gone dead after it delivered them to the boathouse. The freight elevator wasn't working, either. He had started down a staircase only to have Gamay pull him back.

"It's no use," she said. "There isn't time."

"Listen to Gamay," Zavala agreed. "We've got less than four minutes."

Austin knew they were right. He would die and jeopardize their lives if he attempted a futile rescue. He led the way out of the boathouse onto the pier. The guard sat outside dozing in the sun. He got up and tried to unsling his gun. Austin, who was in no mood for Marquis of Queensberry rules, rushed the terrified guard. He slammed his shoulder into the man's midsection and knocked him off the pier.

They piled into the boat. The key was in the ignition, and the gas tanks were full. The motors started right away. They cast off, and Austin gunned the throttle and steered the boat on a direct line for the Nevada shore. He heard a shout from Zavala and turned his head. Joe and Gamay were looking back toward the pier, where the lake bubbled like water boiling in a pot.

There was a muffled roar, and a blood-red geyser shot hundreds of feet into the air like a water spout. They covered their faces with their hands against the scalding rainfall and the cloud of steam that followed. When they dared to look they saw that the pier had completely vanished.

A wave at least ten feet tall was rolling in their direction.

"These boats are supposed to be unsinkable," Zavala said tensely.

"That's what they said about *Titanic,*" Gamay reminded him.

Austin brought the boat around so the bow was facing into the wave. They braced themselves, expecting to be swamped, but the surge simply lifted them high in the air and rolled beneath them. Austin remembered that even a *tsunami* doesn't amount to much until it hits the shore. He hoped the power of the wave would ease before it hit the Nevada side.

Things were happening on land as well. A plume of smoke rose from the forest where Austin had seen the turrets of the building complex from his parasail. As they watched, the smoke changed in character, becoming thicker and darker. Austin reduced their speed and stared at the great black billows streaked with red and yellow flames that were rising high above the trees.

"Götterdämmerung," he murmured.

Gamay overheard him. "Twilight of the Gods?"

"I was thinking more of a *goddess."*

They were all silent, the only sound the drone of the motors and the hiss of the bow through water. Then they heard a hooting like a deranged owl and turned to see a red, white, and blue confection steaming in their direction. The *Tahoe Queen* blew its whistle again. Paul's tall figure could be seen waving from the top deck. Austin waved back, goosed the throttle, and pointed the Whaler toward the oncoming riverboat.

EPILOGUE

Libyan desert, six months later

THE VILLAGE ELDER WAS AS THIN as a stork and his leathery face so creased by decades of desert sun that it would have been impossible to find room for one more wrinkle. Years of malnutrition had reduced his inventory of teeth down to two, one up and one down, but the lack of dentures didn't keep him from smiling with pride. As he stood in the center of his domain, a cluster of yellow clay hovels and a few palm trees marking a muddy oasis, he could have been any big-city mayor presiding over the ribbon cutting at a public works project.

The village was located far to the west of the Great Pyramids at Giza in one of the most inhospitable regions in the world. Between Egypt and Libya lie thousands of square miles of hot, dry sand broken here and there by the bones of panzers left over from World War II. A few scattered settlements cling precariously to life around oases of unpredictable reliability. Sometimes the oases dry up, and when that happens the crops die and famine stalks the villages. The cycle between subsistence and starvation had been a way of life for centuries, but all that was about to change.

In recognition of good things to come the village was decked out with colorful banners. Strips of fabric were braided into the tail of every camel. A large pavilion tent striped in blue and white, the colors of the United Nations, had been set up in the square, actually no more than a dusty open space in the center of the settlement. Lined up on the edge of the village were several helicopters. Diplomats from the UN and several Middle Eastern and African countries stood in the shade of the tent.

The village elder stood next to a structure unlikely to be found in the middle of the desert. It was a circular fountain made of marble and consisting of a large basin enclosing a smaller one surmounted by a statue of a winged woman. The fountain was made so that the water flowed from the outstretched palms of the figure.

The elder was ready. With great ceremony he removed a tin cup from around his neck, scooped it full of water, and took a sip. His toothless grin became even wider, and in a frail, reedy voice he called out in Arabic, *"Elhamdelillah lilmayya."*

He was joined by the other village men who took turns drinking from the cup as if *it,* and not the fountain, were the magical source of water. The women who had been waiting rushed in to fill their clay water jugs. The children hovering around the fountain took their mothers' action as a signal to cool off. Before long the basin was full of laughing and splashing naked children. The diplomats and government officials left the protection of their tent and gathered around the fountain.

Watching with amusement from the shade of a palm tree was the NUMA Special Assignments Team and the skipper of the *Sea Robin.*

"Does anyone know what the old man said?" Zavala said.

"My Arabic is pretty limited," Gamay said, "but I believe he is saying big thanks to Allah for water, the wonderful gift of life."

Paul put his good right arm around his wife's shoulders. "Too bad Francesca isn't here to see herself carved in marble. It reminds me of her old white goddess days."

Austin nodded. "From my impression of Francesca, she wouldn't give it a second glance. She'd check out the water tower and the irrigation setup, make sure the pipeline from the desalting plant didn't leak, then she'd be off to get more plants going."

"I think you're right," Paul replied. "Once the other countries see how well the Cabral process works for the Mediterranean pilot plant, they'll all come running with their tin cups out. Bahrain and Saudi have said they're ready to finance something. But the UN has promised to abide by the request Francesca enclosed with the plans she gave you and will make the big push in the sub-Saharan African countries."

"I heard the Southwest states and Mexico are taking the initiative to build plants on the California coast," Austin said. "That should relieve the stress on the Colorado River."

Gamay said, "I think Francesca would be pleased to see some of those who have been fighting over water working together to bring it to places hit by the drought. There's a whole new spirit of cooperation. Maybe there is hope for the species yet."

"I'm optimistic," Austin said. "The UN has promised to speed up its usual bureaucratic pace. They did a good job setting up a refining plant for that new anasazium site in Canada. Francesca's plans are amazingly simple. From what we've seen of how fast and cheap this plant went up, any country is going to be able to bring in low-cost fresh water."

"Ironic, isn't it?" Gamay said. "Anasazium came out of Los Alamos where they were working on weapons of mass destruction."

"It came close to being just that in the hands of Gogstad," Austin said.

Gamay shivered although the temperature was in the nineties. "Sometimes that giant woman, her two dreadful henchmen, and her horrible lair seem like a dream."

"Unfortunately they were very real, and that wasn't the Emerald City of Oz we barely escaped from."

"I just hope some malignant cell didn't lodge somewhere where it can grow like a cancer."

"Not much chance of that," Austin said. "Gogstad no longer has its leader, its scientific expertise, and the powerful men who were the engine powering this thing. People around the world have realized what they almost lost and are reclaiming their sovereignty over their water rights."

Jim Contos had been listening to the exchange with interest.

"Thanks for inviting me along. At least I know that my two submersibles were deep-sixed for a worthy cause."

"Glad you brought that up. Joe?"

Zavala smiled, extracted a sheet of paper from his shirt pocket, and unfolded it. "This is only a preliminary sketch," he said, "but it will give you an idea of what we've got in the works."

Contos's eyes widened in astonishment. "Hell, it's beautiful."

Zavala grimaced. "I wouldn't go *that* far. It looks like a deformed guppy, but it will go deeper and faster and carry more instrumentation and mechanical functions than any submersible in the sea. It's going to require extensive testing."

"When do we start?" Contos replied.

"The preliminary work has already begun. I've got a date with the Smithsonian. They're planning a memorial to the last pilots of the flying wing, and they've asked me to do a few fly-bys to publicize the campaign. But after that I'll be free to help plan the tests."

"What are we waiting for?" Gamay said.

"That's a good question," Austin said. "Francesca's process is going to turn this sand pit into a garden, but it's no place for a bunch of ocean scientists." He started walking toward a turquoise-blue helicopter with "NUMA" printed in black on its side.

"Hey, Kurt, where are you headed?" Zavala said.

Austin turned. "C'mon," he said with a wide grin on his bronzed features. "Let's go someplace where we can get our feet wet."